This book was donated to the

BO
F O

D0008161

...Or Not

For my mother, Claudia W. Mandabach

...Or Not

Brian
Mandabach

Woodbury, Minnesota

First Edition
First Printing, 2007

Book design by Steffani Sawyer
Cover design by Ellen Dahl
Cover image © 2007 Kris Timken/Blend Images/Punchstock
Editing by Rhiannon Ross

Summer's Almost Gone
Words and Music by The Doors
©1968 Doors Music Co.
Copyright Renewed
All Rights Reserved   Used by Permission

Flux, an imprint of Llewellyn Publications

The Cataloging-in-Publication Data for *Or Not* is on file at the Library of Congress.

ISBN: 978-0-7387-1100-3

Flux
Llewellyn Publications
A Division of Llewellyn Worldwide, Ltd.
2143 Wooddale Drive, Dept. 978-0-7387-1100-3
Woodbury, MN 55125-2989, U.S.A.
www.fluxnow.com

Printed in the United States of America

Journal One

Alone
From childhood's hour I have not been
As others were; I have not seen
As others saw; I could not bring
My passions from a common spring.
From the same source I have not taken
My sorrow; I could not awaken
My heart to joy at the same tone;
And all I loved, I loved alone…

—Edgar Allen Poe

20 August

In my attic room, the heat surrounds me even as my fan blows in the cool evening air. I'm holding a small hunk of granite, shot with milky quartz, and I place it next to a dried *Amanita*, deep cherry, and a northern goshawk feather, smooth and barred with gray. These are my tokens of the mountains, my antidotes against toxicity, my quiet space amid layers of noise.

And this is my new "Sketch Diary"—seventy plain sheets of acid-free paper bound with a wire. It is to be my canvas, my confidant, my Big Chief tablet. It is my testimony, my not going out with a short rope and swinging from a tall pine tree. It is my not ending, my beginning.

I've had the journal for ten days—a gift from a friend I miss too much to tell about—but I haven't written until now. I have only looked at the drawings of the two of us in the front, and re-read her admonition to write. And now, I have begun.

At dinner tonight, Mom and Dad wanted to know all about my first day of school. So I told them it was brutal—moronic kids, teachers offering, what? Rules and procedures? Couldn't I just go back to the cabin and live by myself?

"How about the *walk*, Cassie?" said Dad. "Did you have a nice walk to school and back home?"

My father is very smart, and he likes to ask penetrating questions.

"The walks were okay," I said.

I wanted to add "hot and smoggy and noisy," but I was getting tired of complaining. And since I suppose that's what journals are for, among other things—complaining—here's my portrait of day one, grade eight:

Everybody's early, thronging around under the big blue spruces and the Chinese elms on the over-watered but still splotchy grass. Many of the boys are suddenly as tall as I am, and all the eighth-graders are somehow swollen. Girls show off their summer swellings with their fresh, tight Abercrummy T-shirts and low-rise jeans. For two long years we have waited to rule the school, looking up to the tall, the bosomy, the rude. They were our inspiration, our role models—and now, we'll become them.

Classes are the first-day same as ever. In our seats well ahead of the almighty bell, everybody listens to the teachers, which is a shame because they all say exactly the same thing.

The one difference this year lies in our new responsibilities. First, we must conduct ourselves like good role models. Surely, we remember how we looked up to our older peers. So we must rise to this occasion. And we will, usually by setting the standard of rudeness and cruelty. The second responsibility is preparing for high school. High school will be different. High school will be hard. High school is practically the real world, and it will be a lot easier for us to "slip through the cracks."

Several kids perk up at this—they like the idea of unnoticed failure and wish it could begin right now. But they don't like the next part about having to earn credits by actually passing classes.

So, with this small difference, it's the same as it ever was. Kids fresh and clean and listening to their teachers' rules and suggestions for success. Kids optimistic about having a good year. Kids having high hopes about friends and grades and girlfriends and boyfriends and sports.

Don't they know that everything will be the same?

The smart kids will stay smart. The dummies will goof off. And the popular people will chirp in their little flocks, have their little pecking parties, and then run crying to the counselor.

The school year spreads before me like an endless pool of thick, green Jell-O, through which I am going to have to swim.

I should try to sleep.

Sleep and *try* don't work together, as I should know. I'm going to put on a record—headphones so I don't keep anyone up—and tell how I got into records.

One Saturday in May, just before the end of fourth grade, we stopped at a garage sale. My brother Sean had seen a bundle of fishing poles sticking up out of a barrel with baseball bats and hockey sticks, and he and Dad are always on the lookout for old fly rods.

This time they didn't see anything good, but just as we were about to leave, a few crates of records and a turntable caught my eye.

"Bet you've never heard an LP record, young lady," said the man.

"Oh, I allow as she has," said my dad, who has a few favorite records and a turntable on top of the CD player. "But she is a child of the digital age."

For some reason, I didn't like that "child of the digital age," and I didn't think it was true. I liked the look and feel of Dad's old records, and the sound of them too, so for fifty dollars—a good chunk of my life savings—I bought the record player, two big old speakers, and all the records.

21 August

Homework finished: math and a language worksheet. I read ahead in the history book, American history this year, which is cool, though the teacher is a flag-waver with a whole "Proud to be an American" wall. I consider myself patriotic, but I doubt he would. And why should I be proud just because I happened to be born in the USA?

But I *am* a privileged American child with a super-cool room. I have the third floor attic and even my own bathroom. The walls have a steep slope and there are lots of cool angles. Two windows and a skylight give me light and air, but on summer days, the heat builds up 'til it's sweltering. A big fan in my north window makes it just bearable, and I can always go out onto my little iron-railed balcony outside the east window. There's just enough room to lie down and look at the stars, and the giant spruce trees at the end of our yard screen me from the alley and the old mansion across the way.

I must have dozed off there, because a moment ago I woke up all freaked out by Mom kissing my head. Why is it that when you get to a certain age your mother's kisses are like needles sticking in your spine?

"I just came up to wake you for dinner, sweetie. Fifteen minutes," she said.

Are you sure it wasn't to prick my flesh with stingy nettles?

"Okay, Mom, sorry. Can you leave me alone now?" Trying hard to be nice, I still sounded like a brat.

She creaked across the floor and down the stairs. Our house is one hundred and ten years old and sounds like it's auditioning for a role in a ghost story. I love it, though—it's old and wooden and real, with high ceilings and old windowpanes that give the view a slight distortion. Mom says it's like her vintage cello, the wood supple, mellow, and resonant with age.

Even though our family seems small since Sean went off to college last year, we still have a family dinner unless Dad is in trial or Mom is in rehearsals with the symphony. I have to give my parents credit for not bugging me too much, but I don't like being the only child. Too much pressure.

Tonight I said school was fine—using the old monosyllabic teen routine. It killed me when Sean went through that—I was just a little kid when he started acting freaky. Dad called him Mr. Monosyllable and challenged Sean to actually pronounce it himself. According to Dad, it meant that Sean wanted to be alone and *was* as good as alone even when he was in the same room. Dad would say this right in front of him, which, of course, made him sulk off.

So I said my day was okay, school was fine, homework was easy and done. Was I tired? A little. Did I want to watch a DVD with them? Not really, I'd just go upstairs.

So here I am, listening to a scratchy Todd Rundgren record, using the cover—featuring a rainbow-haired Todd—as a surface to write on.

The summer I got the record player was the last time I was really close to my former friend and soccer teammate Jenny.

I quit soccer after that season because I would rather be in the mountains than driving all over the state for tournaments. Jenny, on the other hand, joined a more competitive league.

Mom and I were close that summer, too, because she drove us to practice and games, and we didn't get up to the cabin with Sean and Dad very much.

Sometimes Jenny came to the mountains with us, but she tended to get bored. And at home, I tried to interest her in my new record collection, but she was obsessed with boy bands and had no interest in obscure classical LPs, jazz-fusion, and the endless synthesizer solos of the seventies. She thought the seventies were cool, of course, but not real seventies stuff—just the TV seventies.

So maybe the end was already in sight, but we still had some good times: summer days at her country club pool, sleepovers, and early morning practices. I remember how we'd sit on my balcony under the stars until way past midnight, whispering, giggling, and discovering infinity. We could just cram the both of us out there, lying back on pillows under sleeping bags, each with the legs of the other along one side.

"Have you seen the stars in the mountains, Jenny, how bright they are? Just think how many we can't even see. And past them, more, and past them, more, and past them, more…"

"Where do you think they end?"

"They don't."

"But that's impossible…"

"That's the fun part," I said. "Trying to imagine infinity—what's beyond the beyond."

It seemed that we were the first kids to play with these thoughts, that we were onto something special and profound.

But then Jenny decided that it made her feel small to imagine the enormity of the infinite universe. She spoiled it by claiming that God knew the number of the stars, God had created them all, and beyond them was God, who was also within them and within us—Him and the Father and the Son and the Holy Spirit.

Jenny's mother had told her this, but what made it worse was that Jenny had asked. To me, these were our private thoughts, and I felt betrayed.

"Then God is infinity," I said, trying to preserve the mystery.

"I don't think so," she said. "I'll ask my mom."

22 August

Today was wonderful—the first and hopefully the last time I open my big mouth in a class "discussion." Dad says I "don't suffer fools gladly," but suffering them silently is a lot easier than trying to reason with them. Especially since I seem to have only two modes: mute and rant.

Here's what happened:

In my reading class, we were supposed to be talking about an article from *Natural History* magazine. Mr. Sinclair asked us to read the article, one page titled "What Is a Species?" Then, he said, we would have a different kind of discussion. He would start us with a topic—the main idea—and let us take it from there. This sounded interesting for a change, but I had no idea how interesting it would get, especially since the topic was so dull. Come on—didn't he know that the seventh-grade teachers had rammed main ideas down our throats and made us puke them out on about seven hundred standardized practice tests?

Anyway, the main idea was that scientists were having a hard time defining species, and the article outlined the various definitions and the problems with each. It wasn't easy, but I spent the summers in the mountains with my dad's collection of natural history books. Call me a freak—I like that stuff.

But I wasn't about to raise my hand.

"I don't believe in evolution," was the very first comment, courtesy of Stephanie Seabrook.

"Okay," said Mr. Sinclair. "Matthew."

"I think Darwin was wrong."

"Anyone want to respond to that?" He was looking puzzled, maybe because his question had been about the main idea. He matched a raised hand with a name on his seating chart.

"Kallie."

"I agree with Matthew."

"Because…"

"I just don't think it's possible for life to evolve. It's not like we see life evolving now."

"We're supposed to be discussing the main idea or ideas of the article," said Sinclair. "And one way to get there is to ask yourself what it's about. I'll stop talking now and turn it back to you. What is this article about?"

Half the kids in the room had been sticking their arms in the air, and now there wasn't one hand up.

"Well, I think this shows that maybe things go better when the teacher keeps out of it. You have a lot to say, then I tell you what I want you to talk about, and you all clam up.

I still think we should start with what the article is about. We need someone to be brave and tell us."

He searched his chart again, to find me, shrugging off cowardice with a hand in the air.

"Cassandra."

"Cassie."

"Sorry, Cassie. What's the article about?"

"The definition of species, not evolution."

"Matthew."

"I disagree with Cassie because the article quotes Darwin."

"Christine."

"Darwin's dead and God isn't."

"Okay...Shelly."

"You go, girl!" Shelly said, and she and Christine did a high-five.

Several others in the room flashed righteous smiles.

"Interesting," said Sinclair. "Rae?"

"I thought fossils prove that life evolved."

"Matthew."

"Then how come monkeys aren't evolving and becoming people today?" And then he started making chimp noises. "Ooo-ooh! Ooo-oo-oo-oooh."

A bunch of other people started making ape noises and scratching themselves. Monkey see, monkey do. They didn't realize it, but they were doing a pretty good job of proving their primate status.

"Okay, wait a minute," said Sinclair. "Hush, everybody. Attention." He waited for quiet. "Let's let Rae respond."

"It takes millions of years."

"Christine?"

"I just don't believe that the earth is a million years old."

"What about the fossil record, carbon dating, basic geology?" I couldn't stand it anymore. "Wasn't that you I saw in science today?"

"Please raise your hand, Cassie. Jenny?"

"Actually, the earth is six thousand years old, Cassie. All the fossils came from the time of the great flood, and most of the animals from the Ark are still alive today."

"What about dinosaurs?" I said. "How the heck did Noah get *those* guys on his boat? I would have loved to see that—ol' T-Rex chompin' down the breeding stock."

"What about *dragons*, Cassie? They were sighted at least until the Middle Ages."

"Okay, hold on a minute, girls—"

"You're kidding right? Dragons? We're talking about dragons?"

"Cassie—"

"Holy mother of the living God, you guys are a bunch of—"

"Cassie! Class!" Sinclair tried to gain control, but I couldn't shut up.

"—freakin' morons. I cannot believe we are talking about dragons. And how do you figure six thousand years old? The *Bible?*"

"Cassie, you can take a time-out in the hall."

"Seriously—*dragons?*"

"Out!"

"Okay, okay—I'm sorry—I'm going."

So I got to stand around in the hall like your average dummy. Beautiful.

Eventually, the bell rang. Rae was the first one out the door and she passed by me without looking at me. And do you suppose my other classmates were warm and jovial?

Done with my homework now, and I don't feel like writing. If I were up at the cabin, I would hike up to the rocks to watch the sunset. But the thought occurs, what's to stop me from walking now?

What's to stop me?

Parents. It's their *job*.

But mine is to argue, so it worked out okay.

"I'm going for a walk, Mom," I said, walking past her door. "Be back soon."

"No, sweetie, it's getting dark."

"It's twilight, I'll be back before dark."

"No way," said Dad, from the bottom of the stairs.

"Da-ad." I hated the sound of my whiney voice.

"No-o." His mocking really helped.

"I'll come with you," said Mom.

Please, no.

"Unless you want to be alone," she added.

"Of course she wants to be alone," said Dad. "But she should be alone indoors."

"Oh, that's healthy advice," I said.

"It's safe."

"Maybe we should let her go for a short one, Gale." Unexpected help from the maternal quarter.

"Deb…Cassie…"

The problem is that Dad, as if being a dad wasn't enough to make him worry, is a public defender. I guess it would be the same for any criminal lawyer, but with the high PD caseload and twenty years in the system, he's defended more than a few people accused of doing very ugly things. So, he has a hard time letting me out in the big, bad world. Too many crime-scene photos.

I knew this was what he was thinking about, and I started getting nervous and scared myself. But I still wanted to go—even more, maybe.

"Just a short one, Gale. It isn't dark yet, and we don't want her feeling like a prisoner."

"Take my cell phone," Dad said to me. "Be aware of your surroundings. Don't talk—"

"—to anyone or look at anyone you don't know," I cut him off and finished his sentence.

"Why does your mocking not reassure me?"

I ran down the stairs, took the phone, and reached up to kiss his cheek.

He put both arms around me, hugging me hard. "Be back in twenty minutes."

"Will do," I said, and I made for the door.

Unlike every other kid in the American universe, I have never bugged my parents to buy me a cell phone. So I didn't instantly fire off a three-way call to my two best friends to gossip about the next best two. (Who would these friends be, anyway?) When it comes to consumer electronics, I'm not interested. I prefer real life to mLife or any other campaign for "digital enhancement of emotional life significance." That's actually what they called it—I Googled it once, mLife, though I'm not sure I understood it any better than I had before.

Do people really think they're more alive if they are digitally connected to everything? And what are you *really* connected to if you're *virtually* connected to everything?

Cassie Sullivan, asking those tough questions—so you don't have to.

By the time I got out the door, I forgot why I wanted to be out so bad. Was I upset about the incident at school, or was I just ready to jump out of my own skin because I couldn't stand being in here anymore?

Asking those tough questions.

Less than ten minutes away, in Valley Park, there's a good hill for catching the sunset, so I made for that. It looks out on a greenway along the creek, which has been converted from a wandering stream along the seam of the mountains and the prairie into a riprap and concrete-walled ditch that drains our acres and acres of pavement. Red gravel jogging and bike trails thread along the creek and split off along the edges of ball-fields, woods, and playgrounds. Past the creek is the huge and terrible Interstate highway, a constant source of noise, pollution, and other violence. And past that are more of the semi-real neighborhoods, where people live their semi-real existences, and then the mountains rise—mine-ridden, road-scarred, over-recreated, but still grand—to a horizon where the peach sky glows with sunlit smog. Beautiful.

Up there on the other side of the peak is our family's own little piece of ground with our cabin and my tipi. This summer—last summer, I guess—Sean and I would have been up on the rocks, bathing in the last rays as the sun sinks into the glacier-white of the Collegiate Peaks.

We sit for a while.

The sun sets.

We talk a little, then walk slowly back, leaving our flashlights off, as it grows darker and darker, cooler and cooler, and bats skim the beaver pond to make ripples that shimmer reflections of the suspended stars.

23 August

Another wonderful day at school, Diary. I was getting stuff together for class when Matthew, whose locker is next to mine, started acting all nice.

"Good job expressing your opinions yesterday," he said. "I don't agree, but it sure made the discussion interesting."

I laughed, relieved. "Well, it certainly was that."

"But there's one little thing I wanted to make you aware of," he said with a grin.

"Yeah?"

"*You're* going to *hell!*" And he slammed his locker.

He high-fived Nathan McMahon, who had apparently been watching (morons always high-five—it's tribal code), and they took off down the hall.

In reading class, Sinclair gave us something a little safer, a story from the lit book, and we had another discussion. Or they did.

People were trashing the story, one by Hemingway about a little boy who thinks he is going to die when he gets the flu. He hears the doctor say his temperature is 103 degrees, and he remembers some kid saying that you die if you go over 44 degrees. Trouble is, he's been living in Europe, where they use Celsius.

Some of them didn't get it, and Sinclair let the others explain. Then they thought there wasn't enough detail. They didn't like the dad going out quail hunting. They thought the ending was random. They thought it was boring.

Though he didn't say so, Sinclair looked disappointed that they weren't into it.

"What did you think of the ending, Cassie?" He tried to get me involved, but I wouldn't play.

"I agree with *everyone*," I said.

24 August

Saturday today. I was hoping that we could go to the cabin this weekend, but no. Stayed up last night listening to the Mamas and the Papas but didn't feel like writing. Slept until noon. Infernally hot up here. Stupid today. Math homework took forever. It's easy, but I'm just stupid.

I feel a little better now that it's late, cooler, and everyone is in bed. I have a record on low—some freaky Pink Floyd, which also seems to help.

Earlier, I was getting the same feeling of stupidity that I've felt before. It started in sixth grade and became even worse in seventh. When Mom noticed that I "wasn't myself," she took me to the doctor—who couldn't find anything wrong with me—then hit the bookstore and loaded me up on vitamins. Maybe the vitamins helped, or the walks she forced me to take, or maybe the increasing light of spring brought me some relief. One of the books Mom got said that Seasonal Affective Disorder (they call it SAD—real funny) and PMS combine in some women for a double whammy. But a vegan diet was supposed to be good for it, so I got some points there.

Summer's always better because that's when I get to be in the mountains, wandering along the creek, hanging in my tipi, reading on a flat rock in the sun. After my first really rough winter in sixth grade, I read a bunch of Native American stuff like *Black Elk Speaks* and *Crazy Horse: The Strange Man of the Oglalas*. I loved the reading, but there weren't any happy endings.

Dad told me not to "romanticize the American Indian." I said at least they had some respect for the land. He said I was lucky I wasn't born a couple of hundred years ago into the Lakota nation because instead of lollygagging around reading and daydreaming I would be working. As a female, he said, my job would be "processor of bison," so I'd be spending every waking hour in hard labor. That is, if I was lucky, and the men had been successful on their hunts. I said, anyway, it wasn't fair the way we took their land and tried to kill them all, and he had to agree with that.

"But," he said, "you have to understand. Two cultures collide. They have two completely different ways of dealing with the world—and one was stronger in numbers and technology. The result was inevitable."

"Genocide is inevitable?"

"I didn't say that genocide is inevitable—I said in this instance, in these circumstances, at this point in history, the end result of the American Indian losing this continent was inevitable. And as the Talking Heads said, 'Same as it ever was.'"

"Sean," I said, "please instruct Mr. Sullivan to answer the question."

"Mr. Sullivan, you will answer Ms. Sullivan's question."

"Yes. Not here and now, but somewhere right now, genocide is happening and it is inevitable. There is nothing you or I can do about it."

Then he tried to backpedal, saying that just because it had been that way didn't mean it had to be that way—by doing what's right and protesting what's wrong, things can change. So, although he tried to take back the part about there being "nothing you or I can do about it," the message I got was that melancholia is not entirely a matter of hormones and sunlight. Things happen—things that cause it. It's not just me—it's the *world* that is wrong.

So I tell myself in the midnight dreary, as I ponder—yes, weak and weary—over many a quaint volume of my own forgotten lore. And wait for the raven's rapping at my door.

25 August

Slept in again today. And I'm dumb again.

Raven rapping? I'm pretty funny. Or pretty stupid.

It's hot. I'm on my balcony. If I wanted to do anything it would be to walk, but it's almost dark and I'm a prisoner. I had to FORCE myself to eat and try to act normal tonight. The monosyllabic routine works best if I'm faking it, but now I don't have the energy.

I imagine the drifting away at the end of "To Build a Fire," and I wish I could just fade away like that:

"How'd you sleep last night, pal?"

"Wonderful. Felt like I slept forever. Slept myself right back to camp, right back to you boys. Too bad about that dog, but I'd like to have a word or two with that old timer at Sulphur Creek."

"Looked like you was sleeping the sleep of the righteous—or the sleep of the damned—one."

"Heh, heh, heh! You always was a real good pal, Buddy. Now I'm just dozin' off again. Just dozin' off..."

27 August

It's been taking all the energy I have just to, I don't know what, exist?

28 August

*Why **will** you say that I am mad? The disease had sharpened my senses—not destroyed—not dulled them. Above all was the sense of hearing acute. I heard all things in*

the heaven and in the earth. I heard many things in hell.
How, then, am I mad?

—Edgar Allen Poe, "The Tell-Tale Heart"

Do I tell you everything, Di? Do I reserve no secrets? Are we thick as thieves? Will you betray me, like a true friend? Is this life or mLife? Can I text you?

Maybe I'm not as stupid today. I feel angry and sarcastic—I guess that's a good sign.

And I want to play records—that's good, too. I love my records. I love to clean them with my Discwasher, move the needle-arm over to the right spot, close the dust cover, and lower the needle with the little lever on the side. At first I got tired of getting up to turn the record over every twenty minutes, and the pops and scratches grated on my nerves. But I got to like even those parts, if the scratches aren't *too* bad, because they make it more real than computerized music.

Reading over the last couple of pages, it looks like I was getting maybe a tiny bit depressed. It's still summer so it can't be the double whammy. But my winter mood started early last year, too.

That's when Sean took off for college in the great Northwest, and though we tried to be excited for him, we were all SAD then. There was a big empty space in the house. Mom and Dad turned to me, trying to be subtle about it, but I felt them watching me. It was supposed to be a good thing—having the house and my parents to myself—but the pressure made me want to be alone more, even while it was harder to do so. If I kept getting good grades, at least they couldn't bug me about that. So I forced myself to do what needed to be done, though I didn't care about any of it.

I hid in my tower on the third floor, reading and listening to my records and looking out on the world. I read *One Flew Over the Cuckoo's Nest* in the fall, and I felt a little crazy, thinking of my room at the top of the house as my cuckoo's nest. In *my* institution—school—I wanted to be like Chief, tall but invisible, and I experimented with pretending not to be able to speak. Sliding through the halls, I imagined Chief Broom's fog. His voice ran through my mind, murmuring about machinery and the sinister something he calls "the combine." And strangely, he made sense.

If, as I compose this missive to wherever, I've been able to conceal how messed up I am, I guess I should drop the pretense now. Reading that last section, it seems clear that I've got more than a few bats in my belfry.

Not that I've tried to pretend that I go along with the herd, but I do act like I'm cool in my own world. And usually, I am—when I don't feel like jumping off a cliff—but I have strange ideas, weird thoughts.

For instance: hearing the machinery in digital media.

Now, to make that sound less weird, let me explain. A record or a tape is a *recording* of the music. And because analog carries a full spectrum of the sound, *all* the music is there.

Digital, on the other hand, isn't really a recording, it's a *sample*. So a CD has sampled bits of each frequency, not the whole sound. Imagine a piano that has ten little keys for each note instead of one single key. That is to say, each of these ten keys combines to make the sound of one note. Now deaden every third micro-note. You only have two-thirds of the sound. My fractions may be off, but that's digital.

Why do CDs sound so good, then?

The samples are high quality, there's no background noise, and the human ear isn't sensitive enough, we're told, to hear the spaces between the samples. But vinyl nuts, like me, can hear the difference: records have a warm tone that digital can't match.

That makes sense, doesn't it? But if I make a leap and say that when I listen to digital music, I hear machinery, then it sounds utterly mad. "Why *will* you say that I am mad?"

I don't actually mean that digital media is a part of the combine, that it implants some sort of machinery, even virtual machinery—

Ahhh, it's too late for this, and I can't think.

Let me get away from Chief Broom and the ticking of "The Tell-Tale Heart" and simplify:

1. Digital music sounds robotic to me. It's too clear, too clean—it's virtual music, not actual music.

2. People are used to it. They like it. They think music is *supposed* to sound that way.

3. Since environment has an effect on organisms, digital music *could* change the way the brain works.

Now, number three may sound like Chief Broom, but maybe, just maybe, listening to digital sampling trains the brain to hear in a certain way. And *not* hear in another.

Is there anything wrong with this? I don't know—but CDs began to sound sinister to me, so I stopped listening to them.

Now if I were *mad*, I would think there were mental viruses hidden between the bits in digital samples. There could even be microchips in our brains that are triggered by digital media to produce thoughts like: "Drink Sexy Cola and be Powerful!" "You must buy things to truly exist!" "The virtual and the actual are ONE!" "Security is Freedom is Marketing is Art is Power is America is Right is Peace is Security is Strength is Truth is Might is Liberty is Lifestyle is Property is Happiness is Automobile is Independence is Globalism is Diversity is Oneness is Jesus is the Almighty Clean of Dr. Bronner's Peppermint Castile Soap—Dilute! Dilute! Dilute! Dilute! Dilute!"

But I'm *not* mad. So I *don't* think that.

Journal Two

29 August

A new journal. I had no idea, when Ally, Sean's girlfriend (and my self-adopted sister), gave me the first one, that it would become such a habit. I'm getting so wrapped up in all this writing that I'm afraid I'll get behind in my homework.

But the question arises, since I hate school, why should I be totally compulsive about homework?

Exactly.

Once you ask the question, it starts to make sense.

The logic is backwards, but that lends the concept a foxy sort of stealth, and as long as I have straight As, I can relax in my own superiority. Not a noble aspiration, I admit, but maybe a small comfort. It's not all that fun to be cleverer than the low-achievers, but I like to think that I am cleverer than those who actually believe in the whole thing: grades, goals, achievement, the Olympics, whatever, *et cetera,* whatnever.

The only ones who might have the edge are those who are sharp enough to do well, but who choose not to.

I used to think that those smart kids who got crummy grades were too messed up to get it together. But Chris Quillen might be an exception. Is he faking? Is he pretending to be together enough to achieve but too rebellious not to fail?

On Monday, Quill, as they call him, came into stride next to me on the way to lunch and said, "I heard about your anti-Christ freak-out, Cassie." Quill talks in character most of the time, and he was using a creepy surfer/stoner/horror voice, not breathy or nasally exactly, but with strange accents:

"I *hearrrd* aboutyer *ann*ti-Christ *frreeak*-out, *Caaa*ssie."

Sometimes, I'm afraid it really is the way he talks, as if he started acting that way and it gradually stuck, like if you cross your eyes too often.

"Whatever," I said, and immediately hated myself. Whatever? "Or what*never*." I tried to amend it to sound clever. It did, sort of.

"Cool," he said.

"What's cool?"

"*Eev*erything, *duuu*de."

I had to laugh. "Yeah, well it doesn't feel too cool to be the school anti-Christ."

"Yeah, well it *iis* cool. *Youu* should come sit with *uss*."

I looked over at the corner table where he sits with long-haired DJ, blue-haired Kelly, and died-black-haired Liz. Liz lives down and across the alley from me, but we've never been friends. She's also in my reading class. It must have been Liz who told them about my dragon rant.

I was tempted, but while Quill got in the food line, I took my lunch over to my usual spot with Sophia and Gwen. You might think from what I have written that I have no friends at all, but I do, sort of. I have my lunch group, three of the quietest, least gossipy girls in the school. When I was freaking out last week after the anti-Christ incident, two out of three didn't even know about it, so I actually told them.

The strange thing is that those same two are very religious. Sophia and Gwen are Mormons, which the bad side of me has a hard time with, but it's impossible to have a hard time with Sophia and Gwen because they are so good. They should not belong to a religion that is in any way comparable to the Christian hypocrites'. The hypocrites wear WWJD bracelets, but it's just for show. They only want to act righteous and be part of the herd, while Sophia and Gwen actually act from goodness and love. Or so it seems—maybe it's just brainwashing.

Anyway, I told them at lunch how my whole reading class was mad at me because I actually answered the teacher's question and everybody else wanted to talk about evolution.

"Good job talking in class, though," Sophia said. "You hardly ever contributed last year." We had been in a lot of classes together, and they knew how quiet I was.

"Yeah, but I got a little worked up," I said. "First of all, the article did mention Darwin, but only because it was about definitions of species." I was on shaky ground here—we had never discussed this. "Then, I got into it with Matthew and Jenny because they were not being scientific—totally ignoring the fossil record."

"Which is full of gaps."

"Unconformities—unlike middle school," I said. "But it was insane. Jenny actually brought dragons into it—*dragons*— as if they were real, as if there were evidence that dinosaurs had lived until medieval knights killed them."

"It is *possible*," Sophia said. Then she saw my face. "Though, granted, unlikely." She talks that way, sophisticated. She loves Greek mythology and all kinds of old tales and lore, which is strange because I thought that all Christian people were terrified of pagan stuff. Not that I knew anything about "LDS," as the Mormon kids call themselves, except that they don't drink alcohol or caffeine and had been run out of just about everywhere except Utah.

"Don't you wonder what inspired the stories of the dragons?" she said. "And what about Nessie?"

"Watch out." Hannah sat down. "You're going to piss off Miss Darwin Junior here."

"You heard."

"Something about you being the devil and screaming about dragons. You don't believe in them, but you do believe in dinosaurs."

"I think we should talk about something else."

Later—

It was just about a year ago that I came up with what I called the Invisibility Code. Although it's not easy becoming invisible when you're a seventh-grade girl who's pushing six feet, I decided to try. After all, if a giant like Chief Broom could do it, I figured I could too.

The rules go something like this:

1. Flat shoes—easy since I had no desire for super-cool platforms.

2. Loose clothes—something I learned about in fifth grade when my chest started to mushroom.

3. Show up and do your work—difficult in those instances when you'd rather crawl into a pit and never come out, otherwise, no problem.

4. Speak only when spoken to or when not speaking would make you more visible.

I relax the last rule when it conflicts with number three. And last week, of course, I broke it completely. Like an idiot. Just because morons are dominating the discussion, and just because they're pissing me off, doesn't equal me being able to accomplish anything by opening my big, fat trap. All I do is make myself a target, but even so, I think I'm ditching the Code. Not only does it sound sort of dumb, but I'm afraid I'll keep doing stupid things like ranting about dragons. Maybe hanging around Ally has changed me more than I realized. Maybe I *want* to rant about dragons when I feel like it. What sucks is that nobody understands me like she does, and since she is a thousand miles away, I might as well be talking to myself. Hence the compulsive journal writing.

The Code seemed to make sense last year, but I was having a number of strange thoughts. I couldn't keep certain images out of my mind, for example, like my own body, in free-fall, as if I'd slipped into one of the photos that froze people forever in their tumbles from the World Trade Center. I kept this very strictly to myself, and I lied beautifully in the "depression assessment" Mom set up after the doctor couldn't find anything physically wrong with me.

The fibbing became number five of the Code. Since I figured that I would be okay if people would just let me alone, I tried to tell them what they wanted to hear. If old Randall McMurphy (Chief Broom's buddy in *Cuckoo's Nest*—the hero of the book, who gets lobotomized) had done that sooner, he wouldn't have had a hunk of his brain scooped out. I should remember him the next time I want to mouth off.

Anyway, the depression questions were either about recent changes, or were matters of degree. I had been bummed out for more than a year, and how sad is too sad? How are people supposed to feel?

The conclusion was that, aside from some perfectly natural fears and sadness over 9/11, I was within the normal range for moods. Some counseling might be a good thing, but I was able to talk them out of it.

The tricky part in all of this was having enough energy to do what it took to keep people from bothering me. Third quarter, I almost got a B in math, the fear of which put me in a panic that gave me energy to do extra credit until I got my percentage up. "Math Mates" worksheets—gotta love 'em.

Then the Gifted and Talented lady kept trying to get me involved, which was the last thing I wanted. One day she pulled me out of class for a chat.

"I work with students who need a little more challenge," she said. "Do you think you might fall into that category?"

"I don't know." Keep it short, noncommittal—they'll get tired of you.

"Is school boring for you, Cassie?"

"No, it's okay."

"Come on. You have some of the highest test scores in the school. You get straight As, yet your teachers say you put in almost no effort."

"I do my homework."

"No class participation, nothing beyond exactly what you're asked to do."

"I don't like to talk in class."

"Why not?"

We were sitting at a table in the library. A class of sixth graders came in and charged the books. One of them waved to the GT lady.

"Hi, Ms. P.!" he said in a little piping voice.

"Hi, Devin," she said.

"Can I get back to class now?" I asked.

She looked a little startled—even the good kids in Gifted and Talented probably don't want to rush right back to class.

"Of course you can," she said. "It was nice to meet you."

"Nice to meet you too, Ms. P." I turned on a little sweetness and bailed out of there.

Soon an invitation came, asking Mom and Dad and me to attend a GT breakfast before school, where we learned about exciting opportunities such as the Knowledgemaster Open, Battle of the Books, and the National Geography Bee. I didn't want to be bothered with any of this stuff, and when I told Mom and Dad it wasn't my style, they didn't push me to participate.

Ms. Price made one last-ditch effort get me "involved."

"What's your favorite class, Cassie?"

"They're all good." Really they were, every one of them, awful. This is why number five is essential. If I told her that every single class was tedious torture for no apparent purpose, what could she do? Could she stop the teachers from reviewing the same things I've heard since fifth grade? Could she stop them from saying the same things over and over again, every day, several times a day? Could she stop the endless test preparation, sample questions, practice tests, and the innumerable standardized tests themselves? Could she stop half the kids from being morons and the other half from being mean? Could she get me a chair that wasn't an instrument of torture for a girl my size? I didn't think so.

"Well, what do you like to do outside of school?"

"Go to the mountains, hike, read."

"Sports?"

"I'm not talented in sports. Or gifted." That gave her a smile.

"You like hiking," she pointed out.

"Yes. I can walk. But that's not a real talent now, is it?" *Careful.* But I loved playing with that snooty English inflection: that's not a *real* talent now, *is* it?

"Do you ever feel, I don't know—depressed?"

I thought I had avoided counseling—what the hell? *Steady* . . .

"Depressed?" Who, me? "No." What could possibly make you think so?

"Come on, we all get down sometimes. But you seem…"

"I'm just a normal girl." I was going for a light effect, a non-depressive affect. "Just ordinary me."

"I think you're more like *extra*-ordinary. I looked in your portfolio—at some of your writing. You may be normal, but you're not ordinary."

I didn't like this woman pawing through my stuff, and yet who can object to being told she's wonderful? And yet again, short of little chats in the library, what could she do?

"Thank you," I said, the mannerly child. "But I'd prefer that you didn't go through my work. Can I go back to class now?"

"Yes, Cassie, but let me tell you," she leaned forward, and her smoothly dyed, reddish-dark hair swung forward as she tapped the table for emphasis. "I said your reading scores were high—the truth is that they're higher than anyone else in this school. Your writing is probably too *good* to score that high."

She reached over and put her hands on my arms, which were folded in front of me. Her hands were warm, with a big diamond on a wide gold band dwarfing her short finger. Her perfume was something expensive, like the symphony ladies who blanket the lobby of the theater with their reek. I felt sick.

"If I were you, school would be *killing* me," she said.

It was not appropriate, but I started laughing. Her *perfume* was killing me. And yet, school was too. She patted my arm and drew her hands back with a puzzled smile.

"What?" she said.

"Thank you," I said. "I just want to be left alone. I mean—" I had to play this just right. "I'm fine. Thanks. Really. And today's math is kind of tricky," I fibbed. "I ought to get back to class."

"Okay, Cassie. I'm here if you need me."

"Thanks, Ms. P."

"Bye, now."

It was partly with Ms. P. in mind that I pulled my stealth rebellion when the big state tests came around. I figured she wouldn't be bothering me if my scores weren't so high, so I decided to throw the tests.

I was in a foul mood—we had been suffering day after day of practice and drill for months, peaking at a pre-test frenzy that included teachers showing peppy "Rock the Test" videos produced by the elective classes. I wanted to retch every single day.

Quill and his friend DJ were dumped in the in-house suspension hole for changing it to "Fuck the Test!" during our pep assembly, which summed up the way I felt, though I wouldn't have shouted it at the top of my lungs in a gym full of people.

These tests are important, we're told, and I'd always tried my best because that's what I do. Also I guess I liked to show off my smarts. But they don't affect your grade. They don't keep you from passing. You don't even get the results until the following fall. So who cares? I was breaking Invisibility Code, but no one at school really cared what *my* scores were. They wanted the school's average to go up—which was why we were drilled and psyched to the breaking point—because the teeth of the government testing monster were chomping on the *schools*. If a few kids had to get thrown to the beast to save the institution, well, sometimes you have to think of the whole rather than the individual.

So bombing the test was an act of revolution—not just a bad score. Or so I told myself when it occurred to me that Mom and Dad would be devastated.

On the first day, the school was giving everybody sausage biscuits and Egg McDuffins. I asked for a vegan snack and got a pesticide-ridden, wax-coated apple. See what I mean? The whole thing is, as Dad would say, a charade (which he would pronounce *sher-aád*).

The first test was math. We had been told over and over again that showing the work and explaining your answers was just as important as the answers themselves. So the easiest way to throw it would have been to darken random circles and leave all the workspaces and written parts blank.

Trouble is, the teacher was walking around making sure everybody was filling in every blank. So what I did was to carefully work every problem in the wrong space, then choose the wrong answer. Some of them were really very hard, but my brain seemed to be working better than it had all year. Stuff that I'd have had to look up in the book when I was doing my homework just came to me out of the blue. I was enjoying myself for the first time in a long time, especially on the explanations. On those I made sure to write a lot of stuff that didn't make any sense at all:

To find the area of a sphere, various formulae are needed. Not the kind of formula you give to a baby, you dumbbell! **Math formulas!** *(But for baby, breast is best.) Anyhoo, you must circumnavigate your particular globe, which will necessitate more math, in the form of triangulations with or without a sextant. Not sex—SEXTANT—like in Captain Cook? But since the globe is a sphere, and not a triangle (even though pie is cut in triangles) you need to use the formulae for them. (Spheres, not babies!)*

I'd never write something like this on a paper that would be graded by a teacher I knew and possibly be seen by Mom and Dad. But these tests were sent off to be graded by strangers and never seen again. It was great.

Every ten minutes on the dot, Mr. Stephens would get up from his newspaper to pace the aisles. Since I was so hard at work and was filling in all the blanks, everything looked great to him. I knew he would never bother to actually read what I had written.

On the literature test I did the same thing. There were a couple of decent stories and poems among the usual garbage, but I pretended to have no clue whatsoever of how to make sense of any of it. The written answers were again a particular source of enjoyment and pride.

When it came to the writing test, we'd been trained to stay on topic, and if they asked for an expository essay, we must be sure not to write a story; if they asked for a story, we mustn't do an essay. Guess what I did? The topic was a persuasive essay, so I wrote a story that had nothing to do with it. I scrambled all my punctuation, garbled my grammar, and didn't paragraph anything. I capitalized all the wrong words. I also took a lot of trouble with my spelling: I nailed somnambulist, but misspelled sliep wocker. It was a blast.

There were two two-hour testing blocks per day, three days per week, for two weeks. By the end of the first week, my energy was flagging, but I kept with the program.

I debated telling Mom and Dad, especially when they asked how the tests were going. I had been complaining about all the prep during the previous weeks, and they were surprised at how chipper I seemed once the actual testing began. Dad said standardized tests are a crock of Cheez Whiz, anyway. But Mom was sympathetic to the school and pointed out how tickled Dad got when his little girl brought home the astronomical scores.

"And she'll have a lot more tests to take before she's through," Mom said. "She'd better get used to them."

After the tests were over, the remainder of seventh grade dragged on. I perked up a little when spring came around, and we took more weekends at the cabin. Sean was due back for the summer right after school was out. And he was bringing Ally—the love of his life, as Dad quipped—for a week's stay, and we were all curious about meeting her.

30 August

Mom has rehearsals this weekend—big concert on Monday—but Dad and I are heading up to my favorite place on earth: our cabin in the mountains.

Years ago, before Sean and I were born, Mom came into some money from her grandmother, and she and Dad put it into land. *Land.* It's a funny word when you look at it. Earth, ground, dirt, soil, acreage. Property. "The Earth does not belong to us; we belong to the Earth," said a bumper sticker stuck on a car that was spewing carbon into the earth's atmosphere. People.

Dad still talks about how his grandfather lost all the family land in the depression, how land is the only thing that comes close to lasting, how the cabin will belong to Sean and me someday and we will *never* sell it. "Land is part of your own body," he says, "and your children's bodies, and their children's. So, selling is amputation. Do you think I'd sell my arm? Or even worse, yours? The land is part of you—you don't sell it."

But somebody must, because he and Mom were able to buy our little valley, nestled under the western shoulder of the Peak. Until they got the cabin built, they camped out, taking vacations and weekends to work on it.

Dad is very proud of doing all the building himself—with light help from Mom, since she wasn't too eager to smash her fingers with a hammer—and he likes to scoff at people who say they are "building" houses. He offers to put on the old tool belt and help them with the framing until they acknowledge that they're actually *having* a house built.

Back to our little home away, the cabin started out as one room with a loft. To make space for kids, they added an extra bedroom leaning against the west side, and eventually partitioned the loft, giving Sean and me some privacy.

The only other improvements have been a solar-cell/battery system for electricity and a composting toilet in the old outhouse.

I prefer my tipi, but on a rainy day or a snowy night, it can be cozy to get a fire going (more carbon—I know I'm a hypocrite) and curl up on the old couch. In addition to shelves and shelves of books at home, we have a well-stocked bookcase at the cabin: kids' books, paperbacks, field guides, natural history—

"Halloooooooooo!" calls Dad. Time to go.

Ahhh! This makes all the difference. I'm up in the cabin loft in the quiet world of the mountains—not silence, exactly, but machine-free quiet where I can hear only the songs of insects and wind blowing in the window.

The cabin sits on a gravelly slope above the creek where Sean and I learned to fish—pulling little brook trout out of the pools beneath splashing falls—and it faces south where the creek flows from spruce and fir woods in a narrowing valley that rises up to a shoulder of the Peak. The cabin is at ten thousand feet. A thousand feet higher, the trees grow sparse among huge, lichen-covered boulders and then give way to the alpine tundra. A western spur of the Peak dominates the valley with its rocky cone that we call the Goat-horn.

Dad comes in from his bedtime trip to the outhouse. "I'm turning in," he says, craning up so he can see me, lying on the bed, scribbling away. "Are you going to keep that up all night?"

"No, I think I'll actually sleep."

"You don't need the white noise of machinery to lull you?"

"*Au contraire, mon père.*"

"What about your silly records?"

"Good night, Dad."

For some reason, as he put out the light downstairs, sleepiness fled from me. After a few minutes, Dad was already snoring, so I decided to go for a walk.

I pulled a sweater over my T-shirt, stepped down the ladder, and grabbed Dad's blackthorn walking stick. On the doorstep under the stars, I laced up my boots, and then I set them to the East Meadow trail.

I like this trail at night because it's so open, and I am afraid of mountain lions. Under the trees, I can't shake the feeling that a catamount is going to drop on me from above, and I get so freaked out that I see one crouched in the crotch of every shadowy limb.

I also carry a stick, because I'll fight like a wildcat myself, if I have to. And, because I'd rather warn them away with my boldness than startle them, I sing when I walk alone. Also because I like to sing.

Railway line to the top of the world—
Why you got to go so high?
Might step out now, my sweet girl,
Off'n the edge of the sky . . .

At the top of the meadows, before the trail winds into the trees and rocks and disappears into threading deer trails, sits a wide, flat-topped slab of granite. It's as liony a place as any in the meadows, and as I approached I sang louder.

Freight train clattering through the night,
Timbers on the bridges sway,
Carry me right on through my fright
And on in over the day . . .

We call this place the Carrock—the rock in *The Hobbit* where the Eagles of the Misty Mountains deposited Bilbo, Gandalf, and the dwarves. The broad surface still held some warmth from today's sun, and I stretched myself out, stunned by the masses of stars above.

The first time I came up here alone at night was in the summer after fifth grade. I'd crept out of the cabin like I did tonight, enthralled by the brilliant stars—not washed out by the false twilight of the city—and at once thrilled and terrified by being out alone. When I got to the Carrock, my heart raced from the altitude and the hike, and my blood pounded at my throat.

But as I lay on the bumpy rock under the stars, catching my breath, I relaxed and remembered sky-watching on my balcony with Jenny. It was so much better here where the stars were bright, and so much better alone. Alone, I didn't have to feel separate. And in the mountains under the sky, being different felt good.

Still, there had been something missing that night: a true friend to share the solitude. So I thought again of Jenny. I'd been angry when she asked her mom about infinity, but contemplating it under the stars, alone, my anger seemed silly, and I was glad she wasn't there. She didn't understand, I thought, and maybe she wasn't as grown up as I was. Maybe she never would understand.

Remembering all this tonight, I felt embarrassed by eleven-year-old Cassie, but I'd been right. Jenny will never grow up. She'll always ask her mother, her father, the other kids, her pastor, her husband...

And whom do I ask? On the Carrock, illuminated by the stars, whom do I ask?

No one.

I watch and I listen, but I don't need to ask anyone how to be. Even when I'm feeling all wrong, the way I am is right.

That night two years ago—just two years ago—I wondered why Jenny, if she was so religious, didn't ask God, instead of her mother. That's what she told me, that she had this personal relationship with Jesus. Why not ask Him about infinity?

So I thought I'd ask. But not Him. I gave the question to the sky, the stars, the planets, and to the bowl of the valley, empty but full of plants, rocks, openness, distance, *space*. And the bowl of the land felt suddenly alive and pulsing—each rock, each insect, each bunch of grass perfectly placed, held taught in an invisible electric web. The rock below me vibrated without moving, and the stars went fuzzy, clear, fuzzy, clear—and I felt an answer.

So I suppose I do ask someone, some thing: the land, or the presence I feel strongest in the land, always here, but hard to discover and harder to describe. I have tried to get it back—the awareness that I felt that night—and sometimes it comes, usually by surprise, and never so strong as that first time.

I tried to call it up tonight. I let my eyes go fuzzy on the stars, and I knew it was there, but it didn't come to me. At least the memory was strong tonight and real. Sometimes it seems faded by time, lost in empty words I have attached to help me remember it. But tonight it was beyond the words, and yet the words were a counterpart to the experience, like a slight breeze turning aspen leaves on their supple stems.

31 August

When I got back last night, Dad was no longer snoring.

"Go to sleep," he said.

"Sorry to wake you."

"Go to sleep."

But I had to write for a while, of course, before sleep could take me away. And I slept good and late.

I was breakfasting on a bowl of cereal and soymilk when Dad came in from fishing.

"'She goes out walking, after midnight,'" he sang, pumping some water in the sink.

"What?"

"What?"

"Stop it."

"Stop it."

"Stop mocking me, please."

He scrubbed his hands. "Fish slime," he said. Then, "I have a sixth sense about my shillelagh."

"Oh."

"How was the Carrock?"

"You followed me?"

"Well, when you didn't come back I got worried."

"I thought the sunset provision didn't apply up here."

He sat down at the table, across from me. It isn't so cool having a lawyer for a father sometimes. Even though he plays defense professionally, when his kid is involved, he works for the prosecution.

"There is no provision of the sunset law," he declared, "that nullifies it in this environment."

"Why didn't you make me come in?"

"I didn't want to interrupt your reverie." He smiled. "But...I don't like you sneaking out."

"Oh, Cassie's a sneak. Yess, preciousss. Cassie's a ssneak, *Gollum.*"

"Why did you go out without telling me?"

"Gollum doesn't know, Sméagol doesn't know. She's a ssneak."

"All right, that's enough, Sméagol."

Now he was on the bench in his judge's robe. "I know you need time alone, so you can go out as long as you walk loudly and carry a big stick. I don't want you entering the food chain just yet. And don't climb any rocks bigger than, or go any farther than, the Carrock."

I couldn't believe my luck. Maybe it was the Gollum routine, but then again, I didn't want to push it, so I stifled the impulse to grovel and cringe and say, "Yes, preciouss, we'll be good! Nice Sméagol never sneaks up nassty, cruel rockses."

"Also," he went on, "I want you to tell me where you're going and when you'll be back."

"If you're in the snore-zone, can I leave a note?"

He gave me a look with his light eyes, blue with tiny pupils contracted from the sunny windows. "Yes," he said. "But bring your watch and don't get so lost in reverie that I have to come out looking for you."

"It's a contract." I reached over, and we shook on it.

After that, Dad worked, and I went out to my tipi. I tied the sides up a little bit, so the breeze could come through, and set up my cot with my thick foam pad and blanket—just try putting a pea in there, just try it.

The tipi became more *objet d'art* than tent when Ally and I painted it last June. I'd had illusions of painting a mural over the whole thing when I first got it, but I became disillusioned about halfway through when I realized how awful it looked. So I covered it with white and tried to forget about it.

In the beginning of the summer, when Sean brought Ally back from college, she loved the tipi. She helped me set it up and then surveyed the damage I had done. I explained.

"It was not a perfect creation," Ally said, "so you obliterated it?"

"I didn't want it to be *perfect*, just *good*."

"If you don't care about creating a masterpiece, then why don't you cover it with patterns and symbols. Peace signs, yin-yang, hearts, smiley faces, flowers."

At this point my jury was still out on the girl. I watched her gazing at the tipi, her long brown hair in braids, wearing an Indian print skirt and one of Sean's white V-necks, no bra. Serious church of latter day hippie.

"Trouble is," I said, trying to be clever and biting, "smiley faces might nauseate me more than what I did before. I'm not trying to create a set for 'That '70s Show'—"

"You're right," she laughed. "What about Indian stuff, Native American, very flat shapes—you can't mess them up. I see thunderbirds, lightning bolts, brother salmon—"

"Cliché."

She laughed again, sort of a, "You're right, I'm silly," but not in a fake, annoying way. She really thought it was funny. And maybe she was impressed that I wasn't.

"I was thinking of easy stuff you could do yourself, but if you'd let me help you—I mean, I've got nothing better to do for the coming week except tag along with the fisher of fish here—"

"Ally *is* an artist, Cass," Sean said. "You should take advantage of her talents."

A very accomplished lady, I thought. A master of all the hippie arts: rolling of the marijuana cigarette, painting of the smiley face, Phish music on the pianoforte . . .

"Okay, well here's my concept," she said, "take it or leave it: no symbols, just an abstract of land and sky. Colors and shapes—some in contrast, some blending into one another, beginning with earth browns at the bottom, changing to red to green to blue, with a sudden sun at the top of the cone, possibly rays shooting down into the rest."

I had to admit, to myself, that it sounded kind of cool.

"It wouldn't stand out too much?" I worried. "All that red and orange?"

"Just a little of those—and we'll mix the colors of the landscape."

She struck a professorial pose. "The piece will enhance the environment, reflect its beauty without attempting to upstage it." She broke her pose and pointed to the Goat-horn, still wearing its snowy cap, shining against the blue. "How can you compete with that, anyway?"

And right about then I started to like her a little, though I didn't let on.

"Won't this masterpiece take some time?"

"It doesn't have to be a masterpiece, it just has to look good, right? And we can do it in under a week. Come on," she said. "Let's see if those paints you started with are still any good. What did you use?"

"Liquitex?"

"Perfect."

So while Sean went out on his first few guiding jobs of the season or fished by himself, we painted. We had to start early in the morning because it rained most afternoons. We got some giant sheets of plastic and wrapped the whole thing when the clouds came. Then I slept in my plastic-wrapped art object while they stayed in the cabin.

I'll tell more about Ally later—writing about her gets me alternately energized and depressed. Though I resented her at first, we ended up very close. Just in time for her to go back to college with Sean, a thousand miles away. So I'm alone again, substituting a diary for a friend. I think it helps me feel that she isn't so far away after all, as if this book is a long letter to her.

When the shadows were long, I went down to the beaver ponds with Dad. I sat under the fir trees above the pond, tired after eating, and watched him sneak up under the dam. He waded in the creek below, played out some line as he waved his rod back and forth, and laid it out flat on the surface.

Splash! A fish hit his fly, and he raised his rod, which bent under the strain and zigzagged back and forth as the frenzied trout fought its unseen enemy. Dad brought it to the top of the dam where it splashed as he reached in, freed it from the barbless hook, and released it without pulling it from the water.

His next fish took the fly and ran for the far side, then straight back at him as he furiously stripped the line in by hand. He netted this trout, and had some trouble removing the hook, holding the fish out of the water and talking to it as he worked the hook free. Then it flipped out of his hand, and he continued talking to the surface of the water where the trout held still below the surface before flashing away into the unseen world.

Watching Dad talk to the trout, I remembered the huge drought we had when I was six. Big fires burned all over the West, and a massive one started about twenty miles northwest of the cabin. From the city, it looked like rain clouds were building up in the northwest. The whole sky turned yellow with smoke and stayed that way for almost two weeks. We couldn't have windows open for the filthy air and had to stay inside in the heat. It only rained once during that time—a brief but intense storm from clouds seeded by ash and smoke. There was a thrashing wind and rain, then hail stripped the garden, piled up on the ground, and lay melting amid a scent like water poured on a campfire. That was the worst of it, I think, the one thing that made it seem like doomsday: rain that smelled like fire.

Just after the fire started, Dad took Sean and me to the cabin to clear a firebreak, and before we went home he insisted on fishing. We followed our little stream—running at less than half its normal flow, down to where Two Mile Creek added its pathetic trickle, summing to a stream that would support fish—barely. The peaks that watered our valley with snowmelt had long gone dry, and all along the bank, usually lush and boggy, only a few blades of green grass poked through last year's dry growth.

Sean went off downstream, while I sat watching my dad,

smelling smoke on the air and feeling that everything was dry and dying. When he got a fish on the line, he called me over. I waded in next to him, cool water on my feet and ankles, as he pulled out a brook trout as long as his hand.

"Hey, little trout, you go talk to the rain clouds, will you?" He lowered the fish into the stream and it darted to the shadows under the bank. "We need rain, little brother—you need it, we need it—the land is thirsty. So go swim upstream and bring us some rain."

He did this with every catch, not many with how low the water was. And before we left, he poured out the rest of our water bottle, wetting the lichen on the rocks and splashing some into the creek.

I'd seen him do these things before, talking to fish and sharing water with lichen and pouring off the top of his beer in an offering. It's strange because he's not religious, and doesn't—except for these rituals—seem interested in the mystical side of nature. Geology is his science, along with ecology, so when he claims that the rock is alive, he means that it changes and rearranges itself in its own cycle. He doesn't mean that the rock has soul.

Or does he? And do I? I don't know, Di, I don't know. And what is spirit or soul, and who cares? I don't know, Di, I don't know. Sylvia Plath talks about the incandescence of things, "sudden tricks of radiance" and sometimes they do shine. But sometimes they are dull and dead. And if it's just me that makes them dull and dead because I can't see their light, is it also me that makes them shine?

Oh, yeah. Asking those tough questions.

1 September

We took the car down to the big river today, and Dad's wading down the canyon to the deep holes where the wise, old trout live. I'm perched on a rock jutting into the stream. Though I was going to, I don't feel much like hiking. I can't put it out of my mind that we're going home tomorrow. There will be Mom's concert in the afternoon and then, on Tuesday, back to school.

I never was a kid who loved school—though I did have a shining moment in fifth grade. I mock eighth grade because I'm outside of things, and I can see the shallow pride and the mean attitude. Back in fifth I was an outsider, too, but I wasn't aware of it. I sailed along in my own world, feeling smart and awake and alive.

One reason I liked school then, for a few minutes, was because of all the independent projects. The teachers ditched the textbooks and taught us by letting us do things. It was a little like my Montessori pre-school when I got to pick up beans with a pair of tongs and drop them in a bowl.

In writing center, I got to write whatever I wanted, and I made up all kinds of stories and poems. But the projects were the best part. You had to include every subject plus one of the arts, and you researched whatever you wanted. My first project was on vegetarianism, titled, "Should Things with Faces Eat Things with Faces?" My second was going to be "Beyond Vegetarianism—Faceless and Hidden Meats," but they said that was the same topic.

Then I went on to more animal rights stuff, and one of my favorite things was making up titles:

Love Your Pets—Set them Free

Of Course I Love Animals!
But If it Means a Closer Shave,
then TORTURE the Little #!**&#$*&%$!

(Why Cosmetics Users Should
Have Products Tested on Themselves)

Fab, Fab Fur—
Inside Animal Concentration Camps

My projects were sort of inflammatory for fifth grade, I guess, and the last one was nixed for political incorrectness: how dare I equate a mink farm with a death camp?

"This really happened," my teacher said as he leaned forward, his face drawn. "The Nazis tortured and murdered people, *people*, do you understand?"

I did understand. I had just read Anne Frank's *Diary*, and I used to look at those smiling pictures of her, that girl that they murdered. I know it was typhus, but they killed her just the same. And not just her—millions like her.

I didn't see the difference that gave us the right to torture and kill animals. And I couldn't explain it to my teacher. "That's not what I meant," I mumbled, about to cry. "I know about that. But it doesn't mean we should hurt animals. I'll change it. I'll change it."

"It's okay, Cassie, I just wanted to make sure you know. We have to be sensitive."

"That's what I'm trying to say."

"Okay," he said. "That's good. Same topic, different title, and stay away from the concentration camp thing. Stay sensitive."

I went back to my table, thinking, What about you? Were you sensitive to your bacon this morning? And what about the chickens who laid your eggs, their claws locked around the cage wires, pumped full of drugs and blinded by artificial sunlight? *Stay sensitive!*

2 September

At the concert in the park:

Aye, 'tis hot, Di, down here on the flatlands. The park is filled with people enjoying a "pops" concert. My mother is beautiful on stage: straight back, dark hair up above her slender, pale neck, and most of all, her concentration on the music.

I've brought some poems to help me forget the seething crowd—Sylvia Plath, Galway Kinnell—but it doesn't work. The "rare, random descent" of the angel in "Black Rook in Rainy Weather" just pisses me off, probably because I'd like to feel some sort of enlightenment myself, and it's so far away.

I wonder if other people keep it away: the angel, the radiance? Not always, because I have seen it burning on them. And in a crowd like this I have seen it too, but it separates me from them because they don't see it.

Why do I hate them for that?

Another question is, do the smug, self-satisfied Christian soldiers see it? Does Jesus give it to them, does he give them the light? Do they only see it through him, and is that why they want to kill the world and die and go to pure light while the rest of us sinners are left behind in a toxic wasteland? Do they *want* to kill the world?

As usual, no answers, but good ol' Cass keeps askin' them questions. So you don't have to.

I come across another poem, "When One Has Lived a Long Time Alone." This one helps a little more, but it makes me envy the poet. I need to live alone—in my tipi with no one, not even family around—and for months, years, if I want to get to the point described at the end, when "one wants to live again among men and women." At this point, I feel like the poet does in the first stanza, hesitating "to strike the mosquito, though more than willing to slap the flesh under her…"

After a nice post-concert dinner at home, Dad grilling up some tempeh for me along with their chicken and wine, I came upstairs to read.

I could have brought my book with me this weekend, but I saved it for tonight. I've read it before, Lois Lowry's *The Giver*, and knew I could polish it off in a night. My lit circle group picked it, and it's easy and good, a futuristic story of a "community" with no problems and no freedom. Also no differences and no prejudice, no history, no sense of future, no choices, and no books except for a book of rules.

Only "the Giver" has real books. He is an old man who also has, through some sort of psychic ability, memories of all time. After being the "Receiver of Memory," he now becomes the Giver, transmitting those memories to the protagonist of the story, Jonas.

One thing I noticed reading it this time is that there is no nature in the community. A river runs along one border, and there must be a sky because there are fighter planes, but there are no hills, no animals, nothing except "sameness."

The other thing that struck me was how the Giver's previous apprentice, who happened to be his daughter, committed suicide. I could imagine that, after being raised in a society in which "I take pleasure in your accomplishments" and "I enjoy your company" are considered better word usage than "I love you" (an ancient phrase that no longer signifies), learning real emotion might be hard to handle. Was it really the memories of despair that brought her to despair, or the memories of bliss and love that, once her training was over, she could never share?

I have to come up with two questions for discussion, so I'm going to ask:

What do you think about the first receiver's decision? And,

In 100 years, will our society be more like or less like that of *The Giver?*

3 September

A morning of garbage trucks in the alley.

Though I'm not sure what things will be like in 100 years, I can imagine that in the not-so-distant future, we'll have a trash quota. All garbage will be weighed and measured to ensure that everyone is consuming enough and throwing enough away. This will inspire all citizens to do their part to make America great. X-ray screening and random checks will prevent people from faking their garbage quotas, but most people will participate honorably and enthusiastically. Nothing shows "patriotism" better than good, old-fashioned garbage!

School today was okay; my lit group is not too heinous. Mr. Sinclair made the groups after my little blow-up, and mine seemed designed to help me avoid the people who hate me. Todd and Maddie had questions that took about thirty seconds to answer, lame stuff like, "Why don't they get to choose their husbands and wives?"

Everyone except me thought the receiver who committed suicide, Rosemary, was weak and pathetic and made the wrong choice.

"I think it was her dad's fault, too," said Todd. "He said—what did he say?—that he gave her memories that were bad."

"Too painful?" I said.

"Yeah, and she can't get any of that pain relief."

Mr. Sinclair pulled up a chair. "Relief of pain," he said. "You're talking about?"

"It's Cassie's question," said Maddie. "She wants to know if what's-her-name—"

"Rosemary."

"Whatever—made the right choice. Obviously not. She's dead."

"But wasn't it her only out?" I wanted to know.

"Suicide is a permanent solution to a temporary problem," Maddie said.

Really? That was original!

"And it was cowardly," said Evan. "She wasn't strong enough to solve her problems."

"But," said Mr. Sinclair, "doesn't the Giver think she was courageous?"

"That was because she gave herself the needle," said Evan. "She didn't need the nurses to stick her."

"I still think it was the Giver's fault," said Todd. "He said he gave her too many memories of pain."

"Do you guys remember," I said, "what memory it was that she couldn't handle?"

Evan grabbed his book. "Wait, I know—where is it?" He flipped through the pages.

"Despair," I said.

"I don't think so...Got it! Loss. Loneliness. A child taken from its mother. But that wasn't the last one." He skimmed the next page. "It doesn't say. Finally, one day after a hard session, she acted all calm, but she went to the medical center and before the Giver knew what was going on, she was dead. He watched it on video.

"Wait," he continued, grinning, "shouldn't they have DVD by this time?"

"I thought it said despair."

"What's despair?" asked Maddie.

"Hopelessness."

"Well, where there's life, there's hope," she said. "And what she did was wrong because only God has the power to take a life."

Here we go again, I thought. And luckily the bell rang, because I was about to ask her if that meant God had killed Rosemary. If only God can take a life, doesn't it follow that

God kills everyone who dies? And if God kills everyone, didn't God kill Jesus too?

So I survived that okay, Di. Where there's life, there's hope. Or despair.

Now I want to go back to what I was saying about fifth grade:

Each of my animal rights projects had to be presented to the class. Some kids laughed at me, but I didn't care. I'd always been a loner. There were a few kids I could play with at recess, but always off to the side, the edges, the corners. If I tried to get into a four-square game with the perfect kids, the social elite—and this group existed even in kindergarten—forget it. I wasn't fast enough to get a square in the beginning, and as soon as my turn came, they all bombed me. I never got any further than the "baby" square.

But the fifth-grade Shakespeare performance, *Twelfth Night*, put me right in the center of things, if just for a moment.

The tryouts were an assignment: everybody had to memorize a section of the play and present it. From that, the teachers decided who would play whom. Everybody got a part or some other job, from stage crew to costumes, and the whole fifth grade put on the play—not exactly as it came to us from the Bard's own quill, but a fifth-grade version with as much of the Elizabethan language as they thought we could handle. The big parts were divided up, and I got Viola for the final two acts.

This didn't change my reputation overnight. There were several girls who thought they should've had it, some who'd had drama classes and acting experience, and they were not exactly in love with me. But as the rehearsals went on, I was lifted up, I became their Viola (or Cesario) and they *did* start to love me. So much that the other girl who played the part dropped out and insisted that I do it all. It didn't make sense— I don't know why they latched on to me, but they did.

One thing I know they loved was the way I said the lines, the way I used an English accent and even went back to the original script for some of the speeches. Their favorite was,

And I, most jocund, apt and willingly,
To do you rest, a thousand deaths would die.

It killed them. Who knows why, but they loved it, they couldn't get enough of it. It's written all over my little fifth-grade yearbook—just the "most jocund" part—along with instructions to call over the summer and not forget them in middle school.

But as it turned out, *they* forgot *me*. Boys who wrote in my fifth grade yearbook, "Your cool, letz get 2gethuh!" looked right through me in sixth. It wasn't that they suddenly turned mean, these popular people who had embraced me, it was just that *I* thought I had become their friend, but they had no further use for me.

Not that there wasn't meanness too, but that came from my old friend, former friend, Jenny. Since I'd dropped out of soccer, we didn't see much of each other that summer, but when we did, it was okay. Then, in the fall, she turned on me. She would pass me in the hall and say, "Hey, Drama Queen" or "Your Ladyship," and her new group would all laugh.

I was baffled. I had been laughed at before, but this was different. It was cruel, not thoughtless. I feared and avoided

Jenny and her friends, but I still felt the burn of shame whenever they were near, even after they got bored and ignored me.

So that was my little rise and fall. It was cool to have all that energy, first my own for animal rights, and second, the energy of the crowd, as they made me their star. Then, sixth grade was a year of falling, and after that, seventh grade—an abyss.

Journal Three

4 September

A fall chill in the air this morning, Di, and birds are flocking. Starlings have filled the trees, making a huge racket, chattering and calling in ascending and descending whistles like the silver whirly-siren I used to have.

School really rules, know that? It just rules. I have two electives this quarter—Español, which is way too easy, but in a tolerable sort of way, and choir. I like to sing, and Mom insists that I take some kind of music. Though I tried piano and cello, I don't have the knack for instruments. Too uncoordinated.

The show choir is a bit silly—we have to wear these dorky tuxedo uniforms and do little dance numbers. All the parents love it, and we do sound good, except that the boys never really sing loud enough and only care about being paired with some Q.T. for the dance routines. I dropped down into the regular choir for about a day, but I could not handle how slow they went and how bad they sounded. If Mom is going to insist on choir, at least I want to be in the good one.

I sound like a snob, Di, I know. Cassie is better than everyone. Too cool for the show choir, too musically sensitive for the other one. But I'm not proud of it. I just don't fit in with the over-achievers or the regular people. I'm just weird me, and it gets worse.

"Guess what new song we're learning in choir?" I asked Mom and Dad tonight.

"Give us twenty questions," said Dad. "Animal, vegetable, or mineral?"

"Animal. Mom?"

"Is it bigger than a bread-box?"

"Much."

"Have we heard it before?"

"Oh, yeah."

"Was it written in the last one hundred years?"

"Yep."

"When are you going to perform it?"

"School Assembly. September 11 memorial."

"Was it written in the last twenty-five years?"

"Yes."

"Is it about pride?"

"Yup."

Dad burst into the chorus, "'I'm proud to be an American, where at least I know I'm free!'"

"I thought," said Mom, "that you were *learning* a new song. This one won't take much of that, now will it?"

"There has to be the usual choral arrangement," Dad said. "Some snappy dance steps—come on, Deb, don't be so elitist."

"If it's elitist to hate that song, then I'm guilty. Couldn't Mr. Kimble have chosen some more significant music?"

"'America the Beautiful?'" suggested Dad, and I was about to say that we're doing that one too, but I couldn't get a word in.

"Yes, 'America the Beautiful.' It's overdone, but there's music to it, and the lyrics are at least poetic and written locally. But for a memorial I was thinking more along the lines of a requiem."

"What about that new Toby Keith thing?"

"*Who* is Toby Keith?"

"Cowboy dude, blond," said Dad, "goatee, acts like he has a trademark on the American flag?"

"Cassie," she said. "What do you think about the song selection?"

"Well, we're doing 'Beautiful' already—not that anybody asked—"

"I did ask, darling."

"And since you did, I don't mind 'America the Beautiful,' but I despise the other one."

"Why don't you just move to I-rack then, little missy," said Dad. "Move to I-rack and see how you feel about Suh-day-um then."

"Shush, Gale. Honey, we despise it too. Why do you?"

Now came the critical thinking exercise. Their attitude is that it's good that I hate what they hate, but I have to explain it myself. It's almost enough to make a Republican out of me. Just to see them freak out.

"Well," I said, "I agree that a requiem would be more fitting. If we had time to learn one. And the song is lame, musically."

"Is that enough to make you despise it?" said Dad.

"Yes." Approving nods here. "But there's more." Expectant looks. "Everyone hates us, right? I mean, not everyone. So many people around the world felt terrible when we were attacked."

Now the silence. They weren't going to feed me any hints to help me out. As if they hadn't already brainwashed me to their point of view.

"I just think that saying you're proud because you know you're free doesn't have anything to do with freedom. There's nothing wrong with being proud, I guess…but it's not about freedom. It's about being all patriotic."

"So you're not patriotic?"

"Yes, I am. But standing up and yelling about it? I mean, while people are singing these patriotic songs, our civil liberties are being eaten away, one by one."

"You're just saying what I've been saying," said Dad. "Word for word. And I'm glad you've been listening to your dad, but what about you?"

This was tougher than any test I took at school.

Mom stepped in: "What are your feelings on 9/11? Why doesn't the song seem right to you?"

"My feelings…Okay. I think about what I saw on TV: firefighters going up the stairs, flight after flight, while people were coming down—" This was one of the images that kept coming back to me. "And then the towers just going down."

Dad reached over and put his hand over mine. Mom got up and rubbed my shoulders, stroked my hair back away from my neck. I shrugged her off.

"And then we go over there and just start bombing Afghanistan. I mean, the Taliban was terrible, but what about all those kids," I choked, "those innocent little kids who got blown up? And everybody here is all fired up and proud to be an American, but why does everybody have to kill each other?"

I was about to lose it.

"Okay, honey, okay." This time I leaned back into her as she stood behind me, hands on my shoulder, bending to kiss the top of my head.

"But *why?*" I pulled away again.

"We don't have any answers, Cass," said Dad, "but you're asking the right questions."

"You give us hope, honey," said Mom.

"How can I? I'm so pathetic."

"Why do you say that?"

"Because I *don't* have any hope. There is none."

"You are wrong, daughter," said Dad. "You're right about everything else—but about that one thing, you're mistaken."

I wiped the tears I'd been trying to hold back and blew my nose. Common sense told me not to argue with him on this point, but he's the one who is wrong. He's right about everything else, but about this one thing, he's mistaken.

5 September

Not too bad today. I was so nervous that I wasn't really stretching the truth when I told Mr. Kimble that I felt a little sick and asked if I could sit down. I felt better after they rehearsed the hated song, which was coming together marvelously, probably due to the quality of the karaoke soundtrack they were singing with. Now that's what I call music.

Dad said tonight that he would call my teacher, get me excused from the song. Usually, he said, he would have me fight my own battles, but this was clearly too upsetting. And what good was it to have parents, especially one who's a lawyer, if they didn't argue your case for you? I said no, told him if he made so much as one call to the school I'd try out for a solo on the hated song, just for spite.

6 September

Instead of being sick today, I just stood there and didn't sing. When Mr. Kimble started looking at me, I mouthed the words a little bit. I probably shouldn't have, but I haven't decided what to do. For sure I don't want Dad to call. But what's the alternative? I've always been taught to stand up for what I believe. Not that it does any good.

Back in fifth grade, I stood up for my beliefs by trying to convert my family to veganism, mostly by spoiling the meal with information about what they were eating.

"Enjoying your dead, skinned, charred bird, Mother?"

"Father, did you know that cheese is made with the lining of a baby cow's stomach?"

The trouble is, he did.

"Yes, daughter, I know what rennet is, and so did you, even before the Persons for Eatable Table Animals got ahold of your mind with their online brainwashing. In fact, we sat at this very table and read about rennet when you were five. Have you forgotten your Laura Ingalls Wilder?"

"Actually, Gale," said Mom, "I think you're forgetting too. Your Cassandra was pretty upset by the pig and calf butchering."

"And after *Charlotte's Web*," said Sean, "she was a vegetarian for a couple of weeks. And that was when she only ate five things."

"You're right," said Dad. "Removing hot dogs and bacon from her diet limited her to milk, bread, and fruit."

"Which is really—" I began, only to be interrupted by Mom.

"And candy—anything sweet was always the fifth food group. I blame it on that nurse who put sugar-water on my nipple to try to get you to latch on. You were even fussy on the breast. Anything I ate, you could taste."

"Do I have to hear another conversation about Cassie the Picky Eater?"

"Do we have to listen to another sermon," said Dad, "about poor animals and the barbarisms of food production?"

Discouraged by the futility of talking, I tried direct action and had my own little Boston Meat Party. On trash pickup day, I threw away every animal product in the kitchen. Cans of tuna, frozen steaks, eggs, macaroni and cheese—all of it in the trash. The milk and cream I poured out into the sink, leaving the empty jugs in the fridge for dramatic effect.

Mom and Dad were stunned.

"Cassie, I can't believe you would waste all that food," Mom said.

"I don't consider carrion to be food."

"But think of all the people in the world who don't have enough of any kind of food? It's an insult to them—and to the animals who produced it."

"If you took all the grain that goes to feed livestock, and used it for people instead, then people wouldn't have to starve," I replied.

"This is insufferable," said Dad. "To be tyrannized by an eleven-year-old! I'm going to the store to get some steaks, a rack of lamb, twenty pounds of veal cutlet, a wheel of extra-rennet Brie, and probably a fur coat. And you, little girl, will get no allowance until you've paid restitution."

I wasn't really taking him seriously because he was going off like he always did. So I pushed it a little more. "The tyranny is us over the animals, Dad. I'm just being the voice of the voiceless—"

When I saw how he was looking at me, I stopped. I looked at Mom. She was really mad, too.

"Cassie," she said. "What are you trying to do here? Exactly what do you hope to accomplish?"

I wanted a "cruelty-free zone." I wanted nobody to eat animal foods or use products made from dead animals or tested on live ones. What I got was months of no allowance and extra chores until I had paid for everything that I ditched. They might have eaten a little less meat and looked at their labels a little more carefully afterwards, but they weren't big carnivores to begin with.

And I guess I didn't learn my lesson, because that year I ruined an old tradition in the cause of animal rights. Every year on New Year's Day, no matter what the weather, we went fishing in the Canyon. Some years it's been miserably cold, and we've spent more time warming up with coffee and hot chocolate than standing in the freezing river fighting the wind. But this year, fifth grade, it was sunny and warm when we started on the trail to the bottom of the reservoir dam.

In previous years I had come along as a fisher-girl, but this year, I was giving it up. Despite the fact that in our family we rarely kill fish, I thought it was cruel. Catch and release is worse than fishing for food. What's the point of fooling the poor things just so you can make them fight for their lives and then, godlike, release them?

We had a lot of discussions, with me asking things like,

"How would you like it if your steak had a big metal hook in it, and you got dragged by your lip to the top of the sky?" But their fly-fishing was the only thing that connected them to their primitive roots, the mystery of the hunt or some such nonsense, according to Mom. So I pretended to be resigned to it, just coming along for the ride.

But as soon as they rigged up and were ready to try out the pool below the dam, I let fly with a big rock that splashed, gloriously, just where Sean was about to cast.

Sean and Dad looked at the river as a big, ringed wave raced outwards, lapping the bank and dispersing into the fast current of the channel. They just stood there, and I almost regretted it, seeing their high spirits decline along with the waves from my rock.

Dad gave me a hurt look. Sean carefully put down his fishing rod. And then he came after me, lumbering up the hill in his waders and big felt-bottomed boots. Before I thought to run, he was on me, pushing me down on the gravel scree.

"You little brat! You're such a brat!"

"Go ahead, beat up your little sister, just like you beat up the poor fishies."

Since my down jacket had me cushioned, he wasn't really hurting me, but he was scaring me a lot, sitting on me and practically spitting into my face.

"I should, you brat, you stupid little brat!"

"Go ahead, tough guy!"

"You've ruined it! Ruined it."

Dad strolled up, and instead of pulling Sean off, he put a hand on his shoulder.

Sean stopped yelling and grinding my arms into the ground. He got up.

It's the only time we ever had a physical fight—if you can call it that. And I gotta say that it doesn't feel great to bring your sixteen-year-old brother to violence. It might if he were a mean brother, picking on me and ditching me when his friends were around. But Sean was always the sweetest brother in the world. I guess I reduced him and Dad to enemies in my crusade to, as they saw it, keep a few trout from getting sore lips.

I know there are cruel fathers in the world—dads who would have given us both a couple of cuffs and maybe devised something really bad for me, like making me wade into the icy river and retrieve the stone I had thrown. But all mine did was stand looking at me, using his silence to tell me how far over the line I had strayed.

"Let's go home, kids," he said, finally. "No fish will bleed this day."

7 September

Great news, Di—I'm surrounded by the freshness of morning in the mountains, with the sunshine streaming in my tipi door. When Dad came home last night, he said he'd gotten a plea bargain on what was going to be a mother of a trial on Monday. So we came up here after all. He and Mom were for going this morning, but I talked them into coming up last night. We hit the Tex-Mex in Woodland Park for dinner and went to bed in the mountains.

I got my tipi the summer after the terrible New Year's, and we all spent a lot of time at the cabin that year. I had given up soccer, and Sean spent almost the whole summer up here by himself. He was doing a lot of guiding, taking tourists out fishing. Most parents might not want their seventeen-year-old kids at their cabins alone, but Sean is not the party-boy type.

I loved the tipi because it was my own private place, and because it was just one step closer to being outside. On rainy days, I would stay out here reading and listening to the drops on the canvas. On sunny days, I would open the smoke-hole and roll up the sides, feeling the cool breeze as I lay around in the shade.

I read up a storm that summer, mostly novels I brought with me but also some of the cabin books. I admit that I was exaggerating when I said before, all cool, about natural history, "Call me a freak—I like the stuff." I'm not some Thomas Jefferson, devouring scientific and philosophical texts for hours on end. The only books I *devour* are novels, but I started to enjoy a sampling of nature writing that summer.

As I read about the land, I began to read the land itself, exploring with Mom, sometimes with Sean or Dad. Mostly I hiked alone, carrying a notebook to record my "observations." I was almost twelve then and was allowed on solo walks as long as I didn't climb any rocks taller than I was or steeper than 45 degrees. I also had to leave a route and return time.

I've known this place my whole life, but I *really* began to know it that year. I came to see how all the little valleys and meadows and high ridges connected, what the easy ways around were, and what climbs led to dead-end rock walls or sheer drop-offs. Toward the end of the summer, I had the comforting sensation of coming by new routes to familiar places, then returning home by the old paths.

Dad accused me of becoming a Taoist hermit and called me "Cassandra Wannabe Pocahontas"—or was that the next summer, when I read Lao Tzu, Black Elk, and the biography of Crazy Horse? I guess that summer it was "tree-hugger" and "Abbey's Acolyte," though the gist of it was the same: he teased me for not hanging out at the mall with my friends because he was proud that I was different, but maybe a little worried as well.

Mom encouraged me to share my interests, to find friends who would dig the mountains the way I did. Right.

And I suppose it's no wonder that I was in for it when school started in sixth grade. My head was still in a cloud wrapped around the summit of the Goat-horn, and I was suddenly tall enough to tower over everyone else in the hall. Among the other barbs flung at me by former friends, I forgot to mention "Mountain Girl," which seemed to be some sort of double- or triple- entendre.

I have since wondered what I'd done wrong. Was I acting stuck-up? I don't think so, but I have to admit it: I thought there were more important things than shopping, boy bands, and whatever else they obsessed on. Mostly I was oblivious to them, which must have made me a target, right? I didn't notice things like the fact that my jeans were floating four inches above the ground until I was being teased about it.

Fortunately, Mom had given up on dragging me to the mall. She took my measurements, gave me a stack of catalogs, and made me circle at least fifteen things I would wear. That has become the tradition, twice a year, whether I need it or not.

And with the way I was growing, Mom became obsessed with my nutrition, reminding me that my health was more important than my ideals. I wasn't convinced this was the case, but I knew better than to argue.

"Two glasses of soy milk only give you half the calcium a normal person needs. With the bone mass you're adding, you need four times that. Your genes have programmed you to be tall—you can be tall with strong bones, or brittle and stooped."

"Okay, don't get hysterical."

"Well, your calcium is still sitting here and so is last night's iron."

"But iron makes me sick."

"Take it with food. A young woman needs iron."

Since I had done plenty of research on veganism, I didn't think she needed to be so obsessive about it. But it did look like I was going to shoot up to about six feet in six months, which is what happened, and thanks to all the soy milk and fossilized seashells she jammed down my gob, I think my bones are solid.

School that year doesn't warrant more than another paragraph. I did my work and kept to myself. My teachers were pretty nice if they weren't in bad moods. By mid-year Sophia and Gwen had invited me to eat with them, so at least I didn't have to pick my way aimlessly through the hostile lunch tables. Then Hannah found us, and we had the safety of numbers.

It's just starting to rain, after half an hour of rumbling thunder and wind gusting around outside. I'm going to make a dash for the cabin before it gets too bad. Must be about dinnertime too.

"Did you know that Mr. Griffin sponsors two clubs?" Mom said as she poured herself some wine and topped off Dad's.

"I don't wish to belong," I said.

"He does a writing club and also has a Tolkien group. Sean loved him. I was so upset when he went down to seventh grade and you couldn't have him."

"So here's your chance," said Dad, "to hang out with the coolest teacher ever."

"Just go to one meeting of each. See if you like it."

"Okay," I said.

"A little belonging wouldn't be such a bad…"

"I said okay, Mom. I'll try it."

It was still raining when I went back out to my tipi, and I had a little leak dripping down one of the poles. I shifted my cot over to the other side, put on my rain parka, left the obligatory note, and went out to the Carrock.

The scent of willows rose in the misty air along with the sound of water trickling in the meadow wash. The rain stopped, but since the Carrock was slick and too wet for sitting, I stood beside it watching the clouds blowing free of the stars.

A coyote gave a series of barks, rising into a thin, yipping howl.

I waited to hear an answer, but none came. Then a breeze swept past me, upslope, and the clouds blew off the moon. Little coyote got himself going again, and the Goat-horn shone with new snow under the half-moon, as answering howls drifted from the sunset rocks and ridges in the east where the city light glowed. All else was still as the land and the plants absorbed the rain, and the clouds again covered the moon.

8 September

Though I was afraid we'd have to leave early, Mom and Dad wanted to linger, too, and Mom and I took a long hike up to the saddle beneath the Goat-horn.

We followed the creek until it veered west under the Goat-horn ridge. The trail ends there, and we angled our way through the worst part: a steep section under the trees where fallen timber lies all over the place and big boulders stand in every gap. Traversing back and forth, climbing over, under, and around logs and squeezing between trees and rocks, it was impossible to judge distance or direction. The grade of the mountainside was our only guide—so we just went up.

When the trees thinned into scattered limber pines and bristlecones, we emerged right beneath the saddle. Today's new snow lay unmelted and undisturbed all over the north-facing bowl like brilliant and slippery icing. We made our way slowly up, and on the ridge-top we found a snug, south-facing niche where we stopped for lunch.

The view was glorious—high peaks distant and near. To the west, the Collegiates, to the south, the Sangres, and to the east—across and above us—the Peak stood huge and snow-dusted, one giant piece of granite. Below us, two little reservoirs reflected the blue.

I remembered a trip to the reservoirs with Sean the summer before last. He'd hauled all his fishing gear up there, and while he fished the upper lake, Mom and I looked for wildflowers, then settled in on the rocks like lizards in the sun. It was mid-July and—unusual for that altitude—windless and hot.

"Wish we had swimming suits," I said.

"Sean's busy at the upper lake—we could skinny-dip."

I scanned the slopes above us, looking for hidden watchers. "Didn't he and Dad say they saw some other fishermen up here?"

"I don't see anybody today."

The truth was that I wasn't too keen on baring my birthday suit in front of my mom, even if there were no other eyes upon us.

"Come on," she said. "Don't be such a prude."

"I don't think so, Mom."

Our rock jutted out into the water, and she was dangling her feet in, testing it.

"It's so cold, a dip is all we'll be able to stand—"

"I don't think so."

"Well, I'm cooling off."

She stripped, and slipped into the water, whooping, to her shoulders, then shot out again, hauling herself back onto the rock.

"Wheeeeeeeee-hooooooo! More like *freezing* off. Once more."

This time she kicked off from the rock and did half a dozen strokes out into the lake, her pale bottom mooning on the surface, before turning and racing back.

She came up sputtering and blowing, dried herself a little with her sweatshirt, and got dressed again. I cooled off by wading in up to my thighs and dunking my face and hair, but I felt lame, chicken, and as Mom said, like a prude.

Today, Mom and I braced ourselves against the wind, gazing down at the blue lakes amid patches of snow.

"Skinny dipping?" I suggested.

"Now you're up for it," she said, reaching her arm around my shoulder and pulling me over to her, "when there's too much cold and not enough time."

She held me next to her for a minute, leaned her head against mine, and then kissed my head through my cap.

"Come on," she said. "We'd better go down."

9 September

Dearest Di: school was amusing today. I got a hard time in my lit circle for not finishing the new book, *A Light in the Forest*. I could have, but it was making me mad—another story about settlers and Indians, and guess who wins in the end?

So, I had to sit out the discussion and read, which served to remind me that showing up and doing your work is the best way to avoid being bothered. But as I skimmed the rest of the book and wrote my questions, it occurred to me that this wasn't so bad. Maybe if I was always behind, I'd always get to skip out on the group discussion.

Next was choir. When it was time for the hated song, I got down off the riser—I'm in the back row—and sat over in the corner. Mr. Kimble waved me back up, but I shook my head no.

After they went through it once, he came over.

"Are you okay, Cassie?" He squatted by my chair, speaking low—a little private chat.

"I'm all right," I answered.

"What is it with this song? I'm beginning to notice a pattern."

"A pattern?" All innocence.

"First you get sick, then you're mouthing—you think I can't tell? Now you just step down. I think I've been indulgent, maybe *too* indulgent, but we are per*form*ing the day after tomorrow. It is time for you to sing. So get back up there and sing this song."

I remembered how he'd taught us diaphragmatic breathing—I was using it now to help steady myself.

I shook my head.

"Get back in your spot and sing," he said. His face was red, like he was holding his breath—while I continued the deep belly-breaths and shook my head again.

Then he exhaled a long sigh. Kids were turning around to see what was going on.

"May I ask why not?"

"It's personal."

"Well, take your *person* out into the *hall* until you're ready to *sing*."

"Yes, sir," I said, but I'm afraid it came out in a mocking tone. I must have overdone the pseudo-sincerity.

This was the second time I had been sent out into the hall this year. It isn't so bad, really.

I waited until I heard the opening chords of "America the Beautiful," then I slipped back in and climbed into place. I sang loudly and clearly—just to prove my patriotism. We sang right to the bell, and I slipped out with the crowd, which delivered me some strange sideways glances. I think Mr. Kimble wanted me to stick around for another chat, but I was gone.

10 September

In English today, they came and got me. I'm used to seeing kids get the orange summons to the office, but it had never come for me.

Dr. Hawkens, assistant principal for discipline, motioned me into a chair across from his desk. He pressed a couple of buttons on his phone and slid his mouse around a little, clicking here and there as he listened to the phone and scanned his monitor. Then he put down the phone and turned to me.

"Cassandra Sullivan—I haven't seen you up here before. I think the only time we've met is when I've read your name at our honor assemblies. No previous discipline referrals. Four point-oh GPA. Advanced on all your CSAPs, though last spring's aren't in yet." He looked at me, smiling a little close-mouthed smile. "What's the sudden insubordination and disrespect for staff and students—what's this all about?"

"What do you mean?"

He waved the referral in his hand. "Choir yesterday."

"I wasn't disrespectful."

He folded his hands on his desk. "Why don't you tell me what happened in there."

"What does it say?"

"Asked you first." He grinned. "I just want to hear your side of the story, then I'll tell you what Mr. Kimble had to say."

"Well—" I couldn't believe this. I've seen kids throw punches at each other and be back in class the next day. Once a kid told the teacher to fuck off, and he was back in half an hour. I was getting busted for not singing?

"Insubordination means refusing—" he began.

"I know what it means." I heard Mom's voice in my head, *Steady* . . .

"Good," he said. "You're a bright girl. Tell me what happened, Cassandra, and we'll get this worked out."

"Nothing to tell."

He turned back to his computer, clicked away at his mouse for a while, and heaved a sigh. I was getting good at making these people sigh.

"Cassandra—"

"Yes, sir."

"That's one thing: Mr. Kimble said that you refused to sing, and when he assigned a time-out in the hall," here he began to read, "'Miss Sullivan said YES SIR! in a loud and sarcastic tone audible to the entire class.' What do you have to say about that?"

I shook my head.

"Don't want to make this any easier, do you?"

I shrugged.

"Well, what would you like to see happen?"

I gave him another shrug, but he kept trying.

"I'll tell you what. Mr. Kimble wants you out of that group. His position is that the show choir is an elite group, our *crème de la crème*, if you will, and he will not stand for rebellion among the ranks. As for myself, I tend to agree. However—"

A measured pause here, then he leaned forward, resting his arms on the desk. "However, let's imagine a different outcome. How about you apologize. How about you sing the song, loud and strong, and agree not to pull a stunt like this again. I think we could, then, let bygones be bygones, water under the bridge."

Back to the little smile—so confident that this was just a little bump that could easily be smoothed.

"Sound like a solution?"

Sounds like a crock of Cheez Whiz, I wanted to say, but again, I shook my head.

"Yeah," he said. "Okay. Fabulous. One day in-house suspension, for starters. We'll also transfer you to another elective. Is art okay? Excellent. He's always got plenty of empty chairs—lot of kids run crying to the counselors to transfer out of *there* when they get their schedules. Unfortunately, this would be your transfer-quota for the year, so don't ask. That suspension can start right now, by the way. I'll send somebody down to get your books."

So I spent the rest of the day in the little in-house suspension room. They collected my assignments for me, and I was done with them before lunchtime. The school security guy, Mr. Bad they call him—short for Badagliaccio—actually escorted me down to my locker to get my lunch.

As everybody in the hall gawked, I got the first taste of peer admiration I'd had in a while.

Quill swerved over across the hall and tried to shake my hand.

"Cassie the Antichrist!" he said. "Public enemy."

"Okay, that's enough," said Mr. Bad. "Back to the hole."

Quill erupted in laughter at this, and really, come on: *back to the hole?*

Mom and Dad were angry at first, getting a call about "insubordination" and "disrespect for staff and students." But when I told them the whole story—swearing that I had not been disrespectful when I was talking to Mr. Kimble and saying that maybe I should have made nice to Dr. Hawk—they seemed to understand.

"So, what happens now?" said Mom.

"I just want it to blow over as soon as possible."

"I can accept the insubordination," said Dad. "But how were you disrespectful to the students?"

"Maybe he thinks I'm disrespecting them…"

"Disrespect is not a verb, Cassie. Don't disrespect the language."

"Yes, sir. He always says that it's disrespectful not to give your best to every song."

"Okay, in principle, but—"

"I'm just disappointed that you're out of the choir," said Mom. "I enjoyed hearing you sing, you're good at it—"

"And she looked so fetching in that tuxedo outfit," added Dad.

"Are you sure you don't want to apologize and get back in?"

"Not if I have to sing that song."

"Performers don't get to choose the program, Cassie. I hate to see you giving up your music over this."

"Choir is not *my* music, Mom. It was *your* idea."

11 September

This morning I got to hang out in the hole until Doctor Hawk was ready to see me again and readmit me to class. I polished my apology letters, removing all traces of sarcasm, trying to keep them simple.

Dear Dr. Hawkens,
I apologize for my rude and disrespectful behavior yesterday.
I'm sorry for behaving in such a bratty way.
Respectfully,
Cassandra Sullivan

Dear Mr. Kimble,
I apologize for my disobedience and disrespect to you and your
students. I did not mean to be disrespectful to you or to them. I'm
sorry for being such a smart aleck.
Respectfully,
Cassandra Sullivan

I think those are some heroic words, Di. I worked long and hard on them, agonizing over such things as the contraction "I'm" versus "I am."

The doctor barely glanced at my notes and wrote me a pass to class. I'm not sure what my teachers had heard about this thing, but Mr. Math accepted my homework without a word. As for my peers, their eyes were drilling me hard. Quill's friend DJ sits next to me and asked me what happened.

"Nothing," I whispered. "I just had to change my elective."

"What'd you get?"

"Art."

"Have fun. He, like, hates everybody."

I thought that sounded funny—how can you like/hate at the same time? I was about to ask DJ which it was, like, like or, like, hate when we were rudely interrupted.

"Miss Sullivan," said Mr. Math. "Maybe, after missing

almost half the class, we'd better concentrate extra hard on our work instead of telling stories?"

I bent over my book, letting my hair slide down like blinders, wondering why I got yelled at when DJ was talking too.

At lunchtime, I went to Mr. Griffin's *Lord of the Rings* group, grateful to have an excuse for avoiding the cafeteria. When I showed up, there were a few seventh-grade girls in his room along with Quill, DJ, and their friend Kelly, sitting on desks in two separate groups, chatting and eating.

"Cassie Sullivan, welcome," said Mr. Griffin. "Everyone, this is Cassie. I had her big brother a few years back, and I understand she is quite the scholar of Middle Earth."

"I thought she was just the school Antichrist," Quill said. "Excellent."

"Cassie, today we are discussing the *Fellowship*, book two, Rivendell through Moria."

"*Khazad-dûm*," said DJ.

"Deep are the wells of *Kheled-zâram*," said Quill.

"Cold are the springs of *Kibil-nâra*."

Mr. Griffin tried to get everybody into a circle, and then people read passages out loud from the book. DJ read the song, written by Bilbo:

> *Eärendil was a mariner*
> *that tarried in Arvernien . . .*

It was really long. A couple of the girls were whispering through it, and people kept breaking off into side conversations, but it was cool anyway. When lunchtime was over, half of them hadn't had a chance to read their parts, so next week we're going to stick with the same section.

"You read something, too, Cassie," said Mr. Griffin. "And not some endless, obscure poetry."

"You don't like Eärendil?" DJ said to Griffin.

"*I* do," I said. "But I like Sam's poetry better: 'Troll sat alone on his seat of stone, and munched and mumbled on a bare old bone.'"

"Yeah, yeah," said Griffin. "See you guys next week."

Then it was back to reading class where, instead of lit circles, we had a September 11th writing prompt:

Now that some time has passed since the terrorist attacks, what are your thoughts on what has happened and what has changed for you and your country since then?

It looked like, with the assembly seventh period, the rest of the day was going to be devoted to this topic. Trouble is, everything you say about that day sounds like either understatement or hyperbole or both. I still cry sometimes when I think of all those firefighters going up while everybody else is going down. I still get freaked when I see a plane in the clear morning sky, and I think I'll always carry the image in my mind of people falling from the windows of the twin towers.

But did anything change?

People seemed nicer for a while. The pain brought us together, everyone said, and I felt it myself. I also felt it fade—into pride and the big psych-up for war and blood.

I remember hearing of the Taliban leader's children being bombed. "How does it feel now, Mr. Mullah?" I remember thinking. "How does it feel when it's *your* kids?"

But it wasn't the little kids' fault, and how can we hate them for killing our innocents when we turn around and kill theirs? Isn't it the same?

After we wrote, we had to read aloud. It was the usual stuff: people telling about where they were when they heard and how sad and afraid they were and how much television they watched. It has changed us, they said, by bringing the country together, making us stronger, making us value our freedom, blah, blah, blah. One girl's dad was in New York, which would have been scary—and one guy's cousin was killed—not that he sounded that broken up about it. One of the goofballs said that we should nuke the Middle East, an idea that inspired a great deal of clapping and hooting.

Then Sinclair asked me to read what I had written, and did I decline? No, I just opened my big mouth and went for it:

The silhouette of a jet
In the blue morning sky,
Confetti. Ashes. Dust.
People flying out windows,
Caught by the camera,
Confetti. Ashes. Dust.
Frozen in the sky,
Falling forever,
Confetti. Ashes. Dust.
Never to land,
Never to escape,
Confetti. Ashes. Dust.
That blue sky,

That black smoke,
Confetti. Ashes. Dust.
Never to escape,
Never to land,
Confetti. Ashes. Dust.

That's how it was.
That's how it will remain.
What has changed?
What will change?
An eye for an eye, and a you for an I, a cry for a cry, a
child for a child, they must die for
a die until the last dying cry.

W.
W.
J.
D.

I didn't expect a lot of enthusiasm, so I wasn't disappointed when my reading was followed by a less than polite silence. Sinclair was mumbling something about liking the repetition when Jenny burst out with, "What is her problem, anyway?"

"No personal attacks, Jenny."

"I'm *sorry*," she said. "But that is just wrong."

"I thought it was cool," said Liz Pine. "Like, totally twisted, but cool. It reminded me of Nine Inch Nails, or Marilyn—not that I'm into them anymore—"

"Who else would like to read?" Sinclair said. "We have just enough time for one more."

Next was art. Before we went down to the assembly I met my charming new teacher, got a spot on his seating chart, and received a little advice:

"We're here to study art, Miss Sullivan. You do your work and be quiet about it and we're not going to have any problems here. Do we understand each other?"

"Yes, sir," I said. No need to worry about sarcasm here—I got the impression he wasn't hard-wired to pick it up.

My peer group was remarkably well behaved at the assembly, and our principal expressed her pride, declaring that the future of America was in good hands with patriots like us coming up.

One of the counselors gave a sort of eulogy for the fallen, which was followed by "America the Beautiful." Both were very solemn and accompanied by teary eyes and some sobbing by assorted girls. It's awful to be so cynical, Di, but I have a hard time swallowing my bile when a group of these girls, all BFF (best friends forever), get hysterical together. There were a bunch of them clustered around the counselor afterwards. This was after a rousing version of the hated song got everybody up and singing. I remained seated, just like for the pledge of allegiance, but I'm already paying for it.

On the way out, some girl I don't even know said to her BFFs in a very well-projected stage whisper, "Hey look, you guys, it's *Osama O'Sullivan*." And everybody laughed.

Journal Four

12 September

Pretty much the same crew showed up at Mr. Griffin's room for writing group this morning as had been there at lunch yesterday. He had a big box of donuts, which are one of the few non-vegan foods I really miss. You can make them vegan, but you can't buy them that way.

We circled the desks and passed out copies of a story by Julia, one of the seventh graders. It was about a girl who stumbles through a time portal or dimensional shift and finds herself with a dagger in her hand instead of a pencil. She seems to be somehow chosen or appointed to rescue another girl who is held captive by the Evil One—or she is the captive's twin sister, or she is the captive, but in another dimension. It was interesting, but a little confusing.

A couple other people read short things they'd written in class, some cute poems and deep thoughts. Then Mr. Griffin suggested an assignment.

"An assignment!" said Tarah, another seventh grader. "We have enough homework already."

"Okay, okay, don't have a cow," Mr. Griffin said. "Let me rephrase that. I had a story idea that you can all try out. It's not homework, but if you're not willing to put some time into your writing, you don't have any business coming here and eating my donuts."

Silence.

"You want to hear the idea?"

Various "okays" and "yeahs" showed how enthusiastic they were.

"I call it The Triumvirate," he said. "You take one set of characters, one problem, one beginning, and you write a story…"

"And make it your greatest triumph," said Quill.

"Always, but that's not what triumvirate is. What about the prefix, *tri*?"

"Three of something, like a trio or a triad?" I said.

"Or triage, like DJ's face." Quill again.

"Shut up, man," DJ said, "or I'll send you to tri-hell."

"Shut up, man, or I'll send you—"

"Both of you shut up," said Mr. Griffin. "Yes, Cassie. It is a tripartite plan. I got the idea from a movie I saw once—*Run Lola Run*. Anybody see it?" Blank looks. "Good, it's too old for you, but it's a cool idea. It was three stories in one, starting exactly the same, but with one little tweak that made the timing different for everything else, so the endings were all different." More blank looks. "For example, in the first story line, Lola is running across a street trying to get to her boyfriend to save him. She dashes across the street about fifty feet in front of a glass truck."

"How can a truck be made of glass?" a seventh grader wondered.

"It's *carrying* glass. But anyway, in the next one, she is a few seconds later, so the truck slams on the brakes and a big piece of glass comes flying off and shatters on the street."

"Cool."

"Excellent."

"I get it."

"So you'll write the same story, three different ways. Just make the beginning the same and the characters the same.

Don't change the characters—the point is to see how the same characters react to the different things that happen. Also, it's going to force you to revise. I'm sick of all these rough drafts."

"What about the endings?" I asked.

"The endings would be different, resulting from the same characters responding to slightly altered timing or circumstance."

"But what if," I said, "the endings were the same? If your character is really strong, or if fate is working, it wouldn't matter what happens—the same end would result."

"Interesting. See if you can pull it off."

"Do we *have* to write this?" somebody asks.

"You don't *have* to do *anything*. But at our meeting two weeks from today, if you haven't, you might as well sleep in because NO DONUTS FOR YOU!"

After writing group I ran into my buddy Matthew. I'd already been called Osama by two or three kids on the way to my locker, but it was extra special coming from Mr. "You're going to hell."

"Hey, if it isn't Osama bin Sullivan," he said.

"That's O'Sullivan," I said behind my hair. "I'm running the IRA as well as al Qaeda."

"I didn't think you looked like an A-Rab."

"Don't say A-Rab, it's not polite."

"I didn't think—"

"You didn't think at *all* then, *did* you, Bible-Boy?" I slammed my locker, and bolted for class.

At lunch, I ducked into the library to avoid the caf, but I couldn't concentrate on reading. I kept trying to think of possible comebacks for the next time I was called Osama, but I only succeeded in inventing a couple of new names for myself. Cassie bin Laden and Cassie O'Samavan were both good, but I had to hand it to that girl after the assembly yesterday—Osama O'Sullivan really rolls off the tongue.

How could I have thought that when I was done with Dr. Hawkens, I could put the whole thing behind me?

"I have been foolish and deluded," said Pooh, "and I'm a bear of no brain at all."

One thing was clear—if I wanted this to blow over, I'd have to swear off calling people Bible-Boy. Then I got to thinking about the poem I'd written yesterday in reading. WWJD indeed.

Turn the other cheek is what I should be doing, I thought, so I decided to make a new list. Invisibility was impossible now, but what if I could just keep my cool until they all got tired of bothering me? Here are the new guidelines:

Avoid political statements.

Avoid religious controversy.

When slapped, turn the other cheek.

Treat others how I want to be treated, not how they treat me.

Pretty simple recipe for getting along with others, don't you think, Di?

I tried to slip out of the library early so I could get my books and avoid the crush, but Mr. Bad stopped me, asked me what I was doing in the hall, why I didn't have a pass, why I wasn't at lunch. This gave me a good workout as far as keeping cool goes. I guess I should add a number five to my new list: stay cool. Or maybe I should just call the whole program Stay Cool. Anyway, Mr. Bad grilled me until the hall filled up, releasing me right into the thick of things where I was promptly given a flat tire and laughed at. I didn't even turn around to see who it was, but kept walking, trying not to lose my shoe or my cool.

In reading, I was told that they'd chosen a new book while I was serving my in-house suspension. I was irritated that they hadn't told me yesterday, but it got me out of class with a pass that I presented to Mr. Bad, who was cruising the hallways.

The pass didn't say when I should come back, so I stayed in the library to read. Not in peace, however, because the office of my old friend the GT lady opens into the library.

"How's eighth grade treating you, Cassie?"

"Fine," I said. *Hello? I'm reading.*

"What's the book?"

I showed it.

"*Number the Stars?* That's a little fourth grade for you, isn't it?"

"My lit circle chose it when I was absent."

"I hope you weren't sick."

Was she fishing, or was she out of the loop? My other teachers had all been briefed on my activities, judging from their attitudes over the past couple days.

"Not really."

"But I should think eighth graders would be on *Anne Frank* for that subject matter."

"I've read that too—fifth grade."

I had just gotten rid of her when our new librarian came over.

"I hate to interrupt someone who's reading." She smiled. "But did I see your pass?"

This is why I need to stay cool. At least she knew she was bugging me—she wasn't so bad.

"Sorry, here it is."

"Does your teacher want you back, Cassie?" She smiled again.

"I don't think so, I have to catch up on the reading."

"Okay. Well, I'm Ms. Tayebnejad. I saw you here at lunchtime, too, and you're always welcome. I want the library to be open to anyone who wants to read."

"Thanks, Ms. Tay..." I looked at her ID badge, but I couldn't get it.

"Tie," she said, "-yeb-neh-zhad. It's Farsi—Iranian. Tie-YEB-neh-zhad"

"Tayebnejad—Nice to meet you." See, Di? I can be civil.

"Charmed," she said. "Now quit chatting and read!"

I got back to class just before the bell. Sinclair didn't mind me staying in the library to read, but he did check the return time on my pass, which Ms. Tayebnejad had added with her initials.

Dinner conversation tonight centered on my birthday, coming up this Saturday. I could have chosen dinner at the Mountain Café, my favorite good-karma restaurant, but I want a weekend at the cabin. Though they're being mysterious about my present, I figured out that it's one big thing, instead of several little ones.

Mom was happy to hear that I'm enjoying Mr. Griffin's "extra-curricular activities." They wanted to hear my ideas for the story assignment, but I don't have any beyond the premise that the characters, the beginning, and the end should all be the same. Dad started going off on Shakespeare and the Greeks, wanting to know how I had become a fatalist. He's a lot of fun, but I wasn't in the mood for it.

I came upstairs feeling restless. Homework done, I'd already written all about the day—I was starting to feel bored, and I *don't* get bored. So I tried to call Ally but just got the answering machine.

It was in the end of last May that I first met her. She and Sean drove his rattletrap station wagon in from Oregon, hitting a few rivers and hot springs along the way.

We had all wondered what she was going to be like, especially since Sean hadn't had a serious girlfriend before. In high school, he'd spent most of his time with Charlie, his best buddy, and Jane, Charlie's girlfriend.

About Ally, whom he'd met last year, he wouldn't tell us much. When grilled over the phone he'd say, "She's great, really smart, really cool, she's an artist, you'll love her."

The night they got here, we had a big welcome dinner out on the patio, with Dad grilling steaks for everyone and a veggie-burger for me.

"Why are you a vegetarian," asked Ally, "health or moral reasons?"

"Vegan," I said.

"And for which reason?"

"Both," I said. "My morals and the animals' health."

"Cool," she said. "So *your* needs don't fit into the decision at all?"

"Not really."

"Cassie's not concerned with self," said Dad. "She would rather pine away and cease to exist than bind herself to the Karmic Wheel."

"Impossible," said Ally.

"Precisely," said Dad.

"You two lay off, already," said Mom. "Cassie's very concerned about her nutrition—she educated herself when she gave up animal foods, didn't you, Cass?"

"Sure, Mom."

"And what about you, Ally?" she said. "Tell us about yourself. "

"We've heard precisely nothing except that you exist," said Dad. "Which may be enough for Seanie Kierkegaard, here—"

"Okay, okay," said Mom. "Let the woman speak."

She seemed happy to do so, and we heard all about her. Mom asked the questions and made the polite responses. I sat back and observed, as did Sean, who watched and listened with the stink of the besotted drifting about him. Dad seemed pretty well enamored himself, which is not surprising, because she's everything the ultra-liberal father would wish for his son.

She's from suburban Seattle, a studio art major, the scourge of her conservative parents, and gorgeous. Her big, dark eyes and clear, suntanned skin—no makeup—glowed in the evening light and later in the breeze-flickering candles.

Mom, as far as I could tell, was already half in love, too—moving rapidly beyond the standard questions. She kept the reins of the conversation for a good while, and *my* admiration was for her. She wasn't threatened by Ally, nor was she overshadowed. A few elegant lines animated her fine features, and her fair skin blushed with wine as she listened. Her dark hair fell across her forehead, and her deep eyes went gray in the twilight. I liked looking at her hands best, though. Taking up her glass or her silverware, she touched these things as artfully as she touched the bow of her cello.

"And what do they think, your parents," Mom asked, "about your plans to cohabitate with our son next fall?"

"'If you want to play house,'" she said in a low voice, imitating her father, "'we can't stop you. But we won't support this sort of nonsense either, and you can pay your own room and board with your own money.'"

"And you have the money?"

"From my grandma, though I hate to think of her reaction if she were still around."

"You never know—I told my grandmother when Gale and I moved in together—but not my parents," said Mom.

"Well, *she* didn't despise me," said Dad.

"I wouldn't say that—but I think she trusted me to make my own mistakes." She stood up. "Anyone for coffee?"

"Yes, please," said Ally.

"Yes, please," said I.

"And let me help." Ally jumped up and began collecting plates.

I deliberately sat still as Mom said, "Please don't—Gale cooked, you two have been traveling all day, Cassie will help me with this. "

"I will?" I said.

"No, Cassie," said Ally. "You just chill. Besides, I have to ingratiate myself into your mom's good graces."

"Oh, you're doing okay," I said. "I wouldn't worry about it." And please don't, like, go all cool and say "chill" to me just because I'm thirteen.

Sean got up and opened the door as the womenfolk made their way, loaded with dishes, to the kitchen.

"You got yourself a good woman, there," said Dad. "What do you think, Cassie?"

"She's okay," I said. I didn't mind her personally—I just didn't appreciate the way she inserted herself into the family with such ease. I probably would have liked her better if she hadn't been so confident.

"She was really nervous about meeting you guys," said Sean. "But I can tell she really likes you."

"Could've fooled me," I said. "About the nerves, I mean."

"Don't worry, Sean. She'll come around, your sister will. Either that, or her skepticism will blossom into loathing. But I think her good sense will overcome her jealousy."

"Give me a break, Dad."

"It's only natural. We don't want to share him either, Cass."

"Whatever you say, Dad."

"Thanks for being so agreeable."

Mom and Ally came back, and Dad continued with his silly verbal gymnastics over coffee. By this time Ally was asking them all about their work, and they were pleased to oblige. When she turned to me, on the other hand, I deflected her by getting all mock-teenagerish.

"I, like, *love* school, and I have the *best* friends, and, like, *next* year? *Eighth* grade? We're gonna rule the school because we totally rule!"

"I know what you mean, ugh! Junior high was the worst."

But I was ready to forget my own middle school life and times—I didn't feel like hearing all about hers.

"Yeah, well, it was great to meet you," I said. "Night, everybody."

"Where's my hug and kiss?" said Mom, demonstrating that good old unconditional love.

"And mine," said Dad.

"And mine," said Sean.

I was afraid Ally was going to chime in, but she had too much sense. She just said, "It was great to meet you, too. See you tomorrow."

I felt bad then about being so pissy, so after holding on to Sean for a good long hug, I put a quick and awkward arm around her shoulder and gave her a friendly good night.

13 September

Yippee! Mountain bound. Homework done. No problems at school except half a dozen "Osamas" and three flat tires. I was very cool and did not RSVP.

I have a new friend, it would seem, in the librarian. She came up to me while I was reading at lunchtime and asked me if I ever actually ate.

"I'd rather read," I said.

"You *could* read and eat at the same time, you know," she

said. "I just went to Freshway, and I got the giant V-G—there's no way I can eat more than half of it."

"Thanks, but I try to stay away from dairy, and anyway, I brought a lunch—I'm just not hungry." Actually I was ravenous but couldn't face the caf.

"Well, there's no food allowed in the library, but you can eat in my office, if you ever *are* hungry."

"Thank you, Ms. Tayebnejad. If I ever *am.*"

That was nice of her. I was tempted to go get my lunch right then, but after pretending not to be hungry, I would have felt too stupid.

Today the lit circle was mad because I had passed them and was finished with the book. Just for spite, I "let slip" that the Jewish girl's friend ratted her out to the Nazis and her whole family was killed. Not that that's exactly what happens, or anything like what happens, but I was feeling mean.

14 September—Fourteen years old

Last weekend we did that hike up to the Goat-horn saddle—today I feel like taking it easy, lying around the tipi.

> *Now it is a strange thing, but things that are good to have and days that are good to spend are soon told about, and not much to listen to; while things that are uncomfortable, palpitating, and even gruesome, may make a good tale, and take a deal of telling anyway.*
>
> —J.R.R. Tolkien, *The Hobbit*

It's a true fact that there isn't much of a story to the summer once I got over my antipathy toward Ally. For me, the story lies in the way I found some happiness, how I found a friend for a couple of weeks. Then, of course, I lost it all again to the gruesomeness of school and my regular life. But there are a couple of tales along the way, too.

The day after the welcome dinner, the whole family caravanned up to the cabin. I've told something already about how we planned and executed the tipi painting and how I began to come around to Ally. But the big turning point was how she helped me in my campaign to spend the whole summer up here.

It was supposed to be the way it had been the year before: Sean was going to live at the cabin full-time, guiding tenderfoot tourists on fishing trips, and I would come up with Mom and Dad, commuting back and forth. The wish of my heart, however, was to live up here all summer.

The first victory came because of the tipi painting. When I was whining about having to go home, Ally said to Mom and Dad, "You mean Cassie's going back with you on Sunday?"

"We don't feel comfortable with her up here alone," said Mom.

"But how are we going to get the tipi painted?" Ally said, and filled them in on her vision.

"Couldn't you just sketch it out this weekend with her, and let her finish it on her own?"

"I guess," she said. "Could you handle that, Cassie?"

"You know what happened on my last attempt."

"And Sean is going to be farting around fishing all week," she said. "If Cassie was here, we could hang out."

"Why don't you drop Sean off where he meets his clients in the morning?" Mom suggested. "They all have giant SUVs anyway—they don't want to ride in *his* car. Then you could come down to the city."

"I guess I'd rather be here in the mountains, but thanks for the invite. I just wish Cassie could stay—she wouldn't be alone if I'm here."

"I wouldn't be alone even staying here with Sean, Mom." She turned to Dad. "What do you think about this week?"

"I think it sounds okay," he said.

"Nobody's asking me," said Sean. "I've got a week alone in the mountains with my girlfriend, and now I'm going to have my kid sister tagging along."

"Thanks, Sean, thanks a lot," I said.

"I was just kidding, Littless," he said. "I never mind having you tag along. I think it would be awesome if you were here all summer, but a week would be a good start."

"I'll take good care of her," said Ally. "It'll be just like summer camp. Three round meals a day, good clean arts and crafts activities, early bedtime."

"Well, if you can get *this* girl to bed early, Mary Poppins, you're hired," said Mom.

I couldn't resent Ally after that. I'm good at getting my way, but I had never had someone help me before. It was a great feeling—I remember getting this rush of admiration for her, or gratitude. I just suddenly adored her.

We got to work on the tipi the next day, mixing up paints, experimenting, trying to get the colors we wanted. We measured, made sketches, and figured out how we would do the high parts. Dad has a big ladder that he offered, and we had already made a shopping list for a trip to the hardware/art store.

The rest of that week I remember as a busy, blurry time—a good time that, as Tolkien said, is soon told.

Ally had me out of bed early—it's hard to sleep when someone is painting the walls of your tent. We would paint through the morning, have lunch, and go until the clouds looked like they were about to rain on our creation. Some days we got in another session in the evening. Sean even picked up a brush a couple of times.

While we painted, we talked. I got to hear all about her middle school years, which seemed almost as bad as mine. She'd gone to a snooty private school where you had to be very careful how you acted if you wanted to fit in.

"So I *was* careful—what I wore, what music I liked, what I said—it's very stressful to conform."

"Yeah, Ally, you're a total conformist."

She was wearing a tie-died sports bra and a white cotton skirt, paint spattered, tied in a knot above her knees, showing off her hairy legs. Reaching up with the paintbrush, she displayed her unshaven pits as well.

"Shaving is not natural," she explained to me. "And what's even scarier than women shaving their bodies is that men are doing it now too. Or maybe the scariest is that I think there's any difference. Are we not mammals? But you should see my middle school pictures—perfect lip-gloss, perfect hair: perfect phony."

"So what happened?"

"I got my parents to let me go to the public high school instead of one of the prep schools they wanted to dump me in. But I think any high school would have been better than junior high."

"I just assumed school was always going to be miserable."

"Oh, it will be. Wretched. But high school is so much bigger, with different kinds of people. Some are mean—jocks and socs—but the people who don't fit in can find other people who don't fit in."

"I can't believe I have another whole year of middle school. If only they hadn't kept me out of kindergarten for a year. Then I'd be done with it. I wish this year were over."

"Don't wish that—you're wishing your life away. And if anything were different, everything would be different."

"That's what I *am* wishing for—when I'm not wishing I'd never been born."

"But think about it. If you had been born even a day later, you might not be you."

"So, if I weren't me, I wouldn't exist."

"Or maybe worse, what if you could change one thing, the worst thing that has ever happened to you, but it changed a whole series of events and prevented the best thing that ever happened from ever happening."

"But is it worth it, all the awfulness?"

She stopped painting and looked down from the ladder. The sun was behind her, and I looked away.

"You have to love your whole life, Cassie. Each moment is the only thing that's real. If you damn even one moment, you risk damning the whole thing. Think about it. Each moment arises and then slips away so quickly—if you're not living in the present, if you're living in the past or *for* the future, you'll miss it, because every *now* happens only once."

We have good conversations in my family, Di, I know we do. Sean's cool because he listens to me and doesn't make me feel stupid or like a little kid, but there's a distance now that I didn't notice when I was little. And Dad's great, but he always wants to play and show off, and he really likes to hear himself talk—even in earnest. Especially in earnest. Mom usually wants me to do something or think something—she wants to influence me. And both of them are always *parenting* me. Nothing escapes being tinted by the color of that relationship. I used to think there was something wrong with me, but Ally says once you get to a certain age, you just can't relax with your family. She says it's nature's way of getting us ready to leave home.

But with her, it's how I always imagined it would be with a big sister and a best friend. She took me seriously, she listened to me, and she talked to me, giving her ideas but not pushing them on me. I can't believe how fast I went from seeing her as an outsider to loving her and wishing she would never leave.

Great birthday dinner and great present, Di. I'll start from the beginning.

I woke up after a little snooze in my tipi, and when I went up to the cabin, I overheard Mom and Dad talking about me. So I lingered on the front step for a minute.

"Did you check on her?" Dad said.

"Sound asleep, can you believe it?"

"It sounds like we're talking about a baby, doesn't it? 'Did you check her,' 'sound asleep.'"

"She really looked like our baby—our great, tall baby lying there on her sleeping bag with her eyes closed and her mouth open. Remember those little nursing blisters when she was a newborn?"

"She had the sweetest little lips. I can't believe it's been fourteen years."

"Do you want to go wake her up?"

"Too late." I opened the door. "These burning ears woke me from a sound nap."

"You rat, what did you hear?" said Mom.

"'Can you believe, it's been fourteen years, our little baby girl,'" I mocked.

"Well, happy birthday, darling, thanks for being born." She hugged me.

"Thanks for bornin' me, Ma. What's for grub?"

"Sautéed wonderful bean curd," said Dad. "Smothered in five-meat special flavor."

"Very funny."

"Your mother actually made you a cake," he said. "In these primitive environs."

"Wow, Mom. Thanks."

Dad has always disdained such suburban improvements as a deck, but he did build us a table and some chairs that we set up on a flattish bit of gravel for "outdoor living." We ate out there: all three of us at one end of the long table and my big pink-wrapped present at the other end.

We started with a bowl of good spicy guacamole and my

favorite blue chips, followed by veggie enchiladas in hot red chile. Mom and Dad were drinking Tecates and I had a bottle of sparkling apple cider.

At cake time, though the sun had slipped down behind the mountains, it was still too light for the candles to make much of a glow. But the wind cooperated and left the blowing-out for me. Mom and Dad sang to me, I paused for my wish, and blew out all fourteen in one breath. I wouldn't tell them my wish, Di, and I won't even tell you—I'm afraid writing it is just as bad as telling.

Dad passed me the box, and I peeled off the pink unicorn paper and set it aside.

"This giant box must have taken the last of the unicorn paper," I said. "It's been my birthday theme since I was about six."

"Yup, this is the last of it. Our little girl is growing up."

I gave the box a shake. "Not fragile, is it?" I said, and began to unfold the flaps that were tucked in at the top.

"Um, no," said Dad.

Then I opened the box.

"Not the old box in a box routine!"

Sure enough, inside the first there was another box. Then *three* more and finally a card with a poem by Dad:

> *Of all the Joys we've ever seen,*
> *Of all that in the World have been;*
> *The fairest flower beside still water*
> *Is you, our dear, our loving Daughter.*

And inside was a printout of an e-mail travel itinerary:

Colorado Springs to Portland. I'm going to Oregon to see Sean and Ally! I still can't believe it.

"Happy birthday, sweetie."

"You're letting me go all alone?"

"Well," said Dad, "you all got along so well last summer. And your brother is on the straight side—I don't think he is going to be hauling you off to any fraternity parties. As for Ally, we don't mind her too much. She seemed a little hippiefied at first, but we got to like her okay."

"I thought it was love at first sight."

"I was favorably disposed, but you never know if style is an indication of substance."

"And this was her idea. She certainly is your *ally*, your Ally," said Mom.

"Good one, Mom."

"Well, I took some convincing on this one. I didn't really see what there was for an eighth-grader to do at college, but she talked me into it. You won't actually be at the school anyway, they're taking you to her uncle's beach house," she said. "It seems like it will be a fun weekend for you."

Looking at the itinerary more closely, I saw that the reservations had me leaving two weeks from today and coming back Tuesday. "You're getting me out of two days of school?"

"Don't you want to go?" said Dad.

"No, no—yes. I just can't believe it. Thank you, thank you, thank you." I got up and hugged them both.

"It's a big opportunity for you to show responsibility," said Mom. "You'll have to get your school work done ahead of time and be your most grown-up self on this trip. Do you think you can handle traveling alone?"

"Of course, Mom. Don't worry."

We discussed the plan. I would fly to Portland, Ally and Sean would pick me up, and we'd drive down to the coast. The house belonged to Ally's uncle, who lived in LA and let family stay there whenever they wanted, and it was perched right on the beach.

It was getting cold and dark when the party broke up with many a happy birthday/thank you/love you hug. Then I went up to the Carrock and lay in the chill under the stars before coming back to write everything into you, Di.

Pause.

But for the wind in the trees, all is silent.

And something slips in between the ground and the canvas, or slides down the poles from the apex of the cone, or maybe it seeps out from my pores, escapes with my breath, emanates from the crown of my head.

All is silent.

If the pen on the paper is loud in the stillness, the rustling of my sleeping bag is deafening. I'm so happy, and then in the midst of the fullness, I am empty and alone. I miss Ally so much. What good is a weekend when there are so many hours before and after? So many hours and days and weeks and months and years.

Moments.

That's the worst part. So many "nows" to live through alone.

I'm damning them, Ally, I know.

What's wrong with me? Why can't I just be glad, count my blessings, be thankful, and blah, blah, blah, blah?

NO.

I won't do this.

I won't let my stupid self ruin this.

I have more stories to tell, and if I am afraid of the future, afraid even of the present, I can fill this empty moment with the stories, so the stories of passed moments, past presents, become now again at the point of my pen on the page, now and more real than ever, like a song is real, playing over and over again.

Okay. I can do this. I'm casting downstream and bringing up the brightly spotted trout—up, up, up into my net…

The first week of the summer went fast, with Ally and I painting in the sun and going into the tipi or the cabin when it rained. I took her on hikes all around the place, up to the falls for a splash break, across the Carrock meadows, and down to the beaver ponds for a dip. The ponds had been blown out the spring before when we'd had a big rainstorm on top of the usual snowmelt. The flood washed out the old muck, so once the beavers rebuilt, the water was nice and clear—but cold.

Ally surprised me by just stripping off her clothes, wading into the water, and diving for the deep end of the pond.

Then she came up whooping and sputtering with cold.

"What are you doing?" she said when she saw me wading out in my tank and shorts. "Why don't you take your clothes off?"

"Shy, I guess," I said.

"It's just us, and besides, you'll dry a lot faster than your clothes will."

"I'll change."

"Suit yourself."

"I will—just as you *un*suited *your*self." I launched myself into the water, remembering Mom's dip in the reservoir and wondering why my female role models were always taking off their clothes. My shorts and top were uncomfortable in the water, though, and by the end of the week I was down to, well, nothing.

I can't imagine Jenny or anyone at school hearing about this. Skinny-dipping! It sounds so naughty! Most haven't even read Anne Frank's *Diary*, but when they saw me with it, they were all whispering about the "lesbian" part. How dare Anne actually have an honest thought along those lines. And *this* is the passage that causes outrage?

Our swimming was nothing sexy, anyway—not even like Anne's "ecstatic" thoughts. After the initial shock, I became aware that being naked was not necessarily sexual. We talked about it later, as we painted, and Ally said that it's the hiding of body parts, among other things, that turns them into sex objects.

"What about porn?" I said.

"What have you seen?"

"Just a magazine I found in Sean's room once."

"Really. Was it pretty bad?"

"Not hard-core—I don't think—naked women posing—"

"That's it, though—it's the poses, the 'fuck me' poses," she said. "Seen anything on the internet?"

"I don't use computers if I don't have to, but when I used to search for Greenpeace and PETA sites and that stuff came up, I would just click it closed as fast as possible."

"Good. You're innocent—but that's the way it's supposed to be. The *body* is innocent, it's what they do to it that makes it pornographic: starve it, pump it up with silicone, shave it, and pose it—videos and commercials are just as bad. Worse, even. It's dehumanizing."

"You sound like my mom—Dad too—the feminist party line."

"Really?" she said. "The only message I got was that sex, *if* it existed, was nasty, nasty, nasty."

That would be a good place to stop now, Di. I'm good again—I wrote myself through it.

And I can't believe that two weeks from now I'll be in Oregon with my bro and adopted sis.

Pausing the scratch of my pen on the paper, I hear the silence again. But it's not scary—only the shushing of wind in the firs and fluttering of aspen leaves, until I hear, blending in at first, then rising into a hateful wail at the sound barrier: a squadron of fighter jets on a midnight cruise.

For all we know, oblivious up here, another war could have already begun. A surprise attack on Iraq, or against us—how would we know?

September 15

Morning in the mountains. I stumble out of bed and throw the door open to the sun, then flop back onto my cot. Mom is practicing, playing her cello, just warming up from the sound of it. She knows I won't be wanting to rush back home, so she's getting her work done here.

I feel okay today. Last night's emptiness and fear are like

bad dreams vanished in the brightness of the morning, and they're not as powerful as the good dreams I wrote. I think I'll lie here and enjoy the present for a while, the mellow sounds of Mom's music weaving itself into the warm, fragrant air of the morning, then I'll wash up, get some breakfast, and settle into a little writing, weaving my own music into the day.

When Ally and I were working on the tipi, she wanted some tunes for our painting and suggested we drag a couple of extension cords out here and crank some CDs on the boom box. Beautiful, I thought, pollute the mountains with tech-noise. But what could I say? Already Ally's opinion mattered to me enough that I was apprehensive about sharing all my weird ideas about digital music.

So I tried to keep it fairly normal—explaining that I didn't think CDs were really worth listening to. I preferred the warmth of vinyl, and besides, who needed music with the sounds of nature all around us?

She wanted to compromise, alternate between a CD and an hour of silence.

"We'll start with silence," she said. "Then you pick—anything you want."

"I want nothing."

"Why not?" she said.

"I just can't stand it," I said. "It's not even music—it's digitally sampled sound."

"It sounds like music to me."

"That's because," I said, "you've been brainwashed into thinking so."

So much for sounding normal. I hate getting all emotional and going off, but that's what I did: "You listen to it long enough and you can't tell the difference, and all the time it's filling your head with machinery."

I continued to spout off, saying that this place is as free of pollution as any place I knew. It was bad enough that we had to pollute it by bringing cars up here, by bringing ourselves even, and I couldn't stand to have it polluted by digital music.

The amazing thing was that she didn't look at me like I was insane, didn't patronize me or get sarcastic, didn't say something like, "Tell me how you *really* feel." And it wasn't that she was afraid to call me on it, because she had called me on other things like being a perfectionist about my first tipi-mural. I don't know why, she just laid off.

It seemed as if she forgot about it, but I didn't, and it bugged me all day. I kept wondering how I could explain what I felt so it would make sense to her, but I never came up with anything. The next day, while she was getting the paints together, I found the extension cords and brought them out.

"What are you doing?" she said.

"I was just being stupid yesterday. Or crazy. Or both. I shouldn't hold you to my weird ideas when you're doing all this work for me."

"First of all, I'm doing this 'work' because it's a cool proj-ect—for me, not just you."

"But still," I said. "Alternating is fair—"

"The other thing is that yesterday, once I gave up wanting to hear music, I began to hear a lot of other things. All the little things that make up the silence: bugs, wind, brushes on canvas, your breath, my breath, my thoughts, *your* thoughts."

"Get out."

"Well, not your *thoughts*, but maybe I was more in tune to you without the distraction of music."

"Really?"

"Ever get the feeling that everything people do is just to distract themselves from something else? School, work, entertainment?"

"Yeah—but I never thought of it that way. I just hate everyone and everything they do."

"No you don't."

"Pretty much. I mean, if people just didn't do all the things they do—even things that are supposed to be good—maybe everybody would be better off."

She was mixing blue, yellow, and white in a gallon jug with the top cut out.

"Even art?"

"Nobody does art—except for kids until they find out they're no good."

"Bitter, are we?" She laughed.

"Well, almost nobody."

"At least everyone *consumes* art. I have a professor who has these maxims on what is not art: If you can consume it, it's not art. If it goes with your couch, it's not art."

"So what *is* art?"

"There is no art." She thrust the jug and a brush at me. "Shut up and paint."

Could any friend be cooler? We painted the whole tipi

with no artificial music. Late that day, though, we decided that singing would be okay. Trouble was, we didn't know any of the same stuff. Freakish Cassie had only been listening to her stack of record albums for the last three years, so we started out just singing to each other. I sang her my favorite Burl Ives from an old kiddy tape I still have:

> *Oh, beat the drum slowly,*
> *And play the fife lowly,*
> *Sing the death march as they bear me away,*
> *Put bunches of roses all over my coffin,*
> *Roses to deaden the clods as they fall.*

Kind of morbid, maybe, but pretty.

Mostly we sang old camp songs that we both knew. "Boombiada," "Sarasponda," "Wayfaring Stranger"—we did them all. Some of the spirituals were really good for singing—surprising to you, Di, since I've been raging against the religion machine, but some of those are good songs.

The only time we listened to canned music was in the car, on a couple of runs we made to the store. It was hard for me to get beyond the skin-crawly feeling of the CDs, but I guess the music was pretty cool behind it.

"This doesn't sound good to you?" she said.

"I don't know, not really. The music might be okay—I just have a hard time hearing it."

"I'll turn it up."

The CD was some live Nirvana, but not as head-bangy as what I'd heard blasting out of Sean's room. Before we got back, Ally skipped ahead to a very cool song that she said was her favorite. My record stack has some good blues, and I like the acoustic stuff: John Lee Hooker and Lightnin' Hopkins. This sounded like that, a little, and it reminded me of the pine woods between home and school—which everyone calls "the pines"— because that's what it said in the song:

> *In the pines, the pines,*
> *where the sun don't ever shine*
> *I would shiver the whole night through.*

It was very bluesy and deep and at the end Kurdt just screams:

> *Pines!*
> *Pines!*
> *Sun!*
> *Shine*
> *I'd Shiverrrrrrrrrrrrrrrrrrr!*
> *The whole.*
> *Night*
> *Throooough!*

Sounds awful to describe it, but it was amazing. I forgot I was listening to a CD.

Back on the job—we were up to the blue now, both on ladders, covering the canvas with sky—we talked music a little more.

"If digital music is just samples of real sound," Ally said, "why is analog any better? Isn't it all just pseudo-music?"

"Yes and no," I said, and explained the difference between

sampled bits and full frequency recording, trying to sound scientific as opposed to wacky.

She painted silently for a minute. She had speckles of sky all over her face, arms, and chest from when I'd got too much paint on the roller.

"But basically, you just draw the line between analog and digital—if you were a true purist, you wouldn't listen to *any* recorded music."

"Well…"

"Well, what? It's all fake—it doesn't really exist. Your brother, the philosopher, told me about this guy in one of his books who loves listening to a certain record. This was like a hundred years ago when recording was new, and—it's some existential thing—he loves it because it doesn't exist."

She came down and we moved the ladder.

"But the sound waves *do* exist," I said. "The group played, a machine picked up the vibrations and cut grooves into a piece of acetate, then copies were made from that, and the needle of the record player touches the grooves, which makes a sound that is amplified and played on the speakers. So the song does exist."

"But the sounds from my CDs exist too."

"I guess."

"Don't guess—they do. I hear them, and if I trust my senses at all, I have to believe that the music exists, if anything does, if it's not *all* illusion. Take this blue paint—what is blue? Blue exists only in the mind—the pigment scatters light and we *see* blue—there is light that *looks* blue, but there *is* no blue. You can look for blue, but you can't find blue. All you can find is stuff that looks blue. And isn't music and art just the next level of illusion—sound waves or photons ordered and arranged just to fuck with your senses and send your mind on a trip?"

"No."

"No?"

"No."

Ally was good at getting me to talk about things like my weird ideas on music. She thought that the machinery thing sounded "a little paranoid" but admitted that the brain could be trained to see and hear some things and ignore others.

Another thing she got me to talk about was Sean, which was a little awkward. What was he like as a kid? Was he a good big brother? Was it true that he'd never had a steady girlfriend before her?

I affirmed the last piece of information, saying that he went out some, but never had anything serious that I knew of, though he'd had friends who were girls—especially Charlie's girlfriend, Jane.

"Was he in love with her?"

"I don't think so—I couldn't see Sean doing anything—"

"I don't mean *doing* anything," she said. "I just wondered if he had feelings for her. My last boyfriend's best friend had a crush on me—you can just tell, you know?"

Not really, I thought.

"I just wondered," Ally went on. "He seems like he'd be quiet—watching and enjoying being with both of them. Inside, it would probably be killing him."

I remembered a time when we were up here fishing the ponds. Jane was just learning how to cast a fly-rod, and Charlie's teaching method was to tie on a fly, give her the old Norman MacLean spiel about the clock, and then ditch her for another pond that wasn't being flailed by a greenhorn.

It was Sean—followed by a tagalong little sister—who stayed with Jane and untangled her line. I remember him watching her cast. He said something to her that I didn't hear, and she turned to him with a puzzled look. He said something else, and she reeled in all her line. Then he took her arm, straightened her wrist, and moved her arm back and forth. She concentrated on her cast, gazing out at the water of the pond, but he was concentrating on her face and—it seemed to me— admiring the freckles cast across her cheeks and nose.

"Maybe so," I said to Ally, but the memory seemed too intimate to share. I think Ally liked the idea of him as the platonic admirer, and also of herself as his first love, the one who discovered him.

"Maybe so," I repeated, slopping some paint onto the tipi. "I never really saw it."

"Wait," she said and showed me how to apply the paint in smooth even strokes, blending it into the earlier part, and then smoothing it out onto the bare canvas. I got a little shiver as she took my arm and adjusted the angle of the brush.

"Keep it loose," she said. "What kind of brother was he?"

"The best."

"Why?"

"Well, for one thing, he always let me tag along with him."

"He wasn't jealous of his spoiled baby sister?"

"He spoiled me as much as anybody. And I guess I would have been the jealous one, since he was older and got to do things. I was always saying it wasn't fair if he got to stay up later or something."

"Was he always so quiet?"

I nodded. "He listens."

She painted a while quietly, covering about twice as much tipi as I did in the same time.

"Tell me your favorite memory of childhood with him," she said. "One story that will sum up your relationship."

"'The Last Good Country.'"

"What?"

"It's a story he read to me from his *Nick Adams* book. We used to read it over and over and, since Hemingway never finished it, we'd make up our own endings. Sean would pretend to be Nickie and I would be his sister, Littless. The evil game warden comes after Nickie because of some poaching thing. When he runs away, she talks him into taking her along, and they escape to "the last good country," his special, hidden place. They camp out, fish, read together—just the two of them on the lam."

"Like *Huck Finn* with a sister instead of Jim—or instead of Huck."

"Exactly. And Sean and I were just like them."

"But you weren't on the lam."

"No." I laughed. "But we pretended to be, playing by the creek up here. In the story, they fished with willow sticks, and Nick—I mean Sean—used to say that all he needed was a coil of line and a few fishhooks and he could survive. He made Dad get him a sack of Bull Durham tobacco just so he could dump it out and keep his little fishing kit in it."

"That's adorable!"

"Sean always wanted 'The Last Good Country' to be real. The place I mean. He always wanted to go some place where there were no people, some place where he could live off the land."

"Did you guys read anything else?"

"Everything. But that was our special story."

"How come?"

"Well, I loved the way Littless was described, all golden and sunlit—it made me want to be her. She was little, but brave—whether she was reading something that was 'morbid' and 'too old' for her or worrying about Nickie killing this kid that was spying on them."

I paused, and Ally kept painting, the sound of her brush soft on the canvas.

"I like the way they worried about each other. There's a lot of love in that story."

As Ally and I worked and hung out, I'd been trying to work up the nerve to ask her about sex. Mom had given me plenty of information, but it's not something you really want to talk about with your parents.

It was impossible to ignore the subject, though, spending the week with Sean and Ally. Not that they were making out in front of me. He couldn't keep his hands off her, but he would just hold her hand, touch her back and shoulders—that sort of thing. They sat close as we ate dinner outside, their legs draping over each other under the table. And up at the sunset rocks, she'd lie back with her head in his lap and he'd play with her hair.

They always seemed to want to go to bed unnaturally early too, with a lot of fake yawns and "I'm tuckered outs."

And that was when the fireworks began. On the first night,

I didn't hear much, just a few moans drifting up to the tipi, but I knew right away what it was. I buried my head in my sleeping bag, then peeped out and lay still, listening.

Ally lost her inhibitions completely the next morning, or else Sean was making her feel awfully good. I could hardly face either one of them at breakfast, and Sean, who was the quiet one, seemed a little sheepish himself.

On Friday morning, when we were mixing up the paint, I gathered myself up and said, "So what do you guys use?"

She knew what I meant right away. "I'm on the pill," she said.

"M-hmm," I said, as if I chatted about these things every day. "But that doesn't protect you against…"

"AIDS? No. We used rubbers for a while. But I was Sean's first and, though I'd been careful as hell, I went to the clinic and got a clean bill of health before we stopped using them."

"Oh. Cool." Did I really want to be talking about this?

"You know all about this stuff, don't you, Cassie? Your parents don't seem like the sheltering type."

"Oh, yeah, it's just, you know, I was just wondering."

"Well, you can ask me anything you want. I remember when I was your age. Everybody pretended that either A, nobody's having sex, or B, sex is the most important thing in the universe, and unless you are having it, you don't fully exist."

"Yeah," I said. "That pretty much sums it up."

"I haven't heard you say anything about having a boyfriend…"

"No."

"Would you like to have one?"

"I don't care, sure, any friend would be good, really—people think I'm weird."

"That's because you're a free spirit."

"Yeah, right, *Mom*."

Ally laughed. "Let's be sisters, then," she said. "Moms have to protect you—a sister's job is to corrupt. We'll be sisters of the paint. C'mere."

She dipped her finger in a yellow swirl that she'd added to lighten the sun-color, and she smeared a line across my cheekbones and over my nose. Then she added a line down the part of my hair, and a dot between my eyebrows. "Third eye," she said. "This is your mystic-soul eye, Sister Free Spirit."

"Now you," I said and dipped my finger in red. I gave her cheekbone spots surrounded by yellow rays. She got a third eye, too, and a streak of yellow down the zigzag part of her hair. "And you, with your oh-so-trendy-in-1997 hair-part— dating back to when you were a middle school conformist—I dub thee Sister Dork-Lightning."

"So, now it's official," she said, stirring the paint.

I held the ladder while she climbed up and continued painting, all the while yelling down her advice and answers to my questions.

She was fifteen the first time. Yes, it hurt some, but mostly it just wasn't any good. Good means you're in love, and you trust each other, and you're nice to each other and, of course, both of you come. (Of course!) They all know how to come themselves, but only some of them know how to please a girl.

I think her being at the top of the ladder made it easier to talk, though I kept looking over my shoulder as she yelled stuff down at me with no sense of inhibition whatsoever. Also, it was good that she spared me details about Sean, who was the part in this I tried not to imagine.

She thought it was good that I didn't have a boyfriend because I would be wanting to experiment with him, and I was too young. At my age, she said, I was better off touching myself than touching others.

"That's how you get to know yourself, what feels good," she said.

"Yeah, right," I said. No one had ever gone beyond telling me that it was "normal" to touch myself. Ally was recommending it.

"What if I don't want to," I said.

"Don't let yourself take advantage of yourself. Just tell yourself no, and if you don't listen to yourself, say to yourself, 'Self, no means no.'"

"You're a real comedian."

"Well, if you don't want to, don't. But as the old-school hippies used to say, 'If it feels good, do it.' Do you want to take a turn up here?"

"Not really," I said. "Do you mind?"

"No," she said coming down, "but let's move the ladder."

That was about it for the sex-ed talk. She closed it up by telling me sex was all about love—it was just a deep and powerful and fun way of showing love. It can get weird because it's intense, so you have to really love the person you're fucking, and trust him. She put in a final plug for masturbation, saying you have to trust yourself and love yourself first, before you can trust and love others.

"Okay, MOM," I said. "Are you sure you don't want to talk about my self-esteem now?"

"Maybe," she said, "you should try some affirmations." Then she put her hand on her shorts, closed her eyes and moaned, "I truuust myself, I looove myself, I truuust myself..." We cracked up then—I as much out of embarrassment as humor. When Sean returned later, and the next day when Mom and Dad came up, she kept trying to work self-trust and self-love into the conversation just to make me start giggling.

We had a farewell dinner outside the cabin on Saturday night—it seemed like it had been ages since the welcome dinner just a week before. Everyone, especially me, thought that the tipi looked incredible. There is something cool about the way a tipi looks, set up in the open land. It takes you back, makes you imagine olden days. But now, painted by Ally, my tipi was a giant painting, a work of art—as corny as that sounds. It was vibrant—hugely so—but just as she'd promised, it didn't look out of place. I think we were all in awe of it.

"I need pictures to take back to school," Ally said. "And I wish I had video of the whole process to play at my senior show. But that might have spoiled it. We would have been too self-conscious."

"Yeah," I said, beginning to choke with laughter before I even said it. "I'm not sure I could *trust myself* on video."

"I don't think your particular brand of klutz is capable of self-trust," said Ally.

We started cracking up, but Mom broke in, "You girls seem to think that trusting yourself is a funny idea," she said.

We were maintaining, holding it back.

"But we've always tried to build Cassie's self-esteem."

Okay, so far—still, maintaining.

"And I should think, Ally, that someone like you would trust herself a great deal."

"I do," she choked. "All the time."

"And I hope you would encourage Cassie to trust herself as well."

"She does," I said, as we lost it and couldn't stop. It was all we could do to stay on our chairs. Ally was letting loose with high, pealing giggles, and I was practically sobbing, shaking, and about to wet my pants.

As I tried to catch my breath, Mom was saying that she was glad we were having so much fun. She stays on top of things, but what can you do when somebody has an inside joke? I felt a little bad about it, but Ally told her that what was so funny was that she had advised me, "just yesterday" on the subject of self-trust, which got us going again. When we finally wore ourselves out, I felt like I had been kicked in the stomach, but I hadn't laughed like that in a long time, maybe ever.

I gave Ally and Sean the tipi for the night, their last together, and at least they were quiet with Mom and Dad there.

The next day Sean and I took Ally to the airport. They had a long goodbye at the car, while I looked the other way, and then I walked her inside. I cried when we said goodbye at the security lines, but laughed through my tears when she hugged me and whispered, "Trust yourself." She gave a final wave once she was through the scanner, then she was gone.

Journal Five

16 September

Weekend over, and it's back to school—back to that nurturing place where we can all follow the exciting path of knowledge, where we can all be ourselves within the safety of—oh, forget it. There's really no point in trying to be clever about it. *Today sucked.*

I started out feeling great. All that writing about Ally got me inspired to violate the Invisibility Code, so I braided my hair Indian-style and wore the tie-dye tank that she gave me. Who cares if people noticed!

And first thing this morning, St. Matthew greeted me by saying, "Nice top—you're like a hippie Osama!"

How sweet of little Bible-Boy to notice! And it wasn't just the colorful aspect of my shirt that he complimented—he must have liked the fit, too, because he was talking directly at my boobs.

I thanked him, of course, and enjoyed all the other complimentary looks I got until lunchtime, when I glided into a landing at my usual table. Why should I hide in the library?

"Haven't seen you in a while," said Hannah, looking me over. "Too busy causing trouble?"

"Not at all," I said. "I've just had some reading to catch up on."

"So, what's going on with you?" She dipped a French fry in ranch dressing.

"Even Gwen and I are hearing about you," Sophia said, smiling. Gwen looked inside her lunch bag.

Oddly, I felt uncomfortable. Probably my fault, right? Friends are always there for you!

"I'm fine," I said. "I had a great weekend in the mountains."

"But what about last week?" said Hannah. "Didn't you get in-house or something?"

She's the best, isn't she? Friends don't let friends change the subject!

But foolish me kept trying. "Can we talk about something else?" I said. "It's just that, well, it's kind of complicated."

Gwen glared up at me. "Doesn't seem complicated to me. You blame your own country. Don't you appreciate what you have?" She took a bite out of her sandwich, fiercely, as if it offended her.

"You haven't heard her side of the story," said Hannah, the essence of support.

"It's *complicated.*"

"Okay," I said. "Okay…" I must have been missing something, because now Gwen seemed to be offended by *me.*

"We'd like to sympathize, Cassie," Sophia said. "And we don't believe in gossip, but some people have said some things—"

"Who and what?"

"Well, since we don't repeat gossip—"

"Everyone," Hannah said.

Friends *always* let you know what people are saying about you!

And Gwen must have been mad, not *at* me, but because she was watching my back.

"Who and what," I repeated.

"Almost everyone," Hannah said. "Especially Matthew,

Jenny, Nathan, Shelly—that whole crowd. Also people in show choir. And Mr. Kimble."

"Mr. Kimble?" I said. Great to know that the teachers were watching out for me, too. "What did *he* say?"

"He told the rest of the show choir that he had kicked you out because you disrespect your country. And the kids say that you were happy about 9/11, that you blame America, that you're a Muslim, and that you hate America and *really* hate Christians." While Hannah was listing my crimes, Gwen continued to glare, clearly because she was outraged on my behalf.

But then I got sort of confused, because I started to get the impression, from the look Sophia was wearing, that she was embarrassed because maybe she believed what people were saying.

"They call you Osama O'Sullivan, and," Hannah paused and smirked a little smile, "you have apparently been seen facing Mecca and praying several times daily."

"I never believed that one," Sophia protested.

"What about the rest of it?" I asked.

"Of course not—but I am curious as to how such rumors get started." She looked at me with interest. A good-hearted girl who didn't want to believe anything bad about anyone, especially her BFF, she must have felt there was a misunderstanding—that the gossips were not cruel any more than I was a terrorist sympathizer.

I could tell all, and as my BFF, she would listen. Hannah would, too—though she would enjoy the drama. I could probably even come to a civilized disagreement with Gwen. Weren't she and Sophia both my best girls? Not to mention Mormons, whose people had been stereotyped and discriminated against? Of course they would sympathize!

I imagined an impassioned speech to win them over. But I couldn't make it.

"You know how rumors get started," I said, getting up. "People talk. People listen."

This was a great line for ending the conversation, for ending the charade of Best Friends For Life, for getting up and walking away. But the question was, now that I was up, unopened lunch in hand, where to?

I made my way between the tables and through the door to the outside. Kids were bunched up around the benches or spread out on the grass, yelling for the football. Mr. Bad stood talking to Dr. Hawk. Behind their sunglasses, they registered my presence, like predatory insects, like security-droids. Dr. Hawk spoke and Mr. Bad listened as I turned and walked the other way, and just then the football hit me in the back, the pointy end jabbing me below the shoulder blade. I kept walking as somebody shouted:

"Osama! Little help! How 'bout a little help, Osama? The football, Osama! OSAMA!"

"O-sam-a, O-sam-a," somebody began to chant. Others joined in, then still more. "O-sam-a, O-sam-a, O-sam-a, O-sam-a."

I saw an empty space in the shade against the building, and I drifted over, sat on the concrete, and opened my lunch, but I couldn't eat. I drank some water. Eventually, the chanting faded. The tinted glass of the windows at my back concealed the kids inside, but I felt them there even before someone knocked on the glass. I ignored it.

I was far beyond Stay Cool. I was ice. The knocking got louder, and was joined by more knocks. The glass vibrated against my back like a massage, a massage of hate, and I imagined the glass shattering around me, the whole pane broken up into sharp, gray pebbles falling all around me as my eyes remained fixed on the summit of the Peak, floating above the city, pink rock and behind it, dry blue sky. The pounding stopped. I finished my water.

A whistle blew. The patio emptied and grew quiet.

With no place to go except class, I got up and went, moving behind a few other stragglers toward the eighth-grade wing. The sound of the crowd ahead was dim.

"Let's get to class! Come on, move along, people," Mr. Bad called out. He spoke to me as I passed him, then I went to my locker, entered Sinclair's room, and slid into my seat. Everyone was silent and reading.

As my eyes went over the same paragraph again and again, I tried to comfort myself with my trip to Oregon, but I couldn't get excited by it because the days between then and now were impenetrable.

I imagined the beach but could only think of sand, that I was buried in sand. At first I could move in it, painfully slow, muscles aching, but then it held me fast.

I stopped trying to move and was still, and it became almost pleasant. The cool, moist sand conformed to my eyelids, gently. It was tight against my ribs. I didn't need to breathe. From a spring below, icy water seeped in around my toes, up my ankles, around my calves and shins. And as the tide washed above me, seawater percolated down, the two seepages creeping closer and closer until they met, with a final tickle, at my navel.

The water carried with it a soft, clay silt, filling the spaces between the sand, pressing close against my skin. The silica clay began to seep into me, cell by cell, molecule by molecule, until I became something like a fossil, something like the flesh of an Anne Rice vampire. The sea covered me with layer after layer of sand and silt and the collected shells of a billion creatures as I rested inside a sepulcher of sand, and far above me, the moon shone onto the smooth, swelling surface. The moon pulled the water to it, and the sun pulled against that, but the earth held the ocean close, and I was part of the earth, but I could hear the waves above me singing surcease, surcease, surcease, surcease.

When you're embalmed in sand and silt, a thousand feet below the ocean floor, it's hard to care about discussing a book with your classmates. From that great distance, I heard them demanding to know why I had given them the wrong ending for the book. Why would I say that the Jewish family had been betrayed and killed when, in fact, they had escaped? And I answered that it did end that way for many, even if this book ended well. Someone ratted out the Frank family, and although Anne's *Diary* ends with her saying that she still believes that people are good, her biography reports that, by the time they murdered her, she'd changed her mind.

After writing that cheerful bit about Anne's death, I lay back on my bed, unable to stop thinking about her.

And I'm so tired of thinking.

The writing sort of helps, but then it just seems like thinking on paper, and I have a long night before me, and I want to do something else, but I don't know what.

Maybe I should watch TV. Maybe I should do some online shopping. Maybe I should go to sleep.

I was going to continue my tale of the summer. The past seems more real than the present when I'm writing it, but now I can't seem to get there. I have a beginning, something like, "After Ally left, I missed her all the time and could only think about August, when she was coming back."

But who cares? I can't pretend that I have a life. Maybe I shouldn't even go to Oregon next weekend. I feel so heavy, and I can't even imagine the sand and silt anymore. It's just nothing.

I wouldn't mind hearing my Jimi Hendrix record, "I don't live today. Maybe tomorrow, I just can't say." But I don't want to get up and put it on.

I was fighting, but now I don't feel like I can. I told the story of my day, but so what? Ally said to write in you, Di, to fight in you, to gather everything that I love and hate. To tell the story, to make random life a story, to make art.

If only I could sleep. Maybe I could sleep. Maybe I should eat something. Maybe nothing.

Stupid to feel this way. What happened today? Do I really care about those people? I hate myself—I'm so tired of being me. I can't stand being in my own skin, that barrier with the world that prickles when anything touches it, even my soft bed/torture rack. I want to be out of it. I, I, I, I, I, I, I. Shut up!

17 September

It's not fun, Di. I need to try to gather myself, but I can't.

Suddenly, I hate my clothes. I don't care about clothes—why can't I think of a single thing that I want to put on?

I want to eat meat, I want to smoke something, I want to wear a short, tight, red shirt.

I want to wear a burqa, I want to cut off all my hair...

?

Yes.

It's amazing the difference a little change makes. Just after I dotted a definitive period after that "Yes" up there, I grabbed my scissors.

Then I remembered Dad's clippers—he used to cut Sean's hair—and I knew just where they were. I tiptoed down to the second floor landing. I could hear Mom and Dad in the kitchen, so I slipped into their room and grabbed the clippers.

Since I was going to buzz my whole head, it didn't matter if I made clean scissor-cuts, but it took me a while to get up my nerve. I leaned forward, letting my hair hang down like a tent around my face, and I felt the weight of it, the smoothness of it, and its darkness.

Then I pulled on a hunk and sawed through it. Unlike when I get a trim, and Mom's stylist, Susan, snips neatly, I had to really hack away at it. I held it for a minute, debating whether I should save it, then dropped it into the trash.

Once I had it short—uneven shags all over the place—I plugged in the clippers and snapped on attachment number one, choosing a close buzz over total baldness. Then I flipped the switch and cut a strip from the front all the way back to my neck. Chunks of hair fell into the sink, and I took another swath and then another. The mirror was messing me up, because it reversed all my movements, so I closed my eyes and did it by feeling, going over and over it until I thought I had it all done. I dared a look.

My eyes blinked back at me, huge and surprised looking. It was like looking at my face for the first time, and I thought how surprised Narcissus must have been, encountering his reflection in the pool and wondering who this youth was. Not that I fell in love with myself, Di, far from it—my nose was too big and I had zits on my forehead and the new-shorn look gave me the appearance of a frightened animal.

Fumbling in the mirror, mixing up which way to turn the clippers, I eventually managed to clean up the rough spots. I held another mirror up so I could see the back, and it looked okay.

It was weird in the shower, shampooing my prickly-soft head, and even weirder when I got out and could feel every breath of air on my scalp. I pulled on a pair of jeans and a T-shirt and went to put the clippers away, stopping when I saw myself in Mom's mirror: it was me from my bare feet to about my shoulders, where my hair should have been hanging dark and wet, and then some other Cassie above that. I went through the tops in Mom's closet, passing over all the dark solids and stripes and whites until I found a silky blouse, hand dyed in deep blue and burgundy rectangles with yellow sun-spots, swirls, chevrons, and squiggles drawn over it in gold fabric marker. I was afraid it was silk, which I don't wear, but it was rayon. I whipped off my T-shirt and slipped on the blouse. It barely met the top of my jeans and was tight.

I stood looking at myself when I heard Mom on the stairs.

"Mom," I called in my best casual-daughter voice. "Can I borrow your rayon top?"

"Which one?" she said, and stopped. I could see her in the mirror behind me and see myself trying to manage an innocent smile.

"I cut my hair. Do you like it?"

"Oh, Cassie!" she said. "Why would you? How could you just…" She actually started sobbing, and holding me, and then pushing me away with her hands on my shoulders so she could look up at me. I still haven't gotten used to being taller than her.

Dad's alarmed voice called in, "Deb, are you all right?" And then he came in and saw.

"Dad *burn!*" he said. "Ye ain't got no more hair no more!"

"Daddy, no! I thought something was wrong." I looked in the mirror with feigned horror. "You're right! It's gone! Call 911! Is it like losing a finger? Can they reattach it?"

"Stop it, you two," wailed Mom.

"There, there, Deborah." He put his hands on her shoulders. "It's just hair. It'll grow. And it doesn't look so bad. She's a good-lookin' kid—I think I like it." He reached out and felt my head, "Hmmm. Do you like it?" he asked me.

"I don't know—I guess it's all right. I wanted something different."

"Well, it is different," said Mom.

"Now, Deb, the child's self-esteem—"

"Oh, all right, she's as beautiful as ever. It's just that—" She looked at me in the mirror again, where all three of us were clustered. "I've always loved her hair—it's always been so...so *Cassie*. Remember, Gale? The first time we cut it? I felt like I was cutting *her*. But okay, honey, I know, you're fourteen now. I just have to get used to it—used to my little girl doing things like this. But you might have said something instead of giving me a heart attack."

"It was a spontaneous decision. Can I wear your blouse?"

"It's a little small," said Dad, eyeing my exposed middle.

"It's okay," I said. "Girls at school show a lot more than this and nobody—"

"You're not girls at school."

I tugged it down. "It's okay, Dad. Look."

"She's fine," said Mom. "It's actually nice to see her dressing a little more feminine."

I felt excellent walking into school today, even after yesterday—which I should have dealt with better and maybe wasn't even that bad. Weird looks by the score. Maybe it's cool to be visible.

St. Matt called me "Osama Bald-Laden," and I thanked him for noticing. Quill ran up and started rubbing my head. DJ said, "Ponyboy, your hair, your tuff, tuff hair!" from *The Outsiders*. Liz Pine thought it was "radical."

I sat with those guys at lunch, and it was okay though I wondered what my old lunch friends were thinking—I felt somehow disloyal to them and to my old self.

Even weirder is that I felt like going shopping for some

new clothes after school. I still hate shopping, but I am suddenly bored with my old T-shirts. What's wrong with me?

I tried to call Ally just now to tell her about my new haircut and everything that has been happening at school. Nobody home—I had to leave a message again.

Back to the summertime—

Ally left a big empty space at the cabin, the tipi, the whole Goat-horn valley, and, I have to say, inside both my brother and me. But she did give me a great parting gift by being my ally again and helping me convince Mom and Dad to let me spend the rest of the summer at the cabin.

Strange for your parents to be more worried about you being bored than you are yourself, but they wanted to know what I was going to do all day. Beyond reading, hiking, and writing a little, I wasn't sure. Lie on the Carrock all day and watch clouds grow? Who cares. Boredom, not to mention horror, was living in the city: pavement, automobile exhaust, shopping, television, and a thousand other useless entertainments. But the mountains are filled with miracles: every thunderstorm, every sunset, every wildflower raising its head in the meadow, every patch of lichen on the Carrock, soaking up the sun and the rain and the air.

In the end Mom came around, deciding that she was going to "validate my need for solitude," though she hoped I would think of some friends to invite up or to make plans with downtown. And she would be in and out, as would Dad, so I wouldn't really be alone that much.

In the first week, Sean worked every day and came back tired, but it was nice having dinner together. I began the summer by immersing myself in Middle Earth—and Valinor—reading *The Silmarillion* for the first time and going through *The Hobbit* and *The Lord of the Rings* again. By the end of *The Return of the King*, I was walking around in a kind of daze, with the contours of Middle Earth mentally superimposed onto *this* earth.

Then I read *Desert Solitaire* again—what a contrast! Where Tolkien made his own mythology, Abbey told stories of people and the earth just as he saw them. In one, a vulture is a carrion bird, full of dark symbolism. In the other, it's "the noble turkey vulture," in whose gut any creature might find an honorable resting place.

I remember one night later in the summer: Sean and I sat alone on the sunset rocks, shielded behind our sunglasses. The day was clear except for a few wispy clouds hanging between us and the Collegiate Peaks. Sean had just gotten a letter from Ally confirming that she would come for two weeks at the end of July and beginning of August, then the two of them would have another couple of weeks to take the long way back to school.

"Do you still miss her like you did?" I said, almost calling him "Nickie." It seemed like we were about to have a conversation out of "The Last Good Country."

"Every day," Sean said. "But you get used to it."

"Do you love her a lot, Nickie?" Okay, I thought, I might as well go with it.

"So do you, Littless." He put his arm around my shoulder. "I thought you hated her at first."

"Was I awful?"

"You weren't bad."

"Now that she's gone, I'm used to it too. But sometimes I expect to see her—like I'm down at the ponds and I think she'll be there."

"You make it sound like she's dead."

"No. But she's not here."

"I know what you mean."

He stared out toward the horizon for a while. "Have you ever heard that saying, 'Wherever you go, there you are'?"

"Sounds like something Dad would say."

"He does," Sean said, like himself now and not Nick Adams. "I think of it like this—any place has two components—what's there, and what you bring with you."

"Like in Lorien when Aragorn says that the only evil in that place is the evil that people bring?"

"I don't remember, but yeah. You like it here because, in a certain way, there's no evil here—just like Lórien. You can't stand the messes that people make, and we keep it pretty clean up here. Out there," he gestured off in the distance, north toward Denver, "there's all kinds of shit going on."

The sun began to slip behind the mountains and a breeze moved up the valley.

"But what I really meant was how this place holds her, holds our memories of her. I think you were reading all that Tolkien to escape, so you wouldn't miss her. And now we're sort of used to it, so we don't mind missing her, we even like missing her, because it's the closest thing to being with her."

"Which is going to happen in about three weeks."

"Wow," he said, and I didn't know if he meant Ally coming or the sky, which had taken the colors of roses and peaches, like watercolors washed over the thin clouds.

"Wow," I said, meaning both.

18 September

Images of summertime:

I'm sitting on the beaver dam, still, watching trout flash out of the shadows to take caddisflies from the surface. Mosquitoes bite me, and horseflies, which I slap and flick into the pond to feed the trout. The sun burns me, and the wind squints-up my eyes. Stubble grows on my legs and prickles under my arms until it softens and lengthens. I shower in sun-heated water from the roof of the cabin and brush out my hair as I dry in the sun on the Carrock. When rains come, I wait with everything else, listening to the drumming on the roof or the tipi and feeling the water soaking into the land.

When I think of my summertime in the mountains, I feel strange now, grooming myself for the eyes of others. The mountains don't care, the land doesn't care. The raven seems to watch you, but what are its thoughts as it flaps above the trees and calls to another on a distant rock?

I miss my hair. I want to wrap myself up in it, but there is only my head, exposed and bare. What will I wear today? Suddenly I have to make decisions. I look at my legs, brown and gangly and adorned with dark hairs. I have a pair of hiking shorts that are borderline long enough to pass dress code. And I think I'll hack the arms off a T-shirt, and maybe cut a few inches off at the bottom.

On my way into the school I heard a chorus of "omigods" and shrieks of laughter from a group of BFF girls who were staring at my legs. *Whatnever.* St. Matt didn't let me down—he checked me out at our lockers and said, "Missed your legs when you got rid of your hair, Osama." I was followed by stage whispers and rude looks all morning.

At the Tolkien lunch group, the seventh grade girls giggled at me, but DJ said I looked "tuffer every day."

Mr. Griffin read the part where Gandalf tells Frodo that it was not "a pity" that Bilbo didn't stab Gollum when he had a chance—"it was pity that stayed his hand." He put a lot of emphasis on the bit where Gandalf says that while many who live deserve death, many who die deserve life. "Can you give it to them? Therefore be not quick to deal out death in judgment, for even the wise cannot see all ends."

"And Gollum is so cute!" said Tarah.

"Cute?" I said. "Where is he described as being cute?"

"In the movie, you know?"

"Oh. Haven't seen it."

Nobody could believe this was possible, except Griffin. He said that the first time he saw it he couldn't enjoy it because all he could think about was how different it was from the book.

I read the scene where Sam looks into the Mirror of Galadriel and sees all the Shire being polluted and the trees being cut down.

DJ read about Gimli the dwarf asking Lady Galadriel for a lock of her hair.

"And he's too reserved," said Quill, "but Gimli—I mean

DJ—wanted me to ask you for a lock of your midnight tresses, Cassie."

"Shut up, man," said DJ, hiding his head.

"He wants one of her *dresses*?" asked Tarah.

"*Tresses*," said Quill. "Locks, mane, protein filaments—hair."

"Most regrettably, Master Gimli," I said, "My dirt-brown locks—they weren't midnight at all—have been most ignobly deposited in the trash."

"Bummer, man, he's, like, heartbroken."

When I got home, the phone was ringing. It was Ally.

"Less than two weeks, sister," she said.

"I know, I can't wait. It's the best birthday present ever."

I took the cordless out back to the patio.

"How are you?"

"Great—I mean, up and down, you know. I'm living for this trip. What about you?"

"We could really use a break, too. Sean is studying his ass off—I'm pretty busy myself. Too many classes, not enough art. You're going to love this place at the beach."

There was a pause. I had so much to tell her, I didn't know where to start.

"What's up," she said. "Did you just want to chat? Your message sounded sort of urgent."

"Well…for one thing, I cut off all my hair."

"All of it? How short?"

"Short. Not shaved, but clippered."

"Wow. I bet it's awesome. Do you like it?"

"I don't know—it's different, I wanted a change."

"That's cool. What else? School?"

"What do you think?"

"That bad?"

"I don't know. Yes. The work is easy enough, my grades are okay, but…everybody hates me." I thought about DJ. "Well, not *every*body."

"Oooo. Cassie's in love."

"Am not."

"Who is he?"

"His name's DJ." I told her about the Tolkien and writing clubs and how DJ wanted a lock of my tuff hair.

"How romantic. He sounds sweet. And he must have it bad for you."

"You think so?"

"How many eighth grade boys would ask for a lock of your hair? Are you going to give it to him?"

"No."

"Do you like him?"

"I don't know. Maybe."

"You should give it to him. It's cute."

"Well, I think I can get it out of the trash."

"He'll love it. But what about everybody else—the ones that hate you?"

I told her about choir, and how they thought I was the Antichrist because of the incident in reading. And how they think that I'm a freak because I have more hair on my legs than my head.

"We'll have to find you one of those T-shirts that says, 'You call me a freak—as if that's a *bad* thing.'"

"Perfect." We laughed.

Then she said, "Listen. I had this idea for you."

"For me?"

"Yeah, I was going to wait until you came out here, but maybe sooner is better than later."

"So, tell me!"

"Well, you remember in the beginning of summer when we were talking about how awful middle school is, and I said that high school should be at least marginally better?"

"Trouble is," I said, "how am I going to make it 'til I get there?"

"That's the idea. You *don't* wait. You go to high school *now*."

"You can't—" I said. "How could I do that?"

"Well, you said you were old enough to be a grade ahead, right? Your birthday is just before the deadline. So skip the rest of eighth grade."

"Will they let me do that? They won't let me do that."

"They might. What have you got to lose? Look at yourself—you don't belong in middle school."

We came up with ideas—talking to the GT lady at school, convincing Mom and Dad, going to the principal instead of the assistant, maybe even going straight to the high school.

"I bet your dad could convince the schools," Ally said. "Think how many hopeless cases he's won in court. So your job is convincing your parents."

"That should be easy. Won't they love to think of their brilliant daughter skipping a grade?"

"I don't know—sometimes they don't like you to move so fast."

"But it's too perfect. Now that you've come up with this, I feel like it's the only way I'll survive."

Even as I said that, it sounded like the overstatement of the year, but still, I was filled with euphoria. To be free of that horrible place forever! To be in a big school, with older kids, where nobody will know me or notice me or think I'm weird. Maybe even where people have half a brain and don't always have to be part of the herd.

And yet, I have doubts. I might be starting to make friends, including DJ. I can still see them, though, right? And what if high school is no better? This little voice keeps fretting me, saying it will never happen, and if it does it won't do any good.

My head is swirling with ideas and fantasies as well as misgivings, and on top of it all, I feel so weird with my new haircut and wearing different clothes and thinking about DJ, too. How do I feel about him? It's not like some kind of warm and tingly feeling—it's more that I can't stop thinking about him.

19 September

Writing group was cool, and just for fun, I tied up a lock of hair for DJ. Turns out it wasn't in the trash because Mom had collected it. She is saving it in a little box and gave me some. I tied a ribbon around it, and put it in an envelope.

To Gimli, Glóin's son:
A lock of tuff, tuff hair.

I didn't know how to close it, so I left it at that.

Without even reading the envelope, DJ gave me a smile that said he knew what it was. He slid it into his backpack even as Quill was grabbing for it.

"Stay back, Quillen," he said. "Thanks, Cassie."

"Sure, man." Man? Had I just called him *man*?

I don't know what business I had giving him a lock of my hair anyway, unless I wanted to encourage the crush he seems to have, so I guess I did want to. Maybe I do have a sort of tingly feeling around him. I think I like it, and if nothing else, it's nice to feel admired.

After writing group, before class, I found a note in my locker. For an instant I hoped it was from my admirer, but then I saw it was addressed to "The Bald and Hairy Bride of Osama."

Hey bitch butch ben Ladin! Maybe you can be one of the verjins that Aluh give the TERRERIST !! If you die soon. Oops! Too late for the verjin part you ho! Fuck you, bitch! America Rules! And shave your skanky legs!!!

I'm not sure that I got it word for word, or that I captured all the misspellings, because I decided not to treasure it forever.

I kept getting strange looks all day, mostly from Matt and Jenny's friends. Before reading class, a bunch of them were standing around in a knot outside the door. When I said, "Excuse me," they ignored me, continuing their huddle and giggling. When someone else showed up, they opened an aisle, but closed it before I could slip through. Do you think I made a scene? Oh no, not me. I just got a drink and came back right after the bell. They were inside by then, all in their seats with their books out, and *I* was late.

I had been blaming Matt in all this, but I think Jenny is really behind it. I keep seeing those two, very tight. She was at his locker after school and they totally ignored me, but they thought something was extremely humorous.

So that was my day, Di. I was thinking of the high school plan the whole time, and it's taken me so far away from where I was Monday, buried in the cold sand of my mind.

I should have talked to Sean yesterday—I can't believe I didn't even ask if he was there. I should try him now.

Luckily, he was home and had some great ideas. Since Mom and Dad might not be easy to convince, he thinks I should write a letter to persuade them. At first he said I should include stuff about what a hard time I'm getting at school, but I don't want to get them all riled up about that. Keep it focused on academics, we decided, and I'll have a better chance. My main idea is that I don't fit in *academically* in middle school, so I should move up to the right level. But Sean has some doubts, too—he's not sure this is going to solve all my problems.

They're going to think about it.

I typed up my letter, made some changes, and printed two copies. I couldn't watch them read it, so I paced around the house until they called me in. Dad called it "intriguing," but said they'd need some time to consider. Beautiful. While they're considering, I'm left hanging.

More from the summer—

Back at the end of July, when Ally returned, I'm not sure who was more excited, her boyfriend or her adopted sister. For me, it was like she had never left—as easy and natural as ever. For them, it seemed a little strained at first.

After touching up the tipi-painting and taking a million pictures of it, Ally worked a lot in her sketchbook. She did pencil sketches of the tipi, the Goat-horn, the Carrock, the cabin. She also drew Sean a lot and did a couple of Mom and Dad. Sometimes she would draw me, sprawled out on the Carrock or by the falls. It got a little uncomfortable on the hard, rough rocks, but the really uncomfortable thing was being drawn. I would glance over and see her looking as if she were not really seeing me.

"Don't look at me," she said. "Look at the sky, look at the rock, look inside yourself. But don't look at me."

I tried not to, but I couldn't help it. I'd see her glance at my face, or my foot, or somewhere in between, and it gave me a funny tingle, as if she were touching me. It was a weird sense of being exposed yet safe. I wouldn't have bared myself like that for anyone else. I don't even like to look at myself in the mirror, but I trusted her.

When she showed me the drawings, it was strange, not like seeing myself in a mirror nor yet like seeing myself through her eyes—it was like seeing someone else, someone I recognized but didn't know.

20 September

Morning Di. I wonder if they talked about the plan. I can't believe they wouldn't even discuss it last night. Okay, it was kind of late. I'll see if they want to talk this morning—casually go in to borrow one of mom's hippie skirts and ask if they want to chat.

They didn't. The only thing Dad would say is that after reading my letter, he might consult me on some of his opening and closing arguments. And that my "puzzle metaphor" almost worked. That's good, isn't it?

They better say yes. I'm not sure I can handle many more days as wonderful as today.

I was still trying to Stay Cool, but it didn't seem like it was helping. In the hall I got called hairy-legged mountain girl, which made me think even more that Jenny was behind this. I even began to consider getting some sort of help. Dr. Hawk isn't exactly my best friend—I wondered if the counselor could do anything. Probably just talk to me about my feelings, or worse, make me go to some sort of "problem solving" or "conflict resolution" group. Like that would help. Anyway, I decided, I better not make trouble if I'm really hoping to get out of here. But things were pretty unpleasant.

In math, Steven Boylan, who sits behind me, kept putting his feet up on the legs of my chair and tapping. I was determined to ignore him, but the more I did, the worse it got. I scooted up as far as I could, my desk almost on top of the chair in front of me. Finally, Steven seemed to get bored. He left me alone for about ten minutes, and then all of a sudden he slammed my chair legs with both feet so my neck snapped back, my waist hit my desk, and my desk rammed the chair in front of me.

"Stop it!" I yelled.

"Cut it out," said the kid in front of me.

"Is there a problem, Miss Sullivan?" demanded Mr. Math Teacher.

"Steven keeps kicking my chair."

"Mr. Boylan, knock it off."

"I just lightly rested my feet on her chair," Steven said. "I don't know why she has to get all psycho."

Math heaved a sigh. "Miss Sullivan, you don't have to shriek, do you? I hope I make myself clear—I don't think we need these interruptions."

I was embarrassed, thinking of DJ witnessing my humiliation from the back corner, where he sat now.

"Do I make myself clear?" said Math.

"Abundantly so, sir."

"What's that?"

"Yes."

"Very good. Now, let's get back to work, shall we?"

"Yes, sir."

"Did you really need to answer that, Miss Sullivan?"

"I don't know, sir."

"Be quiet and get to work and do not answer any questions until I instruct you to do so—is that clear? Don't answer that."

I figured I had better shut up even though I *really* wanted to answer. I had taken enough lately and was ready to start dishing. Stay Cool wasn't working at all, but what did I expect if I used some ridiculous Bush administration-type moniker? As absurd as it sounded, I might as well have made it "Operation Stay Cool."

But no matter how absurd, I decided to try to keep on

staying cool. In a week I'll be off to Oregon, and with a little bit of luck, I'll be out of here for good.

At dinner Mom and Dad were finally ready to talk. I'm still in limbo, but I think it went okay. They had been discussing my idea, they said, and what they wanted from me was an explanation of "the whys and wherefores," and then they would render a decision. Here's how it went:

"First, learned Father," quoth I. "The whys and wherefores are identical, the two terms being synonymous—"

"Touché," he said.

"Let's leave it at why, then," said Mom, "and maybe we'll get some answers."

"But even though we haven't had an answer *per se*," Dad went on, "her response may indicate that the child is too big for her britches and may require, shall we say, a larger size."

"If Miss Smarty-pants would let me take her shopping, then we could get her some double XLs, but maybe we should have her start by reading the letter, and then we can discuss pros and cons."

So I read the letter, which I'll paste here for the record:

Dear and Esteemed Parents,

I have an IDEA that I want to share with you, and after talking it over with Sean, I felt that a letter might be the best way to get my thoughts together. I need your support, and I hope after you read this I will have it.

So here it is: I want to skip the rest of eighth grade and go straight to high school. Sounds crazy at first, but read on:

I know you both thought that I should wait a year before I started kindergarten, and at the time, you were probably right. But now, it seems right for me to move back to my age-appropriate level. I know you want what's best for me, your daughter, both socially and academically, and so I will explain why moving immediately to high school will benefit me.

The social reasons are perhaps the least compelling. Since I have felt like a misfit for most of my school years, you may wonder why moving ahead would make any difference. It may not. Yet it may. I have some intelligence on these matters from Ally and Sean, and they report that a middle school is one of the least tolerant atmospheres they have experienced. High schools are also notoriously intolerant, but Sean has told me that Parker—where I would be going—is an exception. There, I am told, nonconformists like me can more easily find a niche.

If it was my lack of maturity that caused you to keep me from entering kindergarten at the usual time, then by now I think you have seen me surpass others at my grade level. Would it not be appropriate now for me to join a group more in keeping with my own level?

I have made a couple of new friends this year, so it would be a drawback for me to leave them behind just as I am getting to know them. But they'll be coming along in another year, and I'm not so close that I'll miss them too much. Another reason that I mention this is to demonstrate that I am mature enough to make new friends. So please don't think that my misfit status indicates that I am not ready to move ahead. On the contrary, I think not "fitting in" means that I'm not in the right place and that I have better chances of fitting in somewhere else.

One reason I think I'll fit in better in high school is that I hope to find the work more challenging. I try not to complain about it, but the fact is that school bores me to the point of extreme frustration. Going to middle school has seemed to be a waste of time from the beginning. I can't remember being challenged since fifth grade. The last two years have been endless review and constant drill for pointless, useless tests. If the purpose of school is learning, then there is little purpose in my finishing eighth grade. It is the increased academic opportunity and challenge of high school that has the promise of fulfilling that purpose.

I realize that, in the past, I have resisted being challenged. You're thinking about accelerated math, perhaps? If I was content to coast by with As in regular math instead of working for them in accelerated, then why am I so anxious for a challenge now? It's hard to say. Maybe I just didn't see the point, and now I do. Maybe not accepting small challenges has made me ready for this big one. I only know that, in my mind, I never saw myself as a show choir kid, or an accelerated math kid—it just didn't seem right for me. But when I imagine myself in high school, it seems right.

So I end with what I thought of in the beginning as the least compelling reason for skipping to high school—a vague feeling that I'm a puzzle piece put away in the wrong box. I could spend the rest of the year trying but never become a part of this picture. Wouldn't it be better to move my piece over to the other puzzle where it has a chance of working?

I have the honor to remain,
Your humble servant,
And Daughter,
Cassandra Marie Sullivan

"Very impressive," said Dad. "As I said this morning, your puzzle metaphor almost works."

"Almost?"

"Just because this puzzle isn't right, doesn't mean that puzzle will be."

"I guess that's my concern too," said Mom. "The academics will be more challenging and varied in high school, and that may help you socially, too—making you feel more at home. But…I don't know."

"It may not be all it's cracked up to be."

"Sean and Ally may be right about high school being a little more open-minded, sweetie—"

"But you do hear a lot of stories about it being just the opposite."

"And I'm afraid it will be hard in ways you haven't thought of."

"You don't think I can do the work?"

"Not the work," Mom said. "Other things."

"Like what?"

"Parker is a big school, we don't want you to get lost."

At this point I became so disgusted I started sounding like a typical teenager. "So we're back in kindergarten, right? 'Cassie's smart, but she's too much of a baby to handle it.' Please! You should have home-schooled me and kept me a baby forever."

"You know that's not what we want, but are you sure you're ready for this?"

"*Please*, Mom. Like I'm going to get lost and not find my classes?"

I actually said "please" again? *Please!*

"I think your mother isn't speaking literally," Dad said. "What she means is sometimes it's better to be a big fish in a small pond."

"Gee, Dad. Thanks for the interpretation. And the vote of confidence."

"You don't have to get snippy."

"Well, I'm sorry, but I need you guys to support this. I was beginning to wonder how I'm going to get through this year, and then Ally had this idea—"

"I thought this might have been her brainchild," said Mom, "although you didn't mention it."

"Is there something wrong with that?"

"No-o, but having an older friend can make you want to grow up a little too fast."

"I am FOURTEEN. I am older than, like, everyone else in my class. I should be in high school *already!*"

"I'm sure there are others your age, Cassie. It's only a matter of one day, it's not like—"

"You don't understand. I can't breathe in that place. I need to get *out.*" I was about to lose it, and I really didn't want to. You can't argue that you're all grown up when you're bawling like a two-year-old. "I'm sorry." I breathed. "I thought you would be excited about this idea too. So, are you saying no?"

"It's all so sudden. We want you to think about this, not rush headlong."

"I have thought about it."

"For one day or two?"

"Why don't you make a list," Dad said, "of the pros and the cons. Write it in your diary. You don't have to show us, but think it over yourself. And if you are resolved, we'll decide tomorrow. Also, you better come up with a plan on how to convince the schools. If you think we're tough, just wait."

So here I am, still hanging. I guess I should make my list of pros and cons. Really, I think they are just trying to make me sweat. They're going to say yes. They have to.

Let's start with the cons:

1. Leaving my new friends, including DJ. (Mentioned that already, in my letter, and I can still see them after school and next year.)
2. Starting in the middle of the semester will be weird, I'll be the new kid. (see pro #10)
3. Starting out behind in all my classes. (I can catch up, no problem.)
4. Classes harder. (But also more interesting, see pro # 3)
5. Big school will be weird and scary. (I'll get used to it. Middle school seemed big at first, too.)
6. Scary juniors and seniors and sophomores, and even freshmen—because now I will be the youngest one in my class instead of the oldest. (If I can handle the evil Tabor kids, I can handle anyone.)
7. What if everyone there hates me too? (But what if they don't?)
8. Getting up earlier in the morning. (pro # 8)
9. People might think I think I'm "all that" because I skipped eighth grade. (I can just say that I started late,

and wanted to come up with the class I should have
been in.)

10. What if I go through all this and nothing is any better
    at all, or what if it's worse? (I have to try, because of pro
    # 11.)

Okay, now the pros:

1. Never see Dr. Hawk, Mr. Kimble, etc. again.
2. Get away from Matt and Jenny and all those people
   for almost a year.
3. New classes, more interesting, possibly get into honors
   and AP and a real French or Spanish class instead of
   just *le bateau, la baguette, le cinema.* (see con # 4)
4. Go out to lunch downtown—open campus.
5. More freedom, adult atmosphere.
6. More open-minded people—more diverse.
7. Finish school and go to college a year earlier.
8. Get out earlier in the day.
9. Study hall, open scheduling.
10. "Fresh start." Don't people want to make friends with
    the new kid? (con # 2)
11. What if it's all just a little bit better, or even a lot bet-
    ter? What if I'm happier?

There you have it. After I did the pros, I went back and
put the positive spin on each of the cons. Mom and Dad really
have to say yes now, because I am more convinced than ever.

Now, how am I going to get the middle school to let
me go and the high school to take me? Ally and I had some
basic ideas, talk to the GT lady, the principal. And Sean said I

should concentrate on the academic aspect. Now I really wish I had taken accelerated math and algebra.

Oh, FUCK!

I was lying here daydreaming, thinking about how it will be in high school, when I realized, with glee, that if I can pull this off, I'll only have two more years of CSAPs. And then I remembered, with horror, what I did last year.

Man, oh man, oh man, that better not come back and bite me in the butt! I've got to move on this *now*, before the scores come in, or I'm sunk. Vanquished. Worsted.

I can't think about that. I still have time, not much, but enough. I hope. Once I'm gone, they can't send me back, can they?

Okay, what's the plan? I don't have a clue. I'll tell Mom and Dad that I can talk to the administrators myself, and that my reason for advancing is just to get back on track with my age group. But I need their support. That sounds mature, doesn't it?

21 September

They said yes!

We had breakfast out back, as nice an autumn Saturday as you could wish for. I think they had already decided because, after I summarized my pros and cons, and we discussed a couple of flaws in my arguments, like the notion that avoiding small challenges prepares you for big ones, they agreed to help me try it. They liked how I admitted that it might not be any better in high school and could even end up worse.

"You realize," Mom said, "that if we are able to convince them, if they agree, and you go up to Parker—that's that. You can't go back. You'll have to deal with that decision."

"You have to be committed to it," said Dad. "For better or for worse."

"It's just a school, Dad. I'm not marrying it."

"But you're committing."

"Yes. I am."

"And don't get your hopes up too high yet," said Mom. "We still have to get this past the powers that be."

"What's your plan for that?" asked Dad.

I told them my vague ideas and gave them my bit about not really knowing exactly what to do and needing their help.

They thought I was right, the first step would be for me to discuss it with the principal. They wanted me to see her on my own first. I should let her know that I had their support, and they would talk to her later.

Now I've got to chill this weekend and be ready for Monday. I hope we can get a decision before I go to Oregon. (One week from today!) Maybe I can even get registered, meet my new teachers, and get my makeup work before I go.

Chill? Just using the word tells me that my brain is anything but.

At the end of the summer, Sean finished his season with a three-day guiding trip. Since he wouldn't be around, Ally and I decided to go off on our own trip to some hot springs in New Mexico.

We stopped the first night at The Valley, a hippie-ish sort

of hot springs club on the way south. Ally said that it was "against her religion" to pay for hot springs, but she was willing to make an exception since we also got a little cabin to stay in. It's a beautiful spot. The network of warm pools on a mountainside of the Sangre De Cristos overlooks a flat valley, blue-gray in the distance, with the San Juans to the west and New Mexico to the south. The pools aren't that hot, but the bubbly spring water is heavenly.

Ally had gone "almost totally" vegetarian since the beginning of summer, and we had some awesome tofu and watercress sandwiches for dinner. The joke was on me because I'd insisted on buying watercress as part of our grubstake, and then we found it growing wild in the stream by our cabin. We also had a twelve-pack of beer, of which I was only allowed one per night. I forgot to mention that I had been developing a taste for the stuff that summer because Sean occasionally let me have one when Mom and Dad weren't around. One beer was enough to get a little bit of a buzz though, just enough to make me sort of mellow and giggly, and that was how I felt after we took a last sunset dip in the springs and then went back to our cabin.

It had been a long time since I had done anything resembling a sleepover, and it was fun to lie in opposite bunks, talking and laughing until Ally fell asleep.

I could hear people outside the cabin, partying around the big pool, and I imagined the night accepting the noise as it drifted across the valley under the stars. It's a lyrical image, or so I thought, and I played with it for a while: the still air of the night carrying the voices as it carried dust, insects, and echo-locating bats. The silly laughter spilled out around the pool, and the drunken shouts were taken by the night air just as our "environment" takes everything we give it, as our bodies take what we feed them, and our minds what we read, what we view, what we hear…

And I lay there a while thinking until, in much the same way, sleep took *me*.

The next day we headed down to the springs in New Mexico. Straight roads took us across the valley to the border, then we followed creeks and rivers through the mountains until we came to the pullout where there was a trail supposed to lead to the springs. The word was that they were "technically" closed to the public, but you could go in this side route and "nobody hassled you." Wrong.

We climbed up over a ridge, losing the trail a few times among pale, sun-reflecting rocks, and I began to wonder why we were sweating and toiling in the heat of mid-day only to arrive at a pool of boiling hot water. It was a scene right out of a mythical place where, I would soon be told by Matthew, I would spend eternity.

But when we got there, it was heaven! Massive cottonwood trees ringed the pool and rustled in a breeze that hadn't existed a moment before. Just a few yards from the hot spring, a stream of cool water flowed, and it had several promising holes for dipping. There was, of course, the fence—easily climbed—and the road downstream. But we were all alone.

First we took off our boots and waded in the cool creek, then we sat in the shade and had some lunch. The cottonwoods were full of birds, and with our sweat drying in the breeze, the hot pool began to beckon.

Because a kind of berm rose up around the spring, we couldn't see down to the creek and the road, and this increased our impression that we were in a special, magical, private place. All the more cruel, then, after stripping off shorts, T-shirts, skirt, etc. and slowly settling into clear, effervescent, almost-too-hot waters, lying back wearing only sunglasses, closing our eyes in utter relaxation—all the more cruel, then, to hear a voice and see three government employees peering at us from under baseball caps.

"This area is closed to the public—you girls are going to have to get going."

I sank myself beneath the water, but looking over at Ally, I could tell it wasn't exactly concealing me. I tried to hide behind my knees and arms, aware that our clothes were across the pool and behind our audience. The one guy talked in a sort of mumble about this area being closed to public bathing, and we were going to have to go, and he should really write us up, but he didn't want to go and do that. Under their caps, the guys were enjoying our discomfort as well as getting an eyeful, and the leader didn't seem to be in any hurry to finish his piece about us getting lost.

"Okay," Ally said. "We'll get going right away now. Would you mind?"

"Would *I* mind? I'm not sure I care for that, miss. Would *you* mind might be a better question since you're the ones climbed in here over the fence onto closed U.S. Government property. Adjacent to the atomic nu-kyuh-lur research facility, I might add, and as such under heightened security regulations due to homeland security considerations of the highest degree. So maybe I'd better write you up after all, though I really—"

Ally must have been getting the same impression I was— that he was just talking as a way of keeping us there. My response was to cower, but hers was the opposite. In the middle of his rambling she stood and strode through the water without any attempt to cover herself. "Pardon me," she said, as she stepped dripping between them and grabbed our towels from where they lay across some willows.

The guys stood stunned as she turned, her own towel over her shoulder—again no attempt to cover up—and waded back in to bring me mine.

"Okay, then, if you're clearing out then, I guess, okay," said Uniform as they turned back down the hill.

Ally held my towel out for me like a curtain as I stood up, and she hugged it around me.

"Did you see their faces?" she asked.

I certainly did, and mine must have been the same when she rose all bare and streaming water like Aphrodite from her shell in the sea foam. She was a sight to see, and no mistake. She sent those guys humiliated down the hill by giving them a straight-up shot of what they were angling to see. They were probably telling stories about it now, in which, no doubt, they didn't turn tail and run, scared of a real, live naked woman.

After that we headed back to Colorado. Ally had her heart set on hot springs, so I suggested Ponderosa Pass. It's a favorite family destination for us because Dad and Sean can fish the nearby beaver ponds while Mom and I soak in the pools. Ally and I made it there an hour before sunset. We checked in for the night and sampled the springs until it got dark, at which time the pool area becomes "clothing optional," and kids are banned. I assured her that I didn't mind if she stayed out at the pool, but I was feeling sort of ditched and depressed, all alone in the room.

After a while, I thought about sneaking out to the dimly lit pools, but there were a bunch of naked naturists out there that I really didn't want to see—even if I was wearing a swimsuit myself. Summer was practically over, and I brooded over my book, not really reading but just dreading the coming school year and Ally leaving and everything. Maybe a taste of too much freedom wasn't so good for me. I felt it all closing in on me like Huck Finn being taken in and "civilized" by Aunt Sally and wanting to light out for the territory, but there wasn't any last good country left anymore for Cassie to light out to.

Ally came in around one, and I pretended to sleep while she got into bed and passed out.

We spent the next morning in the water, but Ally had a hangover from too much beer and hot spring-dehydration, and I couldn't shake my bummer mood. In addition to school coming up, Ally was leaving. I knew it wasn't her fault that she and Sean were taking off for a leisurely trip back to Oregon, but I couldn't help it. I was going to miss her.

So I was pissy, and Ally was hung over, and it was the end of the summer and all, but it had been a fun trip. I just had the blues, right? Running through my head, I had "Summer's Almost Gone," by The Doors, so my mood even had a soundtrack:

> *Morning found us calmly unaware—*
> *Noon burn gold into our hair.*

At night, we swim the laughin' sea—
When the summer's gone,
Where will we be?

We drove back that afternoon, cruising across the wide fields of South Park. Pronghorn floated ghostly on the high plains, and bison stood dark and dumb behind their heavy fences. Home on the range, twenty-first-century style.

Back at the cabin, Ally and Sean started getting ready for their trip. Mom and Dad came up, and the day after that we all left.

We had some good times,
But they're gone
The winter's comin' on—
Summer's almost gone.

Journal Six

22 September

Heavy and dead today. Worried that my grand plan will come to nothing. I've got to get this thing pushed through before my CSAP scores come in.

But what if I get kicked out when they do come in? Should I come clean?

No way. I've got to Stay Cool, out of trouble, and hope for the best.

And what am I going to do with myself today? I wish we were in the mountains. But maybe a long walk in the park— that might help.

Or not. I walked all the way down the creek to the Spring Street marsh and the beaver ponds. The parents probably wouldn't approve if they knew I had gone so far because it's not the best neighborhood. After a couple of miles you don't see any joggers or families with strollers. Just a few hardcore runners and bikers go past the pool, playgrounds, and ball fields. Farther down from there, the creek goes between the power plant and the railroad tracks and the beat old section of town where the homeless people set up camp under bridges and in the groves of cottonwoods that beavers are trying to take down. That's where the springs and the wetlands are, a little oasis for birds and bums. I sat for a while on a bench beside the trail, watching a few mallards and a single Canada goose. Across the water, Sunday traffic raced up and down the interstate and across from that, red, white, and blue balloons sailed above the car dealerships of

Motor City. "WE SUPPORT OUR TROOPS!!" (Because it's good for business!)

A homeless guy with two dogs came out of the woods as I was sitting there. I got scared, but he was all right, didn't even spare change me, although I wished I had something for his dogs. Those poor homeless dogs always bum me out. It's not their fault that their humans don't have a place to live or enough food for them.

I picked up a couple of malt liquor and vodka bottles and dumped them in the next trash can as I hiked home. And now, here I am. Hope followed by dread.

Dinner was hard. I'm feeling so stupid and low. They noticed, of course, and Mom wondered if I was having second thoughts. Just a little nervous, I said. They assured me that I had their support now, and one way or the other, everything will work out for the best. I thought of the homeless guy and his dogs.

I tried to act optimistic, but I escaped up to my room as soon as I could. I don't feel like being around the parents, but up here alone, I realize I don't feel like being alone either. I called Ally and Sean—nobody home and I didn't leave a message.

There is a bit more about the summer I wanted to describe: music and all the CDs that Ally played for me on the trip, and this journal, though I'm on what, notebook number six?

Music-wise, maybe there's not much to say. We listened to a bunch of old Nirvana and Pavement and some new Radiohead and a bunch of other stuff. I guess I'm willing to give CDs their due. They're okay for the car, and the sound is clean with a band like Radiohead that gets a smooth, atmospheric sound laid down—or downloaded or uploaded or sampled.

Even better is the way Nirvana plays so huge and dirty that there's no place for the machinery to hide. I guess it doesn't matter. Ally says that I'm just putting up structures to hide behind, and that's *my* machinery.

But don't we all hide somehow? Everybody wants an artificial environment, everybody needs an SUV like a tank.

And maybe I am doing the same thing with my great, big, vegan cocoon, but I'm just trying not to be a machine. I'm trying to be *alive*, but I still have to die, right? And I'd rather die than become a robot, so I'll just say "no" to robot music.

Everything is easy and clean in the digital world, in the clean-room where computers are born. So you take someone like Kurdt Cobain, and you listen to him in your clean-room, but he's dead then anyway, and aren't you too? And maybe that's what killed him. Maybe he couldn't live in the clean-room. Maybe he was filthy bio-mass that had to be removed to preserve the sterile environment of the giant digital music machine.

23 September

I was awake off and on all night, obsessing, telling myself to mellow out and hope for the best, but it didn't help. Finally, I realized that if I am resolved on my grand plan, I need to gear up for the fight instead of mellowing out. That helped a little. I thought of Frodo and Sam, trudging on toward Mt. Doom, hopeless but still not in despair. Not that this is a great chapter in the battle between Good and Evil—it's just my own little life. But if I can't handle this, what good am I? One way or the other, I'm going to fight the machine and never give up.

I got to school early and went to see the GT lady. As hard as it was to ask her for help, at least I knew her. And as I'd hoped, she seemed pleased to see me.

"What can I do for you, Cassie?"

"Well, I remember you telling me your door was 'always open'…"

"What's on your mind?"

"I guess I should say that you're right." I gave a stupid sort of laugh.

"I'm gifted that way."

"And, like you said, middle school is not a great challenge to me, so I—my parents and I—have come up with an idea."

"Fabulous! How can I help?"

"You see—" I fumbled with how to put it. "I turned fourteen before the official cut-off. I really should be up a grade, in high school already."

"I should have guessed."

"Yeah, well, I was wondering if they ever move people up a grade."

"You *do* think outside the box." She had some little toys on her desk—puzzles and clear plastic containers of colored oils and water that you flip over so that they swirl around. She picked up a magnetic base covered with metal chips and played with it, forming the metal into a tower.

"Is this an academic thing, or do you want to get out of here to avoid certain…social problems that might be troubling you?"

"I can handle those," I said. "It's academic. I, we—my parents and I—believe that high school would be more appropriate."

"I see. Why now?"

I explained that we should have thought of it sooner, last year, this summer at the latest, but that it just occurred to us, probably since my birthday had just passed. I had heard of people moving up and didn't see why we couldn't do it now, the sooner the better, to get me up where I belonged. She said she'd heard of it too, and that it was the right thing for some people, but it was complicated. And, now, since we were more than halfway through the first quarter, the complication increased because in high school you had to earn credits, and middle level work didn't transfer.

"I never came to you before," I said, "because I didn't think you could really do anything more than the contests and stuff, and no offense, but that stuff didn't appeal to me." I had to lay it down hard now. "You were right. Middle school is killing me. I am bored out of my skull, and I need your help. If I have to sit through another lesson on topic sentences or the stop, yield, go, red, yellow, green 'steps up to writing'—if I have to do another CSAP practice test, then—" I had her attention, and she waited for me to finish.

"Then?"

"I don't know," I said. "That's it. I guess I'll do it, right? That's what I'm trained to do. I'll go through the motions over and over again. 'Tomorrow, and tomorrow, and tomorrow to the last syllable of recorded time . . .'"

"Okay," she said.

"Okay?"

"Okay, I'll see what I can do—no promises, this is going to be a hard sell, but I'll talk to Mrs. Trumbull. You had me before *Macbeth*, by the way, but we'll see if we can get you out of this 'petty pace.'" She smiled.

"Can I be there—or could you just be there when I talk to her? But maybe you could make the appointment?"

"As you wish. I'll see if I can get us in today—we need to move on this thing."

She wrote me a pass—I was late by now—and I headed off to class.

The rest of the day was the usual until my meeting with the principal. When I came into lunch I saw my old friends, and I almost, on impulse, sat down with them. Sophia looked right at me, smiling, like she was about to say hi, but DJ came up and said, "Cassie, over here." I gave Sophia a wave and followed him to where he sat with Quill and Liz and their friend Kelly, or Kel as he likes to be called. It felt funny to blow off Sophia, but it would have felt even funnier to sit with Gwen. Though it hadn't been long since I'd met DJ and those guys, and I wasn't sure I really fit in with them, they seemed more like my kind of people.

In reading, when Ms. P. came to collect me for our visit to the principal, I was gratified that Sinclair was administering the latest standardized test preparation lesson.

"See what I'm talking about?" I said.

"Yes, little smarty-pants," Ms. P. said. "Have you thought about what you're going to say?"

"More or less what I said to you?"

"More about your parents thinking this is best for your

academic needs," she said. "And less about you being bored out of your skull here. Remember, this is her school—she won't like you running it down."

Made sense to me. Then before we went into the office, she said, "And she's heard all about you from Mr. Kimble and Dr. Hawkens."

"I guess I figured that. Sometimes I *do* put my foot in it, *don't* I?"

"And can the English school-girl act."

"Yes, mum."

She laughed and we breezed past the secretaries to the head honcho's door.

Ms. P. tapped on it, and the principal looked up from her computer.

"Cassie," she said, smiling, showing a bit of lipstick on her teeth. "It's nice to meet you. I'm Mrs. Trumbull. I understand you have an idea for us—that you want us to think outside the box."

"You could say that," I said.

"Have a seat." She came out from behind her perfectly clean and clear desk—which is a bit suspicious if you ask me—and pulled out a couple of chairs at her round table.

"First," I began, "I want to thank you for meeting with me—I'm sure you have a busy schedule." Though I've never understood what principals *do* that makes them busy. There was a big whiteboard on her wall, full of numbers—that gave some indication, I suppose. One section was labeled, "Enrollment" with current and projected lines. The other had our CSAP scores by grade level for the past two years, with last year blank because they hadn't come in yet, thank my lucky stars.

"My pleasure." She glanced up at the clock.

"Well, to start, I should tell you that when I was five, instead of sending me to kindergarten, my parents decided I should wait it out for a year."

"Lots of parents do that these days, they like to give their kiddos a leg up."

"But sometimes aren't they a little advanced for their peers—I don't mean to sound full of myself—"

"Not at all. That's why we have Mrs. Price, to take care of our kiddos who are a little ahead of the game. And here at Tabor Middle School, we pride ourselves on meeting the needs of each individual student."

Ms. Price broke in. "But we only have the one advanced class, math—"

"Which Cassie opted out of, I believe."

"Yes, I did, and that was a mistake. And I don't mean to say that this isn't a top-notch school, Mrs. Trumbull, but my parents and I have decided that I should be with, that I should move up to the grade that I should have started with—to high school."

"I thought that might be where you were going with this, Cassie, but I'm not sure that's possible at this point."

This was what I expected. They say the door is open, but before you so much as get a foot in, they slam it shut.

"But can you at least consider it?"

She was shaking her head as if she really regretted telling me no, but before she could say it, Ms. Price jumped in again. "Cassie really wanted to do this by herself, Jean—as I said earlier—but in my position, I felt I had to help her out. I have a responsibility to advocate for gifted students, and Cassie is truly gifted—heaven knows why she wasn't identified before this. All her scores show she is far beyond anything we're doing here. For more than two years, she has been suffering silently—until her little incidents with Mr. Kimble and Dr. Hawkens. I know you believe in doing what's in the student's best interest."

"Of course," she said.

"Shouldn't we at least consider this, do a child-study to determine if she really would be better off in high school?"

"Cassie, could you excuse us for a few minutes?"

"Sure. I guess I'd better go back to class."

"No, no," said Ms. P. "Wait out on the bench there. We'll just be a moment."

Waiting outside the closed door I could hear them talking in low voices, Ms. Price's rising to a fierce whisper, but I couldn't hear what they said. I stood when the door opened.

"Miss Sullivan," said the principal. "I'm not sure about this, but I'm persuaded to let you try. I'm going to give your parents a call, explain my reservations, get their take on things. Then I'll run it by the deputy superintendent, and we'll take it from there. How does that sound?"

Why do they always have to say that? And why does it always have to trip my smart-ass wire? Sounds like, I thought, you're not such a tough old broad after all. Either that, or it sounds like you're going to try to make us think you're on our side while you get the whole deal nixed by your boss.

"That sounds excellent, Mrs. Trumbull," is what I said. "I really appreciate your time and consideration. Thank you so much again."

When I talked to Mom and Dad, I found out that, by

the time we'd had our little chat at school, Mom had already spoken with the deputy superintendent and the high school principal. I bet Trumbull was surprised when she found out they'd agreed to consider me!

They told Mom they would look at my records and wanted "feedback" from the middle school as soon as possible. Mrs. Trumbull would distribute "child-study" surveys to all my teachers, then forward them with her recommendation to the high school on Wednesday. They set up a tentative meeting for that afternoon.

Thanks to Mom, things were moving along. Also thanks to Ms. Price. Mom and Dad both thought that "bringing her on board" was an inspired maneuver.

After we were done discussing my grand plan, as if she'd been reading my mind, Mom asked me if I wanted to go shopping. "My things don't really fit you, and you seem tired of your same old, same old," she said. "What do you think?"

"Okay, sounds great," I said.

"What?" she said.

"Yes, I want to go shopping."

"I'm sorry, I thought you said you wanted to go shopping with me."

"You asked me, Mom. You don't have to get—"

"Wonderful," Dad said. "She's finally turning into a mall rat."

"But *not* the mall," I said. "Any place but there."

"Good," said Mom. "How about downtown, and maybe Manitou?"

So tomorrow after school, she's picking me up. What's

going on? Who am I turning into? No more hair, and now, new clothes? And these moods! I'm as up now as I was down twenty-four hours ago.

24 September

What a wonderful morning of middle school. Instead of telling me I was going to hell, Bible-Boy should have said that *hell* was coming to *me*.

When I opened my locker, paper cascaded out onto the floor. There must have been at least twenty notes in there, cleverly folded and stuffed through the vents. Addressed to "Osama's Slut" as well as Osama O'Sullivan—could I be both?—I didn't have to read them to know they didn't have postscripts of BFFL and W/B/S. Leaving open the possibility, however remote, that I'd use them as some sort of evidence in the future, I stacked them in the bottom of my locker.

Then on the way to class, somebody gave me a shove that sent me right into a group of girls who were walking with their arms linked.

Did I miss hearing them yell, "Red Rover, Red Rover—send Cassie right over"? I guess not, because they didn't even try to hold their ranks, just broke apart saying "Eyew!" as if touching me would soil their little AbercrombieFascistEagle uniforms.

Then someone pulled at my books, which fell to the floor, and a few people scattered them with kicks. It was all I could do not to cry, and somehow it got even harder when DJ came over and helped me pick everything up.

"What the hell, man?" he said when somebody kicked my

history book that he was about to pick up. He retrieved it and handed it to me. "Are you okay?"

"I'm fine," I choked. "Thanks, I'm gonna be late." And I bolted for class.

I made it through the rest of the day okay, reminding myself of my shopping trip with Mom, Oregon with Ally, and the possibility of checking out of the hellhole. To make sure things were progressing on the latter, I checked in with Ms. P. and asked if she knew anything.

"Not yet," she said. "But I am urging your teachers to get those forms filled out ASAP—sometimes they don't have a great sense of urgency on these things."

"Thanks again," I said.

After school, Mom and I started our shopping at a downtown boutique full of candles and furniture as well as jewelry and clothes. Very chic for this one-horse town, I guess, and I wasn't sure I could deal with it. Nothing looked right, and I was almost instantly sick of taking off clothes and putting on clothes that were much too old for me and, especially, looking at myself in the mirror. I was just so big and gawky. I started to hate my hairless head, and with all the weird clothes, I hardly recognized myself.

I was ready to bag it—starting to feel irritated and prickly about everything—but Mom suggested the Indian store and then Manitou.

"And afterwards we can hit the Mountain Cafe for dinner."

"What about Dad?"

"He can meet us—or not. He'll survive on his own."

The Indian store was full of wild printed skirts, woolen

jackets from Nepal, little cotton halter-tops, and Hindu and Buddhist statues. I couldn't help relaxing in there, surrounded by Indian classical music and the scent of incense. I got a couple of skirts and tops, including a really cool T-shirt with an eight-armed Hindu goddess on it. I'm not sure which one, but she stands in front of a lion, holding a sword, trident, bow, incense burner, and a lotus blossom, and she is twirling this thing around her finger that looks like the Milky Way.

Then we drove up to Manitou and hit the "natural fibers" store. After trying on a few things herself, Mom found me checking out their display of makeup.

"Makeup?" she said. "All right, who are you and what have you done with my daughter?"

"Very original, Mom. Anyway, forget it, this garbage would look stupid on me."

"No, try it, try it," said a saleslady. "Not that you need it, with your face."

Did she think I was stupid enough to fall for that?

"And Hoyoka Canyon does *not* make garbage," she continued. "Just all-natural skin accents made from all-natural plant ingredients—totally vegan, mostly organic." She swabbed up some lip color from a sample tube. "Come," she said. "Don't be shy."

I ended up walking out of there with a new pair of hemp sandals, two embroidered peasant tops that look nouveau-'70s cool, a couple of probably-passing-dress-code tanks, and, unbelievably, makeup. I know, Di, it doesn't seem like me to me either, but with my new short hair, I liked the look of just a little color on my lips and around my eyes. And it *was* vegan, no animal testing, organic ingredients. So I got a lipstick, lip gloss, mascara, and eyeliner. I even wore one of the tops and some of the makeup out of the store and to dinner.

At the restaurant, our busboy kept our water glasses very full and I confess, to you alone, Di, that I liked the way he kept looking over at me. Mom kept staring at me, too, until I said, "What?"

"I didn't say anything."

"You keep looking at me."

"Well, you're so different," she said. "But I keep seeing my little girl looking out at me from inside this beautiful young woman."

Parents always think their kids are "beautiful"—I didn't really believe it, but I felt my face flush all the same, and I said, dismissively, "I haven't been a *little* girl since fourth grade."

"I know, but all this—haircut, shopping, *makeup* for God's sake…Why?"

"I don't know. I just wanted a change."

"But why?" She twirled some linguine around her fork, using the silence to draw the words out of me.

"I've been trying to be invisible for a long time. Now I want to be seen."

She nodded and smiled, and I was afraid I was going to get another "why," but she just said, "You should be seen."

Throughout the rest of the meal I told about the Tolkien group and the people in it, and I allowed that school was just fine, no more problems with the "insubordination," and the art class was okay. She wondered why I was in the library at lunch when I told her about meeting Ms. Tayebnejad, so I admitted that things were a little weird around some of the kids after getting kicked out of choir. She was so pleased with me, I didn't see any reason to let her know that I was being harassed on a daily basis. And I knew that telling Mommy and Daddy and having them talking to the principal and the counselor was a surefire way to make things worse.

I figure that, even with me changing my whole look, they'll have to get bored with me sooner or later. And if they don't, maybe I'll be gone soon.

I was afraid Dad was going to give me a hard time when we got home, so I almost wiped the makeup off—but Mom wanted to see his reaction, so she helped me re-apply. He was in his office, up to his elbows in files, and didn't even look at us at first.

He was so sweet when he did look up—I can be corny with you, Di—he just smiled and said, "Looks like a successful shopping trip." He came over and kissed my head. "You look very pretty."

"Thanks, Dad. Gotta go!" And I ran upstairs with my bags and hangers, and here I am—feeling totally weird and somehow normal and very hyper.

I haven't started on my three-part story, but I think I'll try a poem for writing group.

Rock and Self

I

Longhaired Cassie on the rock in sunset colors,
Sky and distance filling the land.
Lichen on the rocks, waiting, unconscious—
Nonconscious rocks wait for the rain.

Do they love the frost? Do they want the sun?
Billion years from magma—Do they want to melt?

II
Nonconscious rock,
are you meant
for something else?
Quartz and feldspar,
do you desire
the freezing water
to break you apart?
Streams rolling,
sanding you into sand,
into molecules
dissolved,
dispersed?

III
Is there any dead stuff just to step on and to use,
Or is everything alive?

Teaching a stone to talk, you practice.
I practice the stones teaching me:

Mute, un-conscious-able, teaching me to sing.
There is nothing dead, but everything is alive—the more
silent, the more perfect.

Rock teaches me to sing like sky like stars like rock like
silence like darkness like non-being.

IV

New-cropped Cassie on her bed, alive and breathing.
Back and neck aching on the pillows,
writing, propped.

The princess stretches and considers herself,
Towered high in luxury above her realm.

Below they die like insects, poisoned as larvae—
Born as good as dead as good as dying re-born.
"Tomorrow," she thinks,
"I'll wear my Hindu goddess—"
A T-shirt in their honor—living busy being born.

V
"If I cannot be stone I will be blood-wet and red," she
says,
searching her mattress for that damned pea that keeps her
awake
and alive
too many hours
of every
single
day.

25 September

I'm going to high school. I can't believe they said yes, but they said yes.

Now I'm terrified again, of course. What if it's too hard? What if everybody hates me even more? Who cares, I'm out of here! I wanted to tell DJ, Liz, and Quill, but I didn't find out until after school. I'll tell them tomorrow. I called Ally and Sean. She wasn't home, but he congratulated me and said I had nothing to worry about. He also gave me advice on what teachers and classes to try to get, but it doesn't seem like I am going to get much choice.

Mrs. Trumbull filled us in on everything. I am getting a trial run for the rest of the semester, and if I can keep my grades up and don't get any referrals, it's permanent. The teachers have a choice of transferring my middle school grades—all As—or starting me fresh. I'm going to turn in my books and check out on Friday. I shook Mrs. Trumbull's hand and even hugged Ms. P.

Last year's CSAPs are still a worry. That was the first thing I thought of when they said it wouldn't be permanent until the end of the semester. But if I can do the work, what can they say? Those scores don't affect your grades, and they can't hold you back because of them.

A few other things happened today. It started with the usual "Hey, Osama" and "American Taliban" greetings, and my locker was covered with little American flag stickers. I peeled them off and stuck them to my jeans in a peace-sign design.

Then, on my way to class, I saw DJ, who told me how tuff my flag-peace sign looked.

DJ—I hadn't been thinking about him much with everything that was going on, but seeing him brought me into another round of questioning the grand plan. Too late! I should tell him, I thought, but decided to wait until I found out if they were letting me go. (I hadn't found out at that point.) As we made our way through the hall, he was being shy, not meeting my eye. It was cute.

I sat by DJ at the Tolkien group, and wondered if we were going to be able to see each other if I went to high school. I wasn't sure about my feelings for him, but when I caught a glimpse of him looking at me, full of admiration, let's just say it got the blood flowing and the nerves tingling.

When school ended, I was just removing my sticker-sign for my meeting with the principal (coward, I know), racing with adrenaline, when Quill showed up and started in with his weird voice.

"Most righteous and awesome Cassie," he breathed. "I was just wondering—have you received a missive—in your locker—from my estimable associate—by the name of DJ— referred to by some—as Gimli the dwarf?"

"I don't think so, uh—" I looked down at the stack of papers in the bottom of my locker. "Well, I did get some notes, but I haven't gotten around to reading them." Matthew showed up, and smirking mightily, spun the dial of his locker. "I'm saving them in case I have some time to kill in hell," I said.

"Excellent," said Quill. "But there might be one here from Gimli."

I was embarrassed for anyone to know about the notes, but relieved as well. We sat down on the floor and went through the stack. Some were blank on the outside, most were addressed in unflattering terms to yours truly. I was accustomed to the usual Osamas, but how can you err with that understated, little-black-dress-of-a-moniker, "Bitch"?

"Whoa," said Quill. "They don't like you."

"I wasn't sure—thanks for interpreting."

"But somebody does," he said, handing me a piece of plain white paper, folded three times and fastened with some kind of seal like hard green plastic in a fancy design. I touched it.

"Sealing wax," said Quill. "The dude got it from his mom. He's in trouble, Cass—maybe you shouldn't have given him that hair. Was it bewitched or something?"

I laughed. "Elvish tresses are said to be a perilous gift for a mortal man—or a dwarf. But there was nothing of what men call magic about the gift."

"Cool," he said. "I'll pass that on to DJ—he'll love it." Then he looked at the rest of my fan mail. "Aren't you going to turn this stuff in and get somebody busted?"

"No, please, don't say anything. Who could I bust? Do you think they put their names and student ID numbers on these things?"

He pointed at a gray dome at the end of the hall. "Security camera," he said. "Everyone who slid a note in here is probably on videotape. Just be sure you tell them that Gimli's note was friendly."

"Still—it won't help. Promise you won't say anything. I'm staying cool, giving it just a little more time to blow over."

"My lips are sealed. But Master Dwarf is getting all protective—you'd better be careful."

"Cassandra Sullivan, please report to the office," blared the ceiling speaker. *"Cassandra Sullivan to the office, please."*

"I will," I said. "And tell him 'thank you.' Bye."

You know what happened at the office, and I forgot all about DJ's note until now. I'd better read it.

Wow! Here it is, Di. It's done in cursive, with all kinds of flour-ishes and about half a bottle of whiteout, and it's a poem:

> For Cassandra
> (formerly of the tuff, tuff hair—currently of the tuff, tuff
> head)
>
> In halls of the children of men,
> She walks alone in beauty brown
> Upon her face a solemn frown
> And she is beyond their ken.
>
> A soul of old incarnate,
> With eyes of brown and green and gray,
> With light transformed now fair, now fey,
> And always seeming infinite.
>
> In vain inscribes my pen:
> The beauty of her noble brow
> Flies and flees away and away—
> I say, "Wherefore, my Juliet?"
>   —by Gimli, Glóin's son (DJ)

What do you make of that, Di? I wonder where he got that rhyme scheme—pretty cool. Too bad it's one love poem for every fifty hate letters. He did seem to be mistaking wherefore and where, but I liked it anyway. It demands a response, so here I go:

> My thanks to Gimli for the verse,
> To Glóin's son for glowing words,
> For praise so high as seems absurd—
> Still—to such lines I'm not averse.

You must know, I'm like bait for the sharks.
I drift on the waters of the flood—
All spreading incarnadine with my blood—
But your poem's a rescuing barque.

I pay no mind to the cursed curse,
The mindless utterance of the herd
—Who's naught but animated mud—
But yours is a light in the dark.

Not too bad myself. Okay, I used the rhyming dictionary, but not for my favorite bit, "Glóin" and "glowing."

What am I doing? Is it a good thing to keep encouraging DJ when I am going to be gone in a couple days? I'll have to tell him tomorrow.

I can't believe this is real. I've been putting so much energy into hating school—and being hated—that I don't know what I'm going to do with myself. Everything's changing. It's like I chop off my hair and get new clothes and suddenly I am going to be this totally different person. But I don't feel different. The same me is talking to myself in this book, but everything else has changed. I put these causes in motion and all of a sudden, like magic, presto-change-o, I'm racing forward into the unknown.

26 September

Though it started out pretty cool, today was bizarre.

At writing club, Quill read his triumvirate. It was a scene, "from his novel"—which I hadn't known he was writing—set in a futuristic world of zombie/robots and rebel fighters. Lots of action, but pretty cool.

Before I read my poems, I was going to tell everyone that it was my last meeting. I chickened out, though, thinking I would tell them after. But I chickened out again because of the way DJ was glowing at me.

When I handed him his poem at the end of the meeting, his glow shined even brighter, so I couldn't tell him then either.

On my locker I found one lonely little flag sticker, which I put upside-down on my butt. That's the symbol of opposing Mr. Bush's plans to invade Iraq, not that anybody at this narrow-minded little school would know that. Maybe there is a peace group at Parker, or maybe I could start one. Am I determined to make people hate me there too?

At lunch, DJ sat down and told me that the poem was tuff, and that he needed a dictionary. I accused him of using a rhyming dictionary for his and admitted that I had myself. He asked if he could call me, and because it just seemed too weird to give him my phone number, I told him to look me up, I was in the book. That seemed even worse, once I had said it, and I blurted out that he would *have* to call me, because tomorrow would be my last day at Tabor.

He had seemed really happy, but then his face fell.

"It's not like we can't still be friends," I said. Quill was looking puzzled, Liz was mad.

"Are you moving?" DJ asked.

"No," I said. "I'm going, well…I'm going to high school."

"High school?" Liz said.

"Yeah, you see, I started kindergarten a year late, and…" I explained the whole plan.

DJ sort of checked out, seeming to stop listening about halfway through, and when I finished, he got up and left. Quill followed him.

"You could have told us what was going on," Liz said.

Kelly looked confused and uncomfortable, then he got up and followed Quill and DJ.

"I mean," Liz continued, "here we think you're, like, our friend, and then you just announce you're ditching us."

"I'm not. It's not like that—"

"Yeah, whatever. It's cool. But what about DJ?"

"I said he could call me."

"Whatever. You don't understand. Ever since he got suspended last year with Quill over that 'fuck the test' shit, his mom has been threatening him with Christian school, and he's been miserable. You didn't know him then. He's been so happy lately. I was afraid you were playing with him. And now this. I'll see you later, Cassie. Like, later much." She got up.

"No, wait. Liz—" But she was gone.

Once everyone was gone, I opened a book and pretended to read so I wouldn't feel so stupid sitting there all alone. But I couldn't concentrate and just sat there feeling wretched.

Finally, it was time for reading class, where Liz refused to even look at me.

Mr. Sinclair's usual routine, no different today, is that as soon as everybody settles into silent reading, he slips out across the hall to fill his carafe. Then he makes a pot of tea in his microwave.

Right after he left today, something hit me on the back. I ignored it and kept reading. Then something hit my leg. Without moving, I glanced down on the floor and saw a pink disposable razor. Then all of a sudden it was raining razors: pink ones, purple ones, even a few blue ones. I sat stunned until Sinclair came back.

"What's going on?" he said. "Can't I leave the room for a minute? Cassie, what's this all about?"

"Don't ask me. I was just trying to read."

"Yeah, right," somebody said. "She was just trying to read."

"Little miss innocent."

Unbelievable. They were blaming this on *me*?

"Apparently," I said, "somebody has read *Carrie*—or no, it was on TV, wasn't it?"

"Okay," said Sinclair. "Who is responsible for throwing these?"

Dead silence.

"Cassie, who threw these at you?"

What could I say? Everyone? And what could he do?

I'm outta here, I thought, and I'm not going to start trouble now.

"I was just reading," I said. "I didn't see."

"Nobody saw anything?"

Then Liz, who may have been mad at me, but at least isn't a sheep, said, "Mr. Sinclair, man, it was, like, everyone. I mean, not me and, like, Rae and Tonya, but Cassie didn't do anything except sit there. And blow off shaving for some bizarre reason."

"I see," said Sinclair. "Cassie, what do you think should happen?"

He was asking me? I thought he was in charge.

"Nothing," I said. "Idiocy is its own punishment."

"There's no call for personal attacks here, Cassie," he said.

Really? Wasn't there?

"Okay, class. The next time anybody pulls a stunt like this, I'm keeping you for detention, every last one of you."

Next time? I thought. What about this time? They're just getting away with it? This is why I never asked for help. Nothing would happen and it would only get worse.

"And now everyone will pick up one razor and put it in the trash until they are all picked up. Everyone except Cassie and Liz."

At the end of class, I was surprised when Liz waited by the door for me. "That was weird," she said.

"I'm getting used to weird."

"So is that really why you're taking off?"

"Part of it, but I *am* a grade behind."

She walked with me to my locker.

"Well," she said. "About our conversation at lunch… It's just DJ, you know? I'm sort of protective."

"I noticed. And maybe I should have said something before, but I didn't know until yesterday. I'm sorry, too. You guys have made me wonder if going up to high school is the right thing. You're the only people who have been nice to me in a long time."

"You're not that easy to get to know. You're sort of different—but that's cool. Maybe we can still hang out sometimes?"

"That'd be cool."

"Friends?"

"Of course."

"I gotta go. And you do *not* want to be late to art."

Then she hugged me and took off.

Talk about weird. I have friends? Who stick up for me? And *hug* me?

27 September

It's my final day, Di, wish me luck.

I meant good luck.

Isn't it funny how people wish for good luck or pray for things when it's already too late? When whatever you're wishing or praying for has already happened or not happened, and you just haven't found out?

When I was wishing for luck, my CSAP scores were already there in the stack in Mrs. Trumbull's office. She had already called the principal at Parker High School, and he had already told her that I was no longer welcome.

I got to school early and went to the counseling office to get my checkout paper, but the secretary told me that Mrs. Trumbull wanted to see me. In her office, she was sitting at the conference table with Ms. Price. Stacks of paper surrounded them.

"Sit down and look at this," said Mrs. Trumbull, and handed me three sheets of paper printed in black and green. "Can you explain for us?"

Ms. Price wouldn't look at me.

I shook my head.

"These must be the lowest scores in the entire school. We

have children who are *retarded* who managed to do better than this."

"You threw it, didn't you?" Ms. Price said. "You went from getting almost every single point to missing almost every single point. Tell me this is some sort of computer error. Tell me your score was so high that you blew up the computer. Tell me you didn't deliberately make asses out of us."

Tears were coming now.

"You did this on purpose."

I nodded, shaking with suppressed sobs.

"Why?"

"I don't know," I said.

"Was it just to make idiots out of us?"

I shook my head.

"Why, then?"

"It's all anybody cares about—the stupid test. And it doesn't mean anything."

"It means a great deal to us, Miss Sullivan," said the principal. "We strive for excellence. All the teachers, myself, the students—except for you. It matters. This is such an unbelievable insult. What you must have done—the lengths that you must have gone to in order to do this poorly. You—"

She waved her hands, left them hanging in the air for a moment, then let them drop to the table.

"You cheated. You cheated us. But you cheated yourself too, because as much as I would *love* to be rid of you... You are going *no*where."

"I'm sorry. I won't do it again. I know I can do the work in high school. I can. I won't—"

"I've already spoken with Mr. Buckingham. He does not want a kiddo who is going to blow his scores."

"But—"

"The trial semester was contingent on your not getting any discipline referrals. This amounts to a level two insubordination, your second this year. You'll be finishing the year with us. You'd better pull yourself together and get to class."

"But—"

"It's over, Cassie," said Ms. Price.

And it is.

Mr. Math asked me if I had a checkout sheet for him.

"I'm staying," I said.

"Well, are you moving into my accelerated group?"

"I don't think so."

"Well—are you going to get started on the warm-up, or are you going to just sit there?"

"Get started."

A little while later, DJ stopped at my desk on his way back from the pencil sharpener. "Did I hear you say you're staying?"

I nodded.

"No high school?"

I shook my head, giving him a bleak sort of smile.

He met this with a concerned frown, and went back to his seat.

After class he asked what happened.

"They changed their minds," I said.

"How come?"

I was having a hard time keeping it together, so I told him I couldn't really talk about it, I'd tell him later.

Next period, I got a pass to come to the office and call Mom, but I ignored it until she called again.

She wanted to come sign me out, but I told her not to bother. She said she and Dad were making some calls to see if they can't work things out, but I told her not to bother.

"Darling, this will all work out for the best—"

Really? I thought. How nice.

"I know it sounds absurd now, but in the end, you'll see. We'll get some things sorted out tonight, and then you've got a wonderful trip starting tomorrow. I'll see you after school, okay?"

I managed to avoid everyone the rest of the day. At lunch I went to the library and pretended to read. Ms. Price walked right by me, but Ms. Tayebnejad was happy to see me and reminded me that if I wanted to read *and* eat, I was welcome to bring my lunch into her office. I said I wasn't hungry.

In reading, Liz said she heard I wasn't leaving. I told her the same thing I'd told DJ.

"DJ was looking for you at lunch," she said. "He feels bad for you, but I think he's glad you're still going to be around."

"That's sweet," I said.

"Expect him to call you."

"I'm going to visit my brother in Oregon," I told her. "But I'll be back on Wednesday. Would you tell him?"

Mom had canceled her afternoon lesson and was waiting for me when I got home, ready to talk. Nothing to talk about, I said, since it was all over. She said there were some other options that she and Dad wanted to talk to me about, but I said no. No options. She assured me that there were and that we would talk about them.

I went upstairs to lie down.

I remember my first angry days writing to you, Di, and the hopeful days. I am on my little balcony in the twilight, looking over the houses and up the hill at the tops of the pines. A loud and filthy car goes by. It grows dark, and a planet, who cares what, is somehow able to shine through. It will be nice to go to Oregon and see Ally and Sean. Tomorrow, I think, I'll be at the Pacific Ocean—or I think about myself thinking that, and I write it, and I continue to think how it *should* be nice, but I feel more like going to the cabin. To my tipi. Alone. Up there, the stars begin to twinkle as the wind blows puffs of yellow aspen leaves down on the ground to rot. Coyotes yip and yammer stupidly. Viciously. Hungrily. Anthropomorphically. Whatever.

Dad came home, and we all had dinner and a talk. The first thing we had to talk about was my intentional failing of the CSAP test. They had to know why and how, and then they had to tell me why I shouldn't have.

"First of all," said Mom, "you've hurt yourself badly. You felt the tests were of no consequence, but it was rash to act on that feeling. And second, for your school, it really is a slap in the face."

"Why? It's *my* test, *my* score. What does it have to do with them?"

"You know they're judged by your scores. That's why they

focus so much on prepping you—if you do poorly, they look bad."

"Maybe they are bad."

"That doesn't sound like you, Cassie," she said. "I am trying to say that you hurt these people by your actions."

"Good," I said. "Fuck *them*."

"Cassie!"

"It's okay, Deb, she's pissed off," said Dad. "Good for her, let it out. You and I both know she's right—these tests are bullshit. I admit that I've always loved her being so brilliant at them, but the tests are not important. The education is. And somebody needs to be saying that. If it hurts them, well, maybe that's not good. But if it causes them to think about what they're doing, then maybe that is good."

"I don't know," said Mom. "Wouldn't it be better revenge to do well on the test but understand its irrelevance? Or do well, but write letters of protest to the board, the governor, the papers? As a high-scoring student, you'd have so much more authority. Just look at the door that was open—"

"Don't you think I know that now?" I said. "Don't you think I wish I had kept on being a good little girl and done exactly what I was supposed to do? 'Do your best. Use the test as an opportunity to show what you know. Blah blah blah, blah-blah, blah-blah.'"

We sat silently for a moment until Dad spoke.

"If you could, would you do it differently?"

"I don't know," I said. "Yes. But part of me wouldn't—just because this shows even more, because of *consequences,* how messed up these tests are. They don't care about me…"

"They just want a good score," said Dad.

"Yeah," I said.

"But that's not how we feel," said Mom. "You made a decision. Now you have to live with it and learn from it, and maybe you'll learn more from having sabotaged the test than you would've from acing it."

"So what am I supposed to learn?"

"What do you think?" As usual, Dad turned the question back on me. And I was so sick of it.

"That it doesn't matter. That I'm an idiot. That I'm sick of learning lessons. That I'm fucking fucked."

"Okay, okay," said Mom. "Angry at yourself, angry at the world. I didn't mean that there's an instant moral here—just add water and stir. All I meant was that, in time—weeks, months, years—you will know you are the better for all this."

"If you say so."

"I do."

Next they wanted to talk about options, and I tried to humor them, but it got so tiresome. Option A is that I stick it out for the rest of the year. Option B, they continue to try to get me into high school, presenting a case to the principal there and to the district administration. C would be some special program in another middle school. D is private school. Guess what? They all have pros and cons. Fascinating.

They already had an appointment with the deputy superintendent.

Ridiculous. I just want to be done with it. So the grand plan fell apart—my own fault, yes, but major tragedy? I don't think so. How would the cliquified kids in high school—half of whom have little brothers and sisters at Tabor—have reacted to me, coming in the middle of the semester? Who knows how it would have worked out. I might have been miserable, probably would have been. What's clear is that I am weary of plans and trying. I don't want the options. I just need to go back into my den and lick my wounds and gather my strength. Or not.

I don't even want to go to Oregon. I was excited, it was going to be a little break before I moved on to my next phase, but now...

I guess it's better than going back to school on Monday. At least I'll have a couple of days to get my shit together.

I told them I was going upstairs to pack and then to bed. Early start and all that. Better throw some things in a bag.

All ready to go now, but I don't think I can sleep. I'll put on a record and drag my sleeping bag out onto my balcony. My headphones will stretch out there and I'll lie back and look at the dim stars in the city sky. Or maybe I'll jump.

Undated, inserted after my Oregon trip...

Since I am sticking around the good old middle school, I decided to write my triumvirate story for writing club. It's about my Oregon trip, but I played around with time (like having Ally tell me about her high school idea in Oregon instead of on the phone). I left some things out, too, and added other stuff (like the Three Sisters peaks, which I couldn't actually see from the plane. Mount Hood, though, was awesome).

So here it is—part fact, part fiction: Part One

Three Sisters

Prelude: The Myth of the Sisters

*T*here *might be a story about the Three Sisters Volcanoes that nobody knows anymore or that nobody thought to tell—that the mountains were once three human girls, and before that, they were* ONE. *Inside her mother, she was entire, of a piece, one little ball of cells. They say her mother was a drunk or a Christian housewife or a career woman, depending on who tells the story.*

Everyone agrees, though, that as mother dreamed her, and father's voice called through the walls of the womb, she separated. Maybe it was because the mother alternately dreamed her not there and there again; maybe because the pull of her love was so strong. But as a defense against non-being, she split herself and slipped through the barriers of dimension. And two of her went to live in other worlds. So, you see, she was not like triplets who have different souls and different fates, but only look the same—this girl was one, split into three.

Being incomplete was agony, and while different things happened to the sisters, each thing arose from identical causes and proceeded to the same end. Of course, they didn't know they were the same—each lived in a different dimension—but each sister cursed her fate and took her own life.

And the Great Mystery took pity on her and made her into three volcanoes, the Three Sisters, that would always be close enough to know each other and to know that, though rain fell and snow melted and lava flowed on each a little differently than the others, each essence was the same, each existence was the same, and they would be comforted. Others say that the gods heard her curse and granted it—she would ever be worn down by the wind and the rain and the great Gravity of her mother who would then push new life up through her, and so each would exist, separate and the same, until the world was unmade.

Sister I

Cassie looks up from her journal when the co-pilot announces the Three Sisters, a trio of volcanoes they're passing on their approach to Portland. From hazy green forests striped with clear-cuts, the volcanoes protrude—round and gentle peaks, snow-covered and mammalian, so different from the jagged uplifts back in Colorado.

At fourteen, this is her first time flying alone—meeting her brother and his girlfriend for a long weekend on the Oregon Coast. She gazes out on the great peaks and smiles to think of her smug teachers and their irritation at her missing school for a couple of days.

Hauling her duffel through the terminal, she sees Ally waiting outside security—typical Ally in a T-shirt and long Indian skirt and big grin.

She hugs Cassie, duffel and all, and says, "Wow! You look beautiful." Like everybody, she has to run her hands over Cassie's newly shorn head. "I love it. New clothes, too? Sean's outside circling with the rest of the crew. Did you check anything?"

"No, this is it. Rest of the what crew?" Cassie had thought it would be just the three of them, like old times last summer at the cabin.

"When they heard we were going down to my uncle's place, they begged to come along. I hope you don't mind."

"No, I just thought...I wasn't expecting—"

"Don't worry," says Ally, putting an arm around Cassie's

shoulder. "We're still sisters of the paint—it's only three tagalongs: Bill and Katie, and Jack."

"Okay, that's cool." It's not. "Friends of yours are friends of mine and all that." They negotiate through the crowd. "The more the merrier," she adds.

Ally laughs. "When you start to talk in clichés I know I'm in trouble. But really, you'll love them. Bill and Katie don't pay any attention to anybody but themselves and will probably disappear into a bedroom for the whole weekend. Jack will entertain and annoy. Sean is the strong and silent type—but I guess you know him."

The air outside is soft and humid, and city smells lie heavily within it—exhaust, cigarette smoke, and something that smells to Cassie like the combined scent of people: food and breath and skin. She feels strange here in this different and humid air.

A gargantuan SUV, a Klondike or something, pulls up to the curb, and brother Sean opens the door.

"Welcome to the throng," he says, pulling Cassie close. "Nice head."

"Thanks, bro." By the way he says "throng" she guesses that he's not ecstatic about the extra people either.

"I'm Jack," says the driver. "Heard all about you, Mama Cass, and I dig you real good already." He didn't wait for a greeting on her part. "Hop in and let's ball this shiny black steel jackhammer down to the coast."

"That's Bill and Katie in back," says Ally as Sean settles her duffel behind two sleepy-looking hippies in the back. "They're hard to tell apart at first." Both wear tousled brown ponytails.

"Hey, Cassie," they say together.

"Hi," Cassie says.

"Okay, my peoples," says Jack. "All aboard the black rainbow bus to the beach."

Ally sits up front with Jack, and the two of them laugh and chat. Cassie can't hear much over the music—some anonymous CD. Since Sean has a paper to write this weekend, he withdraws into a philosophy text. Bill and Katie sleep.

Cassie has looked forward to this weekend for so long, and now it's not going to be anything like she anticipated. But she tries to go with the flow, as Ally might say, gazing out the tinted windows, enjoying the newness of the landscapes: brambly roadsides, brown hills of grass and oak, vineyards and berry farms, and finally the coastal forest, impenetrable and dark as compared to the light, dry woods of Colorado. She rolls down her window to smell for the ocean. She almost can. Maybe. Or is it just the dense Oregon air?

"Keep that away from her," Sean says when Jack tries to pass the joint that he and Ally are smoking.

"What about you, Cosmic?"

"Working," he says.

"Herbie's square," says Jack, taking both hands off the wheel, one still holding the joint, to inscribe a square in the air. "How about the lovalicious love birds in the way-back?"

"Crashed."

"Cool. More for the driver and his copacetic co-pilot. Dig this weed, baby."

"Enough for me," Ally says and turns back to Cassie. "How you doing back there?"

"Great."

"We'll be there soon."

Cassie turns back to the window, and suddenly there it is—the

Pacific, shining blue beyond the trees. Heavy Saturday beach traffic has them crawling through Lincoln City on the 101, then they pull into the golf-coursed, gated enclave that will be home for the weekend.

Everybody piles out of the vehicle.

"Follow me, Cassie," Ally says, taking a decked walkway along the side of the house, down stairs past a Jacuzzi, down more stairs through beach grass, ending on a dune above the beach and the sea, shimmering blue under the westering sun. They run down toward the breakers.

"Remember, everyone," Ally turns to Jack and Sean close behind, and Bill and Katie lagging hand in hand. "NO SWIMMING. It's hypothermia-cold with wicked rips and undertows. If you get washed in, you're dead, so be aware at all times."

They reach the firm sand and line up as a wave crashes up to their knees, icy water washing the sand out from under their feet.

"Back to the recesses of the mind," says Sean. "I want to finish this paper."

"Here," Ally gives him the key. "Anybody for a walk?"

"Not for us," says Katie.

"I'm down," says Jack. "Mama Cass?"

"I guess so."

Ally takes her hand, and leads her up to the edge of the firm sand, where the tide has deposited a row of kelp with bits of wood and litter interspersed. "Make dinner, if you need a break from your activities!" Ally calls back. Jack falls in with them, and takes Cassie's other hand. She breaks away and angles down toward the surf, where waves break cold around her legs, the sun warm on her left side.

So this is how it is, Cassie thinks. I fly all the way out here just to be the kid who's tagging along. She runs down into the lee of a receding wave, tiny bits of shell under her feet, then back up as the next one surges.

Forget it—I will not mope—look at this! I don't need Ally.

But as she spins to take in the whole beach, she's gratified to see Jack going the other direction, while Ally is catching up to her. She turns away and keeps walking, ignoring her. But in a few paces, Ally runs to catch up, reaches her arm around Cassie's shoulder, and slurps a loud kiss in her ear.

"Yuck! You're disgusting."

"I'm sorry, Cassie. I shouldn't have let them come."

"It's okay."

"No, it's not. This was supposed to be your trip, for your birthday, just for you. I promise I'm going to blow them off and hang out with you."

"You don't have to do that—it's just not what I expected."

They continue up the beach and it's good again, the two of them sisters again. Cassie is not yet ready to talk about how horrible school has been, so she asks Ally about college.

It's going great, Ally tells her, but she isn't in enough art classes this semester. She wishes she could skip ahead to the point where all her requirements are done and she can do the work she wants.

"Which reminds me," she says, "I have an idea for you."

"For me?"

"Remember we were talking about how awful middle school is, but high school should be at least marginally better?"

"Trouble is," Cassie says, "how am I going to make it 'til I get there?" Ally doesn't know the half of it—the obscene letters in her locker, the daily harassment.

"*That's the idea. You don't wait. You go to high school now.*"

"*You can't just—*" *she says, then pauses.* "*How could I do that?*"

"*Well, you said you were old enough to be a grade ahead, right? Your birthday is just before the deadline. So skip the rest of eighth grade.*"

"*Will they let me do that? They won't let me do that,*" *Cassie says, but she wonders. Would it really be any better in high school?*

"*They might. What have you got to lose? Look at yourself— you don't belong in middle school.*"

They come up with a plan—talking to the GT lady at school, convincing Mom and Dad, going to the principal instead of the assistant, maybe even going straight to the high school.

"*First, you've got to convince your parents,*" *says Ally.*

"*That should be easy. Won't they love to think of their brilliant daughter skipping a grade?*"

"*I don't know—sometimes they don't like you to move so fast.*"

"*But they have to. This is the only way I can survive.*"

"*Good work, Jack,*" *says Ally when they return to the beach house.* "*Looks like you unloaded all the food. And the beer.*" *She pulls one from the fridge.* "*What's for din?*"

"*Totally V-jin pasta and salad. Mama Cass, never fear—the ever sensitive Jack is here.*"

Cassie is feeling better and decides to mess with him. She examines the ingredients spread out on the counter. "*I can't eat any of this, Jackie Chan.*"

"*Why not?*"

"*Don't you know that V-jins*" *—she duplicates his mispronunciation—* "*don't eat any animal foods? Obviously they don't teach any biology at that school of yours. Or could you have forgotten*

*that BEES are ANIMALS! HELLO-O!" She starts picking up
items and dropping them back on the counter. "These lettuces are
coated with bee's wax, the olive trees they use for this oil are pol-
linated by domestic bees—"*

*Jack looks thrown—it's got to sound stupid, but vegans are
known nut cases, so could she be serious? She takes the beer from
his hands.*

*"This looks okay." She takes a large gallolop, then lurches to
spit it in the sink. "Yerch! I'm poisoned! It's goat piss."*

*"Okay, gimme the beer. I was drinking that. Goddamn kid!
Here I make a nice meal for you, and this is the thanks I get? Outta
my kitchen! Out!"*

*The house is amazing—not big and showy, just beautiful.
The kitchen and all the bathrooms have floors of stone flecked with
shiny mica and quartz. The big central room has skylights and a
rough-cedar ceiling. Built-in couches line two walls adjacent to a
huge fireplace fronted with the same rock as the floors. Scattered on
the couches are hand-painted pillows—one side an abstracted fish
or geometric design, the other a colorful face painted with exag-
gerated planes and angles. On the smooth, white walls, dull-toned
paintings and drawings hang, and Cassie sees a few small watercolors by Ally—of the house, deck, and ocean. Windows cover the
entire west wall, facing the sea toward which the sun is sinking.*

*Cassie drags her duffel down to her bedroom, slides the win-
dow open to the cold and the sound of the sea, and unpacks into a
couple of empty drawers.*

*Then it's time to make her promised phone call home. She
takes the portable from the hall and lies back on the white, com-*

forter-covered bunk. Mom picks up, asking about her trip, becoming less enthusiastic when she hears about Jack, Katie, and Bill.

"Put your brother on, Cassie."

She gets Sean, and picks up a good idea of the conversation from listening to his responses:

"She's just too nice, I guess."

"Maybe not."

"Yes."

"I know how old she is."

"No."

"No."

"No."

"It's just very mellow. She went for a walk on the beach with Ally, I have this paper due Wednesday, so I'm working, and Jack is making dinner."

"They're—napping, I think."

"Mom—"

"It's not like that."

"Don't worry."

"Okay. Here she is."

Mom is in mother-bear mode, wants to know if Cassie is "comfortable" with how things have turned out. Cassie tells her that, though she was bummed at first, she's okay with it now, she's fine.

Then she tells about Ally's plan for her to skip up to high school and realizes, too late, that this was not good timing.

"I've had just about enough of Ally's bright ideas," Mom says. "We'll talk about this when you get home."

"But Mom, I'm not a little kid. Middle school is torture. Ally says that high school will be better, and I am fourteen."

"Just—" Mom says. "We'll talk about this when you get home."

Cassie clams up. "Fine," she says. *Treat me like a dumb, teenage kid, I'll act like one.*

"Have a good time, and we'll talk to you soon."

Silence.

"Bye now, sweetie. Be a good girl. Love you."

"Whatnever." Click.

She mopes on the bed until Jack starts ringing a big bell and shouting, "Everybody to the mess hall! Supper's on!"

First thing Sean does is take Cassie's wine glass away.

"Listen everybody—no booze for the kid."

"I thought one small glass would be okay," Ally says. "Half a glass—"

"No way. I'm under strict orders."

"Right," says Jack. "No corrupting Baby Cass. Takes a village, peoples."

Cassie is silent through this and through most of dinner, though Ally gives her extra attention. She doesn't eat much, observing the others, noticing how Bill and Katie sit close, and how Ally and Sean don't. She figures that Sean is mad at her for bringing the others.

Afterwards, they build a fire downstairs and get ready to watch DVDs. Ally tries to get Cassie involved, offering her the movie choice.

"No 'R' ratings, though," says Jack. "We have to protect our Baby Cass."

"It's been a long day," she says. "Bedtime for me."

"Hey," says Jack. "Before you go, will you sing that song from The Sound of Music?

The sun has gone, to bed and so must I-I,
I'd love to stay, and taste my first champay-agne?"

*"Good—though you got the verses mixed up. But how about
this one?*

I am fourteen barely past thirteen,
pure as the driven snow—
Puffers of kind who blow their own minds,
think they're clever, but I don't know.

"Excellent!"

"Thank you," she curtsies and coos, "Night-night, everyone!"

*She isn't really tired at all, so after lying around listening
to the sound of the movie bleeding through the surf, she takes a
Nancy Drew from the shelf. It's bad, but it occupies her mind.*

*Ally comes in a little later and sits on the bed, wanting to
know what's eating her. "Sean told me about his conversation with
your mom. Is that why you're all hostile?"*

"She didn't go for the skipping up to high school idea."

"Is that all? We'll bring her around. I'll talk to her tomorrow."

"I don't think so. I don't think she trusts you anymore."

*"Just 'cause we brought a couple of friends along? She's not
that uptight."*

*"Ally," says Cassie. She fights to bring her gaze up. Ally is
looking down, smoothing the comforter, then glancing up with a
patient, expectant look. Acting just like Mom, Cassie thinks. Is that
too weird? "Ally—I really am tired," she falls back on the sort of fib
that she'd use on Mom. "I just need to get some sleep. I'll be okay."*

"All right. I'm here if you need me."

Another few cliffhangers into Nancy Drew, and it's Sean's turn to come check on her.

"Hey Littless," he says. "I saw your light on."

"Hey, Nickie."

He looks at the book. "Into some heavy-duty literature?"

"It's poor," she says. "But it's entertaining. I never read any of these before."

"I'll give you some of my Sartre. Being and Nothingness— *that ought to put you to sleep."*

"Sounds perfect—especially the nothingness part."

In the morning, Cassie awakes as foggy and rainy-feeling as the day. After the constant sun of Colorado, she thinks it's nice for the weather to mirror her mood for a change. But her head aches, and coffee doesn't even make a dent in it. Sitting on the window couch, sipping a second cup, she can't see through the misted glass and the fog outside to where the ocean, invisible, breaks against the beach.

Sean spends the day hashing out a draft of his paper, while Jack and the hippie twins go to town to look for something to do. Cassie reads while Ally goofs around with her sketchbook. Rain showers down on the roof and streams down the windows. In the hall closet they find some slickers, rubber rain boots, and hats and go out for a walk.

The rain diminishes to a fine shower as they stroll down the road to a path that runs away from the beach and disappears into coastal pines along the golf course. Cassie feels disoriented when they come to what seems like the ocean, but Ally explains that it's the bay that reaches around the other side of the house. They follow the path along the bay—a gray openness as silent as the ocean is loud.

The clouds lift and they see wide mud flats and tidal pools and the silhouette of a heron. Then the fog floats back in to cover all again.

Cassie would like to tell Ally the latest from school, but she can't bear to bring it up. She still feels as gray as the fog but doesn't really mind. The fog covers it—her life at home—and through the fog she can just glimpse the hope of Ally's plan, disappearing.

Mom and Dad would never go for it, especially since she intentionally failed the big state exams last spring. The letter with the results will be coming any day now. And as for the high school, there's no way they'll take her. She thought she was pretty cool writing her stupid responses and carefully filling in the wrong answer bubble for every item. Whatnever. Transferring to high school seemed like such a cool idea yesterday, but she's sure now that it's not possible. And even if it were, would high school be any better?

They walk. Ally talks of inconsequential things, pointing out berries by the trail, rain in pine needles, chattering about memories of their summertime in the mountains of Colorado.

They come back to the road, cross over a dune, and drop down to the sandy shore, returning to the beach house by the seaward side, but just when Ally says they should look for the house up in the lifting fog, they see something beached in the ebb.

It's a young whale, dead.

"Not too close, Cassie," says Ally. "The waves can flip something like that right over on top of you."

The little whale's eye is puckered and the side of its mouth gapes. A few small barnacles break the smoothness of its skin.

"I've never seen a whale before," says Cassie. "What happened?"

"It's hard to say."

"Was it alive when it washed up?"

"No, when they beach themselves, that's different. This one was dead already. It just washed up like everything does."

Cassie begins to cry, and she's not sure why. Not the young whale—beginning to rot in the surf, such a huge animal and just a baby, so much life not alive anymore, washing up like everything does—but partly that. And not herself—why would she cry for herself because the first whale she'd ever seen is dead?—but partly herself.

The reason for crying would have to be everything that is and then is no more—everything. And the whale lies there in the mist that seems like her own head-space—as Ally might have put it—her head-space, foggy and cold, but with warm, alive things in it and green, wet things in it and loud surf in it that was moved by the power of the land and the moon and the sun and moved by itself, by its own mass.

Ally puts an arm around her shoulder, and Cassie reaches with both of hers as sobs shake her. Ally holds her, raincoat to raincoat, and she cries, but it's not a good cry, not a healing cry. Because she can't feel any comfort, because she can't breathe, because the sobs rip from her throat, hurting more and more, she turns away and approaches the whale. It slides up and down with the bigger waves now. The sea is taking it back.

"Stop! Stay away from it." Ally says at her back, but she wades out to it, up to her hips in the trough of a wave, and quickly, before Ally can pull her back, she hoists herself up onto the whale.

Ally yells things at her as Cassie lays her face against the cold, dead bulk of it. Her diaphragm stops spasming, and she can breathe again as the waves rock her gently on the carcass of the whale, her burning temple teary and wet on the cool, dead creature.

Journal Seven

2 October

I'm back.

It seems like it's been such a long time. Was it only Saturday morning that I got up early to catch my plane, depressed over the collapse of the Grand Plan, feeling like there wasn't even any point in going?

But the Three Sisters gave me the story idea I'd been looking for—even if I couldn't see them—and as I hoped, the trip gave me lots of material. After adding and inventing, I was able to save plenty for the other two versions of the triumvirate. I finished up the story on the way home, scribbling away on the plane and staying up last night re-writing.

Back at school today, I found myself the subject of libelous scribbling on the bathroom wall: "Cassie O'Sullivan is Osama's ho." Wonderful. And so original.

I had a permanent marker in my locker, so I went to get it and covered the whole thing with a giant black heart.

As I was checking the other stalls, I realized I was shaking a little. I'd hoped things would simmer down, now that I'm stuck here. Stay Cool, I told myself, out of habit, but I think I'm done with that.

Oddly, the bathroom wall was the only insult of the day. Maybe it's not going to be so bad.

There was no Tolkien group, so I braved lunch to sit with DJ and everybody, who seemed happy to see me. I told them about my trip, and they were all jealous that I got to skip school. When DJ was getting some chips, Liz warned me to be nice to "our Gimli" because they didn't want him hurt. I wasn't sure I was ready for this kind of thing—exchange a couple of poems and tell him he can call me, and all of the sudden I was responsible for him. I don't know why, but I answered this by asking her to come over after school and hang out, if she wasn't doing anything.

She wasn't doing anything, so we walked home together. She lives just on the other side of the block, a few houses down the alley, but I noticed she didn't stop at home to ask if she could come over. It had been so long since I invited someone "over to play" that I hadn't been sure if I should call and ask Mom or not. I decided to ask her when we got there.

Mom was surprised when she came out of her lesson to say hi, but pleased I think, though she gave Liz a curious once-over. Liz is almost as tall as I am, with dyed black hair and a bunch of earrings, necklaces, and bracelets. She'd taken off the hoodie that made her dress-code worthy, so she was wearing a ripped British flag shirt that showed off the black ball ring in her belly button.

"Nice to meet you," Mom said. "I'd better get back to my student. Have fun, girls."

"Thank you, Mrs. Sullivan." Liz turned on the manners. "Nice to meet you, too."

We went upstairs and she freaked out on my record collection. Of course, there wasn't any Nine Inch Nails or Marilyn or English punk or Ramones. My new Nirvana saved us though, and we listened to that. I played some of the *Worst of the Jefferson Airplane,* too, which is one of my favorites. I have the speakers set up on opposite sides of the room, so you can really hear the stereo. Back in the sixties, I explained, stereo was a big deal, and Liz thought it was cool how they separated the instruments. She liked the heavier stuff, "Plastic Fantastic Lover" and "Ballad of You and Me and Ponielle," but some of it was "too mellow." I also played the first Mamas and the Papas.

"That shit's too hippie for me," she said.

Except for making friends with Ally, whom I don't expect to be seeing in the future, I haven't had a lot of girlfriend time lately. So I liked having Liz over, lying around my room, listening to music and talking. It's strange, in a way, that we seemed to have less in common than Ally and I, who are half a decade apart in age. Still, there was school, and I told her about bombing my CSAP test last year.

"That took balls, girl," she said. "I don't really care or try that hard or anything, but you fucked it up on purpose!"

Then she wanted to know all about DJ, what I thought about him.

I was guarded. I liked him, and said so.

Did I want to go out with him?

I wasn't sure what that meant, "going out." Isn't that what kids had been saying since fourth grade, that they were "going out" when they didn't actually go anywhere, or even see each other, just sent messages back and forth by their friends, or at the most, talked on the phone? And what does it mean now, in eighth grade? You text each other all the time? I wanted to see more of him, I liked being with him—

"Do you like anyone else?"

"No."

"Do you want to fool around with him?"

"I don't know." I didn't want to talk about "fooling around."

"Come on, you do, you're hot for him," she teased. "I can tell."

"Shut up."

"You want to go out with him, too. Don't worry, I'll tell him."

"Don't."

"He's going to ask you. That's why he wants to call you, you know that, right?"

"That's enough on that subject, I think. And don't tell him anything. What he wants to know, he can ask me. I won't tell him either, but he can at least ask."

Having a friend over messed up my writing/homework routine, so I took the night off—homework-wise, that is. My math for tomorrow is pretty much done anyway. I started working on the second Sister story—on the computer, believe it or not, just because it's easier to revise that way.

I'll paste it into you when I'm done, Di. I've missed writing in you, though I do like fiction. I like being able to change stuff without reality butting in.

In the middle of my writing, DJ called, and of course, Dad had to pick up the phone and tease me. We talked for a while, and I ended up telling him all about my Grand Plan, and even the whole history of my becoming what Quill calls Public Enemy Number One.

DJ got all riled up, and he wanted me to tell somebody and get people in trouble. I convinced him that I was doing the right thing by letting it blow over. It pretty much has.

The conversation came around to its predicted end, with

DJ asking me if I, like, wanted to go out with him. I resisted my immediate impulse to mock his incessant use of the mindless "like" and tell him that I couldn't possibly go out with anyone who used that word in, like, every other sentence.

I did tell him that I wasn't sure what "going out" meant—did he want me to go out somewhere with him, or to enter into a formal relationship with him? That set him stammering and liking, and I realized that I might have been a little too harsh, so I told him that I liked him and wanted to see more of him, and wasn't that enough? He indicated that it was.

I think the whole point of "going out" is that it's black and white. Kids want something definite. Just as the Bible-thumpers have Him and a set of rules that are supposed to come from Him—rules they don't question, aren't *allowed* to question—DJ wants our relationship to be beyond doubt. Once I'd thought it out, I was glad that I hadn't given that to him. How could I?

I do like him and want to hang out with him, but as Gandalf says, "even the wise cannot see all ends."

3 October

Griffin really liked the first part of my story. He was gushing, all excited about the whale at the end and wondering what it signifies when you find your spirit animal, and it's dead.

Everybody else liked it too, though the seventh graders didn't think Ally should be smoking pot, and one didn't think the end was realistic.

Here's something strange, Di: After I read, and we talked

about my story, I was warm and flushed, so I pulled off my usual baggy hoodie. Then I got almost as much attention for my little Indian halter as I did for my story. Isn't that stupid? Kel was totally staring. DJ blushed. Mr. Griffin gave me this sort of look that seemed to say that he knew I knew I was supposed to be a little more covered up, but he wasn't going to be the one to tell me.

Mr. Math wasn't either, when I got to his class. He took one horrified look at me and left the room. In a minute, he came back followed by another math teacher, Ms. Jennings, who motioned me out into the hall.

"We try to keep our school a business-like setting—Cassie, is it?"

"Yeah."

"And I can't think of any business where that top would be appropriate."

"Really?"

"So, Cassie, do you have something to put on over it, because if you don't, we have a couple of Tabor sweatshirts—"

"Oh, I've got a hoodie, I was just a little warm." I acted innocent, but I was tempted to ask her if basketball uniforms and sweatshirts were really all that business-like.

"Maybe in the future you should wear something cooler, but that, uh, covers you up a little more. Is your hoodie in your locker?"

"No, it's in the room."

"Well, put it on. And keep it on."

Can you believe it, Di? I've seen that sort of thing so often, I couldn't believe it was me this time. But I got sort of a charge out of it. I think Mr. Math was actually scared of me.

Liz invited me over tonight to watch a movie, and Dad said it was okay as long as my homework is finished. Mom's back on symphony rehearsal schedule, so she wasn't around. As far as the homework goes, I'm afraid I am a couple of chapters behind in history, but I'll get caught up this weekend.

Hi, Di. Kind of an exciting night—I'd better start from the beginning.

Liz hadn't warned me, but when I got to her house, DJ was there—along with Quill and Kelly.

Though they had seen it a few times already, Quill and DJ were set on me finally seeing *The Fellowship of the Ring*. I reminded them that Mr. Griffin hadn't liked it the first time, and I was pretty sure that I wouldn't like it ever. They said I had to see it, or I couldn't be against it.

So we settled on the couch down in the basement, where Liz has a giant TV and speakers all over the place.

In the first moments of the movie, as soon as I saw Elrond's begrimed and scowling face, I knew they had gotten it wrong. Even if they hadn't left out half of the most important things and changed half of the rest, you just can't find an actor to portray the wisest and most fair of all remaining Elves. And when they tried to jam almost a hundred pages of background into a couple of minutes, I could hardly stand it. But I tried.

The hobbits were good. Gandalf was great. Aragorn was good too, and Arwen was beautiful—though they magnified her role to make up for the fact that there aren't any major female characters. And again, how can a twenty-five-year-old human actress play an immortal that is hundreds, even thousands of years old, and is supposed to be the image of the most beautiful maiden of all time?

I'll admit that there was a majesty to it, and certain moments were breathtaking. Maybe, like Griffin, I'll have to see it a couple more times to be able to appreciate it for what it is and not just be missing my own true vision of the book.

When we stopped for a potty break, I asked Liz why she hadn't told me DJ would be there.

"Why, would you have worn something *sexier*?" She looked at my top.

"What's with everybody and my clothes?" I said, as we climbed the stairs.

"Nothing—whatever. So Gimli called you last night. Are you guys going out? I thought you were going to shoot him down."

"That's not what I said, I just—"

"I have *got* to pee," she said. "You use this one," she pointed to a door. "I'm going up to my bathroom. Mom-meee! I want an elevator! This sucks, I *hate* exercise!"

Back in the basement, I sat on the couch a little closer to DJ.

I wanted to ask him what he told Liz, but they started the movie right away, and Quill was shushing anybody who so much as whispered. I had a hard time concentrating on the rest of it, because DJ kept inching himself—millimetering really—closer to me, until he finally reached and put his arm around me. I slid way down, since I'm so much taller than he is, put my head on his shoulder, and leaned into him.

It was getting cold in the basement, and it felt nice and warm to be close to him. He was stroking my bare shoulder and arm, and I took his other hand and held it. What you are supposed to do when you hold hands, I'm not sure. He grabbed mine tightly at first, then he relaxed, and I was touching his hand lightly with my fingers. Eventually, he started rubbing my side with the hand that was around me, slowly moving it toward the front. He pulled away from me, embarrassed, when I stopped its progress toward my right breast, but I snuggled back against him and whispered that it was okay, just take it slow.

As the movie was ending, with the fellowship broken and Sam and Frodo heading off to Mordor on their own, Ms. Pine yelled down that DJ's mom was there. I looked up at him and said, "See you tomorrow," and he kissed me.

Then he jumped up and headed for the stairs, "See you, guys. Bye, Cassie, see you tomorrow!"

"Fare thee well, son of Glóin!" Quill called after him. And he was gone.

The kiss was nice, quick, with no smacking or dreaded tongue. I think I kissed back, but it was over so fast, and I was so startled, who knows? I don't think Quill or Liz saw it—they didn't say anything, except that Liz said it looked like the two of us were "getting closer."

I called DJ when I got home, but his mom wouldn't let me talk to him. She said he had already been out too late and it was past his bedtime.

So here I am, Di. I have my first boyfriend—no sense in denying it now—and I just had my first kiss. I'm happy and miserable at the same time. I feel like such a silly, typical teen-ager with my silly, typical teenage drama, the moral of which is always that everything will work out for the best because everything happens for a reason.

4 October

Uneventful day at school. Could it be that they have forgotten about me? No flat tires, no "Osamas," and Matt didn't jam his locker door over so that I couldn't open mine.

At lunch, Quill wanted to know what I thought of the movie. I told him a couple of my complaints.

He thought that the part when Lady Galadriel talked about taking the ring was cool, whereas I didn't see why they had to trip it out with a bunch of computer effects. The moment should not have been so obvious.

DJ was shaking his head in agreement. "I don't know why Peter Jackson has to do that," he said. "It's like when Gandalf made Bilbo leave the ring. It didn't happen that way."

"And what about," Quill said, "when Gimli asks for a lock of Cassie's, I mean Galadriel's, hair?"

"Shut up, man." He blushed.

"Yeah, man," I said, and put an arm around DJ. "He's, like, sensitive about that." Then DJ really blushed, scarlet, and I took my arm away quick, feeling a flush myself. What's getting into me?

"Well, I think the movie's cool," said Liz, "but I haven't read the book."

"Unacceptable," said Quill.

"It was boring. I couldn't get into it."

Speaking of boring, I should catch up on my history.

I didn't get very far. I tried to call DJ again, but his mom said he was "unavailable." What's up with that?

Then I had to break for dinner. No rehearsal tonight, so Mom cooked, and she had some big news. No cabin this weekend for her, because she is joining a quartet!

I'm really excited for her because she has waited a long time for this. Back when Sean was born, she quit her chamber group because the double rehearsals were too crazy with little kids. And though she's tried a couple of others since I started school, she couldn't find a good fit. In this group the players are awesome, and they have gigs lined up already. She'll have to switch her lessons all around and probably even drop some students. They start practicing next week.

Dad and I are going up to the cabin without her, so she can, as Dad put it, devote herself to the muse.

5 October

Beautiful Indian summer in the mountains, Di, and nice to be up here, but I can't settle into anything. Dad did some fishing; I tried to work on the Sisters. I was copying from the first one, and changing it as I go, but it's not coming together. I think I'm going to type it all into the computer at home, and make cuts and changes as I go. It's too unmanageable this way.

Later I wandered along the creek, bringing my field notes from past summers, but I ended up daydreaming, remembering what Sean said, how "wherever you go, there you are." I was lost in my own head, thinking of DJ and what it would be like if he were with me.

It turned chilly after sunset, and Dad built a fire. We hung out reading, made some popcorn. I forgot my history book—

guess I'll catch up at home—so I pulled some old books off the shelf, things that I'd already read, and was looking at them. *The Nick Adams Stories*, Laura Ingalls Wilder, *Captain Underpants*. I should be reading my lit circle book, but instead I read *The BFG* again. "Giants is never guzzling other giants." Now that's literature.

6 October

Now that I'm back home, I've got no excuses for avoiding my homework. Except not feeling like doing it. It was cool to have those straight As when I was trying to get up to high school. And even before, I was always driven, who knows why.

But now? I don't see the point.

Thinking of my history test coming up, I'm starting to panic, but I still can't get motivated. Maybe I can afford to slack a little. I can skim the chapters this week, do my article analysis for science, and finish my "six traits of writing" thing for language. As for math, I got some of it done in class.

Instead of doing homework, I typed my story.

And DJ called. He asked me where I was this weekend, so I told him all about the cabin and my tipi and everything. Then I said I'd tried to call him and asked why his mom never lets me talk to him.

"She's, like…I don't know," he said. "She doesn't want me to spend a lot of time on the phone."

"Are you allowed to get *any* calls?"

"Well, sometimes."

"Like if some nice girl from church calls, or your youth pastor or something?"

I felt bad then because I was just goofing on him, but I should have known he'd take it seriously.

"Cassie, no way, I don't like any girls at church, I mean, they don't call. *And* I don't like them. But my mom, like…she just…"

"What?" I said, gently.

"She doesn't want me dating until high school."

"Oh."

"I know it seems really old fashioned, and, like, stupid and everything, and I shouldn't have asked you out."

"I said no, remember?" I was tempted to tease him some more, telling him that I was saving him from sin, but by now I knew better. "It's okay."

"I guess I shouldn't be calling you or, like, seeing you."

"We should call it that, 'seeing' each other, not dating, not 'going out.' And I'll wait for you to call me, okay?"

"You won't get mad if I can't?"

"Of course not. I'll see you in school, right?"

"Yeah, and, like—" He stopped, then he whispered, "Gotta go. Bye."

"Bye," I said, but I don't think he heard me.

This going out, or "seeing" each other, is complicated. As if DJ needs all this hyper-protection. He's so sweet, I can't imagine him doing anything wrong. But I guess he already is, according to Mommy.

7 October

Today was okay. I didn't have time to finish up the math, so I turned it in halfway done. Mr. Math put a big red line after the ones I had done and said I would get half credit if I finished it. What a privilege! Then I got him mad by reading my lit circle book in class. It's boring, but I didn't feel like listening to him droning on and on. After he made me put the book away, I was really irritated. I actually was half-listening, enough to pick up what he was saying, so who cares if I read? I was more bored than ever, too, so I slipped out of my hoodie. Underneath, I had on a low-cut tank with spagetti straps. I just wanted to see if he'd notice. Did he ever. He trurned back from the board, did a nice double take, then said, "Miss Sullivan, would you put your sweatshirt back on, please."

"I'm hot," I said, which drew a good laugh out of the class.

"Either cover up, or you can go to the office and tell them that you think it's too warm for teachers to enforce the dress code—is that clear?"

Poor guy. As soon as he'd tacked the question on the end, I could tell he regretted it. I decided to let it slide, though, and just act like your average slut instead of your average smartass. So I sighed dramatically and made a big show of getting my sweatshirt off the back of my chair, standing up, and stretching my arms way up as I put it on. I know it wasn't very nice, but he deserves to be messed with.

Later, DJ met me at my locker and we went to lunch together. I smiled and waved at my old friends, and Sophia waved back.

Nobody is bugging me anymore. I guess I was right to let everything blow over.

Mom wasn't home after school. I'm a latchkey kid now that she has afternoon rehearsal. She is off tonight though, so we had a normal dinner. She loves the new group, said that things came together really well.

Gotta get caught up in history. Test on Wednesday.

Still can't do it. Can't focus on the Sisters either. I was hoping DJ would call, but he didn't. I called Liz. She has history tomorrow and was studying for the test. I feel a little better about it because I knew all the questions she was asking me. But they were all on the early chapters, when I was actually reading them—maybe I shouldn't feel better after all.

8 October

Decent day today. There's no school on Friday and Monday, so on Friday we're all going to walk downtown and see a movie. If DJ's mom will let him. His grades were bad at mid-quarter, and he has to get a grade check showing everything is at least a C or he can't go anywhere this weekend. After she let him go to Liz's the other night, his language teacher called. I'm going to meet him at school early tomorrow to help him with his project. I wonder if that would score me any points with his mommy. Doubtful.

Anyway, I sort of have to finish my own language project. I could put it together now, but I might as well do it tomorrow with him. As far as history goes, I think I know the big stuff from showing up in class and being more or less conscious, and I can skim the chapters for details and dates. I also have to do the questions on the last three chapters, but that should be easy.

If it's so easy, then why can't I do it?

Simple—I don't want to. Not that I ever did want to, but I made myself. Last winter I actually got further behind than this. That was when I was deep in the fog, and the only thing that brought me out of it enough to get caught up was seeing my grades. I couldn't imagine getting Cs or even Bs then. Now I think I can. Well, not Cs, but what's the big deal with a few Bs?

Does a grade matter any more than a state test?

I'm a straight-A student.

"Cassie is a straight-A student."

What does that really say about me?

In high school, you have to get good grades so you get into a decent college. But what does it matter now? Who have I been trying to impress? Why have I been so motivated, and why am I not now?

I look at that last question and the answer is obvious. Ooooo! Cassie's in love! But I'm really not. I like DJ a lot, but don't be silly.

The other answer is that I am disillusioned. I was living in that fantasy world of going up to high school, and when that fell apart, I lost my illusions. Now, I see through grades. They're transparent, meaningless, a joke. Any idiot can get straight As if I could. So now, since I don't see the point, I'm not motivated.

Then why don't I *feel* disillusioned? I did for a while. But now I'm all jumpy, unfocused. I can hardly even work on my story, and I believe in that. Though it sounds ridiculous, I'm too happy to be disillusioned. So it's not love *or* disillusionment. Whatever it is, it's freaking me out. I should be doing that history, or my math. What happened to my program of always doing my homework before writing? Out the window with the Grand Plan. Maybe I need a new plan to keep me going through the motions. After being an over-achiever, my new plan will be for under-achievement:

1. Do what it takes to get by.
2. Always have something to turn in.

I might be through with these lists too. Can't I handle under-achievement without a numbered list to follow? Let me have only one principle: Moving up to high school isn't the answer, fucking up middle school is!

All right, I'll do a little math.

Just after I wrote three pages about grades and homework and how bizarre I am lately, Mom and Dad decided it was time for a dinner conversation about how Cassie is adjusting to her eight-month sentence in the prison of middle school. Perfect!

I tried to get away with the old monosyllabic teen routine, but they weren't buying it. When I first got back from Oregon, we'd had a little talk about my "options," which they'd wanted me to think about on my trip. I hadn't thought about them—I knew I was stuck—but I told them that I was going to tough it out, that it wasn't the end of the world after all, that I could deal with it.

At the time, I wasn't sure how things were going to go, or

how much they were going to improve. Now that people aren't actively hating me every single day, I'm actually starting to relax a little bit.

But because I'd never told them about the problem, I was stuck on what to say.

"Before this high school idea," said Dad, "your mom and I both noticed how down you'd been. And now you seem better."

I'd already tried to brush them off, with "okay" and "fine," so now I guessed I really had to answer.

"I guess I am better."

"We thought so," said Mom. "Why is that?"

"Well," I stalled, and then I thought about what I'd written earlier and started laughing, imagining telling them that I was in love—remember I'm not—and that I'd decided that school work was a pointless bother.

"Let us in on the joke."

Then I thought of something to tell them. "It's ironic, I guess. I was so fired up to leave middle school that I didn't realize I was making friends. I thought Ally was going to be my only friend, and her being six years older and half a country away made things seem hopeless. And now I have some new friends. So that makes it bearable."

"Like Liz, right?" said Mom. "She seems interesting."

"Is this the goth?" said Dad.

"She's not goth."

"I never thought," said Mom, "that little Elizabeth Pine from across the alley would grow up to be such a punked-out teenager."

"She's not a punk either."

"Ripped-up Union Jack T-shirt sounds punk to me," said Dad.

"And I can't believe perfect Stacia Pine would stand for the piercings."

"It's just her belly-button. But," I said, "we're doing our eyebrows and lips and noses this weekend."

They weren't falling for that one.

"By the way, there's no school Friday. Can I go downtown with her and a couple other people to see a movie?"

"What's the movie?"

"Not sure—some thing Liz wants to see."

"What's it rated?"

"Unknown. But we don't exactly look seventeen."

"Who are the others?"

I told them.

"This is the DJ who's called a couple of times?" Mom asked.

"Mm-hm."

"What's the story with him?"

"Nothing," I said, "he's just one of the gang."

"Really." Dad lifted his eyebrows, and if I didn't have guilty written all over my face before, I sure as hell did now.

"You can go," said Mom. "Also, I'm off that day, so if you want to come here after the movie, everybody's welcome."

"Thanks, can I be excused? I better get to my homework."

That excuse is not going to work if I start bringing home Bs and Cs.

"Are you happier now, Cassie?"

"Yes, Mom, Dad, I'm a lark."

"What about the school part of school?" Dad wanted to know. "How is that going?"

"Counselor," said Mom. "Isn't that enough interrogation for one night?"

"No further questions at this time," he said. "The witness may step down, or upstairs. Anyway, she's excused from the table."

Then as I climbed the stairs he called after me, "By the way, I know something's up with this DJ character, and next time we talk I don't want to have to ask your mother for permission to treat you as a hostile witness!"

Speaking of DJ, I guess his mommy is watching him—still no call, and it's late.

This is when I would launch into some old stories, Di, but I've told them all. What now? We've already decided not to waste a lot of effort on homework, I'm not inspired by Sisters right now, and I'm tired of all my records. To bed, then.

9 October

DJ was waiting for me in the caf this morning, and then it was hurry up and wait because they wouldn't let us into the library without a pass. Luckily, I saw Ms. Tayebnejad, and she let us go in with her.

The assignment was to find examples of all six writing traits (ideas and content, organization, etc., etc.), copy them down, and explain them. DJ had the first two. I had nothing. You're supposed to find different examples, but I just photocopied the first page of *Tale of Two Cities*. Dad says Dickens is the best, and though it takes him a while to get to the point, that first paragraph does have everything. I just put numbers by the different clauses, and explained each one. For DJ, we took the rest of the examples from Tolkien, Poe, *Teen People* (that was funny, for voice), and another Dickens sentence. We had just enough time to finish his math before we rushed into class almost late. I hadn't done the first part of the assignment myself, so I didn't even bother trying to turn in the six problems we did together.

The rest of the day was all right. Tolkien group at lunch. During reading, I got to go to the library again where I tried to work on Sisters. I'm having trouble with how to change things. I know where I want to go with it, but I'm not sure how to get there. I think I'm stuck. Am I just too happy and content?

Writing club is tomorrow—maybe I can bust it out right now. Mom's at rehearsal and it's strange to have the house so silent, with no lesson going on downstairs. Time to quit blowing it off. Time to hit the computer and tell the story of Sister II.

Three Sisters

Sister II

*C*assie looks out the window and takes in the trio of volcanoes known as the Three Sisters. The mountains rise round and snowy from the hazy forests below, but Cassie continues to brood.

Nothing would have improved, she thinks, even if they had let her skip up to high school. And anyway, now she has a couple of days with her brother and her one true friend. Time to lick her wounds before she's thrown back to the lions.

Outside security, Ally comes through the crowd, hugs her close, and runs her hands over Cassie's newly buzzed head. "I love it. And new clothes, too?"

They negotiate through the terminal, Ally silently leading, then falling back.

"Cassie," she says, "there have been a couple of slight tweaks to our plan."

"Tweaks?"

"Sean has this huge paper due on Tuesday. He can't get away until tomorrow."

"That's okay," Cassie says. "I mean, I'll miss him, but it's only for a day."

"I tried to talk him into coming, but he insisted he couldn't work at the beach with 'the infernal throng.'"

"Don't worry, it'll just be you and me for a day—like our infamous hot-springs trip." Then she realizes she hasn't been listening. "Throng? Since when are three a throng?"

"Well…" Ally winces. "A couple of friends sort of invited themselves along."

"Friends?"

Cassie thought it would be the three of them, then the two of them, and now . . .

"I hope you don't hate me."

"No, I just wasn't expecting—"

"Don't worry," says Ally, putting an arm around Cassie's shoulder. "We're still sisters of the paint—it's only three tagalongs."

The air outside is soft, humid, and heavy with city smells. An enormous Klondike pulls up to the curb and Ally opens the tailgate.

"Heard all about you, Mama Cass," the driver calls back. "Name's Jack. Hop in."

"This is Bill and Katie," Ally says as two sleepy-looking hippies in the backseat turn around.

"Hey, Cassie," they say in dead unison.

Ally sits up front with Jack, the two of them chatting and laughing away. Cassie can't hear much over the music, even when Ally tries to involve her. Bill and Katie sleep.

Cassie didn't expect to be just trailing along with Ally and a bunch of her friends, but she tries to go with the flow. She is, after all, skipping school, and not having Sean there makes it seem even more like an adventure. She gazes through the tinted windows at brambly roadsides, brown hills of grass and oak, and forests.

When they stop for gas, Ally moves into the driver's seat and urges Cassie into the shotgun position.

"Girls in charge now, pal," Ally says when Jack returns. "Move to the back."

That's better, and soon the two of them are sisters again.

"So, when are you going to start your freshman year?" Ally says.

Cassie was hoping not to talk about how horrible school has been and how Ally's idea to get her out has proved to be yet another disappointment.

"August," she says. "Next August."

"But…You said on the phone that it was a go."

"Was. Past tense."

She tells Ally how she had been all set to check out when they got the scores from her CSAP test, which she had purposely bombed.

"I'll bet that was fun." She looks over at Cassie's pained expression. "Until it came back and bit you in the ass."

"So, I'm stuck," Cassie says. "And things aren't getting any better."

She goes on to describe the deluge of nasty notes in her locker and being pelted with disposable razors in reading class.

"The little fucking fascist fucks," says Ally. "They can't handle anyone who thinks, looks, or acts different. Fuck them, the little fucks." She slams her palm on the steering wheel.

Jack leans forward. "Take it easy on the bus, dude. Don't break it."

"Sorry," she calls back. "You've told your parents about all this abuse?"

Cassie shakes her head.

"Teachers? Principal? Anyone?"

"You," Cassie says. "I'm waiting for them to get tired of me."

"Cassie—you can't fight them alone. You've got to get help."

"I don't think so."

As the miles roll away, Ally tries to convince her to get help with the harassment, but Cassie knows that nobody can help. And like her parents, Ally wants her to think about options, what to do next.

But Cassie is so tired of all that. A phrase comes back to her from an Amy Tan story in her seventh-grade book, "raised hopes, failed expectations." That sums it up.

"What about the upside?" Ally says.

"You mean, as in, 'It's an ill will that blows no good'?"

"Exactly."

"Please."

"Well—"

"I know you're trying to help, but there's no upside. It sucks. End of story. Just more raised hopes and failed expectations. School is school. People are people. I am me. Nothing changes."

Meanwhile, Jack rolls a joint and wakes up Bill and Katie to help him smoke it. Ally waves it away when he passes it up, saying, "And keep that stuff away from my sister, too."

"We'll take care of Mama Cass," says Jack in a stoned drawl. "Takes a village, baby."

"Village idiot, in your case," says Ally. "And roll down some windows."

Cassie rolls down a window herself, and when the smoke stops, she's sure that she smells sea salt in the air.

"What about that boy you like?" Ally says. "At least you're going to see him at school."

Cassie is about to fire off another smart-ass, ill-wind reply, but wonders... maybe it will be nice to see DJ.

"Okay. There's one good thing. I think. You never know."

"That's my little optimist! And this weekend, we're going to have SO MUCH FUN, you, like, won't even remember last week!"

Cassie smiles in spite of herself, and suddenly there it is—the Pacific, shining blue beyond the trees.

"Follow me, Cassie," Ally says, as everybody piles out in front of the beach house. "But wait, bring a jacket or a sweater." They dig in their bags for something warm, then follow the decked walkway and stairs down to the dunes and the sea.

"Remember, everyone," says Ally. "NO SWIMMING. If you get washed in, you're dead, so be aware at all times."

They reach the firm sand below the high tide mark and all line up as a wave crashes into their legs.

Cassie and Ally walk the beach while the others open up the house. The sun shines warm and the breeze blows cold. Unlike the Colorado wind that dries everything it touches, this wind wets—a layer of mist forms on Cassie's sunglasses and her face feels salty-damp. She keeps thinking about how, at this point, she was supposed to be skipping up to high school and leaving all her problems behind. Then her thoughts turn to DJ—poetry-writing, lock-of-hair-cherishing DJ. She'll get a chance to get to know him better now. Will that be a good thing?

"Good work, Jack," says Ally when they get back to the beach house and see him in the kitchen. "What's for din?"

"Totally V-jin pasta and salad. Baby Cass, never fear—the ever-sensitive Jack is here."

Moron, Cassie thinks and heads for the stairs.

She drags her duffel down to her room, slides the window open to the cold and the sound of the sea, and unpacks into a couple of empty drawers.

Then it's time to call home. Mom picks up, asking enthusiastically about her trip. Cassie withholds the information regarding the extra people and the absent person, saying that Sean is locked away working on a paper—not exactly false.

Mom wants to know if she's been thinking about the options they discussed.

"Will everybody please lay off the options for five minutes?" she whines. "First Ally, and then you again. I'd be in high school now already if you didn't think I'd been too 'immature' for kindergarten. So now I'm stuck and there ARE. NO. OPTIONS."

"We can talk about this when you get home," her mom says

quietly. "Just have a good time, and you and your father and I will talk next week."

"Whatnever."

Cassie hangs up, feeling like a brat, and lies listening to the surf until Jack interrupts her thoughts with the dinner bell. "Suppertime! Come and get it!" When she comes up, she sees Ally removing one of the wineglasses from the table.

"Listen everybody—no booze for the kid."

"Come on, Ally," says Cassie. "Even my mom lets me have half a glass—"

"No way. I'm under strict orders."

Dinner turns out surprisingly well—Jack can really cook. Cassie remains silent through most of it, though, listening to the others and wishing they hadn't come. She notices how Bill and Katie sit close, their legs overlapped under the table the way Ally and Sean used to do. Is there something between Jack and Ally, too? Some extra bit of attention that he seeks from her and that she gives? But everyone wants Ally's attention, Cassie thinks, nothing special there.

After dinner, they build a fire downstairs and get ready to watch DVDs. Ally tries to get Cassie involved, offering her the movie choice.

"No 'R' ratings, though," says Jack. "We have to protect our Baby Cass."

"Whatnever," she says. "I'm going to bed."

Cassie isn't really tired at all, so after lying around listening to the sound of the movie bleeding through the surf, she takes a Nancy Drew from the shelf.

Ally comes in a little later and sits on her bed, just like Mom would have, tucking her in and kissing her goodnight.

"You were quiet tonight. Everything okay?"

Ally smoothes the comforter over Cassie's legs.

"Yes, Mom. But remember? The big sister's supposed to corrupt me, not protect. You couldn't even let me have half a glass of wine?"

"Well, I have to be extra-responsible without Sean here. Maybe one beer tomorrow, but no weed."

"I don't want that, anyway."

"Okay, sis. Good." Ally kisses her cheek and forehead, leaving her hand to linger on the side of Cassie's head where the stubbly hair is already beginning to grow longer and softer. Ally's eyes are wide and dark. "I'm glad you're here," she says. "I've missed you."

"Me too," Cassie says, closing her eyes, simultaneously enjoying and feeling uncomfortable with the contact—both the eyes and the caress. Not because of anything sexy—she's just not used to being touched.

Ally plants another quick kiss on her head and gets up.

"Night," she says. "Love you."

"Love you, too."

As she leaves, it occurs to Cassie that Ally is the first person outside her family who has ever kissed her, the first person with whom she's ever exchanged the phrase, "I love you." Even if they did leave out the "I." It seems cruel that they're so far away. Cassie knows Ally would counsel her to accept the bitter as well as the sweet, but it's hard.

She tries to read, but Nancy Drew doesn't hold her attention. Cassie's mind seems to drift out the window to the cold surf, and she imagines or dreams that high school is out there, in the mist beyond the shore, on an island—or is it an underwater mountain? Sean is a teacher there, and so is Dad, but where is Ally? Cassie searches, but finds only her mother, who leads a string quartet in crazy modern melodies, each player sawing high and low, out of time and out of tune, and the audience has pale skin and green eyes like lamps, "Like Gollum," she thinks, and opens her eyes.

The room is dark—Ally must have come in and turned out the light.

Cassie stands at the window. Stars hang over the sea and the lights of boats move below them. She shudders and dives back into bed.

In the morning, Cassie awakes as foggy and rainy-feeling as the day. Her head aches, coffee doesn't help, and she is sad, but she doesn't know why. Sitting on the window couch, sipping a second cup, she can't see through the misted glass, let alone through the fog to where the ocean breaks against the beach.

The others go to town to look for something to do. Cassie tries to read, settling on a book she finds on the shelf—Zen poetry and calligraphy. Ally goofs around with her sketchbook, builds a fire, and makes them a pot of tea. They pile pillows by the fire. Cassie keeps looking up at the windows out onto the drive, looking for Sean.

Finally, he calls. He's not going to make it until tomorrow morning. But it will be early—he promises that, whether he sleeps or not, he'll be there to wake her up on Sunday. He misses her, he's sorry, it's just that this paper is killing him.

What's another day? Cassie thinks.

"It's the old Sullivan straight-A syndrome," she tells Ally.

"Maybe so," she says. "Hey, let's get out of here and take a walk. What's a little rain?"

They go out into a fine shower and follow a path through coastal pines with water gathering in every bunch of needles, drops forming and hanging on each downward point. Cassie can't find her bearings in the rain and fog away from the ocean's roar, and she becomes even more disoriented when the mist lifts to reveal the ebb-tide, mud-flat bay, deserted but for a solitary heron in silhouette.

She feels fog-heavy and numb. The headache is worse, her brain a dull roar against the surf as they climb a dune and walk the beach up toward the house. She wants to stay close to the water, to the firm sand, but Ally doesn't want to miss the house in the fog, and they follow the edge of the dunes. She lags behind, and Ally falls back, puts a cool hand to Cassie's face, and says something to her. She pulls her gently by her hand, and the sand is wet from the rain, but dry beneath and soft, and Cassie's legs feel dream-heavy as they walk the last of the sand and climb the steps to the house.

Ally tells her to take off her wet clothes and get in bed. She returns with water and hot tea and presses three ibuprofens into her hand.

"This is a total PMS headache, isn't it?"

Cassie shrugs.

"You need to feed it."

"No food."

"Okay, not yet, but drink this, take those."

Cassie nods.

"No. Now."

Cassie takes a sip of water, pops the tablets into her mouth and swallows.

"Good girl. Now drink some tea, rest a little, I'll be back."

She returns with a big soy-shake—icy with frozen fruit, just like Cassie taught her to make last summer—and lays a towel-wrapped bag of ice across Cassie's forehead. Maybe it's the protein, maybe it's the ice, but soon the weight and the roar inside her head relent a little. Like the crash of the surf after shutting a window, it's still there, but not all-consuming. She drifts off to sleep, and it's about the same when she awakes—bearable.

Coming upstairs, she hears Ally and Jack talking, and she stops to listen:

"Do you think he'll show tomorrow?" Jack says.

"For sure. I know he feels bad enough about missing his sister, but you know—"

"It's gotta be hard on the dude—I wouldn't be here, seeing us together. I shouldn't have come myself maybe."

"But I wanted you here—"

Cassie hears the sound of kissing. She slips back down the stairs to take in this new information.

So things end. And they end quickly. Just months ago, Ally and Sean were in love. Just minutes ago, she trusted Ally.

But Ally loves me, she thinks. That hasn't changed. And I love her. We're like sisters, better than sisters, sisters of the paint...

So why didn't she tell me?

Cassie retreats to her room and stays there, feigning sickness while she runs over everything in her mind, feeling a gradual readjustment inside her until she actually feels clear and cool if not good. Ally brings her food, and she eats it slowly, savoring the aromas of torn basil leaves in coconut milk curry, the way the rice sops it all up, and the way the heat warms her face and brings a sweat.

She drifts off to sleep and awakens in darkness. The house is still. She slides the window open and imagines the tide receding, completing another cycle, again and again, over and over. The spinning earth circles the sun, and the still moon circles the planet, and the different masses pull on the fluid seas as everything changes.

Cassie sees the glimmer of redemption—or hope in cycles of renewal—as a false gleam of fairy lamps in the night. Then she smiles at how everything turns upon itself in paradox, for her image of falsity—the fairy lanterns—suddenly seems more true than the lamps of home, and it is the fairy stories that seem real.

To slip into the forbidden realm is the goal, to slide into the deathless lands below this world. Who could blame the girl in "Goblin Market"—what was her name? Laura? Who could blame her for pining and dying when she returned to mortal lands after tasting the fruit of Faerie?

Yet who could blame her sister for kissing her with antidote-juiced lips? The sister didn't know: saving is losing. Better to slip away because it's all the same in the end.

Raised hopes, failed expectations. Love and trust fading like the inconstant moon.

Too much bitter, Cassie concludes, and too little sweet.

She will not go back. She will not walk the halls amid stares. She will not groom herself for their eyes anymore. She will not go back and try again.

She will not follow the will-o'-the-wisp—wisp-the-o'-will the follow not will she.

Cassie has always felt the lines blur between poetry and story and life. Tonight, they're one. "A permanent solution to a temporary problem," she hears in her mind, and the voice of her classmate sounds like Frost's New England fence-mender, a stone savage who will not look behind the wisdom of his father's saying. Poe speaks to her too: "This fever called living is over at last." For the problem is living and it is terminal—or is it temporary only because it is terminal?

As she walks down the steps to the sea, Cassie wishes her hair were still long. She likes the Ophelia image of long hair in the water, but best not to think of that. The sea won't do pretty things to her. Poor Sean coming tomorrow and finding her gone. Poor Mom and Dad.

"Death," whisper the waves, to her as they did to Whitman, but there is no night-bird here to sing and no moon, only cold sand and wind blowing breaks in the clouds to reveal stars. "Come," whispers the sea, receding back into itself.

Cassie wades down into the falling wash of water, into the pause between the big surges when minor waves break across the receding spill. She remembers playing on the beach in Mexico, waiting for the big ones to come to carry her to shore, but this time it's the other direction.

Before the big one breaks, she dives under its crest, hitting the cold water—it's as yielding as rock, but she penetrates nonetheless. She fights to hold her air, pulling hard against underwater current, eyes closed, mouth closed against the salt. She bursts out, takes air, and not stopping to let the cold take her, not yet, she starts a strong crawl at the surface. She swims into the waves, rising with them, then dropping down, swallowing water and coughing, swimming hard until she's tired and rolls onto her back.

When she does, she feels the shivers come in a violent shake. A cramp hits her below the belly too, as if it's her period finally coming on. She imagines her blood trailing into the salt water, bringing the sharks. Another shake hits, she begins to feel warm inside, her mind dulls, and she wonders if she will bleed after death—is *there blood after death, sweet shark-calling blood? And she hopes the sharks will come and make a neat job of it so there is nothing left: no bloated corpse washing on the beach, nothing for Dad to look at and say, "Yes, that's her," nothing to burn or to bury, just nourishment for the good sharks with their dull eyes and delicate gill-covers, nothing to fossilize but a molecule of her bone's calcium in a shark's tooth—calcium so hard bought, so fought for in supplements and fortified soy-milk. Oh, to let that fight go, to let the calcium go back into the sea where it all came from—barely a trace that she has ever lived.*

Journal Eight

10 October

A bit wiped out from staying up writing last night, or a bit depressed from doing away with fictional Cassie. Or maybe, after the exhilaration of writing, I don't want to face the tiresomeness of life…

But life's okay now. Maybe it's good, even. I'm about to go to writing club, I'll see DJ—I'm actually having fun for a change, but there's one little thing that's still trying to take me down, that's pulling me away from shore. I've been trying, by fictionalizing and revising my story, to deal with (or to avoid) one simple truth:

Ally is gone.

She's more than just a thousand miles away now—she's out of my life. And no matter how I work it out in my stories, it's still not fiction: I've lost the sister I never had.

After school:

Luckily, I'd read my story last week, so I didn't have to today. I like Sister II better than number one, but I didn't want to read it. I did give a copy to Griffin, though. Kel read his today—three short slasher stories that were on the yucky side.

Sinclair isn't going to let me get away with skipping out to the library anymore in reading. He wanted me to switch groups, but I talked him into letting me be a group of one. I'm reading *Frankenstein*, which was a birthday gift from Ally.

The good news is that DJ managed to bring his language grade up to a C, so he thinks Mommy is going to let him go to the movie Friday. I hope so. It would be nice to have a little something to look forward to.

Dinner was just me and Dad. I'm not sure we're going to make it to the cabin this weekend. He has to work on Friday, and Mom is busy, busy, busy. If we do go, I want to invite DJ, but there's no way his mommy would let him. Probably not even for a day.

Just called Quill. DJ can go to the movie! Those guys live a few blocks north and west, up by the park, and are going to meet us downtown.

I don't know what to do with myself. I love the language, but *Frankenstein* is moving a bit slow. Victor Frankenstein is going on about the ardent ardor that brought about his ruin.

I guess staying up half the night working (ardently) on Sister II has made me tired. Yet I'm not ready to sleep because I'm all hyper (if you can be hyper and tired at the same time). And happy, too, now that I know DJ's coming tomorrow. Outside, there's a fall chill in the air, and I long to be out walking in it.

I wish I were on a grand quest to discover the pole like Mary Shelley's explorer. Is that where A. A. Milne got the idea for Christopher Robin and Pooh's "expotition"? I feel more like a bear of very little brain than a grand explorer. Maybe I'll read a little of the silly old bear, that should lull me off to sleep.

Some hours later, just as the night was beginning to steal away, Pooh awoke with a sinking feeling: he was hungry.

11 October

Liz and I got to the theater first, bought tickets, and went inside. She wanted to sit up front, but I talked her into the back row. We sat next to each other, and when the guys got there, Quill sat next to Liz, and DJ squeezed in front of us to sit by me. He put his arm around me as soon as the lights went down, and I slid down and snuggled against his shoulder. I fell right into a nice, comfortable feeling—even though it wasn't really that comfortable with the armrest/drink holder between us.

By the end of the previews, I was hating that armrest. I wanted to be *next* to him. I sat up a little bit and put my arm around him, but that didn't work. Then Liz reached between us and lifted the armrest and slid it back between the seat backs.

"Duh," she said, and we laughed.

I slinked back down and took DJ's hand. We sat like that for a while, just watching the movie, holding hands. Thankfully, he didn't try to grope around with his right arm, but he did take his left hand from mine and rest it on my leg, half on my shorts and half on my bare thigh. I put my hand on his, but together they weighed a hundred pounds, and his palm was sweaty. That wasn't pleasant, but I started running my fingertips lightly up and down his wrist and arm, and then he did the same on my thigh, which was very nice.

I was only half paying attention to the movie, and finally I turned, reached, and kissed him. We kissed on and off for the rest of the movie. We would do some short ones, some long ones, and then just sit back and rest for a while until one of us leaned in and started it again.

What surprised me was that Liz and Quill were doing pretty much the same thing! During one of our rest periods, she leaned over and whispered to me, "Good movie, huh?" and we both burst into a fit of giggling. Then I whispered to her, "What's going on over there? You never told me you liked Quill."

"Just sort of happened," she said.

When the credits rolled around, the lights came up a little, and DJ and I sat still, holding hands. Then the lights came up all the way.

"Excellent flick," Liz said.

"What's next, gang?" said Quill.

"Ice cream?" I said.

"But you don't eat ice cream," said DJ.

"They've got sorbet—that's vegan."

"You're such a Moby," said Quill.

"I think we have to go," said DJ. His mommy was letting him walk home, but he was getting nervous about being late. So we skipped ice cream and started walking.

Luckily, outside the theater, we saw the downtown shuttle coming.

"Stop that bus," yelled Liz. "Exercise sucks!" And we followed as she sprinted after it.

The bus let us off at the college in just a couple of minutes. From there, I led us over to the bike trail that runs along a little creek, up into the pines, and over toward school and our neighborhood. It was a bit of a detour, but we had saved a lot of time by catching the bus.

On the way over, I remembered a hideout in the pines that

Sean showed me when we were playing "The Last Good Country."

"Do you guys want me to show you a secret place up in the pines?" I said. "It's not really out of the way—it won't make you late, Gimli."

"The stout dwarf fears not his mother's wrath," said Quill.

"Yes, he does," said Liz. "Or he ought to."

"It's cool, we're not late yet."

"Okay, but you have to swear that you'll never tell anyone or take anyone there."

"And what shall we swear by?" said DJ.

"Let's seal it with a kiss," said Liz.

I looked at DJ. "We'll swear by the precious."

"Yess, Gollum," he said. "By the preciouss, we swearss by the preciouss."

"The what?"

"The ring, teenaged fluff-ball," said Quill. "We'll swear by 'One ring to rule them all.'"

"'One ring to find them,'" I continued the verse.

"'One ring to bring them all,'" said DJ.

"'And in the darkness bind them,'" said Quill.

"'In the Land of Mordor, where the Shadows lie,'" we finished in unison.

"You guys are creeping me out," said Liz. "Let's just promise, Cassie. We'll never, ever, ever tell."

"Or go there with anyone else or let anyone follow you."

"Swear to God and hope to die, stick a needle in my eye, no crosses count. Now come on, or Gimli's gonna be late."

We cut off the trail and followed the creek, trickling below huge willows in autumn yellow. In a hundred yards we were below a steep bank, and I found the spot where erosion had left a gap beneath the chain-link fence. We scrambled up and under, Liz complaining, "This is exercise, and exercise is work, and work sucks," and then we were in the pines.

Up higher, the ground leveled off and there was a clearing, edged by the ruins of an old stone foundation. Ponderosa pines stood tall and thick around us, screening us from the path above and the neighborhood across the creek. Pine needles blanketed the ground.

"Wow," said DJ. "How'd you find this place?"

"My brother and I used to play up here."

"Awesome," said Liz, and plopped down on the ground. "Ouch! These needles aren't as soft as they look."

"Pillow," said Quill, stretching out behind her and patting his stomach. She lay back resting her head on him.

DJ and I did the same. It was chilly under the trees, and I folded my arms across my chest.

"Here," said DJ, sitting up, taking off his jean jacket, and spreading it over my bare legs.

Then we lay looking at the sky beyond the tops of the trees. A big gust of wind came shooshing through the needles, and the trees swayed.

I heard Liz and Quill kiss.

"We better get going," she said, "or Gimli's going to be on groundation for life."

We climbed through the pines, springy needles beneath our feet, until we got back to the bike path. That fence had been repaired since I'd last been there, and we had to climb.

At the alley behind my house, we split up, the guys in a rush to get home on time. DJ and I hugged, his kiss missing by mouth and hitting my chin, and then the guys went up the alley.

"Call me, if you can!" I yelled. "Oh, wait, your jacket!" He'd made me put it on when we left the pines.

"Keep it," he called back.

And they rounded the corner, walking fast.

I'm wearing the jacket now, and I like it. It smells faintly like laundry, like when you walk by someone's house in the wintertime, and the dryer is venting a steamy cloud into the cold air.

At dinner, Mom and Dad wanted to know all about my "outing." I caught just enough of the movie to tell them about it, and how we walked home—I skipped the pines detour.

"Are Liz and Quill," Dad said, "going out or whatever you kids call it?"

"I don't know. She hasn't really said anything."

"What about you and DJ?"

"I don't care for the term, 'going out,' Dad."

"Are you dating?"

"We're seeing each other."

"Oh, *seeing* each other. So you look at each other, but you don't go out, and you don't date."

"Please, Dad. Mom, can you get him to leave me alone?"

"I'm a bit curious too, honey. But don't tease her, Gale."

"I'm just trying to get the semantics straight."

"Semantics?"

"The terminology."

"Read my lips, then, Father: stop bugging me."

"Just tell us a little about him," Mom said. "And then we'll leave you alone."

I didn't know what to say. Should I tell them that he wasn't allowed to date? If I did, would they tell me I couldn't see him?

"He's in the writing group and the Tolkien lunch club," I said.

"So you share some interests, that's good. What else?"

What else? He wrote me a poem? He doesn't say "like" as much as he used to? He asked for a lock of my hair?

"He's just the sweetest guy I've ever met," I blurted. Then I added, "Except for you and Sean, Dad. Is that enough? I thought so. Next subject, how's the music going, Mom? Are things coming together well in your new ensemble? And Dad, what about you? How's your new case going? The drunk guy who ran into the cop car with its lights on? Do you think the 'moth effect' defense is going to be effective on this one?"

"I'm glad he's so sweet," said Mom.

"There is no boy who could possibly be good enough for my daughter. But if her boyfriend is sweet to her, then I can't complain."

So I survived the parental cross-examination, Di.

The other news is that, as I feared, we are not going to the cabin this weekend. Mom and Dad are seeing each other, dating, and going out tomorrow night.

12 October

Morning, Di.

I hear Mom practicing, Dad's probably in his office working, and I don't have anything to do. I wish we were going to the mountains. I feel the need to do homework, to get all caught up, but I am *not* going to do that.

And I am not bored. I refuse to be bored. Cassie does not get bored. So why am I so bored? I used to love to be alone. I think I'm sick of myself.

In the pines:

Since I was going crazy in the house, I came up here with a blanket, some lunch, and my book. *Frankenstein* is getting good, but weird. Victor succeeds in creating his dæmon, and then as soon as it comes to life, he runs away from it. Because it's ugly? Now he is sick from shock and horror.

This might not be the best place to read. I keep thinking of yesterday, and wishing DJ were here with me. It's cold here in the shade, so I wrap up in my blanket.

In the pines, in the pines,
where the sun don't ever shine...

If DJ were here, we would lean back against the old stonework, close together, and imagine ourselves in some glade in the Shire, discovering the ruins of an Elven palace. Some hint of magic remains in the glade, or not magic, but the essence of the Firstborn, their love of nature and dedication to their art.

That's where Victor Frankenstein went wrong. Like Tolkien's

Fëanor, he was the most skilled in his art (or science), but he was too proud, wanting his creation to surpass God/Nature in beauty and power. And like Melkor—the original Dark Lord—he wanted to create, but all he could do was to twist and corrupt what already existed, producing a mockery of creation.

But art is not evil—science is not evil, not unless corrupted by pride and the lust for power. And is it always? Even when the Elves created the rings of power to deepen their art and their ability to preserve and protect beauty, they were betrayed by Sauron, who made his own ring to control the others.

Back to my fantasy: DJ and I discover the glade, where an essence of magic and love remains. Also sadness, for the undying Elves must witness the decay of all they create, and they must leave the lands they love. Then we hear fair singing, and a band of wandering Elves arrives, and welcomes us, singing songs of ages past, of those who built the walls and have since passed away, as they must also pass away, after a year or a century of reminiscent journeys before they board the ships, never to return.

When I got home, Dad said that DJ had called.

"Upon interrogation," he said, "this DJ admitted that his intentions on my daughter—"

"Dad!"

"What?"

"You did *not* give him a hard time."

"No, I guess I didn't."

"What did he say?"

"He said he'll try to call you back."

"That's all?"

"He wanted to know if you were, like, going to the mountains, or were, like, going to be home this weekend." He grinned. "And, like, that's all."

I can't believe I missed DJ's call. Here I was off daydreaming, and he finally gets a chance. I talked to Liz, who said that those guys want to get together on Monday. We're meeting at her house, and then we'll figure out what to do. I asked her if she could come over tonight, but she has to babysit her cousins.

"So, what's going on with you and Quill?"

"So, what's going on with you and DJ?"

"Asked you first."

"It's kind of bizarre, actually," she said. "I've known him since kindergarten, like I have DJ. We've been friends forever. DJ had a big crush on me in sixth grade, but he was always like a little brother to me. Quill and I are just buds, or were. I guess it did cross my mind. I mean, it makes sense, he did turn hot last year—if you like the Dee-Dee Ramone hair."

"DJ's is hotter."

"Longer maybe, more like Joey's—but, you know, to me, he's still DJ."

"So what happened with you and Quill?"

"It was the night you came over to watch *Lord of the Rings*. After you and DJ and Kel left, we were watching the deleted scenes, and the next thing you know we're in a total lip-lock."

"Whoa."

"It didn't last long because after, like, one minute, my mom yelled down the stairs that it was time for him to go."

"Then what?"

"Nothing. We didn't say a word about it. And then it started happening again yesterday, and finally, we talked last night."

"How was that?"

"Bizarre."

"Because…"

"You know Quill. Have you ever gotten a straight answer from him on anything? He was just acting silly."

"What did he say?"

"A lot of nonsense, weird voices, song lyrics. Eventually, I said, 'We're not really going out or anything, are we?' And he's like, 'Perish the thought.' And I said, 'Because this is just getting bizarre.' And then he got more serious, saying maybe it was a little strange, but it was cool, right?

"I said it was cool with me, but it changes things. Then he's silly again, 'Life is change, the more things change, the more things stay the same,' and a bunch of shit like that. I told him I didn't want to mess up our friendship, that we were like best friends, so where did this leave us now, best friends with benefits or some kind of Alanis Morissette shit? Then he's all, 'Isn't it ironic, I really do think, a little too ironic.' And, 'I'm drunk but I'm wasted, I'm gay but I'm really queer, I'm blind but I'm sightless, baby.'

"I was getting sick of his bullshit, so I told him to knock it off or I was hanging up.

"'Don't,' he said. 'You think it's cool, I think it's cool—let's just see what happens.'"

"So, are you 'cool' with that?"

"Yeah. It's not like I want to marry him, so—yeah, I think I am. Now," she said. "What about you and DJ?"

"I think it's easier because we haven't been friends forever. But Mommy won't even let him call me."

"Not *your* mom…"

"His. What's her deal, anyway?"

"O-ver-pro-tec-tive."

"As if he needs protecting—he's so sweet, almost innocent."

"Don't you get it? She's protecting him from hos like you. He is innocent; *you* are evil."

"Now I get it."

"But how romantic and cool."

"Not really. It sucks. I'm not used to sneaking around."

"Just be careful. If his mom does find out, he'll get grounded or worse. And—don't you dare tell him I told you this—but he is totally in love with you."

"He said that?"

"Are you kidding? But it's true. He says you're so beautiful, so smart, so tuff—not t-o-u-g-h, but t-u-f-f. He even thinks your hairy legs make you cool. 'She's, like, the only true nonconformist in the whole school.'"

"Seriously?"

"I tried to get him to tell me what you guys were doing in that dark movie theater, but he got so embarrassed he almost hung up. So, what *were* you doing?"

"I think I'll hang up now."

"Come on! First base, I know. Did he hit a double?"

"Liz, you weren't paying attention. The movie *wasn't* about baseball. And don't you have to go babysit your cousins or something?"

"Oh, my God, call me tomorrow. Bye."

13 October

DJ never did call again, and I got myself in trouble last night. I spent a restless evening after Mom and Dad went out, wandering around the house, upstairs and down. Eventually, I settled in the living room, lying on the floor listening to Dad's records. I tried one of his old Grateful Deads, then some Miles Davis. *Sketches of Spain* was too orchestrated, but *In a Silent Way* was perfect. The first side is all one piece, eighteen minutes long, very mellow and spacey, called "Shhh/Peaceful"— just what I needed. Two half-full bottles of wine tempted me from the kitchen counter (Drink me!), so I had half a glass of each, which I didn't think they'd notice.

I set the turntable on repeat and got buzzed on the wine, floating along with the electric guitar, organ, and Miles' trumpet so clear and smooth. Next thing I knew, I was waking up on the rug—I'd thought of it as my magic carpet—with the record still playing. Only now it was LOUD.

Mom and Dad were home.

Mom was sitting on the couch holding my wineglass, and Dad was cranking the volume to wake me up. Then he turned it way down.

"Hi," I sort of moaned, still sleepy and foggy from the wine. "Did you guys have fun?"

"How much wine did you drink?" Mom said.

"Half a glass." I sat up and looked at Dad, still standing by the stereo, then back at Mom. Neither one said anything, and neither one believed me. "Two half-glasses, I guess."

"You guess," said Mom.

"Pretty big half-glasses," said Dad. "We checked out the bottles. What else did you drink?"

"That's all."

"Do you think I count the beer and mark the level on the liquor bottles?"

"I don't know."

"How long have you been drinking our booze?"

"Dad, never. Just tonight. Just this one time. I can't believe this—one little glass of wine—"

"Two glasses, more like it."

"It really wasn't." I took the glass from Mom. "It was just up to here."

"That's not the point," she said. "It's a matter of trust. Even if it wasn't upsetting enough to come home and find your fourteen-year-old daughter passed out on the floor with a wineglass—"

"I wasn't passed out, I was asleep."

"Are you drunk?" said Dad.

"No!"

He gave me his best cross-examination glare. "You drank eight to ten ounces of wine, and you weigh, what? One-thirty? You didn't have any dinner, from the looks of things, so it was on an empty stomach. You must be a regular drinker if you didn't feel the effect."

"Okay, I was a little buzzed, but I wasn't passed out."

I sat down across from Mom. Dad stood behind her. They looked at me.

"There are two issues here," said Dad. "Your mother wanted to talk about trust."

"Can this wait 'til morning—"

"No."

"Can I get a glass of water? I'm really thirsty."

"I'll get it." He went to the kitchen. "Dehydration is a side effect of alcohol," he called back. "Did you know that?"

"Yes," I said, "but not as well as you do. How much did *you* drink tonight?" I *must* have been a little buzzed because I don't usually get lippy. Or was I just tired and dehydrated and cranky? Anyway, I didn't stop there.

"This is bullshit," I said. "How many times have I sat here and watched you polish off a bottle—"

"Trust!" Dad yelled from the kitchen.

"It's simple, Cassie," said Mom, before I could start again. "Now that you have broken our trust, we wonder if we can trust you again. And we wonder if you've lied to us before."

"I didn't lie."

"You said half a glass, then it was two half-glasses. I do believe that's all it was, and I believe it was only this time, but…"

"But we wonder," said Dad, handing me the water. "And we'll continue to wonder."

"I can't believe you're making such a big deal out of this." I drained my water.

"You don't think our trust is important?" said Mom.

"I do, it's just—it's not like I was trying to hide it or anything."

"Why not take a whole glass of wine from one bottle, then? Why not leave a note: Dear Mother and Father, I felt the need to put a little buzz on, so I had a glass of wine. Don't wake me up, I'll need to sleep it off. Love, Cassie."

"Sweetie," Mom said. "You're right—this is a fairly small

thing. But it is not okay. We don't want you doing it again. You understand?"

"Yes."

"The second issue is alcohol."

"I had a double Wild Turkey and two glasses of wine tonight," said Dad. "Since you asked. With a meal, and over the course of a few hours. Your mother had two glasses of wine, and she drove."

"After the movie."

"And we are relatively responsible adults. You are a relatively responsible teenager—we want you to stay that way."

"Alcohol is a dangerous drug," Mom said. "Getting a taste for it too young, before you can make good decisions—"

"I can make good decisions."

"Was this a good decision?"

"It wasn't that bad—I didn't steal your car and kill somebody. I didn't..." I struggled to add something. What is it that juvenile delinquents do when they get ripped? "I didn't scratch your records."

"And if you had, we wouldn't be having this conversation. You'd be in a paddy wagon on your way downtown."

"Cassie, you're avoiding the issue. Alcohol is a dangerous drug. You are too young to drink."

"Okay."

The discussion ended with them telling me they were afraid they had given me the wrong message by letting me have the occasional sip, or few sips of wine on special occasions. They don't want me to think that drinking is some cool thing for me to do. But they don't want to pretend that I won't ever drink, and so they want to keep it at home, under their supervision, and to keep it very limited until I'm older. I can earn their trust by my actions in the future, and if I ever do mess up and have too much to drink, or if I'm riding with someone who's had too much, I can always call, and I will never be in trouble.

Is that reasonable, or does it make no sense at all? I sure felt like I was in trouble last night. I haven't had a lecture like that in a long time.

Okay, Di. I'm weak. I wasn't going to do it. I promised myself I was taking a break from homework. But Mom and Dad were awash in the Sunday paper, so I joined them, and I happened to find an article on climate change. It was perfect for my science article analysis, so I thought I might as well write it up.

Guess what it said? The last ten years have been the hottest in the last century and a half, and "paleoclimatic" research shows that the earth hasn't seen such rapid climate change in six to twelve centuries. Before that, abrupt warming of the climate was the result of "known climatic conditions" that were nothing like what exists today.

But who knows if it's really the so-called greenhouse gasses? Who knows for sure, I mean? Science isn't religion after all. It's based on questions, not faith.

Then I thought I might as well do the analysis that I missed last week, so I pulled a piece out of one of Dad's old *Audubons*. After I finished with science, my math and history books were burning holes in my backpack, and I had to have something to do besides hang around waiting for a call from DJ.

Homework is okay, I decided, if you use it as an escape from reality.

I also talked to Liz—we're meeting at her house after lunch tomorrow to hang out. That's about it, Di. All caught up and here I am, stuck with myself again.

14 October

After hanging around this morning and giving my hair a fresh buzz, I went over to Liz's. Quill was there already, and DJ arrived right after I did. It was so good to see him. I got a nice long hug and we went down to the basement and played pool to a soundtrack of very loud Ramones, a band I'm starting to appreciate. "Hey! Ho! Let's go!" Sort of stupid, but fun. We played pool in partners, girls against the boys—an even match because Liz and Quill can play, and DJ and I can't.

Then they all wanted to go to the pines. It was windy and cold, but I was up for it. We trooped off down the alley and through the neighborhood to the creek and up into the secret glade.

Quill brought a blanket in his backpack, and spread it for him and Liz. DJ and I leaned against the old stone foundation, or he did, and I leaned back against him. It felt so nice to close my eyes and lie back as he wrapped his arms around me.

Liz and Quill were in a "lip-lock" right away, and I started feeling uncomfortable as they got into it pretty heavy.

I looked up at DJ, his eyes a deep brown flecked with gold.

Liz gave a sort of shriek and started giggling.

"Want to take a walk?" I asked DJ.

"Yeah," he said. "This is getting sort of awkward."

"You mean us, or them?"

"Them," he said. "Let's go."

We went down through the fence and along the creek. The sun broke out of the clouds and turned the dirty little creek bottom into a golden hall. Sunlight, passing through yellow leaves of cottonwoods and willows, came out like a semi-solid, radiant thing. Gusts of wind tore the leaves free and sent them falling around us, while those on the ground sent the light back up into our eyes from below.

We walked in silence until the creek disappeared into a culvert, and we had to climb the bank up to the bike path.

"I tried to call you Saturday," DJ said.

"I got your message. I hope my dad didn't give you a hard time."

"No, he was cool."

"I guess he saved the hard time for me."

"Did I get you in trouble?"

"Oh, no, my mom and dad are both cool," I said. Then I was afraid that it sounded like I was saying his weren't. "But they gave me a huge lecture that same night." I told him about the wine incident.

"We don't have a drop of spirits in the whole house," he said. "And if my mom caught me drinking, she'd kill me."

"What about your dad?"

"He's in California. Don't see him much."

We were walking side by side. I looked over and saw him shake his head, and I squeezed his hand. "Tell me about it?"

His parents had split up when he was five and his brother

David was eight. They had never said why it happened, and they never talked about each other, which he said was better than stories you hear of parents who keep running each other down. His father was married again but didn't have any kids, and Mommy sent David to California after he got in big trouble his freshman year at Parker. With David, she had been using that as a threat the same way she threatens DJ with Christian school now. But she doesn't threaten DJ with going to his dad—she's afraid he'll want to.

"Do you?"

"No way. Dad's okay, but my brother's, like, a total jerk. He always used to beat me up and stuff. I'm glad he's gone. Mostly. He was cool sometimes—and if he was in trouble, I usually wasn't. But he got me in trouble too, so I'm better off."

He wanted to know all about my family, but I felt sort of bad because I have it so good. I told him all about Ally, the summer, my trip to Oregon.

On the way back, he started complaining about how his mom never lets him do anything. Then he backed off, saying that she didn't want him to mess up like David, how he was all she had now, and she wanted him to stay close.

By the time we got back to the pines, it had gotten late. The sun was behind a bank of clouds over the mountains, and the wind was tossing the trees around like mad. We stopped before we got to the glade and held each other. The ground was steep there, and I was uphill, which made me even taller, so his head was right at my chest. I didn't mind, except it was sort of like embracing a little kid.

"Here," I said, and turned us around to level us out. His soft, fleece jacket had that same laundry-scent, combined with a snowy, outside sort of smell and the piney scent of the woods. I squeezed him and kissed his neck. "You feel so good."

"You don't mind me being short?"

"I don't mind anything about you," I said. "Come on."

"Where have you guys been?" said Quill when we entered the glade. He and Liz were huddled under their blanket against the stonework.

"Just walking," said DJ.

"I bet they have another secret place," said Liz.

"A secret more secret than the secretest of secrets," said Quill.

"Anybody have a watch?" DJ said.

I pulled up my sleeve. "Five-thirty."

"I'm dead," said DJ. "Murdered."

"Let's make tracks, Master Dwarf," said Quill. "And let's think up a good lie."

"Let's just hurry," he said.

We all rushed down from the pines, and when we got to the alley behind my house, DJ bolted, with Quill trailing behind and not so much as a "see you tomorrow" called back at me on the run.

"Why did we have to walk so far?" I said to Liz. "We totally lost track of time."

"He'll be okay. Don't worry."

"But if he's grounded, I'll never see him."

"There's always school."

"You really know how to cheer a girl up, don't you, now?"

She answered with a hug. "Later, bud."

"Okay, see you tomorrow."

I never thought school would be a comfort, Di, but at least we have lunch. Can you believe it? Me looking forward to school?

I just hope Mommy's not too mad. This afternoon was wonderful, and I can't bear for it to end with DJ having to pay the price.

15 October

Tell me: how is it that Kel can write a disgusting and bloody slasher story, and nobody bats an eyelash, but my story has a little weed and a suicide, and everybody suddenly becomes "concerned"?

First things first. DJ is grounded for the week because he was forty-five minutes late. He's off this weekend, *if* his grades are good at the end of the week. He is going in early tomorrow morning to meet me for more homework help. Mommy thinks he's meeting Quill, who she ought to know would be worthless. If she only knew that he is hanging out with Miss Straight-A Cassie, she might actually approve.

Or not. Especially since I'm not Miss Straight-A anymore. I got grade checks in all my classes, and I'd better hope they count the late work I turned in because I have a C+ in history, a B in English, and a C in math. Man, those zeroes add up.

But the real kicker is Griffin. I was in Sinclair's room, almost at the end of *Frankenstein*, when he came and called me out of class. He led me into the teacher's meeting room across the hall, propped the door open, and we sat down.

"I read your story last night," he said, not sounding as if he had exactly loved it.

"What did you think?"

"Incredible."

"Really?" Now I began to think he'd come to talk to me because it was so good.

"Really," he said.

In that case, why did he seem so serious?

"And very disturbing."

"That's bad?"

"Maybe. Maybe not." He had the story on the table in front of him. He looked from it, to me, and back. "Cassie, are you suicidal?"

Why do I have to laugh in these moments? I did, and then said, "No."

"Have you ever made an attempt?"

"No."

"Considered it?"

"Thought about it—as a subject—but not about doing it."

"I'm glad to hear you say that, but I still wonder." He flipped through some of the pages, sighed, and looked back at me. "Let me tell you what I'm thinking. It's clearly fiction, but some of the characters are real people. Your protagonist is you, and though you came back from Oregon alive, it seems like a fantasy that's...becoming too real. So, ethically, I have to tell the principal. Personally, I'm worried about you."

"What about Kel's gory thing?"

He shook his head. "That wasn't serious at all. It's probably healthy—maybe not. I hated the pointless violence—but it's not the sort of thing that makes me think he's going to hurt someone."

"And mine is?"

"I don't know. I wanted to talk to you first—tell how much I respect the work. But I've got to tell Mrs. Trumbull, and I'm going to call your parents."

"Don't, please don't. It's just a story, it's not real. Mr. Griffin, really, I'm not going to kill myself. I'm actually happy now—things are going great, and now everybody's going to freak out on me."

"But what about when they go south? What are you going to do then?"

"I'll just deal."

He looked at me. "I'd like to think that we have our little talk, and you reassure me that you're all right, and you are. But what if you aren't? You understand?"

"Yeah," I said. "But I really am okay."

"Good," he said. "And take this." He passed my story across the table. "If Mrs. Trumbull reads it, she'll probably get sidetracked by the marijuana, so I'm not going to give it to her. Not that I'm saying drugs are okay—but I recognize they're not a concern here. She won't. Sorry about this."

"That's okay."

"Let's get you back to class. What's the book?"

"*Frankenstein*."

"Excellent. You're a romantic. You think you're some kind of existentialist, but you're really not."

When I got home, there was a message from Griffin on the machine. I was tempted to erase it, but he'll get through eventually. I don't want to violate their trust, do I? Especially now that I have to convince them that I'm not about to jump off a cliff.

Why can't everything be normal—DJ not having an overprotective Mommy, me not being a freak? Okay, I like being a freak. But I wish people would just let me.

Mom's at rehearsal tonight, so it's just me and Dad. Maybe I'll surprise him with dinner.

Uh-oh. Griffin got ahold of Dad at work. He just called to tell me that Mom is bailing on rehearsal and they're both on the way home. They're very concerned.

I had hardly written that last bit when they both rushed in the door as if they expected to find me tying a rope to the rail of the staircase. Mom wrapped her arms around me and held me like there was no tomorrow.

"Sweetie, sweetie. What's happening with you?"

"Air, please," I said. "Don't suffocate me."

"Don't goof around, Cassie," said Dad.

"It's okay, don't worry. I'm okay."

Mom let go, and looked at me, tears running down her face.

"Alright," said Dad. "Should we eat first? Before we talk? Have you eaten, Deb? I don't think I can eat."

"I can't eat now, either. I need to know what's going on."

"Okay, let's sit down." He dropped onto the couch. Mom sat next to him, and I placed myself on the chair in front of them.

"First," said Mom. "Tell me what Mr. Griffin said. As soon as I heard suicide on the phone, I couldn't hear anything else."

"Maybe we should hear it from Cassie—"

"Just tell me."

Dad took a breath. "I came back from court and got a message to call Mr. Griffin. I got him on the phone at home, and it appears that Cassie has written a story for writing club, semi-autobiographical he said, which ends in her suicide, or her character's suicide. It takes place in Oregon. He spoke to her and thinks she is all right, but he wanted us to talk to her and read the story. Which, he said, is incredible. But disturbing."

There's no way I'm letting them read that story.

"Cassie?"

"I'm all right. Really."

"Here's the trust thing again," she said. "It could be that you're fine. Or it could be that you want us to *think* you're fine, so that we'll leave you alone."

She was closer than I wanted to admit. How many times had I pretended everything was cool?

"You see what I mean?"

I nodded.

"Which is it?"

"The first."

"Good," said Dad. "Good. We believe you, right, Deb?"

"I think so. But I'm still worried. We should read this story. You have a copy of it?"

I didn't say anything for a moment. I didn't know what to say. All I could think was, There's no way I'm letting you see that story.

But I said, "Yes. I've got one."

"Will you get it for us?"

"No," I said, and she said, "No?"

"I don't think I can let you see it."

They looked at each other. I saw the hesitation—they were shocked, and they didn't know what to say, didn't know what the other was thinking.

"In fact, I know I can't. I can't let you see it." I groped for something to add, something to give them that would throw them off or lessen the stubbornness of my refusal. "Not until I write the third part."

"But what's to say," said Dad, "that you won't change the first two parts, sanitize it so that we won't worry about you?"

"Nothing," I said. "Trust?"

They looked at each other again.

"Or, I'll give you the first two stories," I said, "and I'll trust you not to read them until I give you the third."

"How could you let Mr. Griffin read it," Mom asked, "and the other kids, but not your parents?"

"I just could, Mom. It was easy. They aren't judging me and worrying about me. They aren't going to look at every little thing and see it as some kind of a warning sign."

"Mr. Griffin did. He called us, didn't he?"

"He had to."

"Don't you think he's doing more than covering his butt?" said Dad.

"Okay, he's concerned, but it's different. With you guys, it's personal."

"I don't like this," said Mom to Dad. "I don't think I can sleep tonight. I don't think I can let her out of my sight until I see this story."

"You can't read it," I burst in. "It's mine. I wrote it. You have no right. This is my privacy, and I can show it or not show it to whoever I want. Now I'm *never* going to let you read it, and if you try to steal it, I'll never trust you again."

We sat there for a while. I could tell Dad was surprised, but he also had a calculating expression on his face. Mom looked devastated.

"I'm sorry," I said. "I can't let you read it."

"Let's leave the story issue for a while," said Dad. "We seem to be at an impasse. Anyway, the story was just a way for us to get a glimpse of your thoughts. So instead, why don't you tell us? And then we can tell you some of our thoughts, because we have some strong feelings about our daughter's life. Deb?"

"I'm so upset I don't know what to think. Fine. Let her tell us, if she will."

"Cassie, can you tell us about the story, or tell us how and why you came to write your fictional alter-ego into oblivion, to send her off into the eternal abyss?"

"Goddamn it, Gale. Will you can the bullshit for once?"

Whoa. I was just thinking up something smart-ass, and then, boom.

"Cassie," she said. "Speak."

"Okay. So. You know I'm not the world's happiest person. I mean, I know I really have a great life. So why should I even think about it, right? Why should I hate myself? But I do sometimes. You know I was really down last year. It was like I was walking around in a fog, and—so that you'd just leave me alone—I did try to pretend that everything was cool."

"I knew it," she said, "we both did, but we wanted to believe you were okay. Sweetie, you should have told us."

"Told you what? That I had no friends? You knew. That school sucks? You knew. That I was sad all the time about everything and half the time I didn't know why?"

"Let it out, sweetie, let it all out, it's okay."

"But it's not okay. You always say that, but it's not. The world is completely fucked. We're going to war, *again*, and we're killing the planet, and I can't even walk down the hall at school without some little fucking Christian hypocrite trying to crucify me." I looked up for a moment, and seeing how anguished they looked reminded me of why I don't talk about this stuff. But I went on.

"Sometimes…I can't turn this stuff off," I said. "Right now, somebody is killing one of the last clouded leopards, just so he can sell somebody else a dried leopard penis. And that person will buy it. He'll buy the very last one, and by the time I have children, there won't be any leopards left. And no mountain gorillas. No elephants."

Now that I was talking, I couldn't stop. "You didn't know, but when we went to see that stupid *Wild Thornberries* movie, and I saw those forest elephants, those *cartoon elephants*, I sat there and cried."

"You did?"

"And it was just a cartoon. And I feel so useless—and don't start telling me how wonderful I am." Here was the thing: I felt at once that I was right to cry for the forest elephants and that I was being pathetic. Not just because they were cartoon elephants, though that heightened my sense of silliness, but also because I feel I should be stronger, that I'm just oversensitive. And while I didn't want to be coddled, to be told that I was good and the world was bad, I did want some kind of reassurance. And I hated myself, once again, for needing it.

"We all feel useless sometimes," said Mom.

"Frequently," said Dad.

"So how do you go on?"

"You just do."

"Why?"

"Because," said Dad. "What's the alternative? *Not* going on. You've been exploring that. And you must know that suicide is only one way not to go on. Plenty of people give up, but keep living. But you will never do that, and neither will we."

"Why not?"

"We just won't."

"Love," said Mom.

We sat for a moment, letting the word hang.

I couldn't argue. I was thinking of DJ, of course, but she didn't mean that. Not *only* that.

"On that note, should we eat?" said Dad.

"Yes." I stood up.

"First, come here," he said standing and opening his arms. I came to him, and he enfolded me, and Mom as well.

They helped me finish the dinner I had started—sautéed veggies and pasta with sauce from a jar. The windows were steamy from the big pot of water that had been boiling all this time, and the kitchen filled with a warm garlicky scent from the tortilla garlic toast that Dad always makes when we don't have Italian bread. We ate there in the kitchen, not talking much, listening to the jazz show on the radio.

"Thanks for making dinner," said Mom.

"My pleasure. Thanks for coming home. Are you going to get in trouble for missing tonight?"

"I don't think so."

"That's what she has a union for," said Dad, getting up and taking our plates to the sink. "The contract allows for one suicide scare per season. But we can't do this again. And as much as I hate to, I think we'd better start round two."

Mom wanted to know what I meant by being crucified in the halls at school. The conversation had been so open, I hated to gloss over that little bit.

"Well..." The question was, how much to give them? The real story is that I happen to be weird. Always have been. But once I stepped completely out of line, people saw a reason to attack me—the mark was unmistakable. That it happened to be religion and politics was beside the point. But that's what got this stuff going—it was the only tangible thing I had.

"Well, you know I haven't said the Pledge of Allegiance since fourth grade. I don't stand for the national anthem. I got kicked out of choir for refusing to sing 'Proud to be an American.' That stuff hasn't exactly made me popular. But it's okay now."

"Define okay," said Mom.

"Nobody's bugging me anymore."

"Good," she said. "But you should have let us know what was going on."

"And if that's blown over..." said Dad. "You're sure it has?"

I nodded.

"What about your health?" asked Mom. "How've you been feeling? How have you been eating?"

"Fine," I said. "Though I did have some massive headaches in Oregon."

"Are you sleeping?"

"Lately, yes."

"For me," she said, "part of the shock of this has been that it came up when we both have noticed you—I don't know—blossoming? There's the new style, the boyfriend, and what seems to be a new comfort in yourself. Is that fair to say?"

"I guess so."

"And that's why we're inclined to believe you," said Dad, "when you say you're all right."

"But I'm not going to leave it at that," said Mom. "We've had a good talk, but I think you should see someone."

I knew who "someone" was.

"You have friends, and us, to talk to. But it might be nice to have someone neutral, confidential."

"My diary?"

"The diary is great," she said, "but it's you. If you're depressed, then your diary will just tell you that you have every reason to be depressed."

"Do you think it should be a doctor?" asked Dad. "Somebody with a prescription pad?"

"That's a good idea."

"No, Mom, Dad, come on. You want me to go on Zoloft? Just take a little happy pill and be like one of those bubble-people in the ads?"

"Nobody has prescribed anti-depressants," said Mom. "Maybe you're not depressed—I'm not a doctor."

"And doctors don't know everything. But I know that if you see a psychologist who thinks you're clinically depressed, then you'll have to see a psychiatrist as well. Might as well see one person" said Dad.

"Might as well see no one."

"I think we might let you get away with not showing us your story right now, Cassie. Am I right?" He looked at Mom.

"For now," Mom said.

"But you have to see someone," Dad said.

"This is non-negotiable. You will see someone," Mom said.

"Okay. Send me to the shrink," I said.

"Good," she said, "I'm glad you agree. Is it really eleven o'clock?"

"And time for bed. But Cassie, I know I also speak for your mother when I say this: the worst thing that could possibly happen to us would be to lose you. Or your brother."

"It's unthinkable."

"You have to be careful with yourself. We love you too much."

"Will you promise us that if it gets bad again, if you feel like you want to get out, you'll tell us?"

"We have to know that," he said. "We need your promise."

"Even before—before it gets too bad to talk about—talk to us. Will you do that?"

"Yes," I said.

"Promise?"

"Okay, Mom. I promise. You don't have to worry."

Journal Nine

16 October

Hey, my diary. Should be exhausted today, but I'm feeling pretty up, though Mom irritated me by skipping her small group rehearsal to stay home and watch me until Dad gets home. She was waiting for me with a nice healthy snack, and when I objected to it all, she told me to think of it as being for her, to make her feel better—not because I really needed coddling.

DJ and I met in the caf this morning, but we didn't get much work done. I told him about yesterday's big drama. He thinks my parents are incredibly cool, and I think he is, because he didn't give me a hard time about the suicide issue, just accepted that it was part of the story.

I got a summons to go see the counselor, one of those slips that says NOW in huge letters. I told her that I didn't need to talk to her, my parents were making an appointment for me. She acted interested in my story, but I won't let her see it. Her door is always open, she said, which I was thrilled to hear.

At the Tolkien lunch, Griffin wanted to skip ahead to *The Return of the King*, to discuss Denethor.

This was obviously for my benefit. Denethor is a character who gives up hope and takes his son Faramir—who is afflicted with Black Breath, a kind of terminal despair—to the halls of the dead, and has them both placed on funeral pyres, doused with oil, and set on fire. Gandalf and Pippin save Faramir, but Denethor burns himself alive. Griffin wanted to be sure I knew that the enemy's greatest weapon is despair, and that the heroes keep going even when hope is lost.

Afterwards, DJ and I made our way back up to the eighth-grade wing, holding hands, not talking. Halfway up the stairs, that same teacher who talked to me about my un-businesslike attire called down from where she was policing the stairwell, "No PDA, kids, you know the rule."

Holding hands? Against the rules? And where was she when I was getting tripped and pushed and having my books knocked all over the floor? I should have held on even tighter to DJ's hand and then kissed him right in front of her.

After school, Nathan, Jenny, and Matt were all at Matt's locker, when Matt said, "How's it going, Osama?" I ignored them, but when I was fiddling with my backpack, he slammed my locker shut. He and Nathan and Jenny laughed as they walked off.

"Small amusements, for small minds," I said. "Have a nice day, Bible-Boy!"

"At least I don't worship the Koran," he called.

"Love you, too!"

At dinner, Mom and Dad told me about my appointment with the shrink tomorrow morning at ten.

"You even get to miss half a day of school," said Dad.

"But writing club," I said. "Can you pick me up after that?"

"Our daughter wants to go to school?" said Mom.

Things were almost normal—they were mocking me again.

"More than I want to go to a psychiatrist."

"But you'll still have to see the head shrinker, so we must conclude that you don't want to miss your beau at the writing club."

"What*never*, Dad, I'm, like, so totally *sure*," I said, my mock-teen voice a bit too authentic. "Isn't it possible that I don't want to miss the writing part?"

"I'll pick you up at 9:30," said Mom. "We'll have some paperwork at the doctor's."

"So what's this going to be like, anyway?"

"You vill sit un der couch, unt Herr Doktor vill make direct his obserwations into ze core of your psyche."

"Ya, das iss gudt, mein papa."

"*Her* observations," Mom said. "But actually, she's a certified Mesmerist. I'm not sure if she uses a pocket watch, but she'll put you in a state of profound hypnosis. Then you'll tell her all your secrets. Then she'll tell me."

"Great, Mom, your dream come true," I said, but I was kind of proud of her. Usually it's Dad who comes up with the nonsense. But of course he had to get in on it:

"You forgot," he said, "about how she'll make Cassie bark like a dog."

"And levitate."

"And consume large quantities of meat, poultry, and shellfish."

"And most importantly," said Mom, "you'll be trained to a bell that the doctor will give your parents."

"Right," said Dad. "Absolute, unquestioning obedience. For life."

They stopped and beamed at each other, imagining this last bit.

"Enjoy your little fantasy, parents," I said. "Don't you want her to program me to vote Democrat for life, too?"

"Good Lord, Cassie," Dad said. "We give you some credit for intelligence."

"But maybe she's got a point. What if she gets some kind of brain injury?"

"Or falls victim to demonic possession."

"Okay, okay," I said. "Are you done yet? Aren't you afraid I'm going to blame everything on my sadistic parents?"

"Parent," said Dad. "Singular. That's what psychoanalysis is all about: you lie around on the couch and, whatever you say, the shrink brings it back to an anal-retentive mother."

"I think it's actually the oral-diarrhetic father."

"Seriously," I said. Things were more than back to normal now. I was getting a little sick of it.

"Seriously," said Mom. "I don't really know. But she comes highly recommended. And she said that, though we're making you go, it's really for you, Cassie. You should probably think about what you want to get out of it."

I couldn't think of any appropriately sarcastic response to that, so I guess this shrink thing really is throwing me off my game. And I'm left with the question: what *do* I want to get out of this counseling?

Mostly, to get a clean bill of health. I want to be able to report to Mom and Dad that I am certified non-suicidal and one hundred percent normal. I'm afraid that won't be as easy as it was with the counselor last year.

So what am I going to tell her? After last night, I'm all talked out. I'd say as little as possible and hope to be left alone again, but I think I am going to have to give her something. Maybe I could tell her all about how people were bugging me and my attempt to move up to high school. I'd like to move on from all that, though, and just enjoy what's going on now: relative calm at school, a few friends, DJ. I could tell her about the good things, but she is going to want to know why I was so down that I wrote about suicide.

The more I think about it, the madder I get. It was a story. Just because I write about somebody who kills herself doesn't mean I am going to. I resent having to go through all this. But I do. And now I'm falling back on clichés and advertising jingles. "Just do it," Cassie. Put on your sweatshop shoes—*sold by the company that cares about building your self-esteem*—and get in there and just do it.

17 October

DJ and I ditched writing group so we could work in the library. Though I am a little faster on the math stuff, he doesn't really need my help. His trouble is that he can't get anything done in class, and he can't make himself do homework.

"Daydreaming," he said. "That's all I seem to be good at."

"Well, you better get caught up—if you think your mom's mad at you, just wait and see what I'm like if you're still grounded this weekend."

Unlike yesterday, we were very productive and got all his stuff finished. I wanted to tell him about my doctor's appointment, but I knew that would get us off track. I'm serious about getting his grades up.

About halfway through class, Mom came to pick me up

and take me to Dr. Velez. The biggest question on my mind, as we drove downtown, parked, and rode the elevator up to the eighth floor, centered on the word "confidential." What you say to psychiatrists is supposed to be private, but here my mom is making me go, and she's paying for it. Even though it's supposed to be for me, I had to wonder how much she was going to hear. Especially after that hypnotism stuff.

When we got there, Mom filled out a bunch of paperwork, and I got something a lot like the "depression inventory" that I had done not quite a year ago. I moved all the way across the room so that she couldn't see my answers—though I figured the doc would fill her in anyway.

It was both sides of the page, asking me about changes in my sleeping and eating, how often I had feelings of worthlessness, hopelessness, helplessness, persistent thoughts of death, et cetera, et cetera. You know me, Di, what do you think? All of the above. But to an abnormal degree? I wasn't sure how to answer, how far the truth would get me, how much to tweak my answers. Most of the tricky ones I put about in the middle of the range, which was not too far off.

By the time I'd finished, it was after ten, and the doctor came out to get me. She introduced herself and then asked me to follow her back. Mom was standing there, uninvited, wondering if she should sit back down or follow.

"You can wait here, Ms. Sullivan, or come back in fifty minutes if you wish."

"Okay, I'll wait," she said, and plopped back down into her chair.

I followed Dr. Velez as she led me into her office and shut the door behind us.

"Either the chair or the couch," she said, sitting in one of the arm chairs herself, crossing one leg over her knee, and writing on a clipboard on her lap.

I thought I might as well do this psychiatry thing right, so I went for the couch. I was going to stretch out on it, but it felt too weird, and I perched awkwardly at one end. I imagined her writing something like, "Subject chooses couch. Seems anxious, ill at ease, nervous."

"Why don't you tell me what brings you here, Cassie?"

As if she didn't know. I was tempted to shake my head or shrug, like I had with good old Mr. Kimball and Dr. Hawk. So far her couch-side manner was underwhelming me.

"My mom told you what's going on, didn't she?"

"She did. And although this was her idea, I would like to know why you think you're here."

I might as well start talking, I thought, and sighed. Didn't mean to do it, but it came out long and loud. It was kind of a big question. How far back should I go?

"Long answer or short?" I said.

"Let's start with the short, and then we can go back and fill in the details."

"I wrote a story that ended with the main character's suicide. So my teacher and my parents freaked out and think that I am about to jump off a cliff or something."

"Are you?"

"No."

"Why did the girl—was it a girl?"

"Yes."

"Why did she take her own life?"

"I don't know."

"Of course you do."

"She was in despair."

"Why was she in despair?"

"She had no hope." I knew these kinds of answers weren't going to cut it. But how was I supposed to talk to this person?

"I know what despair means—I think you're circling around the question."

Great. I'm being cross-examined. Shouldn't I have counsel present? Isn't *she* supposed to be my counsel?

"So," said the persistent doctor. "Why'd she do it?"

"It's just a story. It's not me."

"But you wouldn't be a good writer—and I'm told you are—if you didn't know what motivates your characters."

I didn't know how to reply to this. She was right, in a way, and I started to get interested in the question. Not because of the flattery—it was more the way she talked about the motivation of the character. The trouble was, the answer wasn't all that clear in my mind. The Cassie in my story did what she had to do—it was who she was, it was fate, karma—I knew it was right but couldn't really explain it.

"Does something happen that makes her feel that she has to commit suicide?"

"Yes," I said, then changed my mind. "No. That's sort of the point of the story. It's not what happens. It's just what has to happen."

"Why?"

"Because it does."

"You're circling again."

"No, I'm not," I said, getting irritated because I knew it sounded like I was. "You can't tell me," I stumbled. "It's my story."

"Maybe I would understand if I read it."

Here we go again, I thought. Everybody wants to read the story to find out how psycho I am.

"Will you bring me a copy?"

"I don't think so."

She didn't say anything, and the silence began to weigh on me until I felt like I had to say something.

"I went with what I felt about the character—it wasn't all that conscious."

"Ah!" she said. "The subconscious. Now we're getting into real psychiatry."

She smiled, and I liked her showing that she didn't take herself *too* seriously.

"I'm sorry, Cassie. I know this isn't easy for you, to have me grilling you. And I think I understand what you mean about writing it as you feel it. That's probably why it's so good, and why it freaked your teacher out. If you'd plotted it out, or done a bunch of pre-writing on your character's motivations, it might not have seemed so real."

Exactly.

"I have an idea," she said, getting up and opening a drawer in her desk, pulling out another depression inventory. "Why don't you fill out another one of these, but this time, do it in character, answering for the girl in your story. I can look at yours while you do one for her."

Tricky, huh? I took the clipboard she handed me, and got to work. It set my head spinning a little, as I wondered how fictional Cassie would answer the questions. Maybe I didn't have a clear idea of who she was at all. I'd just written her as me, but *more* me. I'd invented things that happened to her and made her reactions more dramatic. By the time I finished the survey, and scanned it over, a clear picture came out—someone who was very depressed in some ways, very strong in others. She was me, as if I didn't already know that, but before the good things that had happened after the trip. And without something that I began to think I might have—maybe just a stronger survival instinct, something that makes me unable to let go.

I passed it back to Dr. Velez, who skimmed down, comparing the two sheets.

"Interesting," she said. "Your character's pretty extreme, huh?"

She looked up.

"But let's get to you. Your character can find her own shrink. How are things going with you, Cassie? Since you wrote the story?"

"Good."

"Why is that?"

"People are bugging me less at school. I have a couple of new friends. Sort of a boyfriend."

"How is your mood?"

"Up and down. Mostly up. My boyfriend isn't allowed to date, but we still get to see each other."

"Any headaches?"

"No."

"How are you sleeping?"

"Okay."

"Eating?"

"Pretty good."

"Any health problems? Muscle aches, cramps, back, neck, shoulder pains?"

"No."

"Do you exercise?"

Hadn't I answered all these questions on the survey? Twice?

"I hike when we're in the mountains, and I walk. But only to get places."

"How is your energy?"

"Okay, mostly."

"Any trouble concentrating?"

"Yes."

"Why do you think that is?"

I picked up a cushion that was lying next to me on the couch, held it on my lap, and traced its Persian patterns with one finger.

"I've been wondering about that. Changes, I think. I have a new haircut, clothes, friends—I just feel like a different person sometimes."

"What's your boyfriend's name?"

"DJ."

"When you do get to see each other, what do you do?"

"Watch movies with our friends, go for walks—I help him with his homework in the library before school. We haven't been seeing each other too long."

"What else?"

"What do you mean?"

"Are you sexually active?"

"No."

"Are you attracted to him?"

"I guess so."

"What do you do about it?"

"How confidential is this, Dr. Velez? I mean, how much of this are you going to tell my mom?"

"I'll give her my diagnosis. And I have to tell her if I suspect that you will endanger yourself or others. I try to keep this as private as I can, but since you're a minor, there are some things I have to pass on. Does that help?"

"I guess."

"So. Though it seems silly, some kids do better with the baseball thing. What base are you and DJ on?"

"First."

"Tell me a little more about your mood. Do you feel better or worse than one year ago?"

"Better."

"Six months?"

I counted the months forward on my fingers, "Better."

"Three months."

"I was pretty happy most of the summer. Maybe about the same."

"Six weeks."

"Better now. Way better."

This sort of thing went on for a while. At first, she seemed to be hitting the questions on the survey, but then she just got me talking. She had a nice manner, once we got going, straightforward, paying attention. I felt I could be honest without making her think I was a freak. I ended up telling her a lot about my troubles at school and how hard I'd had to struggle to keep it together. Before I knew it, my time was up, and we went out to the waiting room.

Mom looked worried, so I tried to give her a reassuring smile.

"After our conversation," said Dr. Velez, "I don't believe that Cassie is depressed or suicidal—at the present time. I think she's had some close calls, though, and that she's not out of the woods yet.

"Cassie, I need to talk to your mom for a minute. Nothing confidential, just more on my diagnosis. Is that alright with you?"

"No problemo."

They went back this time, and I waited, but it wasn't too long. Mom seemed less worried on the way home and told me that I didn't have to go on medication, but I had another appointment for next week. The doctor was "guardedly optimistic." And at home, we need to "keep the lines of communication open."

So that was the last word, Di. I am officially a psychiatric patient now, though at least I am not thought to be in immediate danger. Mom was mostly relieved, but still worried. Since I didn't feel much like dealing with school after all that, I took her up on the offer to skip the rest of the day. Now I better go back to school to get my books. Mr. History is cramming in one more quiz before the end of the quarter, and I want to be ready for it.

Hello again, Di. My homework trip got interesting. School was just getting out, and I ran into DJ and the gang. Mommy must be lightening up, because when she called to check on his grades, they were all Cs and Bs—thanks to yours truly—and she ended his groundation early. They were all going to the track meet, so I called Mom and asked if I could stay.

Unfortunately, my language arts teacher was selling tickets and told me that I couldn't attend school activities after being absent that day.

So we all took off for the pines, which was different with Kel there. The guys went looking for sticks to use as swords, while Liz and I talked. We had a lot to catch up on. Lately, she and Quill have been together non-stop. Her mom never says no when she invites him over because she likes Liz to be at home instead of out.

"So where were you all day?" she asked.

"I got to skip most of the day," I said. "But I had a doctor's appointment this morning. A psychiatrist, actually."

"No way! My mom wanted me to see one of those—or a counselor or something, but I said forget it. Are you psycho, or what?"

"Or what."

"So, what's going on?"

While the boys played sword fighting, I told her about my story, the big talk with my parents, and my trip to the shrink.

Liz and I had caught up and were watching the boys get increasingly violent in their swordplay when Kel got his knuckles whacked, and they quit fencing. Quill and DJ sat by us as Kel walked around in circles holding his hand and muttering. I scooted over to DJ and lay back against his shoulder. Suddenly, he said, "Time?"

Nobody had a watch, so we all hustled back to school. His mom was coming at 5:30, and he had to be there waiting. The two of us walked on ahead of the others, and I got a chance to tell him about my appointment. I think he was a little hurt that I hadn't told him I was seeing the shrink today, but I said I wanted to concentrate on his homework this morning, and hadn't it paid off? No more groundation.

It was only 5:15 when we got back to the meet, but Mommy pulled into the parking lot just seconds later. Very close call. DJ sort of pretended that I wasn't there and ran to meet her. Liz and those guys went in for the rest of the track meet, and I headed home.

Dad and I had dinner alone again, and I told him about Dr. Velez. He and Mom had talked on the phone, of course, but he wanted to know what I thought about it all. Tired of it, already, but relieved that the diagnosis hadn't been worse.

We were pretty much finished eating, though Dad seemed like he wanted to talk a little more, when the phone rang. It was DJ!

He wanted to apologize for cutting out on me without saying goodbye. Sweet.

As usual, we didn't get a long time to chat, but he wants to do something this weekend—maybe without Quill and Liz. The trouble is, what's his excuse going to be? We're going to think about it.

I wish I could invite him over here. I'm so jealous of Liz

and Quill who get to see each other every day. DJ and I aren't even allowed to have a relationship.

Couldn't he just ask if he can come over? Maybe we could lie and say that Quill is going to be here too, although that could backfire if she finds out. So, what if he just asked? He wouldn't have to tell Mommy that we're going out—oops!—seeing each other. He could say that I'm the person who has been helping with his homework, that we're friends, we're going to do some homework, my parents are home, what's the big deal?

I'm going to call Liz and get her take on it.

She doesn't think it would work. Not only would Mommy say no, but if he asked to go over to a girl's house alone, then she'd be on the lookout all the time.

I still think it's worth a try. She can only say no, and then we can lie low for a while. Wait—are we going to the cabin this weekend? That would be perfect. We could invite him up there for the day, say my dad is taking us fishing—that's a good, wholesome activity.

But she won't want to drive all the way up there and pick him up, so we'll have to bring him home. How is this going to work?

What am I thinking? It *won't* work. Mommy will say no. Still, I want to try.

18 October

School was okay, history test felt pretty good, grade updates show me with a B- in math, a B+ in English. We'll see about science and history.

Tonight we're going to Liz's house to play pool; we worked it all out at lunch. I asked Mom and Dad if DJ could come up to the cabin with us, and DJ is going to ask Mommy. Liz still thinks it's a bad idea. Quill thinks we should try, though he suggested that my whole family join their church.

"You don't have to believe," he said. "All you have to do is put money in the plate."

"*And they'll know we are Christians by our checks,*" he sang.

"I'm a pagan," said Liz. "I got this cool book on Wicca from my aunt. But it's all spiritual—there aren't even any spells. Still, maybe we can find a spell somewhere for making parents let you date."

"I think my mom's, like, protected from your goddess, Liz," said DJ. "And don't forget that she prays for you."

"Hey," said Liz, "you really should invite Cassie to church. She couldn't say no to that."

"But I could," I said.

"Suffer the little children to come to me," Quill said. "And the tall and buzz-headed children too."

Before dinner, DJ's mommy called. Here's what I overheard:

First, Mom told her all about the cabin and the property and the fishing stuff, then about how the two of us met in Mr. Griffin's clubs and what a motivated student I had always been. After that, Mom did a lot of listening, mm-hm-ing, agreeing, and sympathizing that ended up with her saying that I never had shown much interest in boys, and how Sean had started dating late too, and how, of course, she did think it was good for kids to have both boys and girls for friends. Finally, Mom said how happy she was that DJ was coming, which set me literally twirling around the room with happiness.

After she hung up, Mom said, "I guess you know that DJ is not allowed to date?"

"Ummmm…that might be one reason why we're only *seeing* each other."

"I'm not so sure I feel good about this, but I didn't let on that you two are a little more than just friends."

"Thank you, thank you, thank you, Mom. We're really not *much* more than friends."

"She's going to find out, you know. It would be better if DJ would tell her the truth."

"But she wouldn't be letting him come if she knew."

"Here's that trust thing. If you're happy with him lying to her, how do I know that you're not lying to us?"

"But *you're* not unreasonable and overprotective, Mom. I don't *need* to lie to you."

"Don't think I don't know, Cassie, how quickly that could change. As soon as I don't give you what you want, suddenly I become unreasonable and overprotective, too. I was fourteen once, and fifteen and sixteen, and furthermore, I will not keep your secrets."

"But, Mom—"

"Nor am I going to call this woman back and tell her. But if it comes up again, I'll sing. You two better straighten this out."

"Okay, Mom, we will."

"Now, how late are you going to be tonight?"

"Midnight?"

"Eleven. It's going to be an early morning."

I got home well before curfew, it turned out, because Mommy picked up DJ at ten, and I decided to go home and not be a third wheel. I also got to meet her, which was interesting. I don't know what I expected—someone like Momma in *Carrie*, someone with holier-than-thou written all over her, someone overweight and pasty with a southern accent. I guess I'm as full of prejudice as anyone.

She turned out to be younger than I would have thought, and pretty, and normal looking, if a little too put-together for ten o'clock at night. But maybe she had been out Bible studying or whatever those people do. She was also very nice and polite to me—though she did have a certain tightness, like her eyes and mouth were smiling, but inside she was a ball of stress.

Before she got there, we played pool and darts and ordered pizza. DJ actually shared my half of the cheese-free pie, which the others could not understand at all. That's about it. I got a nice goodnight hug and some kisses—well before Mommy got there, just to be sure.

It feels like such a luxury to be with DJ all evening and then look forward to seeing him first thing in the morning.

Good night, good Diary.

19 October

What a day. It was damn near perfect.

The ride up was a little awkward—DJ was not exactly at ease with Mom and Dad until Dad got him talking about *The Lord of the Rings.*

I felt a little funny about the fishing—I don't believe in it, of course, and it seemed strange to have used it as an excuse for inviting him to the mountains. But it was something for him and Dad to do together. He got the hang of the casting right away, and landed a couple of brookies, getting all flustered and stripping the line in by hand instead of reeling in. Since I was just watching, though, he quit early, and the two of us walked up to the Carrock. He thought it was incredible that we actually have a carrock, though we speculated that a true carrock might have to be in the middle of a river.

As Tolkien said, pleasant tales are soon told. We basked in the October sun until lunch, taking turns using each other for pillows, but keeping it cool because it wasn't exactly private up there. Then we had lunch with Mom and Dad and went for a hike.

In the shadowy woods along the creek, it was almost cold, but the aspen groves were full of light. The leaves had fallen, but for a few patches of trees that held fluttering gold, and the ground was covered with pale yellow.

We climbed along the falls, then followed a ridge up to the southwest. Just below the ridgeline were some crags that caught the sunshine and blocked the wind, so we took a break there. I have another secret place on the other side of that ridge—a little valley that you can only get to by two ways, and I told DJ about it. We promised that if anything terrible ever happened—terrrorist attack, fascist take-over—we'd find a way to meet each other there.

Meanwhile, we enjoyed the crags, which gave us plenty of privacy. It was strange to be so close in the bright sunlight, but if we closed our eyes it was cool the way the sun came through our eyelids, like we were kissing amidst a red haze. It was a relief to be alone together, and we did some things we hadn't done before—it just felt right.

Before we headed down the pass, we caught the sunset with Mom and Dad—from the sunset rocks, of course—and on the way back we hit the Tex-Mex. In the dark car, we held hands, and DJ fell asleep. I kept holding his hand and watched him in the passing headlights, his dark hair fallen back from his face, his straight nose in profile, and his lips, fallen open as he slept. I wanted to reach out and trace his profile, to touch the little dip between his nose and his upper lip, but I didn't want to wake him up. After I was sort of adoring him for a while, I saw Dad watching me in the mirror. His eyes smiled at me as I ducked back to my own side of the car, out of his mirror.

20 October

Today seems very dull, Di, or like it's going to be. With the new quarter starting tomorrow, there's no homework except for math. I still have the last Sister to write, but…I don't know. I had some ideas, but now that number two has caused such a stir, I don't really want to get back into it. Mom is still bugging me to see numbers one and two, but I'm holding out. Maybe that's why I don't want to finish the series: I said that when I did, they could see them all.

And Mom actually wants me to change the ending of the next one so that my character doesn't kill herself. But that's the whole point—the endings have to be the same. Any other ending would be a lie. Although the first ending isn't truly the same, in my mind, that's her death. She joins the whale, rolled over and crushed in the surf, or swept out and dumped into the hypothermia rip tides.

They don't understand that the story might be what kept me from going for a one-way swim. You'd think that all of Kurdt Cobain's songs could have kept him alive, and Sylvia Plath's poems, and Hemingway's books, but apparently not. Even though I'm happy now, I can see that sometimes all the songs and poems and books and people you love aren't enough. And living is too much. Waking every morning, eating meal after meal, trying to sleep, over and over and over again.

I'm going to get myself all depressed again, brooding about this stuff, or maybe I'm just getting into Sisters mode, preparing to write. I could write it now, if no one was going to read it. And maybe that's the best way—not tell anyone it's finished, not show it to Griffin even. DJ? Possibly. I should let him read the second one too.

Okay then: it's back to Sisters, to the sound of the surf. Loud and constant and always changing. Peaceful and relaxing and sinister and foreboding.

Three Sisters

Sister III

*A*lly meets Cassie outside security, and they are quickly out of the airport and into the humid city air. Sean pulls up in his old station wagon, jumps out and gives Cassie a hug and a kiss on the head.

"Look at my little Littless," he says. "I like your new head."

"Thanks, Nickie."

He settles Cassie's duffel into the back of the car among the cooler and groceries and other bags.

"I'm going to sit in the back and try to work—I have this huge paper due Wednesday—you women sit up front."

Ally drives, and Cassie enjoys the newness of the Northwest landscape. Is that the only thing that's different? It feels almost the same, the three of them together.

"So, how are you?" Ally says. "Are you dealing okay after the collapse of our grand plan to skip you up to high school?"

"It was bad at first," Cassie says. "The whole thing was so stupid—they knew I could do the work, but they had to punish me for messing up their precious test."

"What about the kids—still hating?"

"They've pretty much forgotten about me. It got worse for a while, though."

"But it's better now?"

"Except for the occasional rude comment."

"And that boy you told me about, PJ?"

"DJ," Cassie says. "We actually told Mommy—that's what I call his mom—that we're friends, and she let him come up to the cabin with us last weekend."

"Overnight?"

"No way. But just to spend the day with him was amazing."

"Sounds serious."

"Not really," Cassie says. But she wonders. Is she missing him already?

From DJ, Cassie moves on to telling about her other friends and how she has finally found a group of people who don't think she's a freak—or at least don't mind.

"When everything went to hell with your plan to move to high school," Ally says, "did anyone tell you it would work out for the best?"

"Please. Don't try to tell me everything happens for a reason. I just got lucky."

"No such thing as luck."

"Whatever. Just don't try to tell me that God's calling the shots, or that there's some PURPOSE behind it."

"So why are you happy now?"

"Ask, instead," Sean says from the back seat, "why she was miserable before."

"It prepared her to appreciate this. Made her stronger." She flashed him a dirty look in the mirror.

"I said 'ask,' not answer."

"And what about people who never get better?" Cassie says. "What about the Holocaust, 2,700 people in the Twin Towers, that gay kid who was murdered in Wyoming."

"Yeah," Sean says. "That must have been a hell of a learning experience for Matthew Shepard—being tortured and beaten to death."

"You two are unbelievable. If life is so meaningless, why don't you just kill yourselves and be done with it?"

"Sartre would say that it's no consolation," Sean says. "Even after death, your body would continue, horribly, to exist."

"But I like existing," says Ally, shifting gears, pulling into the passing lane, and stomping on the gas.

"Me too," says Sean. "Mostly. I'm just giving you Sartre's take on it."

"And weren't we talking about how happy Cassie is? Why don't you get back to Being and Nothingness?"

"Sorry for intruding on your conversation," Sean says. "If you want my opinion, in the future, just tell me what it is. Otherwise, I'll keep my mouth shut."

Are they fighting? Cassie has never seen that. Irritation, tension between them, yes, but for a moment they hardly even seemed to like each other.

After they leave the vineyards and farms behind and come into the trees, Cassie rolls down her window and smells the salty sea. They cross slow creeks, and the road winds down through the forest and suddenly there it is—the Pacific.

The wind off the sea blows cold as they get out of the car at the house, so they dig in their bags for sweaters and windbreakers before going down to the beach.

"Remember," Ally says, "NO SWIMMING. If you get washed in, these rip tides will never let you out, so be aware at all times."

She and Ally walk the beach while Sean goes back to open up the house and work on his paper.

"And get started on dinner," Ally yells back to him. "And make sure the beer is cold!"

The breeze is damp, and a layer of salty mist forms on Cassie's sunglasses and face, even in the sunshine. She keeps thinking about DJ, how he would love this beach, and she wonders about things working out for the best. Ally's words, "Why don't you just kill yourselves," keep coming back to her. She's been there before, in the place with only one way out. It's not because there's no God and no purpose. She believes in individual purpose, but not that everything happens for a reason. September 11, The Sand Creek Massacre, Matthew Shepard—that would be too horrible.

(to be continued . . .)

21 October

I went along with Mom on a trip to the pharmacy last night, and I saw the perfect gift for DJ: a watch! It has a tan nylon band, a heavy-duty looking brassy case, and a little ring around the outside of the face that twirls so you can time things. Not only is it going to keep him from being late and getting in trouble, but it's quite handsome.

DJ loves the watch. I was too embarrassed to give it to him at lunch, so I pulled him into the library before. He was so cute when I gave it to him, and the first thing he did was put it on. I helped him fasten it, and it looked great peeking out from the cuff of his flannel shirt. At lunch he kept looking at it until Liz noticed, and then he showed it off to everybody. She thought it was the perfect gift.

"It's good to know you're taking care of him, Cassie. I was afraid you were going to get him in trouble."

"Oh, I'll still get him in trouble," I said, putting my arm around him and making him blush.

We schemed about how we were going to get to see each other this week, but it's not looking good. There's a track meet tomorrow at the big high school stadium. It's walkable, if Mommy will allow. Today we stayed after school to work on homework in the library. The math took us no time at all, so we got on a computer and did *Lord of the Rings* trivia from this website DJ found. Ms. Tayebnejad is cool, she didn't bug us, but guess who took a shortcut through the library and gave us a hard time? That's right, my favorite modesty enforcer. We were sitting next to each other, at the same computer, with me working the mouse with my right hand, and holding DJ's with my left. GASP! Gimme a break. She must be very lonely.

Sister III (continued)
"At least you unloaded the food," yells Ally into the side bedroom when they get back to the beach house. "And the beer." She pulls one from the fridge. "What's for din?"

"You tell me, veg-heads."

"Let's unpack, then we'll cook," she tells Cassie.

Ally hauls her bag into the master bedroom, and since Sean is using the other upstairs room as an office, Cassie goes downstairs and claims one of the kid's bedrooms. There are built-in bunk beds covered with snowy down comforters. A shelf contains Nancy Drew books and troll dolls. She slides the window open and the sound of the surf fills the room.

Upstairs, Ally's cutting veggies. The gas hisses under a big pot of water on the stove and garlic sizzles in olive oil. Cassie pulls a beer out of the fridge.

"No-no—Sean doesn't want you getting all boozed up."

"But you guys always let me have one beer."

"Well, one beer now, or a glass of wine with dinner—your choice, but no more."

The bottle cap digs into her hand, so she wraps a dishtowel around it, then takes a slug—cold and sweet and bitter. Ally gives her a rueful glance. "I guess a big sister's job is to corrupt."

They eat at the big round table in the living room as the sun slides behind the sea. Cassie sinks into her soft chair, the beer making her slow and sleepy. Sean stays away from the wine and stops Cassie when she grabs for Ally's glass, "Take it easy, you. That one beer was more than enough—your chair is about to swallow you whole." He wolfs his food and says, "Back to work—I want to get this thing done."

"Wait 'til your sister opens her birthday present," Ally says, getting up and returning with a flat, square package wrapped in hand-painted paper.

"Records!" Cassie shrieks.

"What makes you so sure about that?" Ally teases.

"She looked everywhere for those LPs, kid," says Sean. "Goodwill, E-bait, you name it."

"If you were a normal kid, it would be so easy, I'd just burn CDs of everything cool—"

"But you wouldn't love me the way you do."

"—instead of hitting the streets of Seattle and Portland, scouring the bins. Open it."

Cassie carefully unfolds the wrapping, which is magically folded so that it's secured without tape.

Inside are two Nirvanas and a Pavement.

"I didn't even know they did this on vinyl," Cassie says, sliding out Live in New York—*was it mastered on analog?"*

"That I don't know. But you better not turn up your snobby little nose—it cost me a pretty penny. Put it on."

Sean withdraws back to work while they crank up the speakers downstairs and build a fire. The beer wears off, leaving Cassie a little headachy as they put their feet up on the hearth and listen to Cobain's complaint, "Jesus don't want me for a sunbeam..."

That night in the half-world in and out of sleep, she seems to drift out the window on the sound of the surf. Home is out there, past the shore, on an island in the mist—or is it an underwater mountain? Anyway, it is home. And yet, not home. The halls are dripping limestone, and she wanders toward the sound of someone singing. Is it Ally? Mom? She descends along the outside wall of a spiral stairway carved into the mountain's heart while pale people hurry on the inside, rubbing past her, touching her with flapping fingers and peering up at her with green eyes like lamps, "Like Gollum," she thinks.

Cassie awakens to a day as foggy and rainy as she feels. It can't be a hangover from one beer, she thinks, but, oh, this headache!

Upstairs, coffee is on the warmer. She pours a mug and taps on the big bedroom door.

"Come," says Ally, who is alone, propped in bed with a cup of her own.

"Headache," Cassie says, setting her cup down on the bedside table and easing herself onto the goose-down. "Where's Sean?" she says into the pillow.

"He's in the other room."

"Working already?"

"I don't know. Sleeping?"

"But—he fell asleep in the other room?"

"We sort of broke up."

"You—" Cassie peers up from the pillow. Ally gazes at the big stone-covered wall that stretches up to the misted-over triangles of window at the ceiling's peak.

"Last weekend."

"You didn't say anything."

Cassie feels herself beginning to cry and simultaneously asks herself, *Why am I crying?*

Ally opens her arms, but Cassie shakes her head. "So this is, like, the last time," she chokes, "our last time together."

"It wasn't supposed to be—doesn't have to be. We're still the sisters of the paint, always will be."

"But not real sisters. Now everything is ruined."

Sean comes in. "Shove over," he says and sits on the bed. "She told you?"

Cassie nods, her face back in the pillow.

"I'm sorry, Littless. It had to happen."

"Why?"

"We were turning into better friends than we were lovers," Ally says. "It might even be worse on you than it is on us."

Cassie sits up to see Sean giving Ally a look that seems to say, "Speak for yourself."

"But it doesn't have to be the end," Ally persists. "Sean and I are still better than friends, like brother and sister. We'll always have a bond, and so will you and I."

"But now I'll never see you again," Cassie moans.

The rest of the day continues foggy, rainy, and cold. At least *the weather matches the way I feel, Cassie thinks, and I don't have to suffer under that Colorado sun. She realizes why Sean has been working on his paper, and she hates Ally for acting like everything is normal. She hates herself more for being so broken up. Shouldn't she have expected this? Shouldn't she have known it would happen? It sickens her to remember her fantasies of Ally and Sean getting married, of being a bridesmaid, of everyone being family forever. They were kids really, just as much as she was.*

And if they were kids, what about her and DJ? He wasn't even allowed to date, for God's sake—how was that going to end?

Ally makes breakfast and lunch, but Cassie doesn't feel like eating. Ally also makes a big fire to drive out the damp, and pots of tea to bring in the warm, but nothing touches her, and on top of everything, her headache gets worse and worse and she feels her period coming on—a thick, weighty malaise, a full brain and body bloat.

She lets Ally take her out on a rainy walk down the "nature trail"—really just a shortcut to shopping for the summerhouse set. The pines drip, and the fog lifts to reveal the ebb-tide bay and its wide mud flats with herons waiting by still pools, and it's beautiful, but it isn't any good.

(to be continued . . .)

22 October

After wondering whether I could get back into it, I got in so deep that I didn't want to come out. But I like the idea of spreading it out a little bit at a time and revising as I go. Griffin says that revising is the part that most young writers blow off—not me. Maybe that's why I like this triumvirate piece—it's ninety percent re-write.

DJ got permission to go to the big track meet, so after school we hit the path by the pines, cut down to the creek, and ducked into our secret glade. Kel didn't come, so it was just the four of us, and as usual, Quill and Liz plopped down and started making out the second we got there.

"Do you guys ever do anything else?" I complained.

Liz came up for air. "What?" she said.

"But this is the righteous make-out grove," said Quill. "That's why we come here."

"I know you guys have the same problem," Liz said. "There's no place to be alone."

I didn't think, with all four of us here, that it was all that private, but she had a point. And I didn't want to be a wet blanket, but it was kind of weird to be there when they got so intense.

"I think," said DJ, "Cassie and I don't feel all that alone when, like, we're here together with you guys."

"Exactly," I said. "But it's okay. I know what they mean."

"No, that's cool," said Quill. He sat up and shook the pine needles out of his hair. "What do you want to do? We could tell stories. I had this one I wanted to tell anyway."

"I don't know," said Liz.

"Come on. It'll be fun. Once upon a time, a few years ago, in these very woods, a girl was on her way to school."

"Not that one," said Liz.

"But this is the pines, Lizard."

"And don't call me Lizard."

"I think I know this story too," I said.

"I haven't heard it," said DJ.

"Lizzy-bith?"

"Okay," said Liz. "Get it over with."

"So this girl, we'll call her Susie, was on her way to school. But she didn't ever get there. Didn't actually plan to get there. She told Mother that she was going early, to do homework, to see her friends, to get help from a teacher. Strangely, she didn't bring her books. But her backpack was full. With a long rope."

"No, stop it," said Liz. "This really happened. It's horrible. My sister saw her. I won't listen anymore. Let's go to the track meet—I don't like it here anymore."

"Sorry, Lizzy-bith, I thought you were cool with it."

"Well, I'm not, all right?" She was already on her way out of the glade. We followed, Quill catching up to her, putting his arm around her only to be shrugged off.

"So, what happened?" said DJ.

"She hung herself," I said. "From a pine tree by the path, so that everyone saw her on the way to school."

"Jesus."

"Yeah."

"So," DJ said, "do you ever think about it?"

"Well, after my story—which I want you to read, by the way, I'm working on the third part—everybody thinks I'm about to go out and do it."

"But you're not."

"I've thought about it."

"Me too," he said.

"Really?" Somehow I thought it was just me, but of course it wasn't.

"After my brother left. You know how I said that he was such a jerk and everything? Well, I still missed him. He wasn't all bad. And I was pissed that he left me to deal with Mom all alone, and I don't know, I was just freaking out, I guess. For a while there, I thought about it all the time. There was all this pressure, like my mom was always at me."

"She seemed okay when I met her." I felt stupid for saying that, like I was telling him that he was wrong, or shouldn't feel the way he did. It's funny, but I wanted to tell him all the clichés that I hated so much: that he had his whole life to look forward to, so much going for him—all that stuff.

"She means well and everything," he said.

I took his hand. "That's something, right?"

"I guess so."

"But not enough."

We walked along quietly for a while. It was a perfect Indian summer afternoon, so warm that I stopped and pulled off my hoodie, and DJ's jean jacket, too. I was just wearing my Indian top with the spaghetti straps, and the sun felt great on my shoulders. I waved the jacket at DJ.

"Are you ever going to let me give this back to you?"

"Never," he said.

"I'd like to let you take it home and have your mom wash it, and have you wear it for a while. It's losing your good smell."

"I told her I lost it."

"Mad?"

"Nah, she's used to me losing things."

Finally I thought of something that, though corny, wasn't

too cliché: "Well, I'm glad you didn't cash it in, man. I like this jacket."

We laughed and hurried to catch up to Liz and Quill.

The track meet was all right. I saw my nemesis, the modesty cop, and though the school dress code is supposed to be in force at all extra-curricular activities, she looked away when she saw me in my skimpy top. I guess even she gets tired of bossing people around. Then for the hell of it, I put on my sweatshirt hood and draped the sleeve over my face like the veil of a burqa. It was a little warm, so it didn't last, but I enjoyed the strange looks people gave me.

Thanks to his new watch, DJ and Quill were right on time meeting Mommy. Liz and I hung back so she wouldn't see that I had DJ's jacket, then we walked home.

Liz complained about Quill, who knows she hates the story he was telling, but likes to freak her out.

"I'm getting a little tired of him, to tell you the truth," she said. "I hope we haven't fucked up our friendship."

"Interesting choice of words," I said.

"As if." She gave me a sideways look. "What about you and DJ?"

"He's the best. Can you believe I got to spend the whole day with him on Saturday? Maybe his Mom isn't so bad."

"What did you guys do up there?"

"He learned how to fly fish, we went hiking, you know."

"Did you take him to your special secret place?"

"Get out. You are way too nosy."

"Come on, tell Lizzy. You've got to tell someone."

"Let's just say that the relationship is progressing."

"How far?"

"Not too far, but just far enough."

Sister III (cont.)

Back at the house after their cold and misty walk, Cassie listens to her Nirvana record—just the last song, over and over again.

> In the pines, the pines,
> Where the sun don't ever shine,
> I would shiver the whole night through.

It was like the rhyme that kept turning up in the pines near school, stapled or taped or weighted with a rock by the tree where Susie Conners hung herself a few years back. There were lots of stories about her, how kids walking to school on the path through the pines found her hanging in a shaft of bright morning sun, the rhyme tacked to the bark of the tree:

> Where is the voice of Susie Sioux,
> the banshee black and blue?
> In the pines, the pines, in the sunshine,
> she'll shiver the whole day through.

Some stories said she was a punk-obsessed freak, that she wrote the rhyme herself, and made herself up in black and blue before she swung. Some say she wanted to join her beloved Kurdt, others that it was a goof gone wrong when her safety knot slipped, and she slowly strangled, clawing the vanilla-scented bark of the ponderosa pine with her black nails. Still others said that the rhyme appeared after she died—that she was a perfect little overachiever who couldn't take it anymore and was turned into a martyr by the gothic faction. They made up the verse and kept planting it to keep their myth alive.

How awful to die that way, Cassie thinks, how public like a frog, discovered by the hideous and hated herd. Give me a bristlecone high on a peak, eight-hundred years old and lightning-twisted, where the ravens will come and the wind will blow me into a pile of bones in the shade—my hard-won calcium that might have prevented a stooped old-age put to better use—nibbled by deer mice, dropped in the pellets of owls, scattered.

Or give me the sea; give me to the sea.

Cassie refuses dinner but suffers the comforting visits of Ally and Sean to her room. Ally plies her with soy protein shakes, ibuprofen, and ice for her headache. Finally, they go to their separate beds, and Cassie lies listening to the ocean. She pulls her comforter to the window seat and sees that the fog has blown away, and the stars are back, and fishing boats move up the coast like chimeræ of hope. Will-o'-the-wisp. Foxfire.

She thinks that now she's beyond her heartbreak over Sean and Ally, which is good because she doesn't have to hate herself for being so pathetic as to be driven to despair by something so common. And she might be beyond DJ, too: sweet DJ with his waves of dark hair and his brown eyes and his wide shoulders. (Where do those shoulders come from on a skinny boy when he becomes suddenly big, substantial?)

Distance, though. There is already distance between them.

Fast forward, time is video. Skip scenes, time is digital.

She will not live in realtime, she will not wait for the download to buffer realaudiorealvideorealemotionalrealspiritual.

Time is fluid.

Time is a river.

Time is current, rushing her away.

She won't be a fly, cast and reeled
by God,
by destiny plucked
and placed
again and again.
Time is liquid. Time is the sea.
Sweet by and by, sweet bye and bye—
the poetry of death like the sound of the sea.
The elegance and logic of the undertow has taken her.

Cassie pulls on a pair of jeans and climbs the stairs, silent
and barefoot on carpeted floors that don't betray her with a single
creak. A bottle of red wine waits on the kitchen counter, almost
full, the cork jammed back in after Ally's last glass.

"Drink me," it says, and the corks slides easily out, so she takes
a pull.

Back down and out the sliding glass doors to the steps to the
sea, she wraps a big woolen blanket around her shoulders, trailing
the wine, light in her left hand.

Just above the high tide mark, she sinks to the sand, pulls the
cork again, and tilts the bottle back. Warm red wine slides down her
throat, then she shivers and wraps the wool more tightly around her.

Sheep, Cassie thinks. Why shouldn't she enjoy their wool? Or
eat them, even? But at that, her stomach turns, though she sees that
it's all the same: lambs nibble grass and humans nibble lambs. But
not Cassie. She won't eat them, but she will cherish the wool.

Ebb tide breakers wash gently, surge weakly over the sandy flats.
Behind her, clouds slide away from the moon, and the smooth sea
goes silver and the sand glows. Cassie takes another long slug of wine,
corks it, and rises to walk the beach. She angles down to the water,

the sand firm and wet, the waves washing at her feet, soaking her dragging jeans. Her feet go numb, but inside she is warm, wrapped in wool and heated by wine. Alcohol is supposed to make you vulnerable to cold, she thinks, but, mmmmm—it makes her feel so warm.

Down here, she can't see the lights of the boats, only the stars, so bright despite the moon, and she walks, the dippers swinging before her, pointing the way to Polaris, who leads her up the beach.

Here, she thinks, she can let it all slip away. Even in the still of low tide and low wind, the sea is ever loud, dulling her mind while the moon gives everything a clear, crisp definition—colors washed out, leaving only shapes: smooth planes of sand, breaking planes of water, and the sky a dome overhead with the moon hanging and a few clouds floating. Houses on the beach are like those in a make-believe village, the lights dim and comforting, speaking of home and warmth. Someone has a wood fire, and a cedary scent mingles with the saltiness of the sea.

For one moment, though, a small cloud covers the moon; a rushing shadow from the sea, stealing the silver from the water and the light from the sand. In that moment, she feels what was hidden behind the glint of the moonlight—something sinister and unnamed that has no beauty, no love…nothing. A nothing that almost knocks her to the sand.

And for all her brave insistence on the purposelessness of the universe, her denial of a God that wills and guides it, Cassie is afraid, for here is something different from anything she's known. Even in the shadow she can see the workings of nature: the ecological web that doesn't need a god because it is beautiful and terrible and right just the way it is, and even people cannot, in the end, harm it. But within it somehow—nothing.

Then the shadow passes. The moon again scatters pale radiance over everything.

But the nothing thing is still there.

She places the wine bottle, still not empty, at the tide line, anchors it in the sand so she can pick it up on her way back. She wasn't sure that she was coming back, but now she thinks she might.

Cassie continues northward, back to the surf's edge, striding strong on the hard sand. She feels a bracing wind on her bare head, her eyes are strong and bright, and as she walks she's connected, aware, and alive.

This different thing that the shadow showed her meant that she was wrong about death. She'd heard the whispering of death in the waves. She'd heard it as a call, and she'd let herself think that since living was pain, death was relief, "this fever called living is over at last." And she thought there was logic in her equation: problem = life, solution = death. But death was not the point. Just because it always came to everyone and everything didn't make it so damned special, and just wanting to end, wanting it to end, wanting to get out didn't mean anything more than anything else.

Death is only part of it. That's what the shadow showed her. She knew that before, of course, but she had been, what? In love with death? She thought death would save her? She thought death was more spiritual than life? She laughs at herself as she walks and thinks, and she's aware of herself walking and thinking and how the walking helps her think and of the rhythm of her strides and her heartbeat and the waves and everything. She laughs and thinks, what? Was death my Jesus? Was death my saving Jesus?

Because death is nothing.

Pain is something, and fighting the world is something, and having friends and love, and not having them—

My mind's going too fast. It's too full, she thinks.

But I know I don't want nothing. Why did it seem so sweet before and so sinister in the shadow? It's nothing—no thing. But it can't be no thing, everything is some thing. She laughs again because now she is playing games. But she likes it.

The shadow scared her, and that's good. Everything that's alive is scared of death. Survival. She never valued it before.

Cassie's getting winded now, and hot from walking, and tired of thinking in these circles. She lets the wool fall loosely from her shoulders and slows to a stroll. The low tide has left a kind of lagoon, a clear pool separated from the ocean by a strand of sand. Farther up the beach, the lagoon opens and flows out into the waves so that there is a slight current. Larger waves break over the sandbar, and waters leach out of the beach, flowing through and out of the lagoon.

She wades into it, holding the wool above the icy clear water, numbly feeling the gravel and bit of shell beneath her feet.

Suddenly, she steps into a hole, instinctively holding the blanket above her head as she drops to her waist and struggles to keep her balance.

Should've known better, she thinks, after all the rivers I've waded. And this is cold as a snowmelt creek.

The blanket is almost dry, though her jeans are soaked. Testing the bottom before every step, she wades over to the other side, and cuddles up in the blanket on dry sand.

Now what? The moon sails high, and Cassie feels, surprisingly, still warm and good inside, though her legs are chilled. *Well, why not take a moonlight dip? She knows the rules on this beach—NO SWIMMING!*

But she is not going into the ocean, just the lagoon. She strips off DJ's jean jacket and her hoodie, but leaves her T-shirt, and runs into the water, making a shallow dive.

Mistake. The moment she plunges into the water, it sucks the heat out of her body. Breathless, she surfaces, gasping, staggering through the shallows out onto the sand. Shivering already, Cassie removes her T-shirt, wrings it out, and uses it to sop up as much water as she can. She pulls on the hoodie and can barely button the jean jacket.

Got to get moving, she thinks, already taking off down the beach, pulling her hood over her head and wrapping herself in the blanket. Teeth chattering, she begins a chant:

Wool, wool, wonderful wool,

Warm, warm, wonderful wool.

Still only early hypothermia. If she keeps on moving, she'll generate heat, and the wool will hold it—even if those wet jeans continue to suck it out of her. Stupid. How could I be so dumb? I was so happy with myself, getting scared out of my wits, and then thinking I had everything figured out.

She walks on dry sand until her legs burn, and the shivers calm to an occasional shake. She moves closer to the surf, and the walking is a little easier, but the rising tide keeps her from going down to the firmest sand.

Cassie walks. She walks for warmth, for the house and hot tea, for goose-down comforters and Ally and Sean warm in their beds. Maybe she'll climb into Ally's bed to get warm. She'll get a scolding for going out alone, and for drinking the wine, but she doesn't care. Just to get back and get warm. She walks.

She's getting more and more tired but has walked herself out of the shakes until she's warm in her core, when she starts to scan for the shape of the house. Just after the dunes begin to rise toward the bluffs, she should see it.

But they don't rise.

How far north did she go?

Cassie's legs ache and her jeans are chafing horribly, shrinking tight and hard against her so that every step is constrained and the skin of her thighs feels rubbed raw. Even the cuffs are grating against the tops of her feet. Since she's warmer, she risks wetting her feet and ankles again, just to avoid fighting the soft sand with every step. It's better down there, the sand is hard and not so steep. But the jeans are torture. She's got to get them off. She could walk all night, set a pace just easy enough to get herself home and keep herself warm—if only she could stop this chafing.

Cassie stops and tears at the button and zipper, pushes the damp denim down to her knees, and then kicks at the legs. They're stuck, rolled up around her ankles, so she steps on one leg and has almost pulled her foot out when the wave hits.

So big that it has only started to break when it hits her, it sweeps her off her feet and slams her into the sand, driving the air out of her lungs. Then it rolls her up the beach and sucks her back out.

Her empty lungs pull for air but get salt water. She feels bottom and pushes herself up, coughing, but before she can get a full breath, the current grabs the jeans around her ankles and pulls her under.

NO! I just found out—

Cassie fights to the surface. She coughs out water and pukes wine and gets air and coughs again, catching a glimpse of the silver moon, the fuzzy silvery moon through burning salt in her eyes, and she bobs for a moment, getting a half-water/half-air breath before the current takes her down again.

She's too cold.

And she doesn't have enough air.

And the current doesn't let her up, but sweeps her along by her ankles, her jeans like a sail in the wind of the water, until, loosened by the now gentle touch of the tide, they slip off and away.

And, eventually, she cools to the temperature of the water.

Her body is mostly water anyway, and part of everything— water and air and stone. But the spark that was life goes away, sucked into the nothingness she saw revealed in the shadow of a cloud before the moon.

Tomorrow, she'll wash up again, as all dead things do, to warm in the sun and dry in the wind and make people wonder what happened, where did the spark go, and why did the sea have to drown her life? Did she give herself as an offering, or was she taken the way someone must be taken, the way everyone must be taken, sooner or later?

Journal Ten

23 October

Dear Di,

That one kept me up almost all night, and I slept through writing club. I'm exhausted and don't feel like dealing with school at all, but I miss DJ. I wish he could come over here, and we could spend the day together.

When I got to school, DJ met me in the hall, seeming upset with me for missing writing club. I told him that I had been up until after three writing.

"I need to see you after school," he said. "Can you meet me at the pines?"

"Sure, what's up?"

"I don't want to talk about it with anybody else—don't say anything at lunch, okay?"

It was killing me wondering what was going on. DJ did a good job of acting normal at lunch, even when Quill teased him for being all freaked out that I missed writing club. He's so thin-skinned that it must have taken an effort.

I called Mom to tell her I was staying with DJ to do home-work, and she said that it was okay, as long as I came straight home after. I figured that gave me an hour or so at the most before she started getting anxious. This suicide-watch thing is getting old. She has even been talking about quitting the quartet. Obviously, she thinks that I need to be under guard at all times. She moved up the practices, so she can be home after school.

I really wanted to run home and get something warm before going up to the pines—a cold front came through during school, and it was *very* nippy outside—but I knew Mom would be home. I couldn't figure out how to explain why I needed a ski jacket to stay after school and study.

DJ hadn't worn anything warm either. We walked fast, trying to get some warmth going, up the path toward the pines.

"My mom knows about us," he blurted out, all dramatic, as soon as we were away from the after school crowd.

We hugged and held on—both of us were freezing.

"What happened?"

"The watch," he said. "She saw the watch you gave me."

"Oh no, the watch. That was supposed to *stop* you from getting in trouble."

"I know," he said. "It's not your fault."

"Come on," I said. "Tell me about it as we walk."

Every day he had been careful to take it off before he got home, but last night while he was in the bath—he still takes baths at night, Di, is he not cute?—she had taken his jeans to wash them, gone through the pockets, and found the watch. I guess she keeps pretty close tabs on his cash flow. She knew he hadn't bought it, and she accused him of stealing it.

He wanted to admit to stealing it, he said, at first. It's crazy but he thought that it would be "like betraying you, betraying us," if he told about us. But then he realized that there was nothing shameful in what we were doing, that denying me was the truly shameful thing.

So he told her, "My girlfriend gave it to me."

"Your girlfriend?" she said.

"Cassie," he said.

Then she "went, like, ballistic" and reminded him how she

had forbidden him to date. He had the guts to tell her that I said we weren't going out, we were just seeing each other. This didn't impress her very much, and she—big surprise—forbade him to see me.

But he refused to stop. He demanded that she change the rule and allow him to date. He told her he would see me as often as he wanted—with or without her permission. She could send him to Christian school, she could send him to his dad, but she couldn't run his personal life.

By this time he was pacing around the glade, and I was standing there hugging myself and bouncing around trying to keep warm.

"What did she say?" I imagined her breaking into tears at this point, but I guess she wasn't that good at manipulating.

"She kept on forbidding, and I kept on refusing to obey. She said that she's going to call my dad and the Christian school tomorrow but that I am not to see you."

"Does she know you're here now?"

"No."

"Didn't you call her or anything?"

"Are you kidding? Just so she can yell at me?"

"Come here," I said, and put my arms around him. "I think you are one brave dude for standing up to her. I'm proud of you."

"But we're in trouble, aren't we?"

"If she sends you to California, I don't think we'll be seeing much of one another."

"She won't. That's the last thing she wants."

"What about Christian school?"

"I'll still see you. Every day. And she can't afford it, anyway."

"So we've got nothing to worry about," I said, and kissed him.

"It is so freaking cold," he said and held me close.

"Like a witch's teat in a brass bra, as my dad always says."

"Your dad is cool."

"You're cool—freezing, even. C'mere."

But trying to wrap ourselves around each other wasn't really doing it. It must have been in the low thirties, twenties even, and the wind was blowing even in our sheltered grove. Kissing helped a little, our steamy breath together, his face cold, with blotches of pink on the cheeks and his neck warm under his hair and his mouth wet and steamy. But when he put his hand under my shirt, OW! It was cold.

Finally, we gave it up. We decided to go back to my house, but we had to wait until Mom left. His watch said it was almost five, and she was going to be gone by five-thirty. He would wait in the alley until the coast was clear. I found an old blanket in the garage, he wrapped up in it, and I ran inside.

Luckily, she left early, making me promise that I would be okay until Dad got home at six.

Big deal, I told her. Hadn't I already promised over and over again that I was okay?

She took off, I waited for at least a minute, then I called out the back door to DJ. I put some apple juice on the stove and dumped in a bunch of cinnamon and cloves. I was tempted to put some booze in there, but what if Dad came early? I could explain that DJ just got there, I thought, if we were innocently sitting in the kitchen, but not if we were drinking his Wild Turkey.

Then, miracle, Dad called to make me promise I would be okay if he didn't get home until seven.

Big deal, I told him. Hadn't I already promised over and over again that I was okay?

I immediately poured us each a little splash of bourbon in our cider—with that big 1.75 liter, how could he miss it?—and we went upstairs to my room to listen to records.

We had an hour, easy, because it was much more likely that Dad would be later than he said rather than early. DJ had to hear my Zeppelin album, and he thought it really did sound better on vinyl.

For a while, we just listened. It seemed too weird to be on the bed together, so I piled pillows on the floor and he lay with his head in my lap and I played with his hair as we listened to the good, loud music.

Then we fooled around, trying some of the things that we started out on the mountain on Saturday. We ended up on the bed, which, weird or not, is a lot more comfortable than a granite crag.

It felt so good, Di, just to be close together in my warm room on my soft bed. As the clock moved away from 6:30 toward 7:00, we lay holding each other, listening the Mamas and the Papas, which sounded kind of silly after Zeppelin and Nirvana. Then, with time pressing in on us, we forced ourselves to fix the bed and our clothes, wash the whiskey off our breath with mouthwash, and go downstairs.

I called Dad and told him that DJ had dropped by, and

could he stay for dinner? He was a little flustered about me having a boy over when I was home alone, but he said it was okay. We had just broken out the chips and salsa to further disguise our breath—we weren't even buzzed, it had just been a taste—when he showed up. He must have put the phone down and raced home.

DJ had set up some books and paper around the kitchen table while I was on the phone, so we were sitting there acting like we were doing homework when he showed up.

So far, so good, but I was starting to worry about DJ's mom. Sure enough, just when Dad was pulling out some frozen hamburger patties, asking DJ if he was a carnivorous man, she called.

"Yes, he certainly is here," Dad boomed. "Wandered in out of the cold and we're getting ready to give him a belly-full of dinner, if that's okay with you."

"You're very welcome. He's a fine guest."

"We'll see you later then, here's your boy."

He handed the phone to DJ, whose conversation seemed a little less relaxed than Dad's, though he—as Mommy must have been—was trying to make it sound as if everything was normal.

"We're sitting around the kitchen doing homework, Mom."

"Okay, Mom."

"See you later."

"Did she know you were here," Dad said to the interior of the refrigerator, "or was she looking for you?"

"Looking for me, I guess," said DJ.

"I wish you wouldn't do that, son. We parents get worried

if we don't know where our kids are. You're always welcome here, but would you please tell her where you're going?"

"Yes, sir," he said.

"Love this boy's manners, Cassie."

So we had dinner with Dad, who continued to be his personable self. Mommy came an hour or so later, and didn't even seem too mad, which I thought was a little odd.

Dad thanked me for calling him as soon as DJ arrived, making me feel guilty, and repeated to me that he preferred parents know when their kids are coming to our house.

"Your mother tells me that DJ's mother doesn't know that you two are—how did you put it so delicately?—seeing one another. Is this still the case?"

"No, he told her last night."

"Good. How'd she take it?"

"Not well," I said.

"Young love is never easy—"

"Dad? Please."

"Well, it isn't, honey. I'm not trying to be a wise guy—no more than usual, okay?"

"All right."

"I hope it works out well for you kids, and—try to keep some perspective. Don't get too all-fired serious too fast."

"Sure, Dad. I better hit the books."

"Give your dad a hug and kiss."

DJ is in such big trouble—I hope she doesn't send him away. Either California or Christian school would probably mean the end of us. I don't see how we can stay together with him at a different school and her trying to keep us apart.

And I am turning into a major sneak. I haven't done a bit of homework—I can't concentrate at all.

Ugh! I just remembered that I have to go to the shrink again tomorrow. Maybe I can make this my last appointment. I am so beyond that issue. The problem is life, but the solution is not death. That would be way too obvious.

24 October

More bad luck. Terrible luck. Dreadful luck. Abyssmal luck. Vile, ghastly, apalling, fucked-up luck.

No such thing as luck!

Fuck.

Who knows what's going to happen now, but it can't be good. Everything had calmed down with those morons at school—those mean, mean, horrible, horrible people—and today it all blew up again.

And the day started out so great!

DJ wasn't at school when I got there, so after checking the caf, I waited outside—hanging back where Mommy couldn't see my hated self. She dropped him off a few minutes later, and I rushed up to him with a big hug.

"What happened last night?"

"We compromised."

"You're kidding."

"It's not all good—but we actually worked it out."

"How did you manage that?"

"I think it was the report card. It came in the mail and she opened it before she came to get me. Four Cs and three Bs. It's my best one since fourth grade."

She didn't totally let him off the hook, though. The first thing she said was that he was grounded for two weeks for going off without permission. But then she asked him about the grades. He told her I had helped him, not doing his homework for him, but doing it with him. He said that I motivated him. She was so relieved that he didn't have any Fs or Ds that she had to admit that something good must be going on. She is allowing him to see me, occasionally, under supervision.

"But not for two weeks?"

"There's school, and she's going to let us study together, here—but I have to get a note from the librarian or a teacher or someone to prove I was actually here."

And then it happened.

Nathan walked by and just had to make a crack at me.

"American Taliban slut," he muttered, and kept walking.

"What did you say?" said DJ.

He turned around. "You heard me, punk."

"Take it easy, Gimli," I said quietly.

"No way," he said. "This is, like, bullshit." He stood up and stepped toward Nathan. "You need to stop this shit."

"DJ—"

"Do I, punk?"

"You also need to apologize."

"Oooo, and you're gonna make me? Come on."

Nathan gave DJ a shove, and DJ punched him a quick one to the face.

I don't think it connected very hard, and too bad because

it was the last good shot he got. Nathan's fists started flying, and another kid pushed DJ into him. Then they both went down with Nathan on top.

I was yelling, "NO! Stop! Get off him!" but by now a crowd had circled us with everybody yelling.

DJ struggled to get him off, to get away, to protect himself while Nathan hit him and hit him. I grabbed at Nathan, trying to pull him or push him off. "Leave him alone, get off!" I screamed, and I heard kids starting to yell, "Get her, get her off!" Somebody grabbed at me, and I flung my elbow back and felt it connect with something hard.

Then Mr. Bad was there, bellowing in our faces, "STOP IT RIGHT NOW AND GET AWAY FROM EACH OTHER!"

We all went limp.

I moved back and Nathan got up. Dr. Hawk got between Nathan and DJ. Some teacher I didn't know got in front of me and forced me back while Mr. Bad knelt down by DJ. His nose was bleeding, and his whole face was red from crying and being hit. I was crying too, but Nathan was all puffed up, shaking his shoulders and acting like he couldn't wait to get in for another punch.

We were all led off to the office—DJ to get cleaned up, Nathan to wait for interrogation, and me straight into Dr. Hawk's office.

"Cassie, Cassie, Cassie," he said with tired relish. "I didn't expect to see you again, but I should have."

"Can I call my dad?" I said, taking a tissue and wiping my nose.

"They're making the call right now. Why don't you just tell me everything that happened while we wait?"

"I'm not saying anything until my dad gets here."

I was thinking, "without my lawyer," and the thought sent me into a spasm of laughter, and then sobs. I took some more Kleenex. I was determined not to cry in front of him, though the laughter was probably worse.

"If you won't talk until Daddy gets here, you can wait in the in-school suspension room." He called on his walkie-talkie to Mr. Bad, who came to escort me out.

DJ was sitting on the bench, holding a tissue to his nose but looking otherwise unhurt.

"I'm sorry, DJ," I said.

"You didn't do anything wrong," he said.

"But it's all my fault."

I sat and stewed in the hole, pretending to do homework so the monitor wouldn't bug me, and finally Mom and Dad showed up.

Dr. Hawk wanted to handle it, but they insisted on the head principal, so we had a big meeting in Mrs. Trumbull's office with both of them and Mr. Bad. I told what happened, leaving out the "American Taliban slut" and just saying that Nathan was bugging me.

"Is that consistent with what the others had to say?" Mrs. Trumbull asked.

"Pretty much," said Mr. Bad, in his element as security officer. "Except that Nathan said Daniel—or DJ—attacked him for no reason, and then when he defended himself, Cassie jumped on him and attacked him too."

"Come on," I said, "You were there, I was just trying to get him off."

"You should have left that to us. And you threw a pretty good elbow at Stephanie Powers—she's going to have a big black eye."

"Well, she shouldn't have grabbed me."

Dad patted my arm and Mom my knee, as if to tell me to be quiet, and he continued. "Witnesses generally agreed with Nathan, though one of them did say that Cassie had been trying to get the boys to stop."

"What about Daniel?" said Mrs. Trumbull, turning to Dr. Hawk.

"He said that Nathan directed an epithet at Cassie, and when he subsequently requested a retraction, Nathan pushed him, and he hit Nathan. He said that Cassie didn't do anything except try to stop them—but he was protecting her in the first place, so—"

"That doesn't make him any less reliable that this Nathan kid," Dad interrupted. "What, may I ask, was this 'epithet' that was directed at our daughter?"

Dr. Hawk looked at his notes and cleared his throat, "I believe it was, uh, 'Taliban slut.'"

"Taliban slut?" said Dad, and looked at Mom, then me. "Cassie, did this kid call you 'Taliban slut'?"

"'American Taliban slut,'" I said, quietly—torn between desiring dramatic effect and wishing for the ability to make myself invisible.

"My God," said Mom.

"DJ had the right idea," Dad said. "Generally, I go for the

nonviolent solution, but in this case, I might have clocked the little son of a bitch myself." Dad delivered this in a quiet voice that brought silence to the room. I looked at him, my hero— a big man, leaning slightly back, at ease and in control as he turned his eyes on everyone around the table, ending with the principal.

"I understand your feelings, Mr. Sullivan," she said. "And if Cassie has been subjected to this kind of language, then—"

"It's not the fucking *language* that concerns me—" Again, he was cool and quiet, "but the malice it conveys. Cassie, is this the first time such 'epithets' have been directed at you?"

"No."

"Did any of you know this was going on?" Mom asked.

"I did not," said Mrs. Trumbull. "Dr. Hawkens?"

"No," he lied.

"Mr. Badagliaccio?"

"No ma'am."

What about the time somebody threw the football at me and they were yelling, "Osama"?

"We seem to be as surprised as you are, Mr. and Mrs. Sullivan."

"You'd better tell us now what's been going on, Cassie," said Mom. "Did this start with choir?"

"Before that," I said. "But I was handling it myself, and until today, I thought it was over."

"Come on," said Dad. "Spill it."

So I had to talk, and it all came out: the tripping and the flat tires, the bathroom wall, the notes in the locker—which Mr. Bad went to retrieve—the razors, the spilled books, the kicked chair, and what became infamously known as the "epithets," beginning with "Osama O'Sullivan." Dr. Hawk now included the part of DJ's story he'd left out, how DJ claimed that I had been teased and taunted for weeks. Mrs. Trumbull seemed only slightly less horrified than Mom and Dad. I left out my own impression that Bad and Hawk seemed to hold the same opinion of me as my classmates, but I let Mr. Kimball have it for talking about me to the other kids. When Bad showed up with the notes from my locker, there was general outrage all around the room. Some of these were even worse than my first note:

"If you hate America so much, why don't you go suck the dicks of the whole Taliban army then go to Iraq and fuck for Saddam until you bleed."

But they weren't all negative! Some were permeated with love: "I hope that you will repint so that you will not suffer an eternaty in hell with the other muslum sinners."

Nobody could believe that I had been trying to deal with this on my own. Mrs. Trumbull wanted the name of every single kid who had ever said an unkind word.

"Mr. Badagliaccio, run the security tapes from Friday, September 20th and Monday, September 23rd—let's see who was stuffing that locker. Dr. Hawkens, start going through Cassie's list. I want to interview each one personally. Mr. and Ms. Sullivan, I want you to know that Tabor Middle School is not the kind of place that tolerates this kind of behavior. I will personally see to it that we have, as of this moment now, seen the very last of this harassment. Cassie's mistake was in not telling, but now that she has, she will be safe from bullying.

"But," she said, "you know we have a zero tolerance policy

on fighting, too. Given the circumstances, her suspension will only be for the rest of today, which should allow time for the situation to cool off a bit."

"Let me get this straight," said Dad. "My daughter is harassed, her friend is attacked, she tries to stop the attacker, so she gets suspended?"

"She did throw an elbow. What am I supposed to tell the other girl's parents?"

"Fine," said Mom. "Come on Cassie, Gale, let's go home. Mrs. Trumbull, would you call us with the details of how you're handling this? And Cassie may be out tomorrow, too. I'll call the attendance line."

"I'm not sure we can excuse—"

"You're kidding, right?" said Dad.

"Whatever you need to do, Mrs. Trumbull," said Mom. "I'm sure we can live with the consequences."

So we went home for lunch and a little chat. Mom asked me if I wanted to stay home with her tomorrow.

"Oh, don't worry," I said. "Mrs. Trumbull is going to fix everything, right? Nobody's going to bug me anymore—instead they'll treat me with kindness and respect. That's what they always do to people who get them in trouble."

"You did not get them in trouble, Cassie, they did it to themselves."

"Duh, Mom—don't I know that? But that's not how they're going to see it."

Dad had been very quiet since we left the school. "So is that why you kept silent—you feared reprisal?" It sounded so ugly, like I was so pathetic. And that's all it took. I was crying again.

"I ruin everything," I said.

"You ruined nothing," Mom said. "Gale, this is not her fault."

"I know it's not her fault. Cassie, I don't blame you."

"Yes, you do. You think I'm a coward, and now I've ruined everything for DJ."

We were sitting around the kitchen/conference table and now they got up and went into comfort-mode with Mom standing beside me rubbing my shoulders and Dad pulling a chair next to me. Dad said that if he sounded mad, he was, but not at me. They both said that I was very brave, that they understood why I hadn't told, but they wanted me to tell them everything in the future. How could they help me if I didn't share my problems?

They thought that I had been through "a tumultuous couple of weeks" and that I should take Friday off. Mom would skip rehearsal, cancel her lessons, and take me up to the cabin—tonight if I wanted.

But I wanted to see DJ and Liz and Quill, or at least Liz and Quill, since DJ was going to be suspended. I also wanted to go back to prove that I wasn't afraid.

"I never thought I'd see the day," said Mom, "that I'd have to beg my girl to skip school and go to the mountains."

"I just can't stand the thought of you going back," said Dad. "I really wish we had gotten you out of there. To think that some little punk told my sweet girl—my sweet, pure-souled girl—that she was going to hell." He was tearing up. "And then you thought I didn't approve of you. I'm sorry, baby. Don't you listen to them—you are good and brave and better than anyone."

"You are," said Mom. "You're the best."

It's sweet of them to say, Di, but it's just more self-esteem stuff.

I tried to call DJ, but nobody answered. Then I tried to call Ally, same thing. At least I can see Liz and Quill tomorrow. I'm clinging to the hope that DJ's compromise with Mommy will hold, but I'm afraid that she'll send him away now, and once again, I'll be all alone.

Before she left tonight, Mom again tried talking me into taking the day off tomorrow. As if it would be a big selling point, she said that Dr. Velez might be able to fit me in, since we had missed our session today. I didn't tell her, but I am not going back to that shrink. I'm not depressed, I'm not suicidal, I'm just mad.

I called Liz, hoping she could come over. She couldn't. I told her about DJ's compromise, but she didn't seem overjoyed.

"We'll see how long that lasts now," she said.

"We can hope, can't we?"

"I guess so. I don't know—I just wish..."

"What?"

"I told you not push it with her. Now look what happened."

"You're right—it's all my fault. He's going to be in trouble now, and you're mad at me, and I can hardly wait to get to school tomorrow and see what Matt and his gang have in store for me."

"He's suspended, I heard, and a bunch of others too, but you'll hear all about it tomorrow."

"What happened? Tell me now."

"I gotta go, Cassie. I'll see you tomorrow."

Excellent. This is going to be even worse than I thought. I really am all alone.

25 October

It seems that my old wish for invisibility came true today, but it's not what I had in mind when I wanted to be left alone. Only Quill still talks to me, though Liz did for a few minutes.

When I got to school with just enough time to hit my locker and make it to class, I could feel people looking at me. But when I turned to them, they turned away. A few people looked at me with curiosity, but the majority gave me the sides of their heads. I didn't see Matthew, Jenny, or Nathan, and it wasn't until later that I heard the story on that.

In class it was strange too. Though it was nice not to have people saying rude things, kicking my chair, or tripping me as I walked to my desk, it was another kind of insult to be treated as if I wasn't there. The teachers ignored me too, except for Sinclair—not to the point of avoiding eye contact, they just didn't engage me. Or was I being hypersensitive?

I saw Quill after first block, on my way to science.

"How's DJ?" I asked.

"Thank you for greeting me," he said, "in such an artfully mannered manner. I return your salutations." At least he was still normal—for him.

"Come on," I said. "Have you talked to him?"

"Master Dwarf is grimly beset by a host of enemies. But

he is stouthearted and will not fall. The sons of Aulë are made of the very stuff of the mountains, and they will endure. Even in death, 'tis said, they wait in some dark and silent deep, eyes faintly gleaming like bits of phosphorescence in the mountain's heart until the final melodies of the song are heard."

"Do you stay up all night composing these things?"

"And you, good Cassandra, how do you fare? How, noble heart, in this foul, fetid air?" He said fee-tid—or feet-ed? I always thought it was feh-tid. And was he talking in rhyming couplets?

"If Master Dwarf prevaileth, so can I—" I paused, searching for the rhyme. "But I would see him before by and by."

"Good luck," said Liz, suddenly behind me. "He got sent to Christian school."

"No, he didn't."

"Ask Quill."

"Quill?"

"She made him get a haircut." He lapsed back to the stoner-surfer voice. "And burned his CDs, and his Anti-Flag T-shirt. And then, then she fed him to the Christians, at SCCS."

"Oh, my God. She snapped. She totally snapped."

"You know, Cassie," said Liz, and then she stopped. "I gotta go." She turned and walked away.

"Liz?"

She waved back, over her shoulder.

"It wasn't your fault," said Quill. "She should be pissed at DJ's mom. But don't worry, the Lizard doesn't hold a grudge." A rare and serious moment with Mr. Quillen before he turned it on again. "We're, like, late dudess—we better make like bananas and split or, like, we're going to get a detention. Catch you on the flip-flop, pop-top."

I wandered into class half-stunned. Cut his hair? Burned his CDs? Christian school? Mommy had snapped. That moment of reasonableness, all shot because of one little fight, one suspension.

But DJ. My DJ. Would I ever see him again?

Liz was not around at lunch. I sat with Quill and Kel, who told me what I had missed yesterday. The whole eighth grade had been buzzing with excitement, as always happens after a fight. People were getting called out of class and some weren't returning. Some still hadn't today.

Sixth hour, Mrs. Trumbull came to the reading classes. She said that an eighth grade girl had been the victim of severe harassment. Those responsible were being punished, and if anyone had a part in it to confess, they could see her privately.

The harassment was to stop immediately: not one more note, not one more nasty name, not even one more rude look. It all had to stop. If it continued, those responsible would face disciplinary action and possible criminal prosecution.

And furthermore, "That's just not the way we treat people here at Tabor Middle School, kiddos. We're a kind school with kind students."

In Kelly's class, some kids tried to put the blame on me. She told them that I might be wrong, but two wrongs didn't make a right, and they still had to leave me alone.

So that is what they were doing, leaving me alone. It didn't matter much, though.

DJ was gone. Who knows when I'd see him again. I kept

forgetting that, thinking of how we'd talk about all this, and then I'd remember, "Oh, right. He's gone."

I asked Quill to tell him that I was going to call, and that he should call me as soon as he could.

"I hate to sound like Liz, but good luck," he said. "His mom has this blocking thing on the phone so he can't call when she's not home, and she has caller ID for when she is."

"Will you tell him I'm sorry about what happened, that I have to talk to him, I have to see him?"

"He blames himself for getting in the fight, but I'll tell him. As for seeing him—you're not getting past his mom. She's a walking fortress. He might as well be in the dungeons of Melkor."

"But what if I were Lúthien?"

"He thinks you are—but even she couldn't get through."

I made it through the day all right, I guess, phasing in and out of realizing that DJ was not going to be there. I fantasized that Mommy was going to come to her senses, revert back to the original plan. But I didn't really believe it.

When I got home, Dad was happy with my reassurance that nobody was harassing me and my promise to tell if they did. I skipped the news about DJ—I couldn't bear to talk about it.

Now I'm going to listen to every side of my Neil Young triple album. It should help pass the night away. For some reason I've got one of the songs, "Soldier," stuck in my head. Just one looping lyric, over and over, "*Soldier, your eyes shine—like the sun. I don't know why...*" Then, at the end, you can just barely hear that he changes "soldier" to "Jesus." I don't know why.

I also need to hear "Cortez the Killer" because it's so long and slow and has all that sad guitar that pulls me right into the middle of the sadness and somehow makes me feel good about it, right about it, as if nothing else could be so true as long sustained guitar notes and the way they make me feel. I know that any normal girl in my circumstance would turn to Creed or Godsmack for solace in a time like this, but Neil Young is one of the best. He's the one who taught me about the Kent State shootings and Richard Nixon. (Though Dad says Nixon does not have soul, anywhere, no matter what Neil says.)

Dad was tickled when he heard me listening to this record, when I first got it, and he explained the historical references—so I guess I should say Dad taught me, not Neil. He also took me to Red Rocks to see Neil and Crazy Horse, and it poured rain on us the whole second half of the show. During the encore it started raining harder and harder, and everyone was leaving. Then, when the place was three-quarters empty, they came out and played *another* encore. Dad and I were totally soaked, but it was the greatest.

So, Di. Here we are. More stories of yesteryear, and all our yesterdays have lighted fools the way to dusty death. What's going to happen next? Trip to the mountains tomorrow, without DJ. Back to school on Monday, and no DJ. Tuesday, no DJ. Wednesday, et cetera. Tomorrow and tomorrow and tomorrow. Thank you. Good night.

26 October

The cold weather is holding on, and we almost didn't come up to the cabin. Mom thought we'd better, though, because her concert season starts next week and it'll be a while before she gets another chance.

I broke down the tipi for winter, and we're all cooped up inside. Mom and Dad are reading downstairs, and I'm up in the loft, feeling bored. I should make some sort of new plan for dealing with all those tomorrows. But I'm done with plans. I'm also done with suicidal fantasies, and I refuse to get depressed. I think I'll take a nap.

Slept away the afternoon, then there was dinner and the big family discussion.

First was the matter of my report card, which had arrived Thursday, but we hadn't yet discussed. A few Bs aren't the end of the world, but combined with everything else, Mom and Dad don't think it's a good sign.

Then they wanted to know if we could talk about some of those options that they had suggested when my Grand Plan fell through. We might see if there are any spaces in one of the other middle schools or in the charter middle school. We also might consider some kind of alternative high school for next year. They don't feel so good about Tabor anymore, after what has been happening to me there, and they want me to get a good start in high school.

I couldn't muster the energy to put up a brave front about it, but I said that I would rather just tough it out for the rest of the year, and then go to Parker next year. I was not up for another big, intense thing with them, but it was obvious that I was down again. They kept asking me what it was, and I kept saying I was okay. But when they wanted to know what had happened to DJ after the dinner at our house and the fight the next day, I had to tell them about him going to Christian school.

Then they were getting all worried again. To reassure them, I explained my new philosophy on death—how I was over the suicide thing for good, that I realized it was not the answer to life—that living was. They very much approved of this, and thought that it would be good to talk this over with Dr. Velez. My next appointment is Tuesday.

"But I don't need her anymore, then, do I?" I said in my English accent. "I've got it sorted out on my own."

"Just because you have your thoughts together," said Mom, "doesn't mean you don't need to keep going to therapy."

"I don't see why I should."

"Because it is easier to decide what you're going to do than it is to act the way you've decided," said Dad.

"But my mind's made up. I'm going to keep living, but I'm not going to any more therapy. I tried it once, it was okay, but I don't need it."

"How about four more sessions?" said Mom. "And then if the doctor thinks you're ready, you'll be done with it."

"How about none?"

"Maybe six would be better."

"Mom, I'm not five years old and we're not bargaining over M&M's. This is my head that you want to shrink, and I should say if I want it shrunk. I don't."

"We don't want your head shrunk," said Dad. "She's not Nurse Ratched, and we're not sending you off for a lobotomy. We want you to be healthy and safe."

"Good. I am."

"Cassie, I spoke to Dr. Velez," Mom said. "She thinks you are still at risk. And now, you've just suffered another loss—don't you think you should have a little extra support, at least until you see how it turns out? Things are going to be really different for you and DJ now."

"Different? It's over. I'll never see him again."

"But you might—you never know."

"Cassie, why are you so opposed to this?" Dad asked.

Thanks a lot, Dad, I thought. Will the probing questions ever end? Will I ever be trusted to make a decision without the cross-examination?

"Because I am," I said, then foolishly turned the question back on them. "Why are you so *un*opposed to it?"

"Because we are," said Mom.

Okay. I asked for that one.

"Yes," said Dad. "We are. We're taking you to a few more sessions. You can talk to her, and if it helps, you'll thank us. If it doesn't, you won't be out more than a few hours."

"What if I sit there and refuse to talk to her?"

"Then you'll guarantee that it will be a waste of time. But you'll go nonetheless."

"Fine," I said. "May I be excused, already."

"Fine," he mocked. "Be excused, already."

27 October

Last night after writing, I lay around and stewed and tried to read a little. This morning I was still mad about the therapy thing, and I didn't feel like hanging around Mom and Dad.

I hate the way they are watching me now—they didn't even want to let me go on a little hike by myself. Not that it would have been much fun anyway. Wherever you go, there you are.

I'd hoped to find a message from DJ when we got home, but no such luck. I tried calling him, three times, but nobody picked up, and there was no anwering machine or voice mail.

I did have a message from Liz, who said she was "sorry for being such a witch with a capitol B." She promised to call me if she heard from DJ.

Then I called Quill, who saw DJ at church this morning. Mommy isn't letting him use the phone at all, and they couldn't talk much before DJ was whisked away. He starts at SCCS tomorrow. He wanted Quill to tell me that he's going to see me soon—he'll figure something out.

That made me feel better, but not by much. Part of me wants to believe that we can salvage something, the rest of me knows that it's over.

I did some homework, and then I went out to my balcony. It's back to warm autumn weather, the trees bare against the blue sky. We gained an hour today, so the sun was gone behind the mountains a little after four, and the cool air was coming down.

28 October

I couldn't go to school today, Di. Couldn't do it. I was all ready with my books and homework and lunch, but I ducked into the pines.

Okay, I guess it wasn't all that spontaneous. I brought an

extra sweater, though the warm weather is holding, and you, Di. And since I never bring you to school, I must admit that I had this idea in the back of my mind all along—leaving myself an out, in case I decided against school.

Mom has no rehearsal today, so I can't go back home. It looks like a day in the pines—I think my tipi in the mountains or the Oregon beach house are the only places I'd rather be.

I brought my *Fellowship* paperback and spent the morning reading. It was cold at first, but I had my sweater and DJ's jacket. Now the sun is overhead and shines down onto the fallen pine needles in the middle of the clearing. I took off my sweater and jacket, spread them out, and I'm lying down in the sun. There's a layer of warm, sleepy air on the ground, smelling dry and brittle with pine needles. Up in the treetops, the wind is blowing, but down here all is still and quiet except for the drifting screams of recess at the elementary school.

Last time I was here alone, I imagined Middle Earth, and being there with DJ. Now I don't see any point in imagining, and though the book keeps my mind occupied, I'm getting drowsy. Maybe it's time for a nap.

After dozing off, I woke up cold and disoriented—about half an hour *after* school let out. Oops! I rushed home, and Mom was in her studio with a lesson, so I had time to get myself together before fibbing to her about hanging around after school with Liz. I called Liz, in the meantime, half to make sure that she hadn't called or anything.

"Are you okay?" she wanted to know. "Quill and I were worried about you."

"Yeah, I'm fine," I said. "I just couldn't deal with school today. So, I sort of stayed home."

"Is your mom cool with that?"

"She doesn't really know. She left early with my Dad, and just got home a while ago." I don't know why I made that up, but I didn't want to tell her I was at the pines all day. Maybe it seemed too strange, and also, I wanted to keep it a secret. Never know when I'll want to do it again. Like tomorrow.

"So you caught the attendance robot?"

"What?"

"The attendance robot that calls your house between four and four-thirty if you're unexcused."

"Shit," I said. "I'll call you back."

I hit speed dial for the voice-mail as I flew down the stairs to check the caller ID. Sure enough, there was a message: "This is the Tabor Middle School attendance office. Cassandra Sullivan was absent and unexcused for one or more classes on today, Monday, October 28th. Please contact the attendance office. Goodbye." I hit delete, and checked the caller ID. That just said "School District," so I left it. Since she hadn't caught the call, I could say I had called home to tell her I was late.

I rang Liz again.

"Thanks," I said. "You saved my life."

"No problem. You erased the message?"

"Yeah. Will they call again?"

"No, but it's gonna show up on your report card unless you get it excused."

"Not bloody likely."

She laughed. "Yeah, well, I could call in for you, but I don't sound too parental."

"So. Have you heard from DJ?"

"Nope," said Liz. "What about you?"

"Nothing."

"He's gotta be hurtin'. I can't believe his mom harshed out this bad. How are you?"

"Terrible." And suddenly I was. I think I had been in shock. I said before how I would go in and out, thinking I'd tell DJ about something, wondering when I'd see him next, and then remembering that I wouldn't get to. This was the worst yet. I felt all bruised and raw inside.

"I have to go," I said. "Bye, Liz. I'll see you tomorrow."

I stuck my face in my pillow, getting ready to let loose with a few sobs, when I heard Mom creaking up the stairs. I tried to get myself together, but I must have looked a mess.

"How was your day?" she said and then when she saw me, "Oh, sweetie, are you okay?"

"I'm fine, Mom. Just a little privacy right now, please. I'll be down in a minute."

When I came down, I swore that I was all right, just had a moment of sadness. That's understandable, I'm told. It's hard to lose someone you care for, and she could tell I really cared for DJ. But maybe I'd still see him. I should give it time, and keep a little hope that it won't end up too badly.

Inevitably, the subject of Dr. Velez came up at dinner. I didn't fight about it, but I didn't act like I was going to put my best foot forward, which they were dying to hear. I confirmed that I remembered it was at 4:30 tomorrow, with drop-off by Mom and pick-up by Dad.

The other night, I was thinking that I need some sort of plan to get through school's wall of hostility, to get through afternoons and evenings and weekends of time. I'm coming up with a big, fat goose egg. Not only am I done with plans, I appear to be out of ideas.

After brooding on this for a while, I decided that I might as well try to call DJ again. It rang and rang and rang, and I hung up. Then I started calling every five minutes, and letting it ring for a minute. After half an hour, I just let it ring. I put down the phone and went to the bathroom. I brushed my teeth and washed my face and got ready for bed. When I picked up the phone again a voice was saying, "If you want to make a call, hang up and try again."

"Thanks," I said. "I *would* like to make a call." I hung up, pressed redial, and got a busy signal. DJ has got to know that this is me, I thought. At least he knows I'm trying.

But maybe he doesn't. It's just so wrong. You can't keep people apart like this. Ever since I pulled myself together after my last call to Liz, I have been numb and dumb. Now I'm getting mad again, but it's not doing me any good.

I picked up the phone to try DJ again, but Mom was on the line. I'm going to listen to his favorite of all my records, Zeppelin. And LOUD. Was it only five nights ago that we were on this bed together listening to this record?

Oh, God. Here come the tears.

Journal Eleven

29 October

Morning, Di. I don't even think I am going to bring my books today. Why haul all that dead weight up to the pines? I'll go up to the secret glade and read for a while, then I'll double back home. Mom has a quartet rehearsal and should be out of the house by nine. This will all come back to haunt me, I know, but I need some time to myself.

Unbelievable. I hope Liz does get a needle stuck in her eye. I should have known I couldn't trust her when she wouldn't swear by the ring.

This morning, as I came up from the creek, I heard laughter. I thought it was coming from people going to school on the bike path until I recognized Liz's voice.

I climbed the hill, my footfalls as quiet as a hobbit's on the pine needles. The woods are thinner on the lower side, but because of the slope, I could stay hidden until just before I got a view of the glade. As I crept up, I knew it was Liz for sure. Then I saw her, her sister, Lonnie, and three other people—high school friends of Lonnie, I think. I ducked out of sight behind a tree.

I sat there, listening to the laughter float down to me. I smelled weed and then cigarettes on the wind. After it had been silent for a time, I got up and made my way to the grove.

I was surprised not to find any cigarette butts lying around, and glad, though I figured it was because Liz knew I would freak if I found them. Probably her way of being discreet, but it didn't matter. Soon this would be a well-known party site. I stayed and brooded for a while, but I didn't want to spend any time there. It wasn't my place anymore, not that I ever owned it or had any claim on it. Discovery, maybe. I should be surprised that it hadn't been found out before.

I left the way I came and caught the alley up to my house by the downstream bridge. By that time it was nine, and I was sure Mom was long gone, but I checked for her car before I went inside.

It was too good a place not to share, I guess. Not that I forgive Liz. A promise is a promise. Needle eye, hope to die. No crosses count.

I'm up in my room now, and it feels strange to be here in the middle of the morning, alone, on a school day. But the pines feels all sick to me now, so where can I go? I wish I was up in the mountains, lying on the Carrock in the wind. That's where I should be—I could breathe up there. I could think.

I closed my eyes, took a few deep, slow belly-breaths, and came to a conclusion: I'm lightin' out. I'm headin' for the hills.

But how? I don't want to hitchhike. Even if there weren't weirdos to worry about, I don't think the cops would just drive by a kid my age in the middle of a school day—even if I stopped thumbing and was just walking. I wish we had trains or buses or something. Wait—maybe I could take the casino bus and get dropped off at the forest service road up to the cabin.

Well, that was too perfect to work. I cut down the alley, over through the college, caught the free shuttle, and I made the bus stop just as the Gold Rush pulled in. But the stupid driver wouldn't let me ride.

"We don't take unaccompanied minors, kiddo. Company policy."

Now I'm having a coffee at the Feed & Read, while I figure out what to do. Luckily, people downtown are used to seeing high school students around, and I look old enough. I risk running into Dad—but his office is south, by the courthouse, and he's probably stuck in court right now.

I'm resolved more than ever. I've got to get out of town, get my head together, get to a place where nobody will bug me or try to shrink my head. I need to go where the air is clear and cold and free from the sound of machinery. I need to be high in the mountains, tucked safely into a valley of the land and open to the sky.

The question is, how am I going to get to the mountains? I don't want to hitch, but how else am I going to do it? The city bus goes as far as Manitou. But then what? Find some tourists to give me a ride? Hitchhike from there? Walk?

I guess I could take the trail up the Peak, then hike down the back side. But I don't have a tent or sleeping bag. I could stay tonight at Half-Pint Camp—if they'll take an unaccompanied minor—but I don't know if I could make it the rest of the way in one day. If I knew the way. I could get topo maps at the mountain store…

Forget it. It's crazy.

But maybe not. I think I'll check out the mountain store, pick up a map, and then catch the bus to Manitou. That's at least one step closer to my destination.

On the bus—

Insane. There is no way I could do that hike without a tent and sleeping bag, let alone a whole pack full of warm clothes, a flashlight, campstove, water—even if I did know the way. It could snow. It could blizzard. I could be dead.

Hitching's dangerous too, but I think I can choose my rides—avoid anyone who seems bad. Maybe only ride with women.

There's a ramp up to the highway on the west side of Manitou, and the bus stops there, at the Windigo Caverns and Indian Dancing Show. I'll try to catch a ride with someone pulling out of there. Anyone who goes to Windigo can't be a psychopathic murderer. Stupid tourist, yes, but bloody psycho? Probably not.

We're almost to the end of Manitou Avenue. My stop is coming up.

Geronimo.

Hi again, Di. I am riding in a giant motor home, and it's taking me all the way to the forest road. My luck's holding.

I got to the caverns, but they were having a slow day. It seemed like I hung around forever, expecting either the police to drive by or somebody from the caves to come out and ask me what the hell I was doing loitering. Finally people started coming out. The first were two guys, so I hung back and looked away. Then these three hard-living sort of Lynyrd Skynyrd women came out, laughing and lighting cigarettes. When a family came out and piled into a motor home, I went over and waved to the driver, who rolled down his window.

"Excuse me, sir, I need some help. Are you headed west?"

"Woodland Park," he said. "Go 'round the side."

The wife, Sherry, opened the side door. "You ought to be ashamed of yourself, young lady, hitching a ride in times like these. You better thank the good Lord *we* came along. Now, get in here."

"Boys," she said to two kids, about eight or nine, "you make room for this girl and get her anything she wants out of the fridge. This is our boy, Brandon," she said. "And this is his friend, Donny."

I always sort of looked down on motor homes. Dad loves to tell the story about the time he was camping at the Sand Dunes. A big camper pulled into the site across the road, and he and his friends watched as this guy got out, climbed up on the roof, set up his TV antenna, and went back inside. The next morning he got out again, took it down, and drove away. Now that's taking advantage of our National Monuments.

Of course, these people may do the exact same thing— with portable DVD players, you don't even need to get out and set up the antenna—but that's all right by me. They're insisting on taking me all the way to the cabin, about thirty miles out of their way.

I had to make up a story for them about how my brother's car broke down on the way to town. We can't get phone service at our cabin, I said, even cell phone, and I had to get back home to tell my mom what's going on. They scolded my brother for sending me, but I said he's the only one with any hope of fixing the car.

"Silly kids," said Dan, the driver. "Don't you know better than to split up?"

Sherry wanted to know why I wasn't in school, so I told her I was home-schooled. They approved of that, saying they had taken the boys out of school because they're house hunting—and doing some sightseeing—in Woodland Park.

"We're looking for something more like the home-school lifestyle ourselves," said Dan.

"Actually," I said, "speaking of school, I have some writing that I have to do, an assignment."

"Don't let us stop you. You got your education to think about. Boys, get down off that table and let her set up on there and do her work."

So I'm sitting at the table, drinking a Snappy Tom, eating corn chips, and writing. These people are great.

Or not. I had just written that and been offered ham and swiss on rye, and a soda, and some chocolate, when Dan says to me, "Yeah, we think we might like it up here." He looked around as he waited for the light in the middle of Woodland.

"Things are going to hell in a handbasket down in our neck of the woods."

"We're worried about Brandon," Sherry said.

"I keep expecting him to come home with his jeans hanging off his ass and callin' his old man 'home-boy.'" Dan shook his head and hit the gas. "It's time we got on out of there."

He looked back in the mirror at me and grinned. "I hear there ain't but one African in Woodland Park."

African? I thought, and it began to dawn on me. *Does he mean...*

"Too cold up here," Dan said. "That jungle blood runs thin."

He does, I thought. *He means African Americans!* And one of the boys, Donny, not Brandon, whispered to me, "They don't like Africans."

"Thanks," I whispered back, though I had just figured that out for myself.

The next thing I expected the guy to say was, "Now I ain't prejudiced, don't get me wrong..."

"I sort of have to get to work on my writing," I said, before he had the chance. "I'll be in trouble if I don't get it finished."

"Get off there and onto your bunk, Donny, and leave her alone," Dan said. "She's got work to do."

I feel like I should have spoken up, but what could I say? If I had any guts I would have asked them to pull over and let me out. "You've been kind to me," I would say, "but when you insult people just because of the color of their skin, it insults me as well."

Yeah, right.

It made me sick and I didn't want to have anything more to do with them, but I'm as big a coward as anybody else. Is it any better that I am prejudiced against RV-ers? I can hear myself in twenty years, "Now I ain't prejudiced, it's not that they're *all* racists—it's not that they're *all* beer-bellied, Rush Limbaugh-listening nature-haters, but from my personal experience, most of 'em are."

Okay. So I'm a bigot. Whatnever. I have to make nice here,

we're almost at my bus stop. The thing that freaks me out is that they're so *nice*. How can they be that way? Putting themselves out to take care of a stranger, but hating other people for no reason?

Much later, at my campsite:
    After I was dropped off by the kind racist family, I hiked up the road to the cabin and planned my next move. It was pushing one o'clock by then, and in a few hours I was going to come up missing. I'd figured that Mom wouldn't look in my room until I didn't come home from school, so I'd left a note in there. Just to keep her heart from stopping, I wrote in blue marker on the outside of the envelope: *DON'T WORRY! I'M OK!!!*
    Inside, I wrote something to this effect:

Dear Mom and Dad,
    I need a short break from things and some time to myself, so I lit out for the territory (temporarily). I won't tell you not to try to find me (I know you will, but you shouldn't because you won't find me, and I'm coming back in a few days anyway.) but please don't worry. I'm not going to hurt myself—I just need to get away from school and home so that I can figure things out. I guess I know you'll worry too, and I'm sorry about that. Please forgive me, I'll be okay, but I really need this.
    See you in a few days,
    Love,
    Cassie.
    P.S. I really am not going to hurt myself. Do not worry about that. I will see you soon, alive and well.

As I thought about them discovering that I had run off, I realized that my little reassurances wouldn't help a bit, and I started to feel guilty. Dad would rush home, Mom would cancel rehearsal, they'd panic. One would call my friends, I figured, and the other would rush up here. Where else would I go? Because I felt so bad about freaking them out, I considered hitching to a phone or staying at the cabin until they showed up. But that would be pointless. I had come this far, and I intended to take at least a few days on my own.

So, I needed to get in and out of the cabin as fast as I could. I had the perfect campsite in mind—not too far, but very hard to find, with some shade, some sun, water. What else did I need?

I unlocked the cabin with the hidden key, then I gathered up what I needed. Sleeping bag, tent, and water-filter for starters. I'd hoped to make it seem like I hadn't been there, but it would be obvious, so I stopped worrying and took whatever I needed. Last weekend, Mom had cleaned the place out and taken most of the food. There were a couple of cans of beans and jars of pasta sauce, but she brought home the tostada shells, pasta, and other stuff that's not mouse-proof. I took jars of sugar, coffee, tea, and half a bottle of whiskey—just like in "The Last Good Country." From home I'd brought peanut butter, jelly, fruit, some tortillas, a jalapeño pepper, soy cheese, and half a loaf of bread. And a giant bar of dark chocolate. Mom's going to miss that!

I had warm clothes in my drawers up in the loft, so I brought them. It's cold up here. I also packed extra blankets and a foam pad and a tarp. After that I stuffed everything into Dad's big pack and strapped on my tent with bungee chords. I had a big load, but I wanted all of it, and I only had a couple of miles to hike. Most of it uphill of course, some of it over treacherous rocks and scree, but only a couple miles.

I took Dad's shillelagh and hit the trail up the creek. Usually I follow it to the falls, but this time I crossed and went up over the ridge to the west. That sounds easy, doesn't it, just going up over the ridge? Actually I sweated and puffed, following deer trails and cutting across country when they petered out or went the wrong way. Near the top, it got too steep to climb, and I couldn't find the passage through the crags and into the valley on the other side. The worst parts were gravel on rock, very slippery, and I had a couple of moments when I thought I was going to go tumbling back down. Eventually, I found the little gap between the rocks that I was looking for.

I edged along about ten feet of rock on top of a steep scree-slope, then followed a crack up the rock that was doable, but where I probably should have been roped in. I fastened my walking stick under the bungee chords on the pack, and used both hands to make it up the broken granite.

Then it leveled out and fell gradually down to the valley below. The spot where DJ and I had spent the afternoon was a hundred feet higher and half a mile south, and above that, the ridge rose to meet the high crest that Mom, Sean, and I had climbed on our way to the reservoirs. From snowmelt on the high ridge, and maybe springs below, a tiny creek runs through the valley—just enough for drinking water but not enough to support fish. Because there's no fishing, I didn't think Sean and Dad came up here—even if they had managed to find the way in. At the bottom of the valley, the creek disappears into cracks and caves below a steep cleft, so the only way in is either the one I took or a steep descent from the high crest. And why would they bother with that steep descent and climb out when there weren't any fish to torture?

Once I made it into my sanctuary, I looked for a good place to make camp. I had visions of satellite photography and search helicopters spying out my tent—from an overactive imagination, I'm sure—but I still felt I had to find a level spot under the trees. I finally found one, set up my tent, made my bed, and rigged a food cache on a rope between two trees a good distance from the tent. There's a place for a fire nearby, but I don't think I'm going to have one—too visible.

Well, if they find me, they find me. I couldn't face the prospect of a night out here alone without a fire, so here I am by my cheery blaze. Stretched out with my back to the rock after a hot dinner, I'm sipping a spiced tea with lots of sugar and a little whiskey. Everything is much better with a fire. The smoke can be annoying, and the stars get a little lost in interference, but at least I don't feel so lonesome.

There's plenty of dead wood up here, so I gathered enough to last a couple of days. I found a few decent-sized dead aspens and managed to break them up into manageable chunks. Aspen burns quickly, even the logs, but I don't have much else to do besides feed the fire.

After I made the wood pile and got a kettle of water, I hiked up the southern slope of my secret valley, the soft, needly ground rising gradually under the firs and pines to a timbered ridge that screened my camp from the high crest. A squirrel scolded me, and chickadees zipped in and out of the trees as I traversed eastward. Then the sun was suddenly gone, and the coolness floated down from the timberline even as the warm earth gave up a fragrant scent of pitch and dry wood.

Back at camp, I built a lean-to of sticks against one of the logs, stacking the smallest pieces across my frame, criss-crossing larger ones above, and placing a couple of logs on top. I set a match to the tiny, resinous fir twigs, which flared up, setting the bigger sticks snapping and flaming and spreading upward and out.

While the fire burned down to cooking coals, I opened my can of chili beans. Then I shaved an aspen log with the hatchet until I had a flat space to use as a cutting board. The jalapeño was smooth and shiny, deep green and almost black on one side. I held it by the stem and sliced it into rounds, careful not to get the juice on my fingers because there's nothing quite like rubbing your eyes after you've forgotten you've got jalapeño juice on them—you remember real quick. Then I carved off slices of cheese, laying them on the board next to my peppers. Finally, I cut the core out of an apple, leaving the bottom intact. I spooned some sugar into the cavity and poured in a capful of whiskey. Then I wrapped it up in foil. I wiped the knife on my jeans and put it in my pocket.

By this time the fire had burned down, leaving some coals beneath. I shoved most of the flaming wood off to the side and set my can of beans right in the hottest coals. The apple I buried in coals and ashes near the edge. I'd left the lid of the bean can hanging for a handle, and every now and then I pulled it out, wearing a glove, and stirred up the beans. When they were hot, I put the can to the side.

Laying a tortilla on a forked stick, I dangled it over the coals and flames until it was puffy and hot. Then I set it on my cutting board, laid some cheese on it, covered it with hot beans, topped it off with a couple of jalapeño slices and folded it—side, bottom, and side to keep the beans in.

Damn, was it good—the tortilla soft and warm with little almost-burnt parts, the beans and cheese rich and spicy, and the bits of crispy pepper setting my mouth on fire.

Dad had taught Sean and me how to make these camp tacos when we were just kids, and we always had them when we camped out. I ate two more, and I couldn't help but think back on good campfire times with Sean and Dad, and Mom, too. I wondered if Sean and Ally knew I had taken off. I also wondered what Mom and Dad were doing, how they were handling it. Were they down at the cabin, just a couple miles away? Or were they sticking to the phone at home?

And what about DJ? How were things going with him? Did he even think about me still? Had they gotten in touch with him, told him I was gone, asked him where I might be?

After my last taco, I dug out the apple. It was a bit of a disappointment—the sugar leaked out and burned, but parts of it were sweet and good. I made my whiskey and tea while I let it cool, and now I think I'll have another.

The fire is burning low, giving just enough warmth to take the chill off, and above it, the sky is full of stars. If only my DJ were here.

Sigh…gaze into the fire…

It's perfect and beautiful, and I love being here, but while I wanted to be alone, what good is it? Maybe I wanted to be alone because I thought this way I could control everything and slip into my own fantasy without a real person intruding.

But in my solitude, I find myself thinking of others: sharing the camp tacos with DJ, having a conversation about self-doubt with Ally. I can hear myself telling her how I'm afraid that I came up here not to think, not to go to a pure place where I can truly hear my soul's voice, but just to avoid my problems.

The flames fail and I push a log inward so the fresh wood lies amidst the coals. I lay some smaller stuff over that and it all bursts into hot, bright flame.

The fire is mesmerizing. I stop writing every so often to stare and sip my drink, just the way humans have stared into fires for thousands upon thousands of years. In the ash-covered and glowing embers, I see patterns and movement as of something alive, and in the almost-consumed wood I see the fire bring out the shape and the grain of the tree before reducing it to cold, dusty ash.

Cold and dusty ash.

Gollum pawing the ground of Mordor, hissing, "Dusst!"

Almost as much as they delighted in killing, Sauron's slaves relished the destruction of nature. Orcs cut down the trees of Fangorn and hauled them off to feed the forges or just left them lying with uncouth symbols carved in their trunks. And on the plain of Gorgoroth in Mordor, only stunted and thorny things grew.

And here in my own high mountains, the balance is changing—earlier snowmelt and later snowfall and too much water piped off to irrigate the pesticide farms, lawns, and golf-courses where geese forget their millennia of migration and grow fat and saturated with herbicide.

How can I fight, how can I stop it? Oh, Di. I feel it calling me, and DJ's favorite Zeppelin song sings in my mind:

I can feel it calling me the way it used to do.

The fire consumes itself. The fire consumes its fuel and is gone. The fire eats its own body and leaves only elements— elements for new life and new fire. So, why not join the fire? Why not join the ashes and dust—why not be soil and rock and water and air? Not to be fire anymore, not to be burning fuel, not to *be.*

I can feel it calling me . . .

But there it is again, just like on the beach: the nothing. The cold and howling nothing.

On top of the world, my little valley opens to the sky, opens to space like a portal on a starship that bursts open so everything goes screaming into the vacuum.

Can nothing be cold? It feels so icy. And can nothing be dead?

Oh, yes, as sure as dead is nothing.

It's all being sucked out into space and, empty or not, vac-uum or whatever it is, when you hit it, all the water and heat and life and spark get sucked the hell out of you and you're dead, dead, dead, dead, dead, dead, dead.

People who love you will cry because your heat and spark

are gone into the nothing. Only elements remain. Beautiful and senseless elements.

I wanted to be elements before, I wanted to be senseless, but not anymore. I love the rocks, and I believe that even the rocks are alive, but not alive enough to want to *be* them. I need spark and heat, I want fire, not ashes. My blaze will burn out too soon as it is, so why smother it before its time? Why not enjoy the heat while it lasts?

I can feel it calling me . . .

And music—never more to sing a note? How horrible is that? "I can feel it calling me," I sing into the night. "I can feel it calling me, back ho-o-ome."

What a clown I am! A self-conscious, tragic, silly, little clown in the big world. The limber pine in the firelight seems to laugh at my singing out loud, and it throws me into doubt again, telling me to simply be—and I see myself through the eyes of the tree, and I want to be like a tree, to simply be without all this wanting and needing—to be a cold and bloodless tree, watery-thin sap flowing with the seasons, a slow and gradual rising and falling, not this rapid-fire filling and emptying with a hot pump, a hammering heart—

But that's not it either. I got lost again; I followed it too far. Because I love this red pump and this hot blood. If only I could stop thinking for a while.

I closed my eyes and everything went swirly and sick, but it cleared when I opened them and took a few deep, slow breaths. I might just need to sleep and possibly throw up, not die, just sleep and maybe vomit—but keep my red frantic heart squeezing, pushing the blood, hammering the valves, and someday again, I hope, have my heart against someone else, beating against another, warm together in sleeping bags with the cold air outside, beating together and pumping: warm and furry animals, mammals, forgetting the empty space or else loving the contrast of the cold starry night against the warmth of our breath together, breathing each other's breath and making heat together under the cold and distant and elemental stars.

30 October

So this is a hangover. I don't think I'll ever take another drop. My last couple drinks were a little strong, I think. I stumbled to bed after writing that last part, and the tent was spinning around like a flying saucer. I woke in the gray dawn with a terrific thirst and the need to pee.

Went back to sleep, but I'm still thirsty now, and not sure I feel much better. I'll try a couple or three ibus and breakfast.

Ugh. I want to go home. Coffee seemed to help the old hangover for a while, but forget about breakfast. I felt like puking again after I got about three steps out of the tent, and I left the food down on the ground last night anyway. Most of it's gone or spoiled by animals. There's about half a tortilla and some jelly. The coffee, tea, and sugar were safe in their jars, but everything else, which wasn't much anyway—leftover beans, soy cheese, bread, fruit—is gone.

I'm going back to bed. I'll decide what to do later.

I woke up still homesick and whiskey-sick. It's not just physical either—I feel totally polluted. Right down to the soul.

Outside, I found a change in the weather. Clouds have come, hanging down over the southern ridge. It's turned cold, and there's a snowy feeling in the air. It's beautiful, but gloomy and lonesome. I want the wood floors and lamplight of home.

It's going to snow for sure, which fits because tomorrow is Halloween, and it always snows on Halloween.

Memories of Hallowe'en—All Hallows Eve:

Night falls early, hot cider steams on the stove, pumpkin seeds toast in the oven, and a big bowl of candy waits by the door. Little kids' costumes are all puffed up with coats underneath, and Dad gives big handfuls of candy because there won't be too many this year.

I really should be home, not hiding up here. What am I doing? All my mental ramblings last night haven't gotten me anywhere. Or maybe they have. I felt that huge *nothing* again, and I don't want *anything* to do with it. I want my blood warm and red, I don't care how much it hurts.

So I'm going home. I'll stay one more night, and tomorrow I'll go back to face what I left behind and the messes I made by leaving. I don't know what I'm going to do about anything, but I'm going home.

And for now, I'll take advantage of my final hours alone. I'm going outside to lay a big bonfire, then I'll walk, or stagger, up the ridge to where the clouds meet the trees and the ground. I'll breathe cloud-air and mist, and then I'll light my fire and celebrate Hallows Eve at midnight, sending sparks up to heaven.

And then, I'll go to sleep, and wake up, and walk down the mountain.

That's when it's calling me,
That's when it's calling me,
Back ho-o-ome.

By the time I wrote that and came outside, the clouds were even lower. I was, and am, covered over, socked in with misty clouds hanging like a ceiling over my little valley. Earlier, I half-imagined I heard people calling for me, voices drifting in through the mist. But even if Mom and Dad hiked up to the high ridge, they couldn't see me down here now. And I don't think the voices would carry through the weather. I laid my fire and took my walk, stopping every so often to listen, hearing nothing above the sound of my breath and the thumping of my pulse in my throat. Then, because it was getting cold and dark and I wanted fire, I came back to camp.

I'm sitting now in the warm space between the rocks and my blaze. No dinner—I couldn't face the half a stale tortilla and leftover peanut butter, but the tea is sweet and spicy, and I'm bringing the rest of the whiskey home to Dad.

Last night, bright with stars, the valley held a faint glimmer, but tonight I'm blanketed with cloud-darkness and cocooned in the cold. I wonder how I'm going to get home. I wonder if maybe I'll find Mom or Dad at the cabin. I wonder what they're doing now, if they're scared for me, mad at me.

Both.

I don't suppose they'll want to let me avoid the shrink after this. I think they'll keep me on a pretty tight tether when I get back. I guess, like DJ, I'll be on groundation for a while.

Sigh...

Gaze into the fire...

I wonder what DJ is up to and what we're going to do. I have to at least talk to him. They can't keep us apart forever, though Mommy will try to keep us apart until it's too late.

It can't end like this—with no ending at all, no goodbye, nothing. It's as if all the time the two of us spent together has been thrown away. And not just the *time* but the *us*, the DJ and me—because we became *us*, like Ally and I were, like Ally and Sean were: two people becoming part of one another. And now it's as if we've been tossed into the great vacuum of space, the capital N-nothing, and all the life is being sucked out of us until *we* won't exist anymore.

Maybe Mom and Dad can help us to at least say goodbye. Because it can't be nothing. I refuse to accept nothing.

Oh, but it hurts anyway. It's like the ache I felt when Ally and Sean broke up, only worse. I *want* him, and I can't do anything about it.

It hurts to think of Mom and Dad too, and what I'm doing to them. I wish I were back home now. I don't need to be here anymore. I've done it. I've done the poem I read way back in August, "When One has Lived a Long Time Alone." It took me only two days, and I'm ready to go back.

I got up and left the fire's circle to answer nature's call, and I stood for a while in the cold, blind night, facing away from the fire. Scary to be so alone in the bigness of it all, but good. It would have been a perfectly ironic time for a lion to hit me, or a random accident like fictional Cassie and the sneaker wave, and yet I wasn't really afraid—not of anything *happening*. Going home is what scares me: the future, as dark and unknowable as the mountain night.

And the night held comfort, too, as well as fear. I wasn't looking for some big answer from the life all around me—an answer from God—but it was there. Not that I had a big "experience" like that night on the Carrock, but it was enough to hear and feel and smell and imagine the living land: all the plants and rocks, and the trickle of water, and the water of my own body, water that I took from the creek, now soaking into the ground, carrying bits of me into this place ...

I get lost in it all. I follow one thread and get lost in the connections. But here it is: alive and working together. Enough said.

I got some more water from the creek and put another kettle on the fire. The smoke had been deviling me, swirling around on a wind that eddied in the space between the rock and the fire, but when I came back to my place it was rising straight up.

I'm not tired in the least, so I figure I'll be up for another pot of tea. I could go into the tent and read, probably will soon, but for now I'm content to sit here, alternately looking into the fire and writing sentences. My daydreams—up here on my lonesome, but with home on my mind—fill the space with the people who are home to me. I hear Liz's big laugh, and Quill's silly voices. Ally and Sean join me by the fire, and Mom and Dad. And DJ.

Like an answer to wishful thinking, maybe, I see a flashlight bobbing down out of the mist across the way. Like a lamp from some wandering company of Elves, a lamp made of captured starlight, it fades in and out of the mist and the trees. And is that another? It's definitely not Elves, and it's not the search and rescue. But it looks like more people than just Dad and Mom—people between the lights.

Lower now, almost on my level, the lights disappear, lost in the trees, then they fade in and out and do not reappear. I expect to see the lights again, they had been coming straight for me, but maybe they've turned them off.

To ease my nervousness and prepare for company, I take the boiling water off the fire, drop teabags in, and set it within reach. Then I put the other pot of water right in the coals. And I wait.

"Wishful thinking," I say to myself. "The trick of a poisoned brain and a day without food." I stand up, squint through the trees into the darkness, and sit down again.

The wind sends a gust of smoke at me, and snow begins to fall, blowing in swirls of small flakes all around the fire. A few strike my face and melt, and finally the lights reappear, coming toward me, lighting the ground as people come walking.

"Cassie," I hear a voice.

"Dad?" I say.

"Cassie!" he says.

He comes into the firelight first, followed by Mom. Then Sean, then Ally, turning off her flashlight, and beside her, DJ. To say I'm

surprised doesn't begin to explain. Blown away? Flabbergasted? I
expected Mom and Dad, but what are the others doing here?

I stand as Dad strides up to the fire and takes hold of me.
Mom grabs me, too, and we stand there holding on to each other. I
catch a glimpse of Ally smiling and leaning against Sean, and DJ
looks into the fire, his hands jammed into his pockets.

"Damn you, child," says Dad. "Never do anything like this
again."

Mom doesn't say anything, just hangs on.

Ally comes in and puts her arms around all of us, and Mom
and Dad let go. "We were just a little worried," she says. "So we
came out here to join the search."

"Littless," says Sean, pulling me from Ally. "You were supposed
to tell me when you found 'The Last Good Country.'"

"Sorry," I say.

"It took your boyfriend to find you," he says. "He told us about
your secret place."

DJ is still standing there looking into the fire. I take a step
toward him and he looks up. Then we're in one another's arms.
His neck is warm against my lips and he smells like DJ as I drink
in the air that surrounds him, part fresh snow and part wood-
smoke and part him and all warm.

Then I remember everyone else.

"Would anybody like some tea?" I ask, and everybody begins
to laugh. Dad stops, catches his breath, looks at me, and cracks up
again. "I would love some tea," he says.

I pull the other pot out of the coals and throw in some tea-
bags while Mom fishes a set of nesting cups out of her pack.

"We decided," she says, "not to give you hell tonight, if we— when we—found you. We decided to enjoy the reunion."

"Thanks, Mom," I say, and I sit down in my spot by the fire and pour tea.

"Take the place of honor, son," Dad tells DJ, pointing to the space at my left. Ally sits next to him, flanked by Sean. Mom sits at my right, with Dad next to her.

He takes up the whiskey bottle, doctors his tea, and pours a slug into Mom's.

"Share, please," says Ally. Mom passes it around me and DJ.

I'm dying to hear details—of how they managed to pry DJ away from his mommy, for example—but I am so relieved to be found, to have my home come to me before I can even come home, that I am happy just to sit.

Everybody else must feel the same way because nobody says anything for a long time except "I hate rabbits" when the smoke blows our way. Soon the flakes became bigger and the wind dies. Then they become huge, falling from the darkness into the firelight, vanishing into the flames or settling on the ground, on my friend the limber pine, and on my family. We are covered in a matter of minutes, as we sit quietly and watch the fire and the darkness and the snow and each other, leaning out or in every once in a while as if to check that the others are still sitting down the line—the six of us in a line, slightly curved into the fire, between the warmth and the light and the rocks behind.

31 October

I awoke to sunlight penetrating the fabric of my tent, and I blew steam into the green interior. As cozy as it was in my sleeping bag, I didn't linger, but pulled my cold jeans inside and began to dress.

Packing up my little camp didn't take long, and I hurried, inspired by the rumblings in my stomach and the cold, which by now has softened under the sun. Just a few inches of snow fell last night, but it was enough to turn my valley into a world of white. The sky is very blue, the cornices of the high ridge icy-clear, and the still air here on the valley floor carries the close, soft sounds of warming snow falling from trees, the calls of chickadees, and the trickle of water in the creek.

I could use some coffee to start me on my way, but I don't want to take time to set up my stove and heat water—I am only lingering now to write a little before climbing up, down, and home.

But now that it's time to put my boots to the trail…it's not so easy to do. I close my eyes and feel the sun on my face while the cold seeps into my writing hand.

Suddenly I hear a call from the high ridge, small but clear in the wide valley:

"Cassie!"

Could it be a figment of last night's fiction? I keep my eyes closed, clenched now, afraid that if I open them, I'll break the spell, and the call *will* be just a dream. But I open them, and I see a small figure in the snow, far away and above.

"Dad?"

"Cassie!"

"I'm here!"

The End

Acknowledgments

First thanks go to my wife, Lee Hillhouse, for living with me while I wrote this novel. And all that entails. Next thanks to Sarah Scarlett "Spottedstar" Mandabach for patience and inspiration: you're a true Warrior and the hope of our clan. Also to Andy "Candy" Mandabach for forcing the issue by giving me a due date on my first draft: your due date.

And I thank my big brothers for their support and influence: Paul III, Mark, Keith, and Carl Mandabach.

I'm grateful for the guidance of Gary Heidt, free-jazz agent, Rhiannon Ross, Fleetwood Mac editor, and especially Andrew Karre, post-grunge editor.

I've learned so much from my students, ALL of you. Special mention goes to my Lunch in Middle Earth and Three-Broomsticks groups and my writing clubs, including the Society of the Flaming Dagger of L'au Willi-Willi Nuka-Nuka Oi-Oi. Which groups included: Erica Colon (I did not say dagger!), Samster Haeussner, Megan Anderson, Sarah Weiger, Becca Donaldson, Mara Baker, Jared Butterfield, Brian Wallis, Laura Arrington, Holly Tate, Maria Kim, Alex Colerick, Sarah Lovell, Devin Carpenter, Amy Crockett, Rachel Case, PJ Friend, Leah "Not-allowed-to-write-anything-that-doesn't-have-horses-in-it" Simon, Lauren "I <3 Constructed Response Paragraphs" Handlon, Hannah-hannaH Weems, Kaylah "The Devil" Weeres, Hannah "the female George Carlin" Duke, Kacee Eddinger, David Schmidt, Jake "One for the Punks" Schmitz, Danny "Big G" and Emmy "Liddle G" Gradisar, Brandon Shuemaker, Carson Hiltbrand, Nicki Carroll, Gen "Gwenaveevla" Peek, Dakota Myers-Moore, Bethany Barden-Way, Jessica "Tré Jewell"-Armstrong, Jessica Pigeon, Taylor "Liberal Princess" McQlluham, Katy Peek (special inspiration), and Suzie Avant (formerly Avant-Way). I know I've missed a few—sorry!

Thanks also to the great educators I've had the pleasure to work with, who are not at all like the meanie-heads in my book. But especially the best team-mate, mentor, and friend I could hope to have, Nancy Haley. And her husband Tim, who sets the gold standard of silliness.

And great teachers: Dale Griffith, Mr. Nelson, Solace Hotz, Robert Behn, Kent Bowers, Jim Studholme, Joe Gordon, and Ann Haymond Zwinger.

I owe a great debt of gratitude to my chief reader, Samuel Ligon, who keeps the Oak Street Restaurant Vow of our Steppenwolfe Trip to the Art Institute and Anarchist's Theatre. (Not for everyone: for madmen only!)

Ralph Kisberg read a couple drafts of this book and steadfastly encouraged me. Catherine Spicer read a draft, too. Lee read and edited several drafts, most notably the first, at which juncture she steered me away from some of my most serious blunders.

My teen readers were also an invaluable source of wisdom and love: Willyum "Bill" Rivett, Paddy Quinlan, and the Incomparable Becky Simon, who read several drafts and made herself indispensable.

In memorium, thanks to my father, Paul Mandabach, Jr, my sister Janice Allen, and W. Mark Harty, who prefered a feast of friends to the giant family.